An Impossible Marriage

Also published by Hodder

This Bed Thy Centre

The Holiday Friend

The Unspeakable Skipton

The Last Resort

PAMELA HANSFORD JOHNSON

An Impossible Marriage

First published in Great Britain by Macmillan in 1954

This paperback edition published in 2018 by Hodder & Stoughton
An Hachette UK company

1

A CIP catalogue record for this title is available from the British Library

Paperback ISBN 978 1 473 67980 1
eBook ISBN 978 1 473 67981 8

Typeset in Plantin Light by Hewer Text UK Ltd, Edinburgh
Printed and bound CPI Group (UK) Ltd, Croydon, CR0 4YY

Hodder & Stoughton policy is to use papers that are natural, renewable
and recyclable products and made from wood grown in sustainable
forests. The logging and manufacturing processes are expected to
conform to the environmental regulations of the country of origin.

Hodder & Stoughton Ltd
Carmelite House
50 Victoria Embankment
London EC4Y 0DZ

www.hodder.co.uk

'J'éprouvais un sentiment de fatigue profonde à sentir que tout ce temps si long non seulement avait sans une interruption été vécu, pensé, sécrété par moi, qu'il était ma vie, qu'il était moi-même, mais encore que j'avais à toute minute à le maintenir attaché à moi, qu'il me supportait, que j'étais juché à son sommet vertigineux, que je ne pouvais me mouvoir sans le deplacer avec mol.

'La date à laquelle j'entendais le bruit de la sonnette du jardin de Combray, si distant et pourtant intérieur, était un point de repère dans cette dimension énorme que je ne savais pas avoir. J'avais le vertige de voir au-dessous de moi et en moi pourtant, comme si j'avais des lieues de hauteur, tant d'années.'

Marcel Proust

PART ONE

I

(Outside The Door)

I made up my mind that I would not see Iris Allbright again, not after so many years. I do not like looking back down the chasm of the past and seeing, in a moment of vertigo, some terror that looks like a joy, some joy crouched like a terror. It is better to keep one's eyes on the rock-face of the present, for that is real; what is under your nose is actual, but the past is full of lies, and the only accurate memories are those we refuse to admit to our consciousness. I did not want to see Iris; we had grown out of each other twenty years ago and could have nothing more to say. It might be interesting to see if she had kept her looks, if she had worn as well as I had; but not so interesting that I was prepared to endure an afternoon of reminiscence for the possible satisfaction of a vanity.

Also, she had had only one brief moment of real importance in my life, which was now shrivelled by memory almost to silliness. I doubted whether she herself would remember it at all. I would not see her; I had made up my mind.

But it was not so easy. Iris was determined that I should visit her, now she had returned to Clapham, and to this end kept up a campaign of letters and telephone calls. Didn't I want to talk over old times? If not, why not? She was longing to tell me all about her life in South America, all about her marriage, her children, her widowhood – didn't I *want* to hear? She was longing to hear all about me. ('How you've got *on*! Little Christie!') I couldn't be so busy as to be unable to spare just half an hour. Why not this Wednesday? Or Wednesday week? Or any day the following week? She was always at home.

I began to feel like the unfortunate solicitor badgered with tea invitations by Armstrong, the poisoner of Hay. Knowing that if he accepted he would be murdered with a meat-paste sandwich, in constant touch with the police who had warned him what his fate was likely to be, he was nevertheless tortured by his social sense into feeling that if Armstrong were not soon arrested he would have to go to tea, to accept the sandwich, and to die. It was a hideous position for a man naturally polite and of good feeling.

My own position was in a sense more difficult, for no one was likely to arrest Iris Allbright, and I felt the time approaching when I must either bitterly offend her or go to Clapham. In the end I went to Clapham.

I took a certain pleasure in seeing the neighbourhood again. I was born near the Common. I had memories of crossing it on cold and frosty mornings on my way to school; of walking there on blue and dusty summer evenings in the exalted, painful insulation of first, childish love-affairs. I could see the island on the pond, cone-shaped, thick with sunny trees, on which the little boys ran naked, natural and Greek after swimming, until the borough council insisted on bathing drawers. I could see the big field by North Side, the boys and girls lounging in deck-chairs, playing ukeleles as the sun fell into ash and the new moon hardened like steel in the lavender sky; the field behind the Parade, with little low hawthorn hills, where less innocent lovers lay locked by night.

I had not been there since the war.

Now, on that Sunday afternoon in October, I saw it changed, my world laid waste. There were allotments in the big field; the scrawny, shabby cabbages shrivelling on their knuckly stems; tangles of weed lying over the broken earth like travellers thirst-ridden in the desert crawling towards a water-hole. Here and there were tin huts, lop-sided, peeling in the sun; and the row of high houses stretching from Sisters Avenue to Cedars Road had the shabby sadness of women too discouraged to paint their faces or get out of their dressing-gowns. And there were letting-boards. I could not remember anything being to let in my day.

The impression I had of it all was violent, too Gothic to be true – only true, perhaps, in relation to my romantic memories; but I felt depressed, a stranger there myself, and wished again that I had not yielded to Iris's importunities.

She was living on the second floor of a block of mansion flats, built of liver-coloured brick, and roofed in some approximation to château style. The turrets gleamed damply, like gun-metal, on the light-blue sky, and the glazed laurels flashed red and white below in the refracted light from the cars and buses. It was noisy on that corner, as I had remembered it; but far dustier – unless the dust were on the lens of my own memories. I went into the dankness of the tiled hallway, which was like the entrance to a municipal swimming baths, and in the aquarian gloom searched for her name on the Ins and Outs board, faintly hoping that by some accident I might find her proclaimed 'Out' and so have an excuse for going away again.

Iris Allbright. Iris de Castro she was now. She was in.

As I climbed the first flight of stairs I heard a gramophone playing in one of the flats, playing a tune of twenty years ago. I stopped, so certain only Iris could still preserve this record that I wondered for a moment if she were not living on the first floor after all. The world shifted in place and time; I stood against the wall, hearing that tune, seeing nothing but the downward breadth of my own pink dress. He was coming to me now across the slippery floor. I pretended not to know it. I heard Iris humming the words of the song in her small, light, penetrating voice. Every thread in my dress was sharp and separate, each with an individuality of its own. I noted the design of the weaving.

'Shall we dance this?' he said, and I looked up, and Iris was answering him. 'No, no; I'm tired. You dance this with my friend.' 'I'm not dancing this one,' I said airily; 'I've laddered my stocking. I want to stop before it goes any further.' He did not seem to hear me. Iris gave her little shrug, accompanied by the lifting of the right corner of her mouth, the sloping down of her left shoulder. She stepped into his arms and went off as if a breeze had lifted her from her feet. But this had not been her moment of importance, not this one at all.

The world shifted again with a rush of chilly air and set me down on a stair in a dark hallway, above a green-tiled well. I went on upwards and stood before her door. Through the landing window I could see a boy and girl lolling against the railings of the Common, staring at each other. A bus came along. He gave her a kiss and ran for it. She waved after him, until there was only dust to see and the resettling of the plane trees. Then she went back to the railings and sat there, despondent. She raised her hand, let it fall to her side; it was a kind of rehearsed gesture, designed to convince her of her own sadness.

I rang the bell, and at once heard steps along the hall. Between my ringing and the opening of the door lay the whole of my youth.

2

I was out of love: it was insufferably sad. Leslie and I sat on the river's brink, Leslie having no idea of my state of mind. He was in one of his sophisticated moods, conceited, reminiscent. 'I couldn't care for Mabel after that,' he continued. 'I pride myself on being broad-minded, but it was too much. Now it's all merely a part of my past.'

Leslie was seventeen.

It was a freckled, fleecy day, with small clouds like strips of cotton wool running across the bright-blue sky, and the spring wind rattling the leaves. Leslie wore brown-and-white shoes, with Oxford trousers of a purplish shade, which were the fashion that year.

'There are sides of life I hope you will never know, Christine,' said Leslie. His handsome nose, which was rather too long, had caught the sun. His thick, matted ginger hair had caught it also, and the heated brilliantine was giving it a green appearance. 'Little Christine,' he added, on one of his chest notes. He put his arm round me, then withdrew it as though I had burned him. I asked him what the matter was.

'I felt I had no right to touch you with such ideas going through my mind.'

'What ideas?' But I did not really want to know. My head ached. I was tired of Richmond. I longed to get on the bus and go home, let myself in quietly without disturbing my parents and go to my own room, which would be very cool and rather dark. I should have to tell him in a letter; I had not the courage to speak.

'I heard something pretty shocking the other night. I ran into Dicky Flint.'

Leslie made a flinching gesture, probably suggested by Dicky's name. He passed a hand over his eyes. He said in a bass whisper, 'Do you know, *there's a brothel in Balham*?'

I was six months older than he and had read more. I said I had always imagined there might be several.

Leslie leaped to his feet and clenched his hand upon his breast. He was breathing hard. He was not very tall.

'Now what's the matter?'

'To hear such things – from your little lips!'

He presented his profile to the light. A little taken off the nose and added to the chin, and he would have been as fascinating as he thought he was. Even so, he was better-looking than the sweethearts of most of my friends, and I had been deeply flattered when he had first singled me out at the grammar-school dance, for in those days I was far from pretty, and self-conscious about my bust. I had let him kiss me in the gloom of the marquee, and afterwards we had danced in a dream on the square of grass lit by the headlights of the cars parked around it. We had fallen wildly in love. By the time my friends had made me fully aware that Leslie had an ominous mother and was commonly regarded as a little touched I was too deeply involved to break away, and certainly too proud to give my friends the satisfaction of seeing me do so. I believed Leslie could be reclaimed, that he could have sense knocked into his head. I comforted myself by thinking that he only seemed stupid because he was intellectual; he walked about at week-ends with a volume of Nietzsche under his arm. But our affair had now endured nearly eight months, and I knew that Leslie was irreclaimable.

'Oh, don't be silly.'

He looked bitter. He was busy working up a little quarrel, which he was prepared to lead into a lyric reconciliation. He said nothing. I picked daisies and began to make a chain. They looked charming in my green lap, and I was wearing green shoes to match, which was a fashion so unusual that other girls stared at me in envy. They were linen shoes, and I had painted them with oil-colours; the idea was taken from *Little Women*, and I was always afraid someone else would copy it.

Giving up any hope of making me speak first, Leslie dropped on to one knee at my side and laid his hand on my shoulder. He stared at me gravely, with an effect very slightly astigmatic. 'You are so small,' he said, using his chest notes again, 'and so pure. I don't want the world to touch you. I don't want to think of you as – a Mabel.'

'You couldn't,' I said; 'my legs are the right length.'

Leslie said, 'Pshaw', a word he had read in a book and pronounced exactly. 'Little one,' he added. His lip drooped.

'Let's go back. Do you mind? My head aches.'

'Lie in the long grass and I will stroke it away.'

I told him I really would like to go home, and I sucked in my cheeks a little to make myself look wan. He was very disappointed, for our recent Saturdays at Richmond had been rather chilly and wet, and this was the first fine day. 'I wanted to take you on the river.'

This increased my determination to go home. I had once let Leslie row me before, and it was a humiliating memory. We had set out with difficulty, as he had been unable to.leave the bank till the man pushed him out with a boathook. He had then zigzagged down with the tide, catching crabs frequently, and banging into other skiffs; we had been shouted at. This had gone on for about an hour. When we turned back I realised that the wind was hard against us, and that, with Leslie's frantic tacking, we should never get back to our base before nightfall. 'Let me row,' I had pleaded, but he had only bulged his eyes at me sternly and informed me that he did not treat his women like that. We had been battling for about an hour, not infrequently accompanied by shrieks of derision from other boaters, when it occurred to me to ask him if he had ever rowed before. 'Once or twice,' said Leslie with such little breath as he had left. He looked as if he might have a stroke.

'Where?'

'The pond on Clapham Common.'

When we reached the boathouse it was almost dark. The man with the boathook, who had to drag us in, was furious. Leslie was almost in tears, and I was actually so.

'I couldn't let you row me today,' I told him now; 'it would make my head a hundred times worse.'

'Well, then,' said Leslie, 'come home and have tea at my place. My mater's at Auntie's. We'll be by ourselves.' He gave me a soft, suggestive look. 'My kisses will cure you,' he murmured in my ear. His breath smelled of jam.

It was only because I no longer loved Leslie that I assented to this compromise ending to our day. I did not want to hurt him more than I must, and he was miserable enough already. I had begun to realise for the first time that rejecting love, if not so painful as having it rejected, has a shame and an anguish of its own. 'All right. But I won't be able to stay long. And don't let's make love this evening – let's just be nice and friendly with each other.'

'Make love' in those days did not mean what it appears to mean now. When boys and girls in their teens spoke of love-making they meant kissing, and little more.

'I will cherish you,' said Leslie with a strange, episcopal air, helping me to my feet. He picked up the daisy-chain that had dropped from my lap, looked at me meaningfully, pressed it to his lips and stowed it away in the vee of his Fair Isle pullover. He was not, I noted with some satisfaction, wearing the pair of brown-and-white shoes he had bought to go with his sporting attire, as I had condemned them and, after a long tussle of our wills, had forced him to hide away.

When we reached the row of houses in which he lived, on the outskirts of Tooting Bec Common, the light was falling into the ruddiness of a fine evening. The wind had ceased. The red bricks glowed rose red, and over the chimneys the sky was clear as water.

His house was the fourth in the row, a six-roomed villa with a green gate and a hedge of yellow privet.

'We'll pretend it's our own little home,' said Leslie. ' "Just tea for two, and two for tea",' he sang softly, as he put his key in the lock.

But he was wrong, for as we stepped into the fusty little passage we heard his fierce mother roar out, 'Whaur hae ye been, ye silly swine?'

Leslie stopped and shivered. 'To Richmond, of course, Mater,' he cried in a light, rippling voice. 'I told you. Where we always go.'

She came stamping out at us, square and red, her eyes flashing. She had just had a permanent wave, and her black hair looked like a woollen hat. 'Is that ye, Chrristine? If ye've come for tea, ye're too late the noo. As for ye, Leslie, I asked ye to go and get Feyther's harrp from the shop, and hae ye done it?'

Leslie's father was a harpist in a cinema orchestra and expected to be out of work soon, since the first talking pictures had just been shown in London. He was a shadowy little man, with Murillo eyes and reddish hair that lay back in sticky quills, like the feathers of a sparrow.

'His new harrp! That he bought wi' his ain insurance money!'

She turned to me. 'Come on in, then, since ye're here. Why dinna ye tell this silly swine to heed what his mither tells him?'

'I was *going* to get his harp,' Leslie cried; 'that's why I brought Christine back early. I meant to get it.'

His mother had by now herded us into the parlour, where there was just about enough room for three persons and the furniture. 'I should think ye were, kenning that he's got his puir foot in plaster! Gallivanting, that's all ye care aboot. But then,' she added, in a nasty tone of maternal pity, 'ye're only a silly bairn still, though ye talk big to the lassies.'

'Oh, Ma!' Leslie shouted and rushed upstairs to his bedroom, where he slammed the door. He had done this once before since I had known him, on another occasion of his mother's tormenting, and I knew he was going to have a cry.

My head was aching badly now. I should have liked to go home there and then, but felt my duty was to Leslie, to comfort him as best I could; my heart was far more wrung than if I had still been in love with him, when I should merely have been enraged. Anyhow, his mother did not mean me to leave. She had, after all, a pot of tea that was still hot; and she liked me, as she seemed to like all young women, on the grounds that because they were all too good for Leslie they must therefore all be creatures of special quality. She fetched me a cup and sat down to talk to me. Her talk turned entirely on Leslie's shortcomings; her resentment went back to his babyhood, when, apparently, he had invariably been sick after his bottles. Her accent had become far less Scottish, so much so that I began to wonder whether she had really spent her youth North of the Border. Leslie showed no signs of reappearing, so after half an hour or so of her displeasing reminiscences I made it plain to his mother that I was expected at home.

I had barely gone five yards along the street when I saw Leslie coming from the opposite direction. He was pushing a big gilded harp that was mounted on a wheeled platform, rather like the pedestal of a toy dog. His head was high, and he was whistling with piercing nonchalance. As I came nearer I observed that his face was a little swollen; but the smile with which he greeted me was bland. He stopped, giving a backward jerk to the harp, which had run along a little way on its own.

'I do hope Mater hasn't been wearing you out! She's absurd today, isn't she?' He glanced at the harp. 'I thought I'd pop along and get this for the Pater, just to save fuss.'

Two little boys on the other side of the street pointed and giggled. Leslie flushed. 'One would look quite ridiculous with this thing if one cared one way or another.'

'Not at all,' I said.

'Dignity is something one has or hasn't. If you have it you don't mind what you do. "The morality of masters and the morality of slaves." Nietzsche.'

'Leslie,' I said, 'your mother sounds so much more Scotch when she's angry. Was she born in Scotland?'

'By sheer chance, no,' he replied, lifting his eyebrows and looking seriously down upon me. 'She was born in Bungay. But her ancestry goes back and back. Back to the Stuarts,' he added in a hush.

'Give us a tune, mister!' one of the little boys sang out.

Leslie flushed again. 'Well, I'd better roll the damned thing in or Mater will be batey. She never forgets the days when we had servants, you know.'

I walked back with him to his gate.

He wedged the harp with a stone, so that it could not roll. 'A sad day for us, little one. One memory the fewer.'

'There's always next week,' I said, and felt a pang of despair, as I had intended that there should be no more next weeks with Leslie.

'Kiss me.'

'Not in the street. If your mother—'

'The Mater has a soft heart underneath. She's romantic, really, when you get to know her.'

'Silly swine!' said his mother from the doorway. 'D'ye want the wurrld to see ye, standing there like a great gaby? Bring that thing inside!'

'Coming,' said Leslie. She retreated. He looked at me, his pale-blue eyes begging me not to despise him. I put my arms around his neck and kissed him heartily, paying no attention to the renewed jeers of the little boys or to the harp that had lurched away from the stone and was stuck in the privets.

Leslie held me for a moment, encircled. 'Yes,' he said weightily, 'you love your man. You are that kind of woman.'

His mother began to hammer on the window-pane, and I went home.

3

Iris Allbright was one of those 'best friends' sought by plain girls in some inexplicable spurt of masochism, feared by them, hated by them and as inexplicably cherished. She was abnormally pretty; she never went through the stage of childish or adolescent lumpishness, but was always delightful in shape and calmly aware of her own destiny. She was vain and rapacious. Having all the admiration, she could not bear for a jot of it to be diverted, however momentarily, elsewhere. We sealed our friendship in our first term together at school. It was to be our last together also, for I stayed on, preparing myself for a career of business or, if I proved unexpectedly brilliant, school-teaching; and Iris went off to a school for theatrical children at Dulwich, where desultory lessons were given in the morning and the pupils sang, declaimed, mimed, or pirouetted in *tutus* for the rest of the day.

Like others of her temperament, she passionately desired affection of all kinds. She needed little children to crow at her, dogs to lick her hands. From the age of twelve she had little love-affairs with boys, still in short trousers, from the grammar school; if there were no boys about she would divert her flirtatious glances to me, press her sweet-smelling, honeysuckle cheek against mine and beg me to assure her that I would never abandon her for another best friend. As we grew older, as we went walking together on the Common in the soft Sunday afternoons to meet our lads of the moment, my thraldom to her, and my desire to be rid of her for ever, seemed to increase in exact ratio one to the other. My most pleasurable secret fantasy was to imagine myself at her graveside, weeping bitterly because one so gentle and lovely should have died so young.

She spoiled everything for me. If a youth showed the slightest interest in me she exerted every ounce of her charm to draw him to herself. We used to go out with pairs of lads who were also 'best friends', one conspicuously more attractive than the other. Iris at once took the handsomer for herself, assuring me that the other was supremely fitted for me, because he was clever and so was I, and that she could foresee a lifetime of intellectual harmony ahead of us. If this clever boy accepted his rôle as plain best friend (male) destined for plain best friend (female) and even began to show some admiration for me, Iris would not rest until she had got him away from me, at the same time keeping a firm hold upon her original choice. If there were two apples and two to share them, she considered it a fair distribution for her to have both.

And yet, in a way, I loved her. By flirting with me occasionally in lieu of anybody better she forced me into a kind of masculine, protective rôle. It was unnatural to me and I tried to resist it; I wished to be feminine as she; yet sometimes I felt I was beginning to walk with a sailor's roll.

Her femininity was absolute as that of pink roses in a basket tied with pink ribbons. She could wear dresses with flounces and floral patterns, saxe-blue ribbons fluttering from picture hats. Once I bought a bright-green hat of dashing cut, the sort I imagined Iris could not wear, and in it attended a rendezvous with our partners of the day.

'Oh, isn't that the most gorgeous tata!' Iris exclaimed in her popular baby talk. 'And it suits you marvellously. *Doesn't* it suit her, Roger? Peter thinks you look Ooh, so bootiful!'

The boys grinned noncommittally.

'Do let me try it, Christie, please – please – please! Just for once!'

Snatching it off my head, she went to the looking-glass and arranged it very carefully on her own. She pouted at her reflection. 'No, it's not for me! It's Christine's ownest hat. I look a hag. I look like a *horse*.'

'You look marvellous,' said Roger throatily, and of course she did. His throat contracted. Iris gave him a gentle flip on his nose.

'You *know* I don't.'

'Yes, you do.'

'Peter knows I look like a horse! Don't I, Petey?'

'You look all right,' he muttered, as throatily as Roger.

'There! Petey knows. He knows a haggy old horse when he sees one. Christie shall have her property back again.'

And, taking off the hat, she rammed it back on my head, slightly sideways. I adjusted it, my fingers trembling. I believed it made me hideous. She had spoiled it for me and I never wore it again.

Yet . . . yet . . . As I say, in a fashion I loved her. She had secrets with me that she whispered in my ear, tantalising the boys by glances from her steel-bright, fanshaped eyes. When she had a cold she liked me to sit at her bedside, stroking her hand or her brow. And she used often to say, 'There's nobody like you, Christie; nobody but you understands me. And you're the very first person in my heart.'

But when I fell in love for a little with the oafish Peter she abandoned Roger at once in order that I should no longer enjoy what could never be the prerogative of a plain 'best friend'. She made me bitterly unhappy, and when in a dream I stood again at her graveside I gave a harsh laugh and said, 'Ashes to Ashes.'

Leslie was the only lad she was unable to charm. From the first moment he had eyes only for me. Iris tried all her devices

– the teasing ones, such as tweaking his tie out and asking him for a tiny snip of it as a present; the sultry ones, such as turning her back on him and sighing on a long ripple; the malingering ones, such as pretending to turn her ankle and asking him to rub it for her. He remained impervious; perhaps, I sometimes thought, in the hard hours of my disillusionment, because he *was* touched. I could not believe any perfectly sane person could prefer me to Iris.

Nevertheless, the dogged calf-love of Leslie was the supreme turning-point of my youth, and it broke my enslavement to my beautiful friend. Now that I was loved, I began to look more comely. I was relaxed by confidence; I started to buy, without any feeling of making myself ridiculous, softer and paler dresses. I walked more naturally. I danced better. I began to make fewer and fewer appointments with Iris; and perhaps she did not much mind, for her own young men, reassured by the fact that somebody, even poor Leslie, could regard me with unswerving devotion, gradually came to pay me small attentions that Iris found it imprudent for them to spare.

On the evening that I left Leslie to the harp I returned to find Iris on my doorstep. I had not seen her for a month or so; she greeted me with one of her moist open kisses dropped upon my cheekbone. 'You horrible old stranger, you! You might have been dead for all I knew. I thought I'd come and rout you out.'

Dressed in a blue that was softened almost to violet by the light of the falling sun, she looked so charming that passers-by slowed their pace to stare at her. Sensitive to their admiration, she extended her arm to me at full length, jingling half a dozen blue and pink glass bangles, fashionable at the time. 'Tinkle, tinkle, tinkle! Do you like them or do I look like a Christmas tree? Darling, I've been knocking and banging for hours, and not a sound from anyone.'

I guessed that my father and my Aunt Emilie must have gone to the cinema together. She was not really my aunt, but his second wife: the designation was simply one she thought suitable for my use.

'I expect they're both out.'

'Oh, goody!' said Iris. 'I know Aunt E. heartily disapproves of me. She thinks I'm one of those fast actresses.'

In reality, Aunt Emilie did not think of her at all; she thought of no one but my father, for whom she had a humble, stupefied, worshipping love. She had been my mother's friend, a confirmed spinster as she supposed; and to be sought in marriage even by a man who simply needed her in order that his comforts should be uninterrupted and myself taken off his hands seemed to her a miracle and would always seem so. For his part he was mildly fond of her and of me, kind to us both, taking without giving, but taking so gracefully that his thanks seemed largesse in itself. He was a retired civil servant augmenting his pension now by letting the two top floors of the large Victorian house on the extreme edge of the Common, in the borough of Clapham and not of Battersea by the width of a street. When my grandfather bought the house in 1886 the neighbourhood had been much favoured by professional men in some way or other connected with the theatre. At that time the south side of Battersea Rise had consisted of open fields, a few hawthorns, and sheep safely grazing. He had bought his own house chiefly for the view, but within ten years the view had been obliterated by a sudden seepage of lower middle-class houses and shops, and within another ten the seepage had streamed down through stratas of villa and potential slum to the very edges of the river. My grandfather, for twenty years first violin in the orchestra at His Majesty's Theatre, never quite lost heart, and to the end he kept our household as lavish and Bohemian in tone as it was in the days of his prosperity, simply observing to my father during his last and fatal illness, 'When I am gone you can take lodgers in the upper part. But be sure I'm dead first.'

Although my father, Aunt Emilie and I had to live on the ground floor and semi-basement, the house itself had a touch of old splendours – a faded Morris wallpaper still evocative of peacocks and the gold of Danäe; the drawing-room chandelier with three lustres missing, which had been used in one of Tree's productions; a late-Regency mahogany sideboard, massive and simple, adorned only by a wreath of carved laurels; and the black and tarnished Japanese kakemonos, souvenir of a visit to San Francisco, that concealed a bad patch of cracked plastering in the upper hall.

To my friends it all seemed imposing and a little irritating. It makes no one popular to trail the least wisp of bygone glory while being hard up; modest as my life now was, I found a certain compulsion to depreciate the little I had.

'Come into the barracks, anyway,' I said to Iris, 'and we'll make ourselves some tea or something.' I took her in by the door of the semi-basement, grumbling all the while about the house being far too big for comfort.

'But, darling, you can breathe!' Iris protested. 'When I got back home after the theatre I felt I was in a little furlined *box*.' She had just fulfilled her first engagement as a chorus-girl in a musical comedy at the Winter Gardens.

She grew mysterious. Why did I think she had come right over from Winchester Gardens to call on a grump like me? What had I done to deserve the treat that she might, if I behaved myself, offer me? I certainly didn't deserve nice, loyal friends who were always fussing themselves to please me.

The long and short of it was that she wanted me to go to a dance at Hammersmith with herself, her new young man, and her young man's oldest and dearest friend. 'Victor says

Keith is absolutely charming, and he was absolutely crazy that I should find him a really gorgeous partner. So I thought of you.'

'The blind date', the acceptance of an invitation from a partner unknown, was a new amusement that had just come to England from America. I had never tried it myself, and was not eager to do so. (I was conservative in many things.) But Iris was insistent, and at the first sign of opposition from me she began to wheedle in her old, maddening and undermining fashion. 'Victor has wonderful taste in other men, and if he says Keith's all right you can take it that he *is*. And you'll ruin *my* poor little pleasure if you say no.'

I think I might, all the same, have said no had not Iris added, 'I'm sure your Leslie can spare you for *one* night.'

I remembered, then, that I was to be free of Leslie, free for myself, to choose or to refrain from choosing, free from fret and pity and the need for concealment of a mood. This seemed to me so delightful, this new freedom upon the threshold of any adventure or none at all, that I suddenly saw Iris's plan as a delightful one, which for myself would be a secret celebration. 'All right,' I said. 'When is it?'

'There!' she exclaimed. 'I knew you'd come through. I knew you'd never let me down and make me miserable.' Satisfied, she began to discuss what we should both wear, and I kept to myself the belief that my father might be persuaded to buy me a new dress. I could buy nothing yet for myself because, though I had left school, I was still at a secretarial training college. She picked up one of my aunt's fashion papers (which my aunt read fervently, though with no intention of acting upon the advice given) and began to study some drawings of evening dresses, but was diverted by the picture of a somewhat overweight baby with eyes like dark and constant stars, who was staring up into the tender face of a photographer's model unlikely to be his mother.

'That's what I want!' Iris said explosively. 'Nobody knows how I feel inside. I don't want to be on the stage. I want to get married and have a dear little baby just like that, all to my own. I'd like to have four or five babies – yes, I would, and don't look so cynical!'

It was many years before her own life proved the truth of what she had said. Though confident of her own beauty, she was miserably lacking in confidence where her talent was concerned, miserably badgered by her ambitious mother to a goal she felt she had no hope of attaining. ('One day, Iris, I shall see my daughter's name in lights.') For all her scalp-hunting, which alienated her women-friends more and more as time went on, she was sexually cold; her deepest instincts were maternal ones, and she was afraid that she would never be able to satisfy them. ('You don't want to marry too young if you want to keep your figure. There's plenty of time for all that.') When Iris stopped in the street to moon over a baby in a perambulator she did so with all the grace and public prettiness of an actress posing for her picture; yet she was genuinely moved, as by nothing else on earth.

Not realising all this, however, I made no comment upon her stated ambitions, but asked her more about the dance. It was, she said, the annual dance given by Victor's sports club; it was to be held on Saturday week; we would find our own way to Hammersmith tube station, and the boys would pick us up in a taxi.

'Oh dear!' I protested. 'I hate those things where you carry your shoes in a bag. It looks awful.'

'Well,' said Iris reasonably (in some ways she was more reasonable than I and, though I did not guess it, less ambitious), 'I suppose we'll have to wait a bit before we really get the men with cars.'

'You do, sometimes.'

'Oh, stage-door johnnies, in Mother's antiquated phrase. But then, they're not often serious.'

'Is Victor?'

'For the moment,' said Iris, with a curious convulsion of her cheeks that she called 'dimpling' and was the least effective of her facial devices, 'for the moment. He's got such lovely brown eyes, and sometimes I *melt*. . . . I don't believe you melt, Christie.' I thought bitterly that I melted more often than she knew, but had come to conceal these moments lest she be tempted to remove the object of my melting.

'I shouldn't tell Leslie about this jaunt,' she said. She added, with one of her meaningless adjectives, 'He'll only be oofy.'

4

It is the little meannesses of our lives that plague us most. For one thing, we can bear to take them out and look at them. Few of us are strong enough, or silly enough, not to suppress the memory of our major crimes against ourselves or our fellows. The small meanness, the small chicanery, looks fairly harmless, coiled up at the bottom of the Pandora's box which is our past; it is only when, lured by this apparent guilelessness, we take it out into the light that it sinks its fang in us, and we bleed, and we are poisoned.

It torments me now to remember how I got rid of Leslie.

My original intention, sprung to mind at Iris's last remark, had been mean enough. I had intended to ignore her advice, tell him about this dance and my interesting unknown partner, take advantage of the quarrel he would certainly provoke and dismiss him for ever. What I actually did was worse.

Mabel, of whom Leslie had spoken on the river-bank in such ominous terms, was not, as one might have thought, a Messalina or Thaïs. She was a rather stunted little girl with beautiful vacant green eyes, who had walked the Common with Leslie that previous summer. She was a typist in a local candle-factory, five years older than he and something of a favourite with his mother. For the latter had a soft spot for people who were frightened of her, and Mabel was so frightened that she never spoke to her except to admire her wildly and at random in a scarcely audible whisper. She was an excellent dancer, as Leslie was too; and they had twice won the Yale Blues competition at the Rosebud Hall in Brixton.

Mabel's claim to exciting wickedness in Leslie's imagination was the fact that at eighteen she had married a works foreman of forty-five, had discovered that her marriage was bigamous and had run away from him. Leslie used to refer to her in an awed whisper as a *divorcée*, thinking I had not heard the true story; and he suggested that she had once consoled herself by taking a series of lovers. This, however, his mother had pooh-pooh'd. 'The puir girl, she's as straight as a die. Once bitten, twice shy. An' she's no Venus de Milo, at that.'

Leslie's romance with Mabel had ended, as I well knew, shortly before his romance with me had begun; and I also knew that despite his pride in having had for his sweetheart a woman so much older than he ('a woman of *experience*,' he had said darkly, with the astigmatic look) he had lost all trace of interest in her. The only times he seemed to see her now were at the rare dancing competitions at the Rosebud Hall, at which she still partnered him; there was one due on the Monday week that followed Iris's visit to my house.

I spent the next Saturday with Leslie. Luckily it was raining, so we only went to the pictures. I made myself behave affectionately as ever, though now he seemed to me a stranger standing behind a wall of glass, someone I did not recognise and who had nothing to do with me at all.

On the Monday I went with him to the dance. We were well chaperoned at these little dances, for his mother always accompanied us, each time in some new and spectacular dress she had made for the occasion. She was a professional dress-maker, and an adept in salvaging just so much from her customers' materials as would make a blouse or a trimming for herself. Though Leslie would admit it only grudgingly, she was a superb natural dancer, and, if he had bothered himself to teach her the new steps, would have out-danced any young girl in the room. As it was, she had to content herself with the one-step and an 'old-time' waltz for which she was always sought by the M.C., a glossy, stout, smiling, bad-tempered little man called Wilkinshaw. It was Mabel who, generously, used to upbraid Leslie for not encouraging his mother's talent, and reproach him for glaring at her when she insisted on taking part in the Paul Jones. 'I know my own business,' Leslie would say grandly (but not within his mother's range of hearing), 'and it's not becoming for a woman of her natural dignity.'

The Rosebud Hall was built out on some waste ground behind a row of villas. The entrance, surprisingly enough, was actually through one of these houses, and the cloakroom was a converted scullery. House and hall were owned by Mr. Wilkinshaw, who had made quite a commercial success of his dances for years: he provided nothing but a three-piece band, and received a percentage from the café several doors down the street, where the boys and girls went in the interval for light refreshments.

The hall was graceless and gloomy, and the few paper-chains did little to mitigate the effect; but the floor was superbly sprung, and more than one young couple hoping for a professional career in ballroom dancing had done their first serious practising on it. When I had first been in love with Leslie that love had given the hall an Arabian Nights charm of its own, turning to gold dust the perfectly prosaic dust that lay on the window-ledges and the rungs of the chairs; now, in disenchantment, I saw it differently: saw, with a curious crystal prescience, that from this world, the world of Leslie, Mabel and Mr. Wilkinshaw, I must move onwards and far away. I had already deserted it in spirit as I should desert it in time; the knowledge made me both arrogant and ashamed.

Mabel, sitting at my side, looked from me to Leslie's mother and back again with her breathless, humble gaze.

This was the interval before the competition began, and Leslie had retired to change, rather pompously, into some shoes he had bought for this event alone. 'You both look so smart tonight! I wish I had your dress-sense.'

'A lass like yersel' shouldna wear hrred,' said Leslie's mother, 'any colour but hrred. Ye're too peaky.'

'Leslie said I was peaky.'

'Fine worrds from him, the silly fule! And me always on tae him aboot apeerients.'

He came gliding back to us across the floor, self-conscious cynosure of eyes. He was a champion, and he knew it.

'Not nervous, Mabel? Shall we go in and win?'

'I'd feel better if we really practised,' she said, looking down at her short, broad, nimble feet. 'The others do. I felt shaky last night.'

'You were smooth enough then,' Leslie replied. 'Just rely on me now, and remember, keep *smooth – smooth.*'

Mr. Wilkinshaw came into the centre of the floor, held up his hand to a roll of drums. The competition was announced. Leslie bowed to Mabel, who stood up with the electric nervousness of a new recruit, but who, the moment she was in his arms, took on the mask of a bland, blank professionalism.

While they danced, while they were proclaimed the winners, while they were clapped, cheered, presented with a certificate by Mr. Wilkinshaw's wife, years ago a British Amateur Champion, I evolved my shabby plan for escape.

It was understood, after these dances, that Leslie should see me home. We started off towards our tram, pursued by objurgations from his mother that he should not be late, that he should put on his clean socks next morning, and that he should not expect her to call him a dozen times to his breakfast. I suggested to him that we should walk the last part of the way. I had been speaking little and had already made him uneasy.

We walked across the Common. A light drizzle was falling, and the sparse lamps along the path were only the cores of larger, iridescent moons made of mist and gaslight. I said lightly, 'So you've been seeing Mabel again.'

'Seeing Mabel? Of course I have! I saw her tonight.'

'And last night.'

He paused, then said, 'I only looked in on her for a practice.'

'You didn't tell me.'

'What chance did I have? I've hardly seen you alone—'

'We've been dancing together.'

'And, anyway, it didn't strike me as being of the slightest importance. Mabel is nothing more to me than a partner.'

I told him not to lie to me; that I knew he had returned to her; that his concealment of the Sunday practice had proved it; and that I never cared to compete with anyone. He might have Mabel. For us, things were at an end.

'Silly little girl,' said Leslie on a deep, terrified note of tenderness. He stopped and tried to embrace me.

I pulled free of him and walked on. I recognised my own deceit and was ashamed of it. But subduing this shame was a strange pride at having fought my conscience and conquered it. The need to be free was like some violent physical pressure inside of myself; I felt the constriction from my heart to my throat. I could hardly breathe for it. I went on talking, more wildly as I went on. I could not bear lying, bear suppression. I hated dishonesty. I had seen that they were in love with each other, and for all I cared they could go on being so.

'You're mad, you're mad!' cried Leslie. He stopped me forcibly this time, holding me beneath a lamp. I saw the drizzle glistening like sugar on his hair, his forehead, on the ridge of his long nose. His eyes were open and lost, the rainy lashes sticking out from the lids like *chevaux de frise*. Then he said fatally, 'I can hardly help it if she's in love with me. That's not my fault.'

This evidence of a conceit that could override even the instinct to be silent in moments of danger (Mabel was not in the least in love with him, as well I knew) downed the last spurt of my conscience and sent it into a coma from which it was not to awaken for some years to be. I told him there was no need to discuss the matter further. We had come to the end – I had realised that for a long time, and so had he.

Nothing can be crueller than very young men and women when they fall out of love, nothing crueller nor more unimaginative. Much later in my life, when I lost a lover, I was to remember how Leslie had lost me, and to be moved painfully by pity for him and disgust for myself.

But this bursting desire for freedom gave me authority. I told him he must go away now, that I should make my way home alone.

'But you can't, not across the Common, not at this time of night! There are all sorts of bad types lying in wait.'

'I'll risk them,' I said and broke into a trot.

The drizzle changed suddenly into torrential rain. Instead of following the path, I cut into an open field, black as pitch, and ran straight on, guiding myself by the blur of lamps along West Side. Leslie lost sight of me. I heard his voice calling, panicked and desolate. 'Christie! Don't be so silly! Come back! What your father would have to say—' It passed into a trail of sound, a faint horizontal across the vertical bars of the rain, a sound far off, already being sucked down into the years; and then there was nothing at all but the hiss and patter of the night, the chattering of the trees under the punishing spouts of the sky.

The wet grass soaked into my stockings, the edge of my skirt; the soles of my shoes made a suck and a flap as I ran. The coolness was strange and delicious, and so was the dark.

I was free at last, light as air. I might have been running barefoot in the surf of some marvellous sea, along the edge of a land where nobody knew me and I knew nobody. For those few moments in the long field, no one knew where I was, no one in the world. I was to have that sensation of absolute freedom many times more in my life. Once, (I remember) after a period of stress and misery, I was walking in Gray's Inn Road, where some mere accident had taken me, and I had thought, No one can get at me. No one can write me a letter, telephone me, even guess at where I am. Here, in this London street, not two miles from my home, I might be in the deserts of Asia for all they know. And with that thought the bonds of the world had fallen from me and I had known a lightness and joy that was like rising from some crippling illness to discover that limbs would obey the will, were mastered, and were whole.

Yet it was, I think, something more than the exaltation of freedom which took me so strongly that wild wet night, in my eighteenth year. It was the knowledge that I had found the power to reject; that I need not simply take, in gratitude, what I was given. Later in my life I was to need a love so violently that I could fight for it with that strength which can throw pride overboard without a qualm; as if it were puerile and degraded; and could find courage in the memory that I had made my own choices in the past, and that therefore, if this love refused to come my way, I might find some sort of peace in accepting the rough justice of heaven. But that is another story, and not one I care to remember. As I say, it is the small things that plague us most, simply because we have the sense to keep the greater ones under lock and key.

5

I was born two years before the First World War, at the end of my grandfather's days of prosperity. My earliest memories are connected with shortness of money. For instance, there was a big doll displayed at Evans Auction Rooms on which I had set my heart, and my mother promised that she would go and bid for it. She returned from the sale sad-eyed and empty-handed. 'But I was glad I didn't get it, darling, *because I felt that doll had an evil face.*' She looked pathetically into my eyes, as if begging me to be convinced. And then there was the great debate as to whether or not we should have the house wired for electricity, which ended in the curious compromise of wiring the first two floors and, leaving the upper two to gas. 'A pound a point, remember; a pound a point,' said my father, stamping this phrase on my memory with a dark magic it has never lost.

When my grandfather died we found that he had left nothing but the house; and so the stream of lodgers (tenants, we called them) began: Mr. Cosgrave, who was removed hurriedly by night in an ambulance within a week of his arrival, on the suspicion that he had sleeping sickness; Mr. and Mrs. Leake, who were run to earth by the genuine Mrs. Leake and assaulted by her in our own hall; Mr. Smith and his sister, who left us, fortunately, a month before they were prosecuted for the dissemination of pornography through the mails; young Mr. Hope, who drank; and old Mrs. Thomson, whom we all disliked and whom I scared into giving notice by writing 'The Sinn Feiners are coming!' on the lavatory wall. (My mother assured her that there were no Sinn Feiners in Clapham and that this was a childish trick of mine, but Mrs. Thomson insisted on leaving that same day, muttering as she tottered away with her suitcase, 'No child of nine could have *spelled* it, no child could have *spelled* it.)

That was the kind of traffic likely to occur in those days, if you let rooms furnished. It was far too easy for people to rush in and rush out; and though we always took references, these had usually been written by the lodger's close relations, if not by the lodger himself.

I loved my mother, a sad, fretful, affectionate woman who had enormous dreams for me. She spoke of them seldom, but *looked* them all the time. I was bowed by the weight of her hope. It was she who ran the house, my father and the lodgers; all the cares were hers. When she was brought down by pleurisy, which turned to double pneumonia, she looked at me in anguished surprise. 'But I can't die! No one else is fit to manage.'

I was fourteen then, and when she was gone I believed I could never be happy again.

She was right in believing that no one else was fit to manage. I was too young and my father too disinterested. He looked rapidly around for a wife who would manage everything, and rapidly married Emilie, who had been a tower of strength, as my father put it, right through my mother's illness and afterwards. 'Or perhaps one ought, to say,' he remarked, giving his strange, half-hitched smile, 'a cottage of strength. Your Aunt Emilie is too small to remind one of towers.'

In his fashion he was very fond of me; but he had never been an ambitious man, and was not particularly ambitious on my behalf. It had been my mother's desire that eighty pounds of her insurance money should go to training me at a really good secretarial college, where I should meet the right kind of girl and perhaps go straight into a really high-class post. If she had to see me as a secretary at all (and she saw me mostly as a great pianist, actress, singer, writer), then it was as something she called a 'Social Secretary', one who sent and accepted invitations for a duchess, and did the flowers. My father, though he thought the idea silly, did not flout her wishes. He put the eighty pounds down straight away and gave me another twenty to spend on appropriate secretarial clothes – in those days an unimaginable sum.

I was happy at this college, though I made no friends there, for all the girls were richer than I and many of them were doing their training, not in order to earn a living, but to have some sort of career in their hands either to while away the time before they married or to maintain themselves if ever it became necessary for them to leave their future husbands. 'Darling,' one of them said to me, 'you have to look to the future. Suppose he's a brute but not enough to divorce him for: well, you leave him, but you may not get a penny, and then what? It's far better to know that you *can* leave a man at any time, because it keeps him in order.'

No – my friends were the local ones of my childhood: girls I had known at school, boys from the grammar school or the Catholic college of the Salesians. We were growing up together, and life was cheerful. It had been a principle of my mother's that it was far better for me to bring boys home than to meet them surreptitiously around corners. In fact, I did both. But her insistence upon open house once a week for any of the boys and girls of my acquaintance was a good one, for she had an excellent eye to the weeding-out of undesirables. My father continued her custom, less from principle than from laziness. He trusted me, I suppose, whenever he thought about the matter at all. Emilie fretted, but she never dared to say so, and kept guard on me only by waiting up for me with cocoa whenever I went out dancing.

In those years, dancing was a national mania. The Charleston had just reached us from America. We used to turn on the gramophone, roll back the carpet and practise earnestly, my friends and I, till ten o'clock, when Aunt Emilie brought us tea and bread-pudding and put the clock on the sideboard to indicate that it was time the visitors thought about going home. For me it was a free life, an innocent one, a good one. None of the boys and girls were entirely strangers to each other, or to each other's families. Even if some unknown boy had been picked up on the Common (a harmless, giggling, very mildly romantic proceeding) he would usually turn out to be the nephew of one of the women Aunt Emilie knew at church, or a cousin of another boy whose credentials were already accepted.

Ukeleles were fashionable. All the young men tried, with more or less varying success, to play them. Dicky Flint, a blond, strapping lad a little older than the rest of us, and the only one at whom the accusation of 'fastness' had ever been levelled (without justice, incidentally), was famous among us for being able to play 'melody' as well as accompaniment. His ukelele bore a charming knot of ribbons at the top of it, and was quite an expensive one. It was the custom, on warm evenings, for the young men and girls to draw deck-chairs into a circle in the big field by North Side, and for Dicky to play while the others sang the tunes of the day, but these open-air parties Aunt Emilie resented, and she forced a kind of reluctant resentment upon my father. 'Bring them home if you like, but sitting there with them on the Common is *common*,' she would say; she had few synonyms.

'Yes, Christine, don't do it,' my father would echo her feebly, while thinking of something else.

Yet, one blue June evening, when I had disobeyed orders and was sitting with the others, he strolled by, looking rather dashing, as he often did, in his tipped cap; seeing me, he simply raised it, gave my friends his odd, charming smile and passed on, leaving the smoke of his cigar like a blessing upon the love-haunted night.

The week after my dismissal of Leslie was a nerve-racking one, for he bombarded me with letters and even with calls at extraordinary hours. I would not see him, but I did write a long, false letter telling him how precious his friendship would always be to me, though I could offer him nothing more. Aunt Emilie suspected that I had treated him badly, but did not interfere; she would always side with a woman against a man, if that man were not my father. He, on the other hand, conspired with me frankly to see that Leslie did not get beyond the doorstep. 'I never thought that boy was any good to you, Christine, the silly lolloping lump. Plenty of time for that sort of thing. You stick to your shorthand.'

In fact, my mind was full of my unknown partner; my fancy touched such romantic heights that if the dance had been held in Buckingham Palace and Keith discovered to be the Prince of Wales, reality could scarcely have matched my imaginings. Also, I had determined that upon this occasion I was going to outshine Iris, turning her mere prettiness to nothing by my own dignity and mystery. (I had never thought of myself as mysterious before, and it now seemed an excellent idea.) My father was willing to pay for a dress, so I bought a perfectly plain pink one and decided that, as a *coup*, I would wear no necklace, no earrings, no trinkets of any kind. I had read novels in which the heroine's studied lack of adornment had made diamonded countesses seem tawdry and underbred.

Of Iris I had heard nothing, except for a note, dropped in my door, to the effect that I should call at her home on the Saturday evening at seven and that the boys would take us by taxi all the way. She added a PS. 'Victor says Keith really *is* handsome, by the way; *not very tall*, but quite heavenly.'

On the important night I came downstairs stately but full of misgivings.

'You must have been up there a couple of hours,' said my father.

Aunt Emilie took one look at me. 'Why ever do you want to make yourself such a plain Jane? Why not wear your crystals?'

'Jewellery isn't being worn this year by really smart people,' I said. I hoped even they would notice how the absence of it threw my personality into relief.

Emilie prowled slowly round me, as if I were an inanimate object. 'Well, I think you look like a charity child. Doesn't she, Horace?'

'You and I don't know about these new fads. The colour suits her.' My personality did not appear to strike them.

'I still think the crystals, or your silver rose—'

I was shaken: but I stuck to my guns.

'Don't you be too late,' said my father, not specifying how late. 'Yes, I must say pink's your colour.'

'You're not going to walk to Iris's in those shoes?' said Emilie.

'I'm not going to carry a horrible little bag,' I said.

'It's blowing half a gale,' my father observed, 'but please yourself.'

6

It was a March night of tearing moon and cloud, a night so vigorous, so full of movement, that even the far-off ragged edges of the Common seemed to be rising and falling like the rail of a ship. I had tied a scarf over my hair but even so, was afraid I should arrive dishevelled; the wind seemed to fight me back as I crossed North Side and turned into Winchester Gardens, where Iris lived. I hoped I should be early enough to tidy myself before the young men came; I could not afford the smallest physical disadvantage, even a momentary roughening by the wind, in the presence of my friend.

She opened the door to me herself: over-dressed as usual, but making me aware, with a conclusive sinking of the heart, that my studious, hopeful underdressing had been a mistake. I felt as though I had come out in my nightdress.

'Oh, pitty, pitty colour!' she exclaimed, clapping her hands like a baby and eyeing me with an air of mature appraisal. 'You look so virginal, darling. I do wish Mummy could see you, but she's round at Aunt Ada's. Come into the bedroom and tittivate. They'll be here at any moment.'

I looked with one last faint resurgence of hope at my reflection in the mirror, saw behind me, emphasising my unfortunate starkness, all the characteristic clutter of her room: the frilled dressing-table; the pallid, slightly soiled crinoline doll whose skirts formed a nightdress case; the row of soapstone elephants, descending in size, along the mantelpiece.

'You look like a Puritan maid, dear,' said Iris; adding, after a slight pause, 'but why?'

This seemed unanswerable, and I did not attempt it.

She put scent behind her ears and along the hem of her dress. 'Mummy says I've got to have a decent stage-name. Iris is all right, but Allbright's all wrong. She wants Iris Lavallière, but I think it's oofy. I want Iris La Haye.'

I said I didn't like either. 'You're pretty enough,' I suggested, 'to startle people with something very simple. Like Iris Green. Or Grey. Or even Jones.'

'How can you say that! I look like a horse; don't contradict me, I know I do.'

We got in each other's way, each of us fighting for the greater share of the glass, and all the while Iris chattered and chattered, in so high and nervous a voice that I suddenly realised she was uneasy about something.

'What is it?' I asked her.

She set down her hairbrush and looked at me. 'What's what?'

'What's the matter?'

'Nothing. Why should there be?'

'I thought there was.'

'Don't be oofy,' said Iris. She put her arm round me, regarded me with her veiled flirtatious look. 'Say I don't look a horse?' She held herself closely against me; I could feel her heart beating. 'Darling, you know I adore you? You know Iris would never let you down?'

I felt an increase of apprehension. 'There is something!'

'No, darling, not really; because you've got such a sweet nature and nobody's kinder than you, but it does sort of seem that Keith—'

The door bell rang.

'There they are!'

'Keith what?'

Iris spun about in a gust of pale-blue tulle and violet scent. Her bracelets jingled. The colour ran into her cheeks, as it runs into a glass of clear water when a brush of crimson paint is dipped in it, first veining, then suffusing.

'Keith what?' I cried.

Pushing me away, she ran out into the hall and opened the door. She greeted the young men with a kind of wordless chatter, something that sounded as if it were made of real words but was probably not. I came out behind her; and the gust of air from the night sent our hair blowing on our foreheads and flattened our pink and blue skirts against our knees.

'This is Victor,' she announced in a tone of wild gaiety, her eyes looking everywhere but at me. He was a deep-dimpled young man with toffee-coloured eyes; all of him shone.

'And this is Keith.'

I took the shock immediately; my succeeding emotion was one of pure dizzying anger.

Keith was handsome – Victor had not lied about that. He was more than handsome; his face was beautiful, a sad, clear, cold face, the eyes great and blue; questioning; resigned to the answer. But the eyes were below mine, on a level with my lips, and I was small.

He was a cripple, so stunted that a body meant to be broad and powerful had to support itself upon the legs of a boy of twelve. Wedge-shaped, one shoulder sloping down behind his head like a hillside in the background of an Italian portrait, he offered himself in hate and pride to my appraisal. For he knew at a glance that I had not been warned.

We shook hands.

'I hope we're not late,' said Victor, 'but if we are we've got an excuse. We didn't come by taxi. We came in Keith's car. He only got it today.'

'From my father,' Keith said, unsmiling, looking at nobody. 'He promised it for ages, and today he came across.'

Iris opened the door again and peered out. 'Oh, you *lucky*! Doesn't it look gorgeous, crouching there like a tiger?'

'It's only second hand. It was my father's car. But he bought himself another.'

'Aren't we lucky girls, Christie?' she demanded, skipping back to stand at my side. She put her arm around my waist: I held myself rigid.

I was in a kind of terror. I knew that I must conquer my fury, not in an hour's time but now, instantly; that I must not let Keith see it, or, if he suspected it, to be sure of it. The fury was against Iris, for her deceit, her feebleness of spirit: she had known the truth, perhaps belatedly, but had not dared to tell me. I thought: This is all she thinks I am worth; this is the measure of her contempt. And at the same time (this horrified me) I felt some of that rage diverting itself to the cripple, that he should be as he was. I could not help it, though I hated myself for it. And in self-disgust I also knew a pettier self-pity. Somehow the plain pink dress, the device of wearing no ornaments, made me ridiculous in my own eyes, so that I turned from myself in hate not only for the cruelty I could not help but for the silly affectation I could have avoided.

'Make yourselves comfortable while I retire for a weeny minute,' Iris called to us, seeking escape if only for a few seconds; 'you'll find cigarettes in the box.'

'I must say Iris looks terrific tonight,' said Victor smoothly; not so smoothly adding, 'So do you.'

'I don't really try to compete.' I sounded disagreeable, and knew it. I found the cigarettes for him. 'I'd better get my coat.'

I ran to the bedroom, where I found Iris, tight-lipped, putting on some more powder.

'How could you do that!'

'Darling, I didn't really *grasp* it. You know how bad men are at describing each other. I only knew he was a bit lame – or that's what I thought.'

'You knew what he was.'

'Christie, you're not going to quarrel with me? Please, please! You shall dance with Victor quite as often as I do.'

'Victor is a horrible greasy boy,' I burst out; 'I'd *rather* have Keith.'

Iris burst into tears. 'Now look what you've done! You've made me look hideous. You're spoiling everything. Oh, go away! I'll join you in a minute.'

When I went back into the sitting-room I found Keith alone.

I saw that he was older than I had thought; perhaps twenty-four or five. Or perhaps the strain and resentment of his life had added the years to a boy of eighteen.

He stood with his back to the fire, hands locked behind him, his face quiet and still.

'It must be fun to have the car,' I said. My voice sounded normal to my own ears. I was fighting against time to subdue the sick and heaving anger so useless to me, so brutal to him.

He drew a very white, stiff handkerchief from his pocket and passed it between the palms of his hands. The overhead lamp, rather dim, as all Mrs. Allbright's lamps were, shone on his head. His hair was acorn-coloured, thick and flat.

'I'm afraid they didn't tell you,' he said, not a flicker of change in his expression. 'That was fair neither to you nor me.'

I searched wildly for words. There should be words that would not hurt him, but it was no good trying to find them. There was not time. I could only speak, and hope that by luck the words came right.

'You mean, that you're lame. No, they didn't. But I don't suppose people notice as much as you think they do.'

Then he smiled, a tender, eased smile, but having in it nothing that was humble. ' "Lame" isn't really the idea. I can dance – not badly – but I'd as soon sit and talk. It is as you please.'

My anger sank, to be submerged by a pity almost as painful, which had in it a touch of a new anger – an anger for him.

'But I'm going to dance. I want to dance a lot.'

'Victor says you write poetry.'

'I try.'

'I read it. I wish I could write it. He tells me you're extremely clever.'

'I'm clever and Iris is pretty,' I said, out of old resentments. 'We've got our labels.'

'I think you are both,' he replied slowly. 'And I wish I were like other men, so that you could take the compliment seriously.'

He did a curious thing; he held out his hand palm upwards and waited for me to put mine into it. I did so. It was like the first figure of a dance that neither of us knew very well. He pressed my fingers very tightly and then walked away.

Victor came in. He was followed by Iris, determinedly gay and noisy.

'And how have you two been getting on?'

'I have been telling Christine that she looks very pretty,' said Keith. I saw then that he was not a boy who looked older than his years; he was a man who looked younger. He was probably nearing thirty.

Iris reacted to this quite automatically. 'There! Christie getting *all* the compliments as usual and not a word for poor me!'

Keith smiled, and said nothing.

'Oh, we all know you're a horse and a hag,' Victor teased her. He ran his hand over her bare shoulder. She told him not to tickle. She was sensitive. She didn't like to be touched. Especially she didn't want to be touched by people who called her a hag. She made him play out a little scene with her, to get her to forgive him; and by the time she had agreed to do so it was a quarter to eight.

'I think we'd better be going, if you don't mind,' Keith said in his odd, impassive way. 'It's a fair drive.'

So we went down to his car through the battering wind.

'Now, Christie shall sit with Victor in the back,' Iris said authoritatively, 'and Keith and I will tell each other our life stories in front.'

'Oh, I say!' Victor protested.

'No. You'll all do as I tell you. Keith has a down on little Iris and thinks she's nasty, and I'm going to have everyone being friends before we get to the dance!'

Keith silently held the door for her as she stepped into the driving-seat. She managed to whisper to me, 'I'm making it up to you, you see!' Really, she had sensed his disapproval of her, his kindliness towards me, and could not bear that, even by him, I should be preferred. In this kind of behaviour Iris was entirely without cruelty towards the person she attempted to dispossess. She bore no animus. She did not even think of that person. She had grown up loved, admired, worried over, exclaimed over. If she were not first with anyone whom she met, this merely seemed to her a disturbance of the natural order of things that must be set right. I think that if any girl, robbed of her sweetheart in this fashion (and there were many), had turned upon Iris and made a frank complaint, Iris would, with bright, surprised eyes and all her good-nature aroused, simply have accepted the justice of this plea and stepped aside; but very young men and women set great store by something they call pride, which is really lack of courage and self-confidence.

I did not, of course, care if Iris were perverse enough to go to the lengths of attracting Keith from me; I was far more annoyed and humiliated by the behaviour of Victor, who, forced to sit with me in the back, spent part of the time in sulky silence and the other part jerking himself forward to kiss Iris's neck. He did this once just as Keith braked to avoid a pedestrian, banged his face on the back of the seat in front, and made his nose bleed. We arrived at the dance in a somewhat uncertain mood: Keith stiff and silent, Victor holding a handkerchief to his face, and Iris and I displaying the kind of automatic, rather aggressive gaiety that young girls display at parties when the prelude has somehow gone wrong.

7

The ballroom was in the semi-basement of a large restaurant on the Broadway. As we went in I saw at once that when we had left our coats we should have to make our entry down a broad flight of half a dozen stairs, designed to display the charms of confident and pretty girls, but not, I thought, to display me; and at once the uncontrollable, vertiginous fury returned as I pictured myself, uncomely in the pink nightdress, walking down these Steps at the side of a cripple whose head did not reach to my ear. My eyes filled. Iris said something to me, but I could not answer her.

In those days I was given to imagining myself (it is a habit that passed without note as I grew up) not in heroic or splendid rôles but in disgraced and shameful ones. It was one of the bizarreries of adolescence, a thing I only allowed to come to the front of my mind when I was actually driven to indulge it. It seemed to me, that March night, as if these disagreeable dreams had suddenly hardened into reality; that upon this reality every eye was turned, and every ray from the clustered lamps, lemon, rose and gold, garlanded for festivity, was converging upon it. Wildly I considered pretending to feel sick, even to faint; wondered if I might force myself to an attitude of non-participation so emphatic and strange that it could only command respect and endow me with some of that mystery for which I had so idiotically hoped when I set aside the pearl beads, the crystals and the silver rose. (But I had the courage for none of these things.) Choked with tears and anger, I followed Iris into the cloakroom, pulled off my coat and threw it to the attendant, accepted the ticket, passed my hands over my hair and went to wait for her by the door, without so much as a side glance in the mirror. This I could not face.

In a few moments she came and stood by me. She muttered, 'Oh, what's the matter? You aren't going to spoil things, are you? I swear I didn't know. Oh, Christie, you can't still be oofy!' I pushed her away. I was afraid the tears would fall. The desperate thought crossed my mind that if only they would stay within the confines of my lids they might give me sufficient of an illusion of beauty to help me carry this horrible affair through. I did not give a thought to Keith, though I knew I ought to be thinking of him and for him. I was utterly selfish in my own distress, and stimulated by the pride of being wicked enough to accept my own selfishness.

We went out.

This was a larger, more elaborate dance than most of those to which I was accustomed. The sports club, Iris had told me, was for people with pretty good jobs: professional people, businessmen of executive standard, and master tradesmen who owned shops but did not serve in them. Many of the men were wearing tail-coats; the dresses of the women were less fussy than those of the girls at the Rosebud Hall, and a little scantier; but I saw no countesses in black velvet without adornment.

Victor and Keith were waiting at the head of the stairs, Victor wearing his confident, meaningless smile, Keith squat and unsmiling in his shadow. Iris moved towards Victor arms outstretched, as if she were greeting him at the end of a voyage, the blue dress taking a faint rosiness from the lights overhead. 'Darling, have we been ages and ages?'

'Ladies' privilege,' said Victor, with what seemed to me a sickening little bow. My heart tightened. I walked towards the young men.

And then something happened. Keith stepped forward. He said to Iris in a loud, expressionless voice, 'You look magnificent. May I congratulate you?' With a movement so deft that I could hardly follow it, he slipped between her and Victor and placed his hand on her arm, drawing her forward with him. It was with Keith that Iris descended the terrifying stairs and I who followed with Victor, who looked like a thundercloud behind a shocked, bright smile.

My charged heart seemed to burst like an ulcer, infinitely easing, but infinitely weakening. I was filled with such wonder and such gratitude that when Keith asked me for the first dance I could not find words to answer him. I was so sorry now for my callousness towards him (thank God I had not shown it, but had merely let it consume itself within me) that I sought as wildly for means to please him as I had sought for means to desert him. Curiously enough he danced well, better than I (who had never been a fit partner for Leslie), and the pleasure of his competence was soothing. We danced for a little in silence. At last he said, 'It is not gentlemanly to say so, I know, but I do not find Iris particularly pleasing.'

'She's sweet really,' I said, feebly torn between affection for him and the old loyalty to her.

'She wants to take everything from you. Why on earth do you let her?'

'I can't,' I replied, repeating myself, 'compete.'

'Oh, nonsense. Iris is for very young men only.'

This lifted me to a seventh heaven. 'She seems to be for all of them.'

'Again I say, nonsense.' Keith spoke very much as if his lines had been written for him; I had already noticed his aloof trick of substituting 'I cannot', 'I do not', 'I would not', for the more natural 'I can't', 'I don't', 'I wouldn't'. 'She is for very young men, or for men who will always be very young. Would you consider Victor up to your own intellectual weight?'

'I haven't really thought of my intellectual weight,' I answered, deeply flattered.

'You must have done so. You write; you read. Victor says you have already had a poem published.'

'One. But not in anything important.'

'You would always need an intellectual response,' said Keith, looking suddenly weary, 'but that, of course, is all I'm fitted to offer you, and all by itself it will not do.'

The music came to an end. He did not swing me round, as many men swung their partners (Victor, I noticed, had made Iris into an iridescent top), but brought me gently and precisely to a full stop. We returned to our table.

Then Victor danced grudgingly with me, I sat out a dance with Keith, and danced once with some young man who appeared to be the club secretary. We had ices. Keith said, 'Will you excuse me? I've left my cigarettes in the car,' and went away. Victor and Iris took the floor again and I was left alone.

All at once I saw standing at the foot of the stairs a middle-aged, high-coloured woman talking to a young man. Though I glanced at them only casually at first, I felt impelled to look again at the man. At that moment his eye caught mine; he stared at me for a second, looked away.

My heart moved, sending me without warning into such an anxiety, restlessness and desire that I was scared by my own emotion. In a stroke, I was in love.

8

I know through this experience that love at first sight is possible – I have proved it empirically. What I see no reason for claiming is that love of this kind is the best, for the most enduring love in my life, which is no part of this story, did not at all begin in such a fashion. It was upon me suddenly in joy, bewilderment and something like fear, when, after years of knowing, and of complex but unanalysed friendship, I had looked upon the object of it with new eyes.

But this love of my eighteenth year was heedless, irrational and storming. I could not believe in it; it seemed not part of myself, like bone, flesh and fibre, but a hard and alien thing which had lodged itself within me.

He was a slight, fair man, perhaps twenty-seven to thirty years of age, a little below medium height, but with a kind of perching, flexible grace. He had a small face, the forehead high, the nose sharply aquiline, the mouth full and a little surly. His chin was small but jutting. It was a bird-like face except for the eyes, full, blue and analytic under heavy and curious-coloured lids.

His posture, his way of replying to what the woman was saying, simulated a kind of contemptuous impatience; he did not seem, as it were, part of the party. He might have been some kind of inspector, called in to pass an opinion upon the organisation, the band, the structure of the building itself.

There was another girl sitting next to me, like myself unsought; a plain girl, who, I had observed, seemed familiar with many people there. Driven as I could never have been by any lesser curiosity, I said to her, 'I have a feeling I know those two by the stairs. Can you tell me who they are?'

'Well, she's Mrs. Patton; she's one of our vice-presidents. She's awfully rich and helps out a bit if we have a deficit. I don't know who he is.'

'I think she's rather attractive,' I said falsely.

'Oh, do you?' the girl answered with pardonable surprise.

Keith came back with the cigarettes, Victor and Iris from the floor. The dance went on.

In those days the young men had a certain bad habit that may or may not, for all I know, be current today. This was to feel the necessity, at any dance on unlicensed premises, to go out for a drink whether they wanted one or not. It was merely a custom; it established their manliness, emphasised the reality of their trade-union. Victor, I knew, would make a move shortly; I was rather surprised when Keith moved simultaneously, as I had somehow thought he would have grown out of this convention.

'Interval,' said Victor, 'and time for a very quick one. Will you girls excuse us?'

'I shan't let him be long,' added Keith, whose eyes had brightened a little as though even he, this evening, had discovered some kind of enjoyment.

'Aren't they sickening!' Iris complained when they had gone, dutifully leaving us with lemonade. 'Men simply can't keep off the drink. I think they're revolting.'

They were still absent when the band returned to the dais.

'They don't deserve us, darling,' Iris fumed. 'Honestly, I think the world would be far better without men.'

The floor was empty at first. Then one couple took to it, and then another, and the efflorescence grew till it bloomed like a garden.

I saw him picking his way towards us – to me? – walking gracefully, but looking graceless. I was standing against the wall, and I dared not look at him. Instead, I examined my pink dress, discovering that though it was shiny to the eye of anybody else, the pattern of the weaving made it seem mat to anyone wearing it. Shining thread passed beneath dull one, a cross-hatching infinitely small and delicate, giving a low tone to the whole surface. Staring downwards, I could see his legs, two black chimneys fastened to earth.

'Shall we dance this?'

The voice seemed not to come in my direction or Iris's, but to be launched into space, awaiting a response from anybody who cared to make one.

I looked up, jerking myself out of a hot and apprehensive dream.

Iris was smiling like an angel or a child. 'No, no; I'm tired. You dance this with my friend. She's far better than I am.'

He looked at me.

'I'm not dancing this one,' I said, sounding airy, though I was blazing with pride and disappointment; 'I've laddered my stocking.' I explained rather elaborately that it was necessary for me to go to the cloakroom before it went any further.

He did not seem to be listening. He was looking at Iris now, his eyes frankly inspecting her; he looked all over her face in a circular inspection, and she flushed. Then she gave a little shrug, placed a hand upon his upper arm – she had a trick of avoiding a man's shoulder – and a hand lightly on the top of his own. He smiled then, and half lifted her across the strip of carpet on to the sprung floor. She was a blueness among flowers. Her smile sprinkled them like a garden spray.

During my self-imposed retreat to the cloakroom I thought: Keith was wrong. This is not a very young man. She will take everything away from me, all my life. (For the whole of life seemed at that time a crystallisation of years small enough to be held in the hand, a thing for immediate disposal, to be snatched by another, to be thrown away.) Yet (I defended her even then) was it her fault? He had wanted her, not me. Of course he had wanted her. Would not anyone else on earth?

My face feeling stiff as my tightened throat, I went back to the ballroom.

Keith and Victor came back – Keith impenetrable as usual, Victor with a masculine, ingratiating smile, part guilt, part self-satisfaction.

'So sorry! We had to fight our way to the bar.' His smell of beer reminded me a little of Leslie's smell of jam, and aroused in me a pang of quite irrelevant remorse. 'Where's Iris?'

'Someone asked her to dance.'

The music stopped. She came shining down on us, like Marie Antoinette entering the Oeil de Boef, her partner behind her. He bowed to her quickly and went away as if he had a pressing appointment.

'Oh, Vic, I'm afraid I was naughty! But you were late, and Christie and I couldn't be wallflowers!'

'I was a wallflower,' I said, and was surprised to find that I could say it easily and without rancour. I did not believe Iris had been a success this time.

Keith smiled at me. 'Only from choice,' he said.

The band struck up a Paul Jones.

'All in!' Iris cried, standing on tiptoe, stretching her arms above her head and waggling her fingertips. 'And may the best girl win.'

I looked at Keith.

'This is not my dance,' he said, still with the same approving smile, 'though I did hear a chap say once that no Paul Jones was any fun without a booby-prize. However, I shall leave that rôle to Victor.'

Iris clasped me by the hand and pulled me after her into the ring of girls. Sliding, sidling, gliding, bumping one another, eyes bright and shifty, we all revolved. Victor, in the outer ring, was trying to put a space between himself and his neighbours by stretching out his arms, in order that if Iris came his way he should not miss her; but was repeatedly forced forward by the pressure, his arms pinned to his side, his smile protruding as his body protruded.

'—Te-tum te tiddle-y, ta, ta!' the band chorused, and stopped. I looked up. In front of me, having separated himself from the men on his left and his right, as Victor had failed to do, was the man with whom I had fallen in love.

We moved off to one of those slow, somnambulistic waltzes which made the calves ache.

'That was neat, I think,' he said to me, looking over my head.

I saw at close quarters that he was rather lined, as if he had been much in the sun. From below, his nose looked not only imperious but rather utilitarian, like a cutting-edge. His eyes were small-pupilled, the iris curiously composed as if by a mosaic of blues and greys, each infinitesimal section faintly pencilled around.

He said, 'When I ask you to dance, why does your friend take it upon herself to accept the invitation?'

I was much too young to be clever. 'But you were looking at her!'

'I was probably looking,' he replied, 'somewhere between you. This is the first dance I've been to in three years and I'm a trifle gauche. However, I thought my meaning was clear.'

'It wasn't!' I cried, and began to laugh as he laughed. Happiness filled me, and wonder. 'Why did you come tonight?' I asked him.

'One of the big pots of this club is a cousin of mine. She dragged me along.'

'Are you glad you came?'

'Yes. But next time I ask you to dance I hope you'll answer for yourself.'

It was brusque, it was arrogant, and, because he must have known how much younger I was than he, it was a little unkind. But I did not care. His voice had a certain leisurely harshness that enchanted me. Beside him, young men like Victor were miserable little boys. I was sorry for Iris. Really sorry. Poor Iris.

'Damn,' he said.

We were off in the rings again. This time I tried as hard to stop before him as he before me. Iris, on the far side of the room, raised her eyebrows, put a finger to her lips in mock rebuke. But we did not succeed in our manœuvres until the final round, which, because the band was weary, was a perfunctory gallop. As we stopped, breathless, he said, 'Supper-dance next. Will you save it for me?'

At that moment I caught sight of Keith, at our table, alone. He was reading through a programme of the club's future activities, reading it with a kind of concentration which filled me with compassion and strength.

'I'm sorry,' I said; 'I'm booked for that.'

'Break it.'

'I can't.'

'Who's it with? That treacly chap?'

'No.' I nodded towards the table.

He hesitated for a moment, then said, 'Have it your own way, my dear,' and walked away as abruptly as he had walked away from Iris.

I felt desolate.

Keith looked up to greet me. 'Was it fun?'

'So-so.'

'I think you were having a great success.'

'Don't be silly,' I said, with an ungracious fretfulness.

Iris eddied down upon us. 'Christie, you sly old thing! *Quite* the most attractive man positively chasing you round the room! I believe it's a plot.'

'A plot to do what?' Keith enquired.

'Oh, a plot to do – to do anything! You don't know Christie. She's deep.'

'Does anyone know who he is?' I asked.

'I could find out,' said Victor. 'I know Mrs. Patton a bit. He seems to be with her.'

'And he asked you for the supper-dance! I heard him! Christie, you *are* having a triumph.' Iris spoke with the wonderment she might have displayed had all the women taken a fancy simultaneously to Cyrano de Bergerac.

'Well, I couldn't,' I said quickly.

'Oh, you coot!' she exclaimed. Entirely generous in some ways, she really hated me to miss any chance that came my way, provided it was not a chance which she felt to be hers by rights. 'Why ever not?'

'I promised it to Keith.'

He looked at me sharply. For a moment I thought he would tell me that there had been no promise; but instead he said gently, 'It would have been all right.'

'But I wanted the supper-dance with you,' I told him.

It was easy then almost to mean what I said; it was easy to be kind. Yet during that long, over-creamed, over-sweetened supper, sitting in his quiet company while Iris and Victor flirted more and more noisily as time went on, paddling their hands upon each other, sibilantly whispering, going into fountain-jets of that peculiar, tinkling laughter which one always suspects is directed against oneself, I grew more and more irritable, found it harder to take comfort in the mere fact of behaving well. Seated, his stunted legs concealed by the table, Keith seemed less of an object of pity. I tried to concentrate upon the beauty of his face and the stillness suffering had at last brought to it. Surely he had found his own kind of happiness? Hadn't I been too sensitive on his account? Mightn't I have thrown away a lifetime (again that lifetime, that nut of crystal) for the sake of offering him a reassurance he did not need? These thoughts were itching at me, driving me into a new frenzy of resentment, when he said suddenly, 'Don't think I don't notice how good you are. I shan't forget that supper-dance, Christine.'

I told him I was not in the least good, meaning exactly what I said, but giving my words a self-flattering inflection of insincerity.

He paid no attention. 'I shan't try to make another date with you; I never do, with people. But if you would ever like to have lunch with me in London, or dinner, perhaps you could just let Victor know. And I would arrange it.'

I saw Mrs. Patton coming across the room to us in response to Victor's wave. The man walked perchingly behind her, aloof, hands in his pockets. Victor introduced us to her.

'I'm so glad you've come! It's quite a jolly little function, isn't it? Everybody's so friendly with each other. This is my cousin, Ned Skelton.' She drew him forward. He nodded to each of us. 'Ned has to be dragged off to these frivolities,' she added, with a twinkling glance and a tap on his shoulder. 'He's a man's man – brrr! Poona and all that. Ha-ha-ha?' She had an odd laugh, shaped like a rhetorical question.

'Not really Poona!' Iris exclaimed, leaning forward across the table, so that her blue bodice was rucked up like petals about the tender small line of her breasts. 'How too awfully "What-what"!'

Only Iris could be so silly and appear so charming; but he did not show much interest.

He told us he had been for a short time in the regular army and had spent a few months in India.

'Oh, you could have brought me a baby elephant to add to my collection! If only I'd known!'

He observed that there was a heavy customs duty on elephants. He looked at his watch, turned to Mrs. Patton and told her he must be going if he were going to catch the last tube.

'Now you just sit down with us, both of you,' Iris ordered, 'and Keith shall run you home in his car – you wouldn't mind, would you, Keith? The night's still young.'

'Nevertheless, I have to go to work in the morning,' Ned replied. All this time he had not looked at me once. I felt desperate and bitterly cold. 'If you'll excuse me—'

He said good night to us all, then, as if it were an afterthought, turned to me. 'I'll be seeing you again, I hope. In fact, I'm sure of it.'

'Christie,' Iris exploded when he had gone, 'I told you it was a conquest! I never saw anything like it. Now I'll bet you've made Keith jealous!'

In a second even she realised what she had said. She coloured very slightly and briefly, no more than if she had passed by a pane of pink-stained glass when the sun was piercing it. 'Oh well,' she added, with no meaning but to bring the conversation to an end.

Keith said, 'Of course I'm jealous; who would not be?' and we went into the ballroom to dance again in a world that was a desert. Keith made only one more remark that evening which was not a social commonplace. He said, not even mentioning a name, 'He is what one might call a graceful boor; don't you think so?'

At midnight he drove us home. He took Iris to her door first, where she bestowed upon Victor the customary good-night kiss, shrinking and laughing as she gave it, as if it were an unusual experience to her. Then she kissed me fondly, flowerily, her lips open upon my cheek; moved them up to my ear and murmured, 'So it did turn out all right after all, didn't it?'

'Don't be silly. It didn't mean anything.'

'Ned Skelton I'm talking about!'

'So am I.'

'But you've forgiven me—?'

'I suppose so.'

'For the other thing? It wasn't my fault?'

'What are you two conspiring about?' Victor demanded with false joviality. 'We're the world's workers. Our beds are calling us.' He had had his kiss, and the interest of the evening had departed for him.

With a shout and a wave to Iris, we drove away again. When we came to my home, where, of course, Aunt Emilie's light was still burning and cocoa awaiting me, Keith got out of the car and went with me up the steps. He thanked me for the evening. 'It was a happy one for me.'

If he had been anyone else he would have kissed me, this kiss being considered as part of such an evening's routine; he simply shook hands. So I leaned forward and kissed him, without embarrassment and without the blemish of self-approval – because he was kind, and I liked him, and I wanted to kiss him as a friend.

I never saw him again.

9

The succeeding weeks remain in my memory not as a string of pictured moments run together like a film strip but as a faint-coloured atmosphere; a greyness cocooning all manner of hopes, desires, desperations and preposterous fantasies. I ran to the hall in search of a letter I never expected to receive; even a knock at the door would shock me into a new expectation. Every day I dressed with the care of a girl awaiting her bridegroom. If he came he should find me as perfect as I was able to be. Every night I lay down in the belief and unbelief that something might happen tomorrow.

I was genuinely in love.

But the very young cannot love for long with no sort of stimulus. Any kind of stimulus will do – a glimpse of the one who is loved from the top of a bus, the mention of his name by a casual friend, even his surname displayed by chance on a billboard, a shop front. Had I ever heard at that time of Henry VIII's Poet Laureate I should have read his poems with subjective passion, but I had not. For me there was nothing at all. I had not seen Iris; was, in fact, avoiding her. I met Victor once in Piccadilly and mentioned Ned Skelton to him; but he had seen and heard nothing of him, he said, nor even of Mrs. Patton, who had gone to Switzerland for the spring.

So, imperceptibly, the agony lessened into an ache, and suddenly even the ache was gone. I was lonely; I even caught myself regretting Leslie; but I was well again, and my father and Emilie showed obvious relief in seeing me look less peaky.

I ceased to regret Leslie, however, one Saturday evening in May when he called upon me without warning. When I opened the door I found him posed nonchalantly on the step, wearing a new grey suit of cardboard stiffness, a peculiarly small bowler hat and, to my repelled amazement, his brown and white shoes.

I recognised them at once for what they were: a badge of emancipation from my thrall. When we were sweethearts I had flatly refused to be seen in his company until he abandoned them, and reluctantly he had given way. He had loved those shoes. They had seemed to him the essence of careless *chic*. Now he was flaunting them again, and the sight of them quite distracted my attention even from the remarkable hat.

'I won't come in, my dear,' said Leslie at once, though I had not yet had time to invite him. 'I just thought I'd look in on passing for old times' sake. How is the world with you?'

I replied that it was quite all right.

'I'm starting a new job in the City on Monday,' he informed me. 'In linoleum.' I had a pleasing vision of Leslie clad in this product. 'Actually, Lucette – that's a girl I know – suggested it. I merely applied, and *tout va bien*.'

He had also, I noticed, resumed his French phrases, which I had also deprecated on the grounds that he always used them wrongly.

I congratulated him.

'I thought, on the threshold of a new career, as it were' – he smiled, to show me the phrase was merely a mock pomposity – 'that I'd like to be sure there were no hard feelings. You mustn't think too badly of me,' he added surprisingly.

'But I don't. Why should I?'

'It was grand while it lasted. But I shouldn't have been the right man for you. I'm a bit of a philanderer, my dear; you need a steadier chap.'

I felt happier, my last trace of guilt vanishing away. Leslie had convinced himself that it was he who had brought our affair to an end, and I was content that he should have it so.

'Perhaps I do,' I agreed.

'Lucette isn't like you; she's a little flighty. My mater thinks she's a bit of a butterfly. But *pour le moment*. . . .' His gaze wandered away to the spire of St. Barnabas' Church, grey as clay against a sky of Italian blue, a sky burnished by the promise of a hot day tomorrow. It seemed to exalt his thoughts, for he added, 'And there are other things in life but love. Serious things.'

I agreed, and again wished him luck.

'Well-p!' said Leslie – the monosyllable of people who think they ought to go and are reluctant to do so, or of people who wish to speed the departure of others. He held out his hand and I shook it. '*Vaya con Dios*,' he added, with considerable effect, and, raising the little bowler, which in the stress of emotion he had forgotten to raise on greeting me, bolted down the steps in the direction of Battersea Rise and had soon disappeared into the sunset that blazed behind the minarets of St. Mark's and the Masonic School.

I went back into the house, free and cheerful, to find my Aunt Emilie engaged in one of her anniversary hypotheses.

'Just think,' she said to my father, as she stood knife in hand over an ox-tongue, like an abstracted Judith unable to keep her mind on Holofernes, 'if your father had lived he would have been a hundred and two today.' As always, we accepted this in silence as respectful, as marvelling, as if my grandfather had actually performed the feat.

'And your mother,' she added, 'would have been ninety-three.' This, however, seemed an anticlimax even to Emilie, and she summoned us both to supper.

'Who were you talking to just now?' my father asked me.

'Leslie. He just looked in on his way somewhere else.'

'I hope *that's* not starting again.'

'Certainly not.'

‘North Country people would call your Leslie gormless, I believe.’

‘He was always gentlemanly,’ Emilie put in timidly; Leslie had been nice to her, had even teased her a little.

‘What an atrocious phrase!’ my father exclaimed. ‘If anyone called me gentlemanly I should cut my bloody throat.’ He was in one of his racy moods; they seized him whenever his mind wandered back to a brief spell in Central Africa, where his government job had once taken him, but which poor health had forced him to quit. They had been great days of whisky and poker. Some of the men (not he) had kept native girls. They called them, he had told me in a moment of forgetting his audience, ‘black velvet’. I was sorry for him, guessing that the unusual heat of the day had made him restless and reminiscent.

I said, knowing occasional cheekiness amused him, ‘I don’t think anyone would, if they heard you say that.’

‘Now, now, Christine,’ protested Emilie, shocked to the marrow herself but unswervingly loyal to him, ‘your father’s a man.’

‘Am I?’ he said sadly. He added, an apparent *non sequitur*, ‘I wish I’d brought back a parrot.’

And indeed there seemed to be a becalming of our days, of my father’s as well as mine. Emilie’s, of course, were permanently becalmed, and she was happy. We lived together through that hot summer, at peace and utterly disinterested in one another. The boys and girls came in to dance and to eat bread-pudding. There were the usual mild flirtations. Forgiving Iris, I invited her round again, though she could only come on Sunday nights, as she was ‘working’ – she was one of six dancers in a cabaret She took a young man away from my friend Caroline Farmer and Caroline, in pique, married at the age of eighteen someone she did not love and who was to desert her a few years later. Otherwise there was no incident until, in September, my training came to an end and I started out to earn my own living.

10

The training college found me a post as assistant secretary (an agreeable title, borrowing a degree of grandeur from association with the Civil Service) in the West End office of a travel agency, at a salary of two pounds a week. This was as near as I could have hoped to get to my mother's dream of me as a 'social secretary' or 'receptionist'; for the only purely commercial business that we did was cashing letters of credit. Most of the work was concerned with making travel arrangements for our customers, showing them around London and executing any small commissions they might have for us.

Mr. Fawcett, the manager, was a large, gentle, sloe-eyed, shambling man with distinguished social connections in Europe and America and a family of four shiftless sons, who were all doing badly in some professional capacity or another. This gave him an air of desperate conscientiousness which impressed clients, for they could not know that it sprang simply from personal worry.

The assistant manager, Mr. Baynard, was one of those young men who wear the promise of age seamed into their cheeks; he was small, brisk and seemed permanently contemptuous. I disliked him at once, for on my very first day in Waterloo Place he robbed me of my fine title and labelled me, conclusively, the 'Junior'. Mr. Fawcett's secretary, Miss Rosoman, was a beautiful Jewess in her full flowering; she had the ephemeral, perilous wonder of a rose only just bearing the weight of its petals; a rose which, at any moment, at the freak of a cold wind, will be merely a bald and dusty fruit on a dry stem. She was a shrewd, efficient girl, generous-minded under an apparent aloofness and 'devil-may-care'. She had been with Mr. Fawcett during his years with an English agency, and he had retained her for this job only after an oblique and bitter tussle with our office in America which had been uneasy about the anti-Semitism of some of its clients.

For the rest there was an office girl, Miss Cleek, hardworking, timid and peaky, and Hatton the messenger, a big man with an ugly face and beautiful taut body, who dashed around in peaked cap and braided coat and followed like a private detective upon the tail of Miss Rosoman and myself if ever we went to the rooms of a male client to deal with his private correspondence.

'For,' said Mr. Fawcett, with his look of intense anxiety, 'I am responsible for you both to your parents. People are, for the most part,' he gasped, '—ah, more or less gentlemen; but there is always the bad type. The – ah – throw-out of the litter. Your parents need have no fear.'

This conscientious policing seemed to us both rather unnecessary. Miss Rosoman had no parents, and my father would never have wasted on me a moment's worry; but the Fawcett Plan, as we called it, was rigorously carried out, and we never emerged from a private suite in Claridge's, the Berkeley or Brown's without seeing, at the end of the corridor, a guardsmanlike shadow we recognised as Hatton.

I settled down quickly and agreeably enough, realised sensibly that I must resign myself to detesting Mr. Baynarad with the same unemphatic and incurable detestation I should always have for spiders and east winds, and had no particular trouble with anything but the calculating machine. As a general rule, dollars were converted into pounds, and letters of credit cashed, by Mr. Baynard or Miss Rosoman; but on the occasions when they both happened to be out the duty fell to me. The calculating machine was bought mainly for my benefit, as everyone else, including Hatton, could do the sums as rapidly on the edge of a date pad. I, however, had the singular gift of making the machine provide me with wrong solutions. For I had no mathematical sense whatsoever. The numbers the machine turned up were usually correct enough. The snag was that it was my duty to put the decimal point in the right place; and I had not the sort of mind which perceives at once that $750 converted at a rate of $4.35 to the pound is more likely to yield a three-figure than a two or four-figure result. Time after time I handed out preposterous and meaningless sums to clients; time after time they smilingly corrected me, and one or two, seeing my despairing flurry, would work out the sum for themselves or lean across the counter and run it up (almost like a piece of sewing) on the little machine.

Thus this business of the letters of credit became my major preoccupation of a depressing nature; my major preoccupation of a pleasing one was food, and this I shared with Miss Rosoman. Naturally her three pounds a week went further than my two; but then she, being bigger framed and markedly viscerotonic by temperament, needed more to eat than I did. Out of my salary I had to find six shillings a week for fares and ten shillings a week to help Aunt Emilie and my father at home; I spent five shillings on cigarettes (ten a day, for I was a precocious smoker with a genuine craving that was to become worse with time); the remaining nineteen shillings had to cover my insurance stamps, my clothes, my weekly visit to the cinema, my trifling cosmetics and my food.

So the daily lunch (at the ABC four days in the week and at Slater's on pay-day) became a matter for much mouthwatering thought and planning. It was the focus of a dull morning, the background music of a busy one. My favourite meal was scrambled egg on toast (eightpence), a a small, canary-coloured sponge pudding with blackcurrant sauce (fourpence) and a cup of coffee (twopence) – one and twopence in all; and if I had a one-and-sixpenny meal on Friday this brought my expenditure on food to seven shillings and twopence a week, the extra shilling representing tips. Miss Rosoman, concerned for her weight, chose her food more ascetically – a salad, Rye-Vita biscuits; a glass of orangeade; but the quantity she needed to sustain her energy was so much greater than I needed myself that her food bill fell into proportion with her salary.

One aspect of life at the agency was peculiarly trying. Until the end of September we were so busy that a moment of idleness was something disconcerting, something we hardly knew how to employ, something, in fact, vaguely embarrassing. From the first of October to the first of March there was almost no work at all – on some days literally none. Yet Miss Rosoman and I, in the outer office, could not be seen in the act of obvious relaxation because of the faint chance that some official from the Other Side should arrive unexpectedly and decide that Mr. Fawcett's organisation was not pulling its weight. We could relax until ten-thirty, the official opening hour for customers, and from half-past nine until that hour (having written and despatched such few letters as there might be, filed a few cards relating to new customers) we could look through *Time* and the *New Yorker*, make a start on *The Times* crossword puzzle, or even (in Miss Rosoman's case) knit. For the rest we had *to pretend to be busy*.

This was often no difficult matter for me, as my fury of creative energy was growing. I was now managing to sell a poem or two fairly regularly; and I was trying my hand at a fanciful, undocumented biography of Christopher Marlowe. So I could sit and scribble industriously hour by hour upon pink 'second copy' paper, while Miss Rosoman tapped away at her private correspondence and Mr. Baynard, at his desk at the far end of the room, very slowly read 'Sapper' under cover of the Barclays Bank Annual Report and occasionally rose to perform the disquieting action of drying out his sodden handkerchief before the electric fire, for he was much given to streaming colds.

If Miss Rosoman (privileged) raised her brows in protest he would whip round on her. 'All right, I know what you're thinking! But it's perfectly healthy because all the germs go up in the steam.'

'*Filthy* devil,' she would whisper to me. 'He makes me entirely sick.'

But as his colds grew steadily worse towards the winter equinox, so his temper grew more uncertain, and with it his tendency to be purely spiteful.

It was a chilly, saffron-coloured morning in early November. I had been to Brown's (Hatton was running messages in the City) to take a client, who was still perching there like some forgotten swallow, her steamship tickets for next week. Miss Rosoman and Miss Cleek were away with influenza, Mr. Fawcett more than normally anxious and withdrawn because his younger son had just been sent down from Oxford for pathological laziness. I returned, nipped and despondent, to find Mr. Baynard prowling about in a kind of obscure, triumphant rage and almost the entire contents of our filing cabinet strewn about the floor.

'What happened?' I demanded, aghast. The files were my affair.

'We've got to look busy even if we're not. I'm fed up with you girls knitting and scribbling. You can just amuse yourselves putting all these back again.'

'Putting them back?' I repeated stupidly.

'You'd better have your ears seen to. I've noticed before that you're a bit deaf. It may be wax,' he added, with something like a touch of nervous conciliation. He recovered himself from the impulse to retreat. Rage was as thick in him as his cold; it was a catarrh of meaningless rage. 'Better be seen doing the filing than doing nothing. Any of the big pots may look in – they never warn us. How do we know?'

'But,' I protested, almost in tears, 'I'd taken so much trouble with those files. I'd got a better system.' Horror weakened me. 'I was so proud of them,' I said abjectly.

I realised he had planned for me labour as futile and degrading as the labour of the treadmill. I could not bear it. 'It isn't fair!' I broke out.

'Will you remember,' said Mr. Baynard, 'that you're the Junior, and the Junior does what she's told.'

My spirit withered. Almost in tears, shaken by fury, I stooped to my absurd task.

At twelve he went out to lunch. 'You can hold the fort,' he said airily. 'I'll be back at one. And Hatton's due any minute.'

But Hatton was kept by the City manager, and Mr. Fawcett emerged at a run to tell me he had an appointment with a Mrs. Schuyler Loring at the Berkeley. For the first time I was entirely alone, with my files and my savage grief.

I had not been alone ten minutes when I heard the whine and clatter of the lift, and into the office walked a tall, pallid young man in English tweeds and a bowler hat. He gave me his card; I sent him to the rest-room while I looked him up, and found he was my first millionaire, worthy of an A.

We had our own private designations for the clients on these cards, and it was based strictly upon our previous record of their tourism. We knew them as A, B and Query, and Miss Rosoman and I were adept at assigning our clients when they turned up without warning, to hotels consonant with these grades. I saw at once that James R. Dewey III was an A man, a Claridge's man, and that he was not merely a dollar but a sterling millionaire, his father a steel magnate.

This was a client not for Mr. Baynard but for Mr. Fawcett himself. Should I telephone the Berkeley? Would Mr. Fawcett be annoyed to be disturbed in his communion with Mrs. Loring, also an A, and, though less wealthy than Mr. Dewey, a regular client appearing regularly every year with the celandine and departing with the first aster? I stood irresolute amid Mr. Baynard's brutal litter.

At last I went to the rest-room and told the young man that Mr. Fawcett was out on business. Would he like me to try and find him, or was there anything I could do for him temporarily?

He had risen at once with a graceful and rather startling movement, like smoke rising from an unsuspected spark on a still day. He looked down at me with the conscious pleasure of the man who enjoys his own height. 'I can think of nothing you couldn't, I guess.' He examined me frankly. 'Could you accommodate me by cashing a small cheque?'

I told him I should have to work it out.

'You must get pretty deft at all this,' he said, following me into the outer office. I shut him on to his own side of the counter, took the traveller's cheque and went with false confidence to the calculating machine. The sum was an easy one, and I think I should have done the exchange easily enough if I had not first been upset by Mr. Baynard and was not being upset now by Mr. Dewey's gentle, interested scrutiny. He watched me while I scribbled meaninglessly on paper, and then as I set up the metal figures and turned the handle. The result stood there, as usual, literally pointless: and at the idea of having to think where that point should go my nerve snapped. 'Can *you* work it?' I cried.

He laughed right out then. 'You have got a queer set-up here!'

'No, we haven't. It's just that everyone's out. I don't do this usually.'

'You poor little thing!' Mr. Dewey exclaimed. 'It's a shame. You turn that gadget round and I'll fix it.'

He looked at the result I had already achieved. 'I guess you're a mathematical genius, Miss—'

'Jackson,' I told him. 'Why am I?'

'No one else could have got it to do a thing like this.'

'It's the decimals,' I said, at his mercy.

'But even the figures are screwy. Look, shall I give you a lesson?'

He smelled of some kind of toilet-water, or shaving-cream, and also of very clean flesh. His linen was stiff and white as new cartridge-paper.

'Someone may come back.'

'O.K.' He operated the machine himself. 'You owe me sixteen pounds four shillings and threepence. Will you take my word for it? Here, don't you write it down on anything? You'll have to account for what you take from the till. Do you keep the money up here?'

A wild idea came to me that he might be a bank robber. He saw it in my eyes.

'I'm not Jesse James,' he said reassuringly.

'The bank sends it up every day in the pneumatic tube and then we send it down again.' I counted out notes for him and he took them with a stately bow.

'Where should I get some lunch?' he asked me.

This was an easy question. Classing him as A, I suggested three or four smart restaurants frequented by Americans of his own grade.

'Where do *you* go?'

'Oh, anywhere,' I replied.

'Yes – but couldn't I go, too?'

Now this was my first millionaire, and he was asking me to lunch. I was stimulated by excitement to the entirely new sensation of greed. If I were going to lunch with a millionaire, then I would have the best of it. I would not go where I usually went; I would go where he did.

'You wouldn't care for any of my places.'

'Oh, I see. Why not?'

'They're just places for business girls.'

'Called—?'

I did not understand.

'What are they called?' he repeated.

'You wouldn't care for them,' I said stubbornly. I was watching the door. At any moment Mr. Fawcett might return, or Hatton.

'Would you have lunch with me?'

I hesitated.

'I'm harmless. Would you?'

'Well, I'd like to—'

'Then where do we go?'

'There's the Monseigneur in Jermyn Street,' I said, my heart beating.

'The Monseigneur it is. When are you free?'

'Not till one.'

'Shall I call for you?'

No, I said; it would be far better for me to meet him.

It was not that Mr. Fawcett would have refused me permission; anything, within reason, must be done to satisfy the whims of A clients. But he would have sent Hatton to follow me like a shadow, loom just beyond the outer edge of my sight (a mere edge of darkness at the extreme corner of my eye) and then follow me back to the agency again. And I wanted this joy, this Arabian Nights adventure, all to myself.

Mr. Dewey could not have understood all of this, as he did not know our habits; but he understood me sufficiently. 'I'll meet you at Monseigneur, then, a little after one.'

At that moment Hatton came back, the braided cap set

well forward on his bright red hair, his lips pursed in a silent whistle. Mr. Dewey departed quickly.

Hatton threw down a packet of ten Goldflake and held out his hand. This meant that he had won them at darts, in the Coventry Street Arcade; that his victory had cost threepence, and that for fivepence he would hand me the prize. I was saving several pence a week through this arrangement, as he was the champion of Leytonstone, where he lived.

' 'Oo's 'e?'

I told him.

'Cash a cheque for 'im? Get it right?'

'It was quite simple,' I replied with dignity.

'Coming on, aren't you?' He looked at the floor. ' 'Oo made that bloody mook-oop?'

I told him bitterly about Mr. Baynard's scheme for employing my leisure.

' 'E's a young—' Hatton never articulated any word more violent than 'bloody' in my presence; but he would form the others with his lips, leaving me in no doubt as to his thought. 'Coom on, pick your feet up and I'll 'elp you.'

Hatton and I were friends. He was a clever man, his mind quick and neat. He knew the workings of the business as well as Mr. Baynard, operated the calculating machine (which he was not supposed to touch) more quickly than anyone, and had a gift as instinctive as Miss Rosoman's or my own for assigning the right person to the right hotel. Coming through the gate into the outer office, he gave the files a swift glance, glanced as swiftly into the few Mr. Baynard had inadvertently left in their places. In ten minutes he had them all back again in beautiful orderliness, A, B, C, down to Z, green ones for customers of long standing, pink for newcomers, blue for customers heralded by letter but not encountered as yet. 'And if 'e does a mooky trick like that again I'll let 'im 'ave the sole of my boot,' Hatton flung at me, as he marched off to his own headquarters. He would, of course, do no such thing; but it comforted his pride to think he might. I heard him, in the back room with the brooms and the vacuum-cleaner, humming his favourite song:

'*Exercise, Exercise,*
In *the morning* when *you rise.*'

II

By one o'clock I was repenting my audacity in suggesting that Mr. Dewey should take me to the Monseigneur.

To begin with, I was a little frightened. Suppose he was the wrong kind of man? He might make suggestions to me. Never having received a suggestion before, I did not know how I should acquit myself. I was a little too mature to imagine that he might drug my drink (which was a common practice of wicked men, in the opinion of Aunt Emilie) in so public and reputable a place; but I did wonder whether I might not be weak enough to agree to 'go to his room' later, should he ask me to do such a thing, and then, through sheer punctilio, be forced to implement the promise.

More serious than these vague and drifting fears, however, was the fear of being ashamed in his eyes before the waiters. For weeks I had put off mending the lining of my coat, which was now ripped from armpit to hem. Could I insist upon keeping that coat on, no matter how warm the restaurant was? I could tell him that I felt the cold to an abnormal extent. He would find this either interesting or ridiculous, according to the heat of the restaurant. But I should have to risk his findings. I shivered, in my imagination, as I saw the long tear exposed to public view, lying like a ragged snake over the back of a gilded chair. I saw the waiters grinning behind their smooth, exotic hands. I saw Mr. Dewey repressing a contemptuous smile. Whatever happened, I must keep my coat on.

By ten to one I was so apprehensive that my legs were quivering. As if that were not enough, Mr. Baynard did not reappear – and then, with only the barest of apologies – till ten past one, when I had, through a fever of impatience, to give him an account of my stewardship. I had only time to rub some powder on my face, slide anyhow into my hat and the disastrous coat, and run at full tilt up Lower Regent Street to the Monseigneur.

He was waiting for me there (I had even been praying that he had given me up and gone away), as calm, as cheerful as if we had been old friends and I had been punctual to the minute.

He cut short my excuses.

'You're here now,' he said comfortably, 'that's the thing.'

I had not realised that the grill-room was in the basement. When he took me into the little lift, trellised with gold and with gilded flowers, I felt I was being abducted into hell. I could find nothing to say. The tremor persisted in the calves of my legs.

'What's your name besides Jackson?' he asked, as I walked by his side through a hot and golden nightmare, between little tables garnished with rose, carnation, lily. I told him.

'That's pretty,' he said; 'so pretty I shan't need to call you Andy, as I would have done if your name had been Miss Jackson, Euphemia.'

I was too dulled with fright even to understand simple jokes. I knew he had made a joke, and my misery was refreshed by the fear that, since I had laughed only feebly, he would think I had no sense of humour.

I saw a narrow Byzantine face, two lean and prayerful hands. They were sharp upon the general haze. They appeared to want something. 'May I take your coat, madam?' the face murmured.

I said clearly, to Mr. Dewey, 'I won't leave my coat; I feel the cold quite abnormally.'

There seemed to be quite a long silence, during which I realised that the temperature of the room could not be unlike that of the steam-room of a Turkish bath.

'Quite sure?' Mr. Dewey asked in a tone of pure astonishment.

'I've always been like that,' I said. 'Even at home I often keep my coat on.'

'Oh, you do,' he replied.

He ordered the meal; I could not assist him. I could not read so many words on so large a card. He gave me a dry martini, a drink I had never tasted before, and immediately it made me feel much better and much worse. I could talk now, and I did; but I was feeling the heat so intensely that I knew it could be only a moment before it betrayed me by manifesting itself in a sweat all over my face.

'Are you quite sure you're not feeling it too warm?' he asked me concernedly.

'I'm barely comfortable *now*,' I replied. 'I feel just nice.'

I took a mouthful of the second drink, which he had bought without consulting me, and all at once I knew myself to be silvered all over, my cheeks blazing under the glaze of perspiration, runnels of moisture appearing under the brim of my hat.

'I don't get your motive,' said Mr. Dewey firmly, 'but I think we'll have you out of that thing.' And before I knew it my coat was off and draped at my back. I jumped up. Seizing it, I turned it the other way, so that the lining was concealed, and I was resting against the untainted cloth.

'Now why?' he asked.

'The lining's torn!' I said, and stared at him.

He stared back at me. 'Oh, Christine!' he said. 'Oh, Christine, what a girl you are!'

From that moment all was happy, and when he made me the suggestion I had feared I felt not frightened but only proud. It was a suggestion in keeping with the most golden of my romantic ideas. He was flying to Paris that week-end. He would like me to go with him. He thought we should have a wonderful time.

I answered very politely that I should have loved it but that my father would never approve.

'You mean,' said Mr. Dewey, 'that it would be entirely out of your line?'

'I'm afraid so.'

'Yes. Well – plenty of time. And my loss.' He smiled at me sweetly, put his hand over mine. 'Sorry.'

He made no further suggestions (a little to my disappointment), but on the way up to the realities of the harsh autumn day he put his arms around me in front of the lift-boy and kissed me, first on both cheeks and then on the lips.

'I'm off tomorrow,' said Mr. Dewey as we lingered in Piccadilly. 'Then I go home on the *Ile de France*. And after that, God knows. Would you like a flower?'

I hesitated. He seemed to have given me so much – perhaps too much; I was not used to drinking, and I felt I should have to move cautiously before Mr. Baynard.

Mr. Dewey paused by an old woman with a tray of gardenias, petals like kid leather, leaves like emeralds. 'Yes, I think you ought to have a flower.' He said to her, 'I'll take a dozen.'

A dozen, at half a crown a time.

He bunched them up between my hands.

'I can't take these,' I began.

'You have them. Shall I walk back with you?'

I begged him not to.

'It has been very nice, Christine. Thank you very much.' And he gave me a little, fond push to speed me on my way.

Dazed with delight and drink, still shamed by the remembrance of the coat, numbed by the contrast between the adorable, slightly sinister paradise from which I had just come (I could not help feeling a sense of escape) and the barren earth of the office before me, I lingered in Waterloo Place, just behind the Crimea memorial, which looks from the rear like a boarding-house slattern in curl-pins and nightgown. I considered the flowers in my hands. How could I ever explain this redundancy to Mr. Baynard? What would he think? What would Mr. Fawcett think?

For the moment I was paralysed by indecision. How could I get rid of the things? One, even now, seemed to be browning around the edges, as though scorched by an iron. I could not throw them in the gutter; it would make me too conspicuous. Was there any stranger to whom I could give them? Some beggar? Some child? There was none; and my watch said two-twenty-five.

There was only one thing to do. Praying passers-by would merely assume that my great-grandfather had died at Inkerman, I reverently approached the memorial, inclined my head for a moment, ceremoniously knelt down, deposited the flowers on the plinth, and then ran for the office as if bloodhounds were after me.

Mr. Baynard greeted me coldly. 'Do you know you're ten minutes late? The lunch-time of the Junior is one hour and no more. Oh yes, someone rang up wanting to speak to you. A Mr. Skelton. Would you please tell your friends in future that you are not allowed to take personal calls at this office?'

12

Is he going to ring back?'

'I don't know and I don't care,' Mr. Baynard replied. He felt a sneeze coming. 'I didn't enquire!' he added furiously, a second before the explosion.

I sat down quietly, wanting to bring no more anger down upon my head, for my only aim now was to wait for my head to clear and in the meantime to try to contemplate the wonders of this day. I thought of Ned Skelton with excitement and trepidation, though with no resurgence of my first wild love. Indeed, I could hardly remember what he looked like – eight months is a long time. But the afternoon passed very slowly, and I grew tired of starting up each time the telephone rang. The day darkened down. A slant of fog fell across the sky, leaving visible only the first line of trees in St. James's Park. Like wrought-iron they stood against its yellow fur, and not a leaf stirred.

At a quarter-past five he telephoned again. Luckily I was alone, finishing some last-minute letters for Mr. Fawcett. Mr. Baynard, seeking comfort for his cold, had put on his hat at the stroke of the hour and was blinding his way homeward.

'I don't know if you remember me,' said the voice I should not have recognised had I heard it without warning.

'We met at the dance.'

'I ran into your friend Victor playing squash last night and he told me where you worked.' He waited, as if for some response.

I said at last, feebly, that that was nice.

'I wondered if you'd like to come for a drive with me some time. Scarcely tonight, by the look of it.'

'I'd love to.'

'I'd better ring you again.'

'It's not easy for me here.'

'Oh, I see. Well, then, give me your home address. You're not on the phone there?'

On hearing I was not, he said briskly that it was a pity. He usually only knew what he wanted to do at the last moment. As I gave the address to him, I felt a faint bristling of disquieted pride. Why should he speak to me in so assured, so businesslike, so unexplanatory a fashion? He reminded me a little of Mr. Baynard addressing the Junior. So I said, 'My time's not always my own. I don't always know when I'll be free.'

'You'll be free for me,' said Ned Skelton; 'I'll see to it.' And he rang off. It was all disturbing and unsatisfactory; it left me with a tension unappeased and a faintly disagreeable stirring of tadpole hopes that I did not wish to develop into full and lively frogs. I was growing up now, determined to put ungrounded fantasies behind me. Why should he seek to trouble me like this, assuming I was at his call? I had just been out with a millionaire. I had just received the fairy-tale gift of a dozen gardenias. It was a pity he didn't know that, didn't realise that I was the kind of young woman to whom such things happened.

I stacked Mr. Fawcett's letters tidily, the envelope folded upon the top of each, and took them in to be signed.

He gave one of his great irrepressible sighs, the sigh of an animal or a baby. 'I've kept you late, Miss Jackson. You'd better run along, or you'll have trouble getting home. Oh dear, dear, dear, dear, dear!'

I had great trouble getting home, for the fog had thickened and the bus moved at less than walking pace down Piccadilly.

The street lamps streamed up it in their separated rays, and along each ray the fog spiralled and curled. The lights in the windows were dim; even the great fires in the depths of the comfortable clubs were no more than handfuls of round-cut rubies glowing without glitter. This stifling atmosphere and the aftermath of martinis gave me one of those headaches which seem to concentrate the mind to a cold common sense. I knew my millionaire would by now have forgotten me; that however important a figure he had been in my own life, I was a manikin figure in his. I knew that I did not greatly care for Ned Skelton – that he was not gentle, that he would not be kind.

I did not care if I never heard from him again; I did not want him to write to me.

At least, I did not want it then; but in the following weeks, as day after day went by without a word, the old unquiet awoke in me, the forgotten fever stirred and was resurrected. I saw, hallucinated, the future, and I longed for it. I was excited and unhappy.

Yet when his letter did arrive I had to reply that I could not see him, not yet awhile, for my father was dead.

One night, a week or so before Christmas, he rose out of a peculiarly troubled sleep, took Emilie by the shoulder and said, in a voice unlike his own, 'I'm going down to the lavatory, old girl.' She had had a busy day, and he had aroused her from a comfortable dream. She thought vaguely that he sounded odd and that it was even odder for him to wake her with such uninteresting information; but the current of the dream caught her and pulled her down into it. She awoke again a little later with the feeling that it must be nearly dawn, and she stretched out her hand to him; but he was not there. She was alert at once. She jumped out of bed, put on her dressing-gown and went, full of undefinable fears, out on to the landing. Her watch told her it was only half-past one. She had an idea that it had been one o'clock when he left her – probably she had heard the church clock strike. But half an hour was a long time for him to be absent, and as she made her way downstairs she began to tremble.

Then she saw him coming to her along the passage, walking like a drunken man; she saw him by the street lamp that shone through our fanlight. He looked at her, said, 'What are you doing here, old girl?' and was transformed into a stranger by so violent a convulsion of his features that he seemed to be playing some ghastly trick to frighten her. 'Old girl—' he repeated, and collapsed at her feet.

She cried out. I was sleeping too soundly to hear her. She knelt beside him, heaved his head into her lap, touched his sopping forehead, called to him, kissed him, cried to him in the anger of naked fear. She fumbled for his pulse, but could not feel it.

All this she told me.

But what I myself knew was the appearance of Emilie at my bedside, whispering, patting, even at this moment trying to rouse me without shock. 'Christine, it's your father. He's been taken ill.'

Then there was the nightmare of following her into the hall, now blazing with lights, and of looking for the first time upon death; of huddling into my clothes and running out into the freezing streets in search of a doctor; and of all the rest that I cannot write, as it is the routine commonplace of sudden death, the ordinary procedure, and to me the unlookable, the unthinkable.

The damaged heart which had forced him to leave Africa and which he had tended so carefully for years could labour on with him no further – it had revolted, sprung, and stopped.

For two days Emilie seemed frozen. She was an innocent, not very intelligent little woman, ill-fitted for a tragic role; but she had loved with an extraordinary tenacity and concentration, the whole of her being centred upon my father. She would have liked to die with him. Once or twice I came upon her sitting in some dark corner, hands folded neat as napkins in her lap. She was apparently holding her breath. Her breast did not rise or fall. Her eyes were stretched and staring. Only her colour swelled and darkened until her cheeks were like dead red roses. Then, with an explosion of breath, she would suddenly exhale. I believe she was indulging in a fantasy of killing herself by this means.

She went quietly through the inquest, the necessary arrangements, until the day the men came to take his body away. And then she clung to the coffin and would not let go, her little chickeny arms whitening with the strain, her eyes closed, her lips stubbed into a strange, childlike protrusion. I tried to plead with her; she would not let go. She spoke once. 'If I've got him they can't take him. He shan't go. I won't let him go.'

The men were in despair. The minutes went by. Emilie, lying half across the coffin, gripping it with fingers of iron, was silent. At last she opened her eyes wide, looked about her, released her hold and stood upright. She gazed as if in amazement at her arms, bruised in red lines where the edges of the wood had dug at them, and, with a murmur bearing some kind of apology, went out of the room.

13

The funeral was over. The blinds were up. The weather was mild for December, and the muffled sun shone all day. Emilie went quietly about the house, caring for it and for me. We both saw the pattern of our immediate lives. She suggested that I should ask my friends round again, for the usual evenings: but the days of dancing were over. We sat gossiping uneasily over the tea-cups, and the young men and girls found they had to be home earlier than usual.

Suddenly Emilie discovered a game for us. Though I think we all found it embarrassing and silly, somehow the fascination of it caught us and would not let us go. There was guilt connected with it, too. It seemed to me that my friends were entering the house with a touch of shamed excitement, an air of stealth.

It is the game you play with an inverted tumbler in a ring of cardboard letters. The players touch their fingertips to the glass, inviting it to answer their questions; and if they wait patiently it will begin to slide gently back and forth, spelling out words.

Now there are two kinds of players (three, in fact, if you include cheats, which I do not): those who cannot help exerting the will, so that the glass moves through their more or less unconscious agency, and those who remain passive, so that each result is a surprise to them, satisfactorily confirming a belief in the occult. My Aunt Emilie was of the former kind, though she would never have believed it had anyone told her so, but would have denied it with genuine indignation. For in the end the glass inevitably did as she wished.

We would sit together, she and I and perhaps three of my friends (Dicky Flint, sometimes Iris, occasionally the engaged and miserable Caroline Farmer), in the fire-lit dining-room, the reflected flames soaring and falling on the faded morris garlands, sparkling bright in the mahogany sideboard. Emilie would light a candle, so that we should be able to see the letters clearly as the fist of glass poked them out of place. Like a small, countrified, commonplace sibyl she would sit at the head of the table, her arm hieratically outstretched, her stumpy fingers patient, light as breath, upon the thick bottom of the knowing tumbler. My friends (all except Iris, who was superstitious) thought her ridiculous; but the sinister fascination of the game held them. Sometimes the glass would move by their own wills, responding to their private desires.

'Who is there?'

A tentative jerk about the circle, P X A B Y. Too many wills were moving at the same time, which, in this game, is the cause of gibberish. Dicky, with a touch of raucous nervousness: 'Come on, come on, don't be shy. Who's there?'

A long pause. Then: 'AUDREY.'

This was the name of Dicky's latest girl.

Iris, with a terrified spurt of laughter: 'Audrey, do you really love him?'

The glass: 'BIT.'

Dicky: 'Not more than that?'

The glass: 'BIT DICKY IS WICKED.'

And so on.

But for the most part it brought Emilie peculiarly smug and uncharacteristic messages from my father. He was happy in a land of flowers. The sun was hot. There were birds.

'Africa,' she whispered, and the tears on her cheeks sparkled in the candlelight. 'Are you in Africa, dear?'

'YES.'

'Do you think about me and Christine?'

The glass, surprisingly (perhaps moved by an unconscious revolt on my part): 'NO.'

'Oh, you do, I'm sure you do! . . . Dicky dear, you're leaning on it too heavily. Let's try again. *Do you think about me?*'

The glass, obediently: 'YES.' And then, scaring me: 'NOT NED.'

But this, also, I must have compelled.

These sessions seemed harmless enough at first – a consolation to poor Emilie, a slightly daring amusement for my friends and me now that the gramophone, in respect, stood silent. After a while, however, they began to worry and to sicken me. I thought of my father's ironic disapproval, how firmly he would dissociate himself from them if he could know about them at all. And they were becoming, for Emilie, more than a consolation; they were becoming an obsession. All day she moved about in a dream, cleaning, cooking, bedmaking, dealing with the quiet and for once satisfactory tenants of the top floor; but with the approach of evening she flushed and sharpened, grew voluble, her eyes bright and fanatic.

It was the evening of January 1st – a sharp, wet New Year's Day. We were sitting round the glass – Emilie, Caroline and myself.

The glass began straight away to plunge about with a ghastly liveliness; it was so marked that I forced myself to remember my disbelief.

'Who is there?' Emilie's whisper hung on air like the smoke from a cigarette.

The answer, direct, immediate, moved by her will: 'HORACE.'

'Horace! Have you a message for me?'

It stuck, remained motionless.

Caroline muttered in my ear (she had had no chance to speak to me before, since Emilie had opened the door to her and swept her straight into this horrible game), 'Getting married next month. All very quiet.'

'Horace! Have you a message, dear?'

And then it darted off again, as assuredly as before, my will behind it, though I was conscious of no pressure in my fingers.

'STOP THIS DAMTOMFOOLERY.'

Emilie cried out. She was so shocked that in releasing the glass she gave it a flick with her finger. It spun out of the circle, jerked across the table edge, bounced once on the carpet and then rebounded on to the fender, where it broke into pieces. She burst into hysterical sobbing. Caroline jumped up and switched the light on. We both stood blinking in the sudden glare, feeling distraught, ridiculous, oddly ashamed, and profoundly relieved. 'Look here, Mrs. Jackson,' Caroline said,' it was an accident. And it's only a game. Really it is.'

'I'll never play again,' Emilie wept, 'never.'

She pushed us both aside and stumbled out. We heard her moving about the kitchen getting tea; heard, through the clatter of cups and saucers, the harsh rasp of her tears. We looked at each other.

'I should leave her alone,' said Caroline.

Next day Emilie seemed to be herself again, as ordinary, as dull, as unexcitable as ever.

Three days later I received a note from Ned Skelton, telling me he thought I might enjoy a run into the country next Sunday. He did not ask me if I would come; he simply said he would call for me with the car at half-past two.

My thoughts flew first not to him but to what I should wear. I was anaesthetised from all other emotion by the thought of clothes. I was getting shabby again; I had saved very little as yet. Should I spend it all on a new coat or on a new hat and bag? Black would go with anything, and I had an excuse now to wear black. (My grey office coat had been considered sufficient mourning by Emilie, who had not forgotten a jocose remark by my father to the effect that if she got herself up for him like a crow he would haunt her. She herself, much against her will, since she would have felt better in weeds, was wearing a brown jumper in order to mollify his ghost.) Clothes. Caroline had a fur; she might lend it to me.

I took this letter to Emilie, who read it without apparent interest; but she said, 'Yes, do go, dear. You're young. You shouldn't be too much in this house of death.'

'We can't think about it like that always!' I protested, my blood chilling a little.

'No, dear. Of course not. It was silly of me. Poor Horace was always so cheerful, wasn't he? But it would be good for you to go.'

14

Sunday was a day of snow. It lay in a crusting of black and silver beads along the privets in the front garden, clung in lichen patches to the rooftops, and was stacked, hard as steel, in the gutters. The sky looked white and hard; there was sun behind it, but it would remain invisible, would not break through.

When the dinner-plates were cleared away I went upstairs to dress. I had Caroline's fur. I had a new black hat. I felt calm, mature, until I saw, from the top window, the little sports car, bright as a ladybird, slide to a stop. Then I was lost, frightened. My heart began to hurry; I knew I was unbecomingly flushed, that I would not be able to greet him as if he did not matter at all.

I saw him climb out, walk slowly, with his air of delicate, birdlike balance, up the front steps. He was wearing a camel-hair coat and a brown felt hat. The bell rang. Let him wait! I ordered myself. But even as this firm, convincing instruction shot out I was running down into the hall. On the landing I halted, for Emilie was before me, letting him in. She said something in her little dull voice. I heard him answer her easily, his voice smiling. He looked up and saw me. 'Hullo! I don't think I'm early. Anyway, you're ready for me.'

It was hard to meet his eyes. When I did so I saw a kindly shine beneath the heavy lids, something reassuring and a little comical, as if he were including me in a secret.

'Your aunt and I have met already.'

'Where?' I was still unnerved enough to be obtuse. He looked so old, so much older than any of my friends; his flattery in seeking me out seemed almost too great for me to accept. I felt humble, and angry because I was humble. I wanted to quarrel.

'Just this minute, of course.' He asked her if she would entrust me to his driving, meaning not only to that.

'Don't keep her out late,' Emilie muttered, thinking of her responsibility towards me.

'I won't. It'll be freezing later on, anyhow. I'll deposit her at seven sharp. Come on, Christine,' he said, and took my arm, bearing me defenceless out into his unknown world.

As he helped me into the car I could not help hoping that one of my friends would see me and tell Iris. Iris's young men were all so young; it surprised me that she, an actress, should still go running about with men little more than schoolboys.

He told me he was taking me Hindhead way. 'Do you know it?'

I shook my head.

He drove silently for a while, and I tried to study, without him seeing me, his bird-like profile, alert, attractive, discontented.

'I don't suppose you know anything much.'

An alarming phrase, a seducer's phrase, I thought, and I panicked. It suddenly occurred to me that he would want to kiss me, and that he might try to do so in a fashion not accepted by my friends, even by Dicky Flint, who was thought to be fast. '*It is only done in France*,' Leslie had once told me in the shocked and sunken voice he used when mentioning sexual matters. 'No nice man would ever do such a thing. Any decent girl would slap his face.' And then, sunken deeper yet, 'It is a sort of *symbol*.'

So I had thought of this as a kind of ravishing, had thought of it with horror and a kind of guilty yearning; for my youth was becoming uneasy, fretting in me like a covering of buds just below the surface of my skin.

'How old are you, Christine?'

'Eighteen,' I said. I should be that age in two days' time.

'I am fourteen years your senior, my girl. Does that alarm you?'

'Oh no,' I replied. 'That's not old.'

'Not to me. But I could just, allowing for precocity, have been your father.'

I wished he would not talk about precocity, paternity, my youth, his maturity. I felt he was already invading me: that he had plans for me. The fright persisted; yet I was enjoying myself. I wished Iris could see his car, his camelhair coat. He seemed to be richer than most of the young men I was likely to meet. He might take me to places like the Monseigneur – I was glad I had now some slight experience of them. I wondered about his life, felt a thrust of jealousy, sharp, pure and explicit, at the thought of the girls he must have known and kissed (how?); I did not want him to kiss me. I am strong, I said inwardly; I can look after myself.

We were free of London now, and here the snow was vast and cleanly over the land, the horizon barely distinguishable from the sky except where it was marked by the deep blueness of distant woods. All white and blue; I had never seen such ink-blue distances.

He was telling me something of himself. His father was an estate agent. He, Ned, had never liked the idea of going into the family business, so he had become a regular soldier and had served for a while in India. Then ('It was bloody poor luck,' he said, making me wonder whether, even though he was a man and not a boy, it was altogether respectful for him to swear so easily in my presence) they had found a spot on his lung and invalided him out.

'The spot went eventually; I'm all right now, so don't imagine I'm headed for a poetic end.' He looked at me and stopped the car. We were on the Hog's Back, the white world below us and the heavy silence of the snow all about. The sky had darkened a little to a luminous grey with a tinge of russet.

'Pretty, isn't it?' He put his hand on my knee, looked at it in a kind of surprise as though he had expected to find it somewhere else, withdrew it, and offered me a cigarette. He went on with his story. He had still refused to go into the business – anything but that. He had gone to Liverpool with his army pension, with some faint idea of getting on a ship, but all he had done was to get into debt. 'I used to back horses and now I don't. I've learned my lesson. My father saw his chance at once; he said he'd pay my debts if I stopped my nonsense and came into the business. Which I did. And now I'm respectable. A little sordid, don't you think?'

'It's not sordid now,' I said cautiously, after a second's thought.

He laughed. And then he put his arm round me, turning me so that he could look, not so much at my face, but over and into it. I was rigid with fear, desire and love; but mostly fear. The snow was falling again, spinning in little flakes no more than shadows all over the land, throwing a faint and fading lacework over the bonnet of the car. I could not bear that he should kiss me, for I knew I had no strength with which to follow Leslie's sage advice.

He let me go, started the engine, and turned the car in the road. 'Got to be careful, it's like glass underfoot. We'd better hurry or we'll get no tea.'

We had tea at an hotel in Hindhead, a Sunday outing tea of brown and white bread and butter, egg sandwiches, chocolate biscuits, iced cakes, Dundee cake, maids-of-honour and madeleines. Most of the other people in the lounge were men and girls who had also come in their cars; the girls were smarter, a few years older, than I. I felt proud again, and the firelight reassured me.

He spoke to me gently, asking me about myself; his face was kind, and it was easier to talk to him now that he did not so openly admire me with his eyes.

'And what were you doing with poor old Butterworth?'

I did not understand.

'Victor Coburn's friend. The crippled chap.'

I explained what had happened, and felt a little disgusted with myself for doing so. I should not have betrayed Keith like that, simply in order to show Ned that this was not the only sort of partner I could find. I should have pretended that he was an old friend, that I had gone to the dance with him simply because I liked him. And yet, wouldn't Ned know by now that Keith was not an old friend? My self-disgust was eased a little.

'You did your duty gallantly. I guessed it *was* a duty. Otherwise I shouldn't have appeared in your existence again. Would that have been a pity?'

'Of course,' I replied brightly and rather too loudly. Several people glanced at me. I added, quietening myself, 'This is very nice.'

'Very nice,' he repeated. His eyes flashed, blue and teasing. 'Well, we shall have to be moving, or your good aunt will take me for a middle-aged seducer.'

This was so nearly what I myself took him for that I blushed. I looked away quickly, hoping he would not have noticed.

'Which, of course,' he added, 'is very much your own idea. Well, I'm not. You can set your heart at rest.'

'I didn't think anything of the sort!'

'Yes, you did, my dear. I always know.'

I was miserable. I felt, beneath all this teasing, the knotting of a cord. He knew I was too inexperienced, too much at sea, to tease him in return, as an older girl would have done. We sat for a few minutes in silence. Then he called the waitress, paid the bill, and drew me to my feet. We set off home.

It was quite dark now, a windless, moonless night. In the swing of the headlamps, the snow was dirty gold. Inside the car it was beautifully warm and small.

'I like being with you,' he said at last. 'Don't you feel we should get on well?' He did not take his gaze from the road. His hands upon the wheel were small and silvery, lightly-boned, beautiful. 'Don't think absurd things about me. That's for aunties. Not for you.'

'I don't.'

I felt I was approaching the joy, the shame, the ravishment. Unwillingly in love, I closed my eyes and felt the prickling of tears.

'Did you wonder why I took so long getting in touch with you again?'

I asked him, with some spirit, why I should have wondered; I had not expected to see him after that night.

'But I told you I should be seeing you. I don't prattle for the sake of prattling.' He gave me a brief glance, half-smiling, half surly. I had never before seen this kind of authority in a man, and I was both angered and moved by it. I found the courage for obstinacy and silence.

'My dear girl, my dear girl,' he said, 'you've got a lot to learn. No – I meant to find you out. But I had something to get out of the way.'

I did not question him; he continued as if I had.

'A girl. Something that's been going on for years.'

'I see.'

'We weren't engaged. It was just understood by all the bystanders. It's over now.'

'Poor girl!' I exclaimed involuntarily on a flash of understanding.

He stirred. 'Oh, I think she knew all right.'

'Knew what?'

'That something had happened.'

'What had happened?' I cried out.

'You, of course.' His cigarette was out, and he paused to relight it. 'I had to tell Wanda. It was only decent.'

'There was nothing to tell her!'

'So far as I was concerned there was everything. And I wasn't going to look you up again before she had the position clear.'

Even then I sensed his cruelty to this girl, the driving force of his own desires, his own impetuosities; I sensed and resented the assumption that I was there for his taking. I should have liked to leave him there and then, to make my way somehow or other home through the cold and sheltering screens of the dark, to go free. Yet I was so proud that a man so much older than I should have done this thing for me that I could not resist the steady rising of an exaltation which was like happiness. It burst the banks suddenly, flooding out conscience, drowning fear.

'How did you know *I* was free?' I demanded, but now I myself was teasing, and he knew it; knew that, even because I had found it within my power to tease him, his own power had tightened over me. For it could hold the woman as it could not hold the child.

'You're too young not to be. At least, you've been too young up to now.'

We were in the outskirts of London. Its jewelled pincers closed upon us.

'I think we shall get on very nicely,' said Ned, 'extremely so.'

I took the moment into my full experience, knowing instinctively that it would be one of those I should be able to recall in sensory and pictorial detail as long as I lived: the beam of other headlights swinging over our faces; the feel of the leather seat to the hot palm of my hand; the smell of the engine; of the fur around my shoulders in which Caroline's familiar *Paris Soir* still lingered; of his soft, light coat and of his own flesh; the height of my heart in my throat.

We came at last to my door.

Now, I thought, now. I steeled myself, but I am not sure to what – whether it was to accept his kiss (how cheap he would think me if I did!) or to reject it (how young, how silly he would think me if I did not!). He left the engine running, the only sound upon the stillness of the frozen common; we sat within the giant purr, neither of us speaking. I wanted, without reason, to ask him to help me – to tell him that I was, indeed, young. I was for a second not ashamed of my youth.

He took my hand and fondled it. In the light from the dashboard his face was younger, was tender, not at all alarming.

'Thank you very much,' I said; 'I have enjoyed it.'

I waited. The fretting in the buds, close-packed as the microscopic flowers within a paperweight, grew almost beyond bearing – a wonder and a pain. Involuntarily I moved my fingers within his own, and as if this movement had broken a spell he let my hand go, opened the car door and in a second had me out and on to the road. He went up the steps with me and stood there while I found my key.

'Tell your aunt you're safe and sound, and right on the dot of seven. I'll write to you again.'

Then he was gone; the door stood open; she called to me from below, 'Is that you, dear? Did you have a good time? Supper's ready.'

PART TWO

I

Many years afterwards I suddenly saw quite clearly that in those first days Ned had loved me much more than I had loved him. I was simply in love with the idea of him; had his approach to me been more immediate, less cautious, I might have realised this. But a genuine and unselfish fear for me, a doubt of our future together, made him hold off. It was not for three weeks after that drive in the snow that he took me out again; and then it was wrong with us – we had nothing to say. I was scared of boring him because I could not face the suspicion that I was a little bored myself. Another week went by, with nothing more than a brief note about nothing in particular. And another week. So my desire was fed by injured pride, and a second, more urgent, more real love imposed itself upon the romantic dream.

I could not guess that he loved me, but was afraid to claim me in fact as he had already done by the bravado of words. My youngness frightened him. He was slipping away from me and back, as a boat moored in a river slips downstream and then, as if involuntarily, in its own good time, slips back, brought by the compulsion of the current and the rope. For he could neither want me nor want to be free of me.

Meanwhile, living in a sensual fantasy, I moved through the office life, the life of home, of Emilie, of my friends. To my friends I had already dropped a hint or two of Ned, less for the sake of boasting than from the starved impulse to speak his name out loud.

When Emilie observed 'You don't see much of that Mr. Skelton, do you, dear?' it was less of a pain to me than a pleasure, for by mentioning him she assured me that he was real, that he existed for others besides myself.

Iris, however, suspected that I had won a triumph, and she began to pester me for details. She had just dismissed Victor, after a trumped-up quarrel, because her mother had not rested from assuring her, almost every waking hour, that there were far better fish in the sea. She had dismissed him, and now, though conscious of having acted wisely in a worldly sense, she was really wretched.

I had been to supper at her house, and we were sitting afterwards in the glumly lit drawing-room, the two of us and her mother.

Mrs. Allbright was a tiny, smart, faded woman with a curious, sensitive-looking nose, which seemed rather than her eyes to look, rather than her lips to enquire. Her husband had died in the last year of the war, when Iris was two.

He had been a handsome, weak, mother-seeking man; Mrs. Allbright had mothered him with a kind of angry strenuousness. He had been her whole life. Now that he was dead she had nothing to do but mother, with equal strenuousness though less affection, her pretty and fanciful little girl.

Iris, blithe enough, buoyant enough by herself, seemed in her mother's company weighed down by a ballast of too much ambition, too much hope. And she maddened Mrs. Allbright by her unresponsiveness.

'My daughter, Christine, is a great trial to me.' This was spoken as if Iris were not in the same room with us, rocking one foot over the other and flicking at a fashion magazine. 'She gets this cabaret chance: a special song with two other girls, and a verse to herself. Does she leap at the opportunity? Will she try to perfect herself? Will she practise? No. She just moons about the house dusting and doing the beds, as if she were a charwoman.'

Iris seemed not to listen to this oblique bullying. She put a record on the gramophone, a sentimental song made popular by the latest talking film, and hummed the words to herself.

'Do you know, Christine,' Mrs. Allbright continued remorselessly, 'who *goes* to the Café Elysée? The Prince of Wales. Now suppose Iris caught his eye. What wouldn't a word from *him* do for her? I say to her, "If you won't practise for your mother, practise for the Prince." But she's stubborn as a mule.'

'Oh, for God's sake!' Iris cried out, shouting above the wheedling song. 'Anyone would think he was going to marry me!'

Her mother flushed up with temper and a kind of obscure triumph. 'Stranger things than that have happened!'

The needle ground in the groove, *Just you, just you, just you, just you.*

Iris raced to the gramophone, turned it off and banged down the lid. 'There you are, Christie! That's what I have to put up with!'

'They say,' said Mrs. Allbright, 'that he has an eye for a pretty girl. *Any* man who has an eye for a girl may be drawn in further than he thinks. In a democracy anything may happen.'

'Stop it, stop it, stop it!' Iris put her fingers in her ears.

Her mother sighed. 'Oh, well. You see how I'm treated by my own girl. I wish she had your brains. Looks aren't everything.'

'If you're suggesting,' Iris shouted, still with stoppered ears but by no means deaf to her mother, whose lips she had probably learned to read, 'that Christie hasn't got looks, she'll go straight home and I won't have a single friend left. You've already taken Victor away from me.'

'Of course Christine's *quite* nice-looking. But God gave you exceptional looks, and no heart, and no brains. And I don't want to hear any more about Victor. He was common.'

Iris put her hands down and relaxed into moodiness again; but it was a new kind of moodiness, with tears threatening.

'Where's that nice Ronald Dean?' Mrs. Allbright demanded.

This was the young man Iris had mischievously taken from Caroline, and had handed back with lavish generosity too late for the quarrel to be mended. Caroline was married now. She had been bright about it, brave and defiant. She had known that it would be disastrous.

'Don't bring that up again,' Iris said, 'or I'll be having trouble with Christie as well as you.'

'Iris can't help it if men come round her like honey-pots,' Mrs. Allbright said to me in a tone of rebuke. She felt her simile was somehow inexact. 'As around a honey-pot,' she corrected herself. 'And Christine has her own interests these days, I believe.'

Her manner had changed. She was on her daughter's side now, hot on the scent. She smoothed her abundant grey hair, dressed with such elaboration of waves and whorls that it made her head seem too weighty for her body to endure. Leaning back on the sofa in a pose a little like Madame Récamier's, she pointed her intelligent nose.

'A little bird tells me there is an exciting young man in the offing.'

'Christie's an oyster,' said Iris; 'she's a clam. She doesn't trust her old friends, and if you badger her she'll just be oofy.'

'There's nothing exciting,' I replied.

'A little bird tells me he's not one of these callow boys,' said Mrs. Allbright.

Iris was the little bird.

'He's thirty-two.'

'My dear, my dear, I hope you know what you're doing! It's a wise little head on young shoulders, as we all know, but men of that age don't always have the right intentions.'

'It's nothing,' I said, but rejoicing to speak of him. 'I only know Ned casually.'

'He's that *perfect* charmer we met at the dance, Mother, the one Christie took poor little Keith to.'

'And Very nice of her. I like a girl who can make sacrifices.' Mrs. Allbright leaned across to pat the air approvingly, for she could not reach quite far enough to pat me. Her animus against Iris returned. 'I know girls who won't make sacrifices even for their own mothers.'

Iris was, however, too interested in her own thoughts to be distracted into anger. She came from her own chair to mine and wreathed her arm around me, a pretty arm, smooth and faintly freckled, like the shell of a brown egg. 'Christie! I want you to bring him here one night. I want to make sure he's really good enough for you. Please do!'

I replied that I did not know him well enough to take him visiting. 'Besides,' I added just so that she could hear and not her mother, 'I haven't forgotten Caroline.'

Iris twitched her nose. It was shorter than her mother's, and more delicately made, but sometimes it had the same air of living on its own and holding its own opinions. 'Horrid!' she murmured back. She added aloud, 'Well, *get* to know him better. I'll be thrilled to see him! Everyone will be!'

'I wonder,' Mrs. Allbright said dreamily, 'who of all our circle – you young ones, I mean – will be engaged first? Iris, I expect. She has more opportunities.'

'Perhaps Christine will marry Neddy!' Iris cried, on a babyish note. She had a habit of giving intimate nicknames to people she hardly knew or had never even met.

I told her not to be silly.

'Christine has her own way to make. She has to look after her aunt. I'm sure her father didn't spend all that money on her training just for her to go and marry any Tom, Dick or Harry.'

I heard this, but said nothing. I had fallen into a delightful dream of marriage. In a dark room full of the smell of flowers, with a foreign sea beyond, I held out my arms to him in terror and in longing. My thoughts seized hold of one detail of the picture and perversely clung to it. I was trying to decide upon the right nightgown.

Mrs. Allbright retired shortly afterwards. 'I'm feeling sleepy, and you girls like to have your secrets to yourself.' She had a parting shot at the door. 'See if *you* can't make my lazy daughter practise!'

When she had gone I said to Iris, 'I'm not risking anybody with you, not after the business with Caroline.'

Her eyes filled and were grey as rain. She laid her hand against my cheek. 'Darling! I swear I couldn't help it. I tried to put him off, I swear it. And I did send him back, after all. I do think you're cruel!'

On any other night she would have developed this theme, out of secret pride in her own power to charm and waylay, but something else was worrying her.

'You are cruel, Christie,' she added, but she gave it a conclusive air, as if not meaning that we should discuss the topic further. 'Darling, I want to ask you a question.'

'What is it?'

'Only between us. Because we're old friends. I couldn't say it to anyone else. Christie, do you feel you'd want to – you know, let a man do that?'

It was the circumlocution of our day, elusive, nounless. As I have said before, we had no easy word like 'love-making' to help us.

'If you were married, of course,' she added with a prim look. 'We're not tarts.' She took my hand and held it.

I could not answer while she was so close to me; speaking of love, she was the caricature of a lover. I got up and went over to the window. It was a wet night, and the lamps dropped their weighted ribbons into the black seas of the street. A car went by, casting up a splash and spatter as it turned the corner. I said, 'Yes, I should want to. It's ordinary to want to.'

'I don't!'

I turned to look at her. She might have been crying for hours rather than for a few seconds. She looked pale, swollen, almost plain. 'I've got to tell you. I'd loathe it. The thought of it makes me ill. I'll have to bear it when I get married because I want babies, but that's all! I've got to marry, anyway, because I shan't make good on the damned stage, and then I'll have to get away from Mother. But I shall hate it. I don't know how you *can*!'

It was easy to come to her now and let her cling to me.

'But Iris,' I said after a minute or so, 'you kiss them, don't you? Doesn't that ever make you feel—'

'No! I don't feel anything, ever. Except being pleased they like me. I've got to have that. It keeps me going.'

'Is that the only reason you took Ronnie from Caroline?'

But at this she composed herself. Her features tightened. She gave me the smile she gave to the men, veiled, half a secret offered to them, the other half kept to herself. 'How ridiculous you are! It wasn't my fault at all. He ran after me from the moment he met me. If you want to blame anyone, blame Caroline. She didn't do a thing to help herself. She just sat there and watched.'

It was getting late. I got up and went to fetch my coat. She did not go with me to the bedroom, but I found her waiting by the hall door. She gave me one of her planted, fresh kisses in the middle of my cheek.

'One thing,' I said, 'if Ned ever does begin to like me I'll see you don't meet him. As a compliment to you.'

This was meant, indeed, partly as a compliment, but mostly as a joke, that we might end the evening easily. To my surprise she did not take it as such.

'You are strong, Christie! How I envy you!'

Then she said something which seemed to come, not from herself, but from a creature lodged inside her. It had the sound of that prophecy which is only slightly emphasised because it is so sure, and I was to remember it all my life.

'And the people who fall in love with you will jolly well see to it that you go on being strong. You'll never be able to cry on any man's chest. You won't be allowed to.'

It struck me as nonsense, then – a kind of malignant but quite meaningless retort to my remark about Ned. Attracted as I was by his ruthlessness, his force, his lack of any by-your-leave, I could not imagine what she was talking about. Perhaps she could not, either, for she looked suddenly bewildered. Her smile broke out again, sweet, flirtatious, affectionate. 'It's been a comfort to talk. Don't mind me. I'm often silly.'

2

It was spring. My friends and I were mourning the death of D. H. Lawrence. Few of us had read much of his work, besides *Sons and Lovers*, and we grieved for him partly because he had suffered for impropriety's sake. (In those days the standard of impropriety had not yet reached so high a level that a writer would be hard put to it to find enthusiastic persecutors. This was our difficult dawn; this was the first putting-forth of our noses to sniff the air of sexual freedom.) Yet we grieved also because, though we did not fully understand him, though we were frightened of him – sensing perhaps the touch of chill at the core of his savage and sensuous being – we felt that he was one of us. If he had not been, he could not so surely, so remorselessly, have set his thumb upon the sore places of our hearts. Aldous Huxley, we felt, had been for us. He flattered our intellects; somehow he kept his own dazzling cleverness just within our range so that, if we used our brains as he meant us to, we could always pride ourselves on seeing the joke. But Lawrence made us face what was in the dark of ourselves, whether we liked it or not; he showed us the way out of our youth, and showed us that it was hard.

Ned, to whom I spoke of him on one of our rare, becalmed, frustrating afternoons, shook his head at me. 'There's nothing in the fellow. I got hold of a copy of *Lady Chatterley's Lover*, and, believe me, anyone could do that if they put in all the dirty words.'

The chill that came off Lawrence seemed nothing beside the chill that sometimes came off Ned. I felt it the most keenly when I first found the courage to show him clippings of my few published poems. He read them through, half smiling, then handed them back in silence. I put them in my bag. It was an hour later before he referred to them; meanwhile, we had been talking together in the uneasy, profitless banter which it seemed neither of us could escape. He said, 'I haven't got the true artist in my soul, Chris. You'll have to attend to that side of things.'

We went out together once a week, either for a drive or to the cinema. He had kissed me for the first time, an ordinary goodnight kiss, not the kiss I had dreaded and longed for. I was in love with him – but not all the time. There were days when I woke to believe myself free of him. The world had mysteriously shifted into new proportions, as if some great, benign hand had jolted it during the night. On these days I told myself that it would be easy not to see him so often, and eventually not to see him at all. But then, if he did not write to me or telephone me at the office (which he usually did at ten to nine, before Mr. Baynard came in) I would be sick with desire for him, tormented by fantasies in which, without thought for myself, I would put into his hands all that I was, begging him to destroy me and rebuild me to his liking.

Also I was thinking, in a manner precariously balanced between the romantic and the practical, what it might be like if I married him.

We should not lightly condemn the snobberies of middle-class youth. For a girl like myself, born into the stratum that is for some odd reason left undesignated (not lower-middle, certainly not upper-middle, but somewhere as nearly as possible equi-distant), there was not much to look forward to. A few years of business life, which might only euphemistically be referred to as a career; and then, perhaps, a modest marriage into familiar circles, familiar standards; the birth of children, and the same not unamiable, but quite unpromising, cycle all over again. I did not think seriously of a career for myself. A few poems, not really in the latest fashion, seemed little enough to found it upon: and though I professed to find T. S. Eliot freakish and pretentious, I had more than a suspicion that the day of Rupert Brooke, in whose manner I wrote, was done.

I shared, with several other girls whom I knew, the unspoken and rather despairing conviction that the only progress we could possibly hope to make would be a social one, although, being bookish, we would genuinely have preferred it to be professional. Already the suburban dance-halls seemed things of the past; the.proper thing to do was to drink cocktails in the bars of Mayfair, thus romantically identifying oneself, even if only for an evening once a fortnight, with the débutante and the prostitute. (I do not think Caroline could have faced her marriage at all had not her husband felt a strong orientation towards Dover Street.) Ned took me sometimes to the Running Horse; even on one occasion to Hatchett's. And his address was W.1.

He lived in Maddox Street, in a flat above a wholesale dress-house. He had not yet asked me to his home; I had seen it only from the outside, craning my neck upwards on a misty afternoon, hoping no one would see me and wonder what I was doing there. This was one of the days when the ache of longing had become intolerable. Almost without forethought I had found myself, during the office lunch-hour, moving in the general direction of Bond Street, not knowing why, and knowing perfectly well.

W.1. It had a magical sound in those days for the young living far beyond in the greater numerals: S.W.11, N.W.12, S.E.14. Perhaps it still has. It meant an excitement, a dangling of jewels in the dusk, music and wine. It meant having enough money not to get up on the cold, sour mornings and catch the crowded bus. It meant a kind of adventurous security.

I was sensible enough not to suppose Ned was rich or that he lived in grandeur; but I did know that he had been to a minor public school on the south coast, that he had a club, and that W.1, though he was not likely to admit it, would have as much importance in his imagination as in mine.

During that first time of doubt I was often pulled back from the instinct to leave him by the fantasy of myself stylish and safe in W.1. I can set this down without being much ashamed, for the silliness of youth has for me now the older sense of the word – which is simplicity or innocence. There is something cold and minatory about boys and girls who never pass through what we call a silly stage. I am more ashamed to recall that my visions of a smart life were derived less from my sober and conscientious reading (from Henry James or from *Swann's Way*) than from my less publicly avowed reading of Michael Arlen.

But I had another reason, apart from the impatience of youth and the fear of the future, for thinking I might marry.

3

Emilie had changed. She had been one of those mild, contented women with no apparent inner life, but now a deep one seemed to have taken possession of her. At first she had been dulled with grief, anaesthetised by it. In the past few weeks she had grown melancholic, only too aware of misery, only too prone to release it in sudden, soundless weeping. Several times I had come back from work to find no supper prepared for me and Emilie seated in the drawing-room window staring out over the Common, making no attempt to wipe the tears that fell down a face which had once the bright rosiness of a ripe apple, and had now the rosy-brownness of an apple rotten at the core. She no longer seemed content to let me go in and out as I pleased. She wanted to know my whereabouts, to know what time I should be in again. She needed me at last. She hated to be alone in the house.

At first she only hinted at this; soon she made it quite open, often devising strange little treats to keep me in.

'Do you know what I thought we'd do tonight? There's a very good programme on the wireless, so I thought, why not have our supper in the drawing-room, on a tray?'

Or again: 'Today I remembered a game your father showed me – it's such fun. I thought I might teach it you this evening so we could often play together.'

Her behaviour was pathetic and, in its way, comic; I had never known her remember so many hypothetical centenaries. Her uncle would have been a hundred and four on the third of next month, and his wife a hundred and five. Once she bought a bottle of medicated burgundy to celebrate the tenth anniversary of the Golden Wedding her parents had not succeeded in reaching. These thoughts did not seem, as before, to add sadness to her wonder; they induced in her now a kind of hilarity, a flushed, soft-footed good humour. They made her sing under her breath 'Two Little Girls in Blue'.

Caroline, who had looked in one night, happened to find Emilie in one of these moods. She said to me later, when we were alone, 'She's a little odd these days, isn't she, Chris?'

I said I hoped it would pass. 'But if it doesn't I shall have to get married or something. It's a dreadful house to come home to.'

She laughed. She was tall and fair, with the heavy eyes and thick affectionate mouth of the portrait of a girl by Roger van der Weyden, which is in the National Gallery. 'I'd swap my spouse for your aunt any day. You don't know how lucky you are.'

'Why did you do it?' I burst out. I had not dared ask it before, out of respect for her courageous pretences.

'Oh, I promised in a fit of nonsense – and then I couldn't get out of it. You'd be surprised how one can't. The first of us all to marry, and just look at me!'

'It will turn out all right. It must.'

'I tell myself so.' She sighed and rose, shutting herself off from me again. She had always been an oddly abstracted girl, receiving the confidences people felt impelled to give her, yet offering little in return. 'But you stay put. I mean it,' she added, as she put on her hat, pushing it carefully back from her protruberant and rather childish brow. 'The bed part is all right. It's when you get up again that you have your doubts.'

I was looking, not at her but at her face in the mirror, the face which should have been naked only to her own eyes. She had been the most phlegmatic, the most easygoing, the least vulnerable of us all; and at nineteen she had to find her way alone out of a silly tragedy that need never have happened. At this moment she dreaded going home.

'It would be too much trouble,' she said, 'to avoid Iris, because she seems to rear her beautiful head all over the place. But one day I shall lie quietly down on the rug and sink my teeth in her calf.'

I went up, when she had gone, to say goodnight to Emilie. I found her lying fully dressed on the bed in the full glare of the light.

'I thought you'd be asleep by now,' I said.

'I hardly sleep at all. And I wasn't sleepy.'

'Why did you go up so early?'

'I knew you wanted to be alone with your friend. You don't need me now. Nobody does.' She stared open-eyed into the burning lace of the gas-mantle, like an eagle staring at the sun or (I thought, with horrible literary appositeness) like Regulus lidless on the Carthaginian shore. 'You don't want me,' said Emilie with a kind of revolted scorn.

After scenes of this kind it was a relief to go to the office.

4

The day began propitiously. I was reading, in a flush of excitement and discovery, a new American novel brought to me by Take Plato. (This was a friend of Dicky Flint's, a handsome, black-avised youth of passionate intellectual ambitions, whose hair grew bison-like upon his forehead, and whose nickname had arisen from his habit, at one time, of appearing to begin every sentence with these two words.)

'This is wonderful, Christine! You've got to read it! It's greater than Tolstoi; it's greater than Katherine Mansfield!' His admirations were eclectic.

'I've been hearing about nothing but his wretched book for a month solid,' Dicky had said, giving his long shy grin. 'We'll be having to change his name if this goes on. We'll have to call him Crying Wolfe, only it sounds like a Red Indian.'

The book was *Look Homeward Angel*, and the copy, sent to Take Plato by a friend in Illinois, was the first American edition. I was intoxicated by it. I could not put it down even to eat my supper, despite Emilie's disapproval of reading at mealtimes. I took it to the bathroom and read it while I lay soaking, pausing now and then, as the bath grew too cool for comfort, to add some more hot water. I even read it on the top of the bus, though the jolting print made me feel sick.

It was a book for us, for our age, for our time; a book for youth, for the silly, the loving, the yearning, with their intimations of immortality, their hot hearts and hot heads. It was formless, as we were. Like us, it was filled with vaulting ambitions, noble aspirations; with the frustration of beholding the world beautiful and entire, in the knowledge that we should never be able to communicate this entirety, should be lucky if we could stammer out even an impoverished hint of it.

I was intoxicated by it – and in this delightful drunkenness arrived at the office to find a note from Ned, summoning me to lunch with him that day at the Trocadero; to find Mr. Baynard cheerful and musical because he had been chosen to play the most interesting of the young men in *Hay Fever*, which his local dramatic society was to produce that summer; to find Mr. Fawcett beaming with joy because he had been able to announce the engagement of his least satisfactory son to a widow who would be able to keep him in the comfort to which he had been accustomed.

'Spring is in the air,' said Miss Rosoman. 'What a lovely day!'

And indeed it was one of those spring days which, even in London, are of a colour between blue and green; a sparkling, pretty day to bring the women out in flowery dresses.

'Seems a pity to have to work,' said Miss Cleek timidly, as if afraid we might think this an audacious sentiment on her part. 'Though, of course, one has to,' she added quickly.

Miss Rosoman stretched her arms over her head; her full breasts rose and hardened. 'I'd like to be out with my boy today, on the river at Sonning, or something like that.' I was too happy to flinch snobbishly at the phrase 'my boy', which was one neither I nor my friends would ever have used.

' "*Thou the stream*
and I the willow,
Thou the idol
I the clay," '

Mr. Baynard sang in his frail, throaty voice. Knowing the song, I joined in with the 'seconds', waiting for his 'Thou the—' before cutting in with my descending 'Thou the stream'.

In the waiting-room Hatton was humming 'Exercise', to the droning accompaniment of the vacuum-cleaner, and the sun poured through the office windows, laying its quiet golden rectangles across the shining floors. Nothing could have begun more propitiously. My thoughts balancing between Thomas Wolfe and Ned, I worked that morning with the beautiful precision typists are often able to achieve in a state of trance. I took letters from Mr. Fawcett without hearing a word he dictated, so that when I came to transcribe them they appeared quite unfamiliar and interesting. At twelve o'clock (my normal lunch hour) I went exultantly to meet Ned.

He had never taken me out to lunch before, chiefly because my time was so short; this seemed a special occasion. The restaurant, to me, was a smart one. I was glad to be wearing my new grey costume and hat.

'Nice,' he said appreciatively, looking me up and down. He took me out of the daylight into the warm and lamplit grill-room. The smell of roasting meat and poultry made me hungry. It was pleasant to feel, at the same time, hungry, beautiful and in love.

As usual, he began to draw me out about my life, my habits, my tastes, my likes and dislikes, about my few childish love-affairs; about my friends, Iris, Caroline, Dicky, Leslie and Take Plato. The way I talked amused him; his eyes were sparkling and steady, full of affection and irony; but behind them was something else, something new and purposeful.

'Not a bad record for a small girl,' he commented, having edged me into telling him the names of four boys over whom I had respectively wept between my twelfth and my sixteenth year. 'I shan't put up with any more of it, you know. Dicky goes, Leslie goes, Plato goes.'

'There was only Leslie, and he's already gone.' I could not help laughing. We were comfortable together; I was flattered by what I supposed to be his pretence of jealousy, and time went quickly.

'I must be going,' I told him; 'there's such a fuss if I'm even two minutes late.'

I hoped he would call the waiter, but he did not. 'Let them wait for once. I've a piece of news for you, such as it is. I'm going into the house-selling business on my own.' He told me he had long hated working for his father – 'It's as bad as one of your relations teaching you at school' – and felt he would do better working for himself. His mother and father had agreed to lend him some capital, in addition to what he had already managed to save. 'I shall start pretty modestly and then build up. I know the ropes. And I shall have something to fight for.'

Had he said 'work' instead of 'fight' I should merely have assumed that he meant his own independence; his choice of the word told me that he meant something more, and I felt a stab of panic and excitement. He took my hand and kissed it, then stared straight at me. The rest of the room was blotted out by a haze of dark gold and darker rose. It was very hot. The babble of voices seemed far away. 'We'll be talking about this again.'

I was taken with the shyness that is a part of early love, one of its dreads and delights. My own voice sounded forced as I told him how glad I was for his sake, how much I hoped for his success. I added that I really would have to go; that if he didn't mind I would leave him to pay the bill while I rushed back to the office.

He held my hand firmly. 'But I do mind. You'll go when I go.'

I was shot through with so intense a pleasure that it seemed to me shameful. I could not meet his eyes. But however much his air of authority pleased me, I was forced to resist it. I suffered from a sort of pathological punctuality, either inherited from or patterned upon my father. Wherever I was going, I allowed for at least half an hour more than was necessary to get there. Not to arrive on time for an ordinary friendly meeting distressed me enough, but the idea of being late for the office (I had had no martinis this time to protect me against Mr. Baynard, for Ned never drank before the evening) was a torment.

'I must go. I've got to. I shall get into such trouble!'

'Sit down, Chris, and don't fidget. How long have we known each other? Not counting the dance – since we went to Hindhead?'

'Five months.'

'All that time I've been trying to make up my mind about us.'

'Ned, you must get the bill!'

'All right.'

He called to the waiter, who said, 'Half a minute, sir.'

'I've sown my wild oats. You haven't begun to think about yours,' he went on.

'Girls,' I said faintly, 'don't really sow them.'

'Some girls do. I've known girls who have.'

I hated them all.

'Not girls like me.'

'Not so young, anyhow.'

'It's not a matter of being young,' I insisted, to put the girls he had known into their proper places (as a crowd of unworthy demireps); 'it's a matter of principle.'

He smiled. 'Have it your own way. Anyhow, what I'm trying to say is that I don't want to be accused of baby-snatching.'

The term seemed to me vulgar; for a moment I felt the chill of it. 'So far as I know there's no reason why you should be,' I replied, I fancied with dignity.

'Don't you? I really think you should.'

The crisis I had awaited so long, with such trepidation and desire, was plainly imminent: and now my only thought was for my lateness; the only figure in the forefront of my mind Mr. Baynard.

'Ned, is that waiter never coming?'

He did not budge. 'He's taking his time.' He glanced at the clock on the wall, a little white face set in a curly-rayed sun. I had thought it a beautiful clock; now I hated it. He added, with a touch of unmistakable malice, 'And, what's more, that clock's ten minutes slow.'

I was aghast. 'Oh, it isn't! It can't be!'

He compared it with his watch. 'Twelve minutes slow, to be exact. Oh dear, you are in trouble, aren't you?'

I was almost crying. 'I have to go, I tell you! You don't know what it's like for me.'

'Neurotic,' he said, shaking his head. 'A distressing sight in one so young.'

I got up. Before he could stop me I left the room, raced up the stairs and ran as hard as I could go towards my fate. He caught up with me quite easily just as I had reached the corner of Jermyn Street.

'Don't get in such a state, Chris. It's exaggerated. I'll come and put things right with old What's-his-name.' He held my arm firmly, forcing me to slow down.

'You mustn't!' – though as yet I could not believe he meant it. 'It would make it much worse!'

He said: 'I'll come with you.'

I grew desperate. He was being cruel, and I knew it. Later, the memory of it might excite me, might seem to me delicious proof of his strength and manhood, but at the moment it was merely frightening. I kept begging him not to; my voice grew louder and louder.

'You don't want to cause a public sensation,' he said. 'They'll be having us up for obstruction.'

On the office steps I made one last appeal.

'Nonsense. It was my fault, anyway, and I'm going to see you don't suffer for it.'

'But I'll suffer worse!'

'The more you argue, the later it's getting,' he replied sturdily; and as if that were not enough, the pathetic fallacy came into operation, for quite suddenly the bright day dimmed, as if a shovelful of dust had been cast across the sky, and a few great drops began to fall.

Even in the lift he held my arm, was still holding it when we went into the office, to find Mr. Baynard awaiting me, rigid as Nelson on his column and in very much the same attitude.

5

'Exactly half an hour over time, Miss Jackson!' he shot at me in the staccato intonation he must have been rehearsing inwardly since one minute past one, simply altering the time named in accordance with the realities of the situation. He was too enraged even to notice Ned; or he may have thought (not perceiving the policeman grip) that he was a client who had happened to follow me in. Mr. Baynard never minded offering a rebuke in public.

Miss Rosoman, in pity for me, bent her head and typed furiously. Miss Cleek, who had just put her head round the door of the cloakroom, withdrew it. She would hide until the storm was over.

'This is the second time in six months!'

'That doesn't sound very impressive, if he but knew it,' Ned muttered in my ear.

'I'm sorry, Mr. Baynard,' I said. 'I couldn't help it. I couldn't get the bill—'

'You should leave time for getting bills! I'm not going to be flouted like this by the Junior. I won't have it. I *will* have my authority respected.' His lip quivered. Rage always brought him close to tears. He turned to Ned. 'Yes, sir? What can we do for you?'

'I'm with Miss Jackson. It was entirely my fault that she was late.'

Betrayed into using to a friend of the Junior's a tone he would normally only have used to a client A or B, Mr. Baynard's fury knew no bounds.

'Miss Jackson's no right to bring her friends in here! And she's no right to go out to lunch with friends if she can't get back in time! This is a business office! I won't have it!'

Ned let go of me. He took a perching step to the counter and leaned upon it, looking up at Mr. Baynard with deceptive mildness. 'The trouble is,' he said, 'that you are rude. I don't like that.'

'Who are you? What are you? Who do you think you're talking to?'

It struck me suddenly as a little pitiable, for Mr. Baynard was scared. He was afraid of being made ridiculous in front of the girls.

Ned was in no hurry to reply. Miss Rosoman had slowed her typing to a beginner's pace because she did not want to miss anything. The cloakroom door, open half an inch, indicated the interest of Miss Cleek.

Ned said, 'I am going to marry Miss Jackson. We decided it at lunch, which I thought might have been a good enough excuse to satisfy any reasonable person if you'd given me a chance to offer it. My name is Skelton.'

Mr. Baynard saw the way of escape and took it. 'Oh, I see! Well, that makes some sort of difference. I suppose I must congratulate you, Miss Jackson; But it mustn't happen again.'

'I should be annoyed if it did,' Ned murmured, with an appearance of courteous jocularity. He put a hand upon my shoulder.

I felt myself at the core of a tenacious dream, unable to think, to speak, having no strength to force myself awake. It must be a joke: Ned could not make me marry him by this means. Yet I felt proud. Though the dream was terrifying, I could not be certain that I was not enjoying it. I do not know what I should have done or said if I had not been saved by the percipience of Miss Rosoman, who told me afterwards what had come to her in a flash: that this was the first I had heard of my own engagement.

She came to the counter, leaned across it and kissed me, having to heave both her feet off the ground in order to perform the feat. 'Christine, I'm so glad! Why didn't you tell us? Oh, Mr. Baynard, isn't it exciting?'

Baffled, he agreed that it was very exciting. Miss Cleek, flushed, appeared in the passage and sidled her way towards her little desk.

'I'll see you tonight,' Ned told me. 'I'll call round about eight.' He kissed my cheek, nodded to Mr. Baynard, gave Miss Rosoman his open and charming smile, and went away.

'We can't let pleasure interfere with business,' Mr. Baynard said, 'even great events. You'd better hurry up and get your things off.'

When I came back to my seat he had taken hold of himself, and so, to a degree, had I. He put me at once on to the most disagreeable task he could find, which was to copy some faintly soiled index cards on to some new ones. And when Miss Rosoman came to ask me all the exciting details, he told her sharply that I could not be expected to get on with my work if people constantly interrupted me.

'You're out of luck,' she murmured to me, on the way back to her desk. 'They rang up this morning and said they weren't doing his play after all. Probably stopped the whole thing so they shouldn't have to see him act.'

Certainly he was filled with some sadness from a source independent of my bad behaviour. During tea I heard him singing 'Thou the Stream' again under his breath, but this time in a minor key. I felt very sorry for him. I, too, had once enjoyed acting, and had been broken-hearted when the part of Hippolyta was taken away from me and given to a rather fat girl called Freda.

That I could find time that afternoon to be sorry for Mr. Baynard is indicative of my state of bewilderment. I could scarcely believe what had happened to me and to what I had been publicly committed. My twitching thoughts were sharpened only by a flow of visual images, slotting their way like the lighted carriages of a railway train through a far-off landscape by night; of myself in W.1, strolling between meals in a black dress fluent and slim as a liquorice braid; of the wedding-night in the mysterious room above the sea (the phrase came to me, *Le Collier des Perles*); of a day of knowledge, flat in the unromantic light, and two people ordinarily dressed, making conversation at a deal table in a prison with no doors at all and no clocks upon the walls. To feel sorry for Mr. Baynard was simply one way of relief.

I dreaded seeing Ned that night, and at the same time felt the hours would never pass. I did not know what I should say to him. I put my trust in God (I actually prayed; I asked him to send me some healing inspiration) and in the spur of the moment.

But the day, being one of those overheated days in which curious forces work with a kind of involuntary frenzy, brought me into further trouble – this time of a ridiculous nature.

It was my duty at five o'clock sharp to collect the remainder of the petty cash, together with the day's accounting, put it in a cylinder and send it back to the bank through the pneumatic tube. So far as I knew at the time I did as I had always done. In retrospect I rolled up notes and debit slip, slid them into place, and fastened the cylinder-cap, which was of metal with a coating of dingy felt.

Mr. Baynard and Miss Rosoman had gone home; Miss Cleek had taken the letters to the post; Hatton had not yet come back from delivering his messages. Mr. Fawcett was writing personal letters in his room, and I was just putting on my hat, when the inter-office telephone, between ourselves and the bank downstairs, began to ring. 'I say,' said Mr. Harvey, the cashier, 'we haven't had your dough. What's happened to it?'

I had sent it down, I told him, as usual.

'Half a tick, then; someone else may have got it. I'll go and see.' After a pause he returned. 'We've got the cylinder and we've got the lid. But no money.'

I was invaded by alternating tides of heat and cold. 'It *must* be there.'

'It's not. You can't have screwed the cap on, that's what.'

'But I did!'

'My dear girl, you can't've.'

So I went to tell the story to Mr. Fawcett, who, with that look of consternation commonly associated with people who have observed psychic phenomena, eyes protruding, hair (it seemed to me) vertical upon his scalp, darted out without a word. I heard him ringing repeatedly for the lift.

When he returned, he was not wearing his normal air of friendly abstraction. 'Do you know what you've done? *There are three hundred pounds whirling around in the motor, being torn into little pieces!*'

Unable to defend myself, I put my head upon my arms and cried. I had had a terrifying vision of Paolo and Francesca in the eternal whirlwind. Three hundred pounds! It was a sum I had seen in one piece often enough, that I had counted out in fives and tens. Only now did it assume for me its appalling reality.

I could have done nothing wiser than to put myself at Mr. Fawcett's mercy.

He stood above me. I could just see, through my fingers, his huge, hanging, helpless hands.

'All right, all right, it can be fixed. They'll have the numbers downstairs. But don't do it again, and for heaven's sake stop crying! Do stop. The world hasn't come to an end.'

So he tried to comfort me, speaking in tones more personal than he had ever used; more personal probably than he had ever supposed he could use to a subordinate without distaste. He scolded and consoled by turns, treated me by turns as a child and as an adult who should be ashamed of herself. Finally, unable to arouse me from my nervous frenzies, he said loudly, 'Look here, it really doesn't matter a damn! Besides, you're upset enough, anyway. Mr. Baynard told me you'd just got engaged. That's enough to upset anyone. You oughtn't to be crying, you ought to be happy. Oh, please stop it, Miss Jackson! Go home and have a drink, if you do drink, and enjoy your dinner and think no more about it.'

He was a good man, but cowardly. He said quickly, 'I'm going off now. You get along, too. Hatton will lock up.' With a whisk about of his body that disturbed the surrounding air, a sigh of relief at having decided to struggle with me no longer, he was off and away.

I raised my head to discover, with some surprise, that my eyes were dry, though at what point I had stopped crying I could not guess. The office was quiet. The rain had ceased, but great glutted drops still sagged from the balustrade on to the veranda outside. I considered, with a kind of detached, intellectual interest, the bank notes eddying in the machine below, which I could conceive only in Wellsian terms as a sort of Martian dynamo. It was a fatal thing to do, for suddenly, without my volition, two of them turned into Ned and myself, spinning in permanent giddiness and supernatural, irrelievable nausea, in the whirlwind created by Dante out of his divine spitefulness – the whirlwind in which the modern mind can never believe (since it has made God into a tolerant fellow, a sort of senior clubman) nor the prophetic soul of the lover ever cease, in its secrecy, to fear.

6

When he came that night I believed I was ready for him. I should tell him lightly that a joke was all very well, but that I should look foolish when I had to break the pretended engagement next week. I should rebuke him smilingly for giving me so much trouble, and when he had begged my pardon we would both have a good laugh over the dilemma of Mr. Baynard, the effectiveness of Miss Rosoman, the embarrassment of Miss Cleek. I should tell him about the notes in the machine.

He came springing up the steps, two at a time, smiling all over his face. Reassured, I went to open the door.

Then he kissed me as he had not done before. I could not bear to raise my head – I was lost.

'What a way for it to happen,' he said, in a voice not like his own. 'I love you, Chris. Now you tell me.'

I told him. It was a moment of drenching terror and joy. Neither of us seemed able to move.

Then Emilie came along the hall, and when she saw us cried out as if she had seen murder done. Ned let me go. Advancing upon her (she stood with her weight upon the balls of her feet so that the trembling ran through her, one hand upon the newel-post, the other thrust half-out), he kissed her on both cheeks. 'Aunt Emilie, Chris and I are going to get married.'

'But you can't,' she said after a pause. Her gaze flitted between us. She put Ned away from her. 'Christine is too young.'

'My mother was married at seventeen,' he replied, which was not true, but is a thing commonly said upon occasions such as these, when it is necessary to stopper criticism.

'It was different in those days,' Emilie answered with a curious dreaminess. Her eyes were not dreamy. The pupils were like specks of quartz.

'I know you're surprised.' He did not seem to regard this as an understatement. 'But you must have guessed what I felt about her.'

'She's too young for you.'

'She's a bright girl for her age, Aunt Emilie. And I shall train her in the way she should go.'

She moved past us into the drawing-room. We followed her. She was standing precisely under Tree's chandelier, as in a place of judgment; but she was overcome by feebleness. 'I can't spare Christine. I've no one else.' It did not occur to her then, or at any later time, that she could exercise the right to forbid my marriage till I was of age.

'You can come and live with us, then,' Ned said loudly, with an overriding force.

'I don't know what to say.'

'Well, you could wish us happiness.'

'It won't be soon?' She raised her eyes to him confidingly, as if she felt he were more of her generation than mine. Her colour had faded; beneath the permanent patches of withered rose she was pale.

'Not too soon. I've got my own way to make first. I'm setting up for myself. Come on, Aunt Emilie, say something nice!'

'I congratulate you,' she said. She touched his arm. 'I congratulate you,' she said to me. I kissed her. I was full of guilt. I felt as though I had submitted her to some outrageous indignity.

Ned had come prepared. From the pocket of his mackintosh he brought a half-bottle of whisky. 'We shall all drink to ourselves. To me and Chris and Aunt Emilie.' He sent me off for glasses and water.

Aunt Emilie would drink water only.

She asked us what our plans were, what Ned's mother thought, again insisted that the wedding should not be soon. She had accepted it, and she was desolate. He was gentle and reassuring to her throughout this dismal celebration, but he could not stand too much of it.

'And now I want Chris to myself for a bit, which you'll admit is reasonable. I'm going to run her out to Richmond, and I promise not to be late. I'll be with you in a minute,' he said to me, 'so get your coat on', and went upstairs to the bathroom.

'It's a shock,' said Emilie. 'It's such a shock.'

'It was to me, rather, but we shall both get used to it.'

'Yes. Are you sure about it? Are you happy? I wish your father was alive!'

'I'm terribly happy,' I replied, and it was true. I was at the peak of a happiness so intense that it sent the whole room out of focus. Her pinched face was the only clear thing upon the romantic haze.

Then she said in a loud, terrified voice, as if driven by Conscience to something hateful, 'If you don't know about the Act, *I* couldn't tell you. You'll have to find someone else. I suppose you'll have to know now—' and ran from the room.

Ned came back. 'What was all that about?'

'Nothing.'

'But she was in such a state!'

'She thought I mightn't know the facts of life,' I said reluctantly. 'It was all she could think about, with me getting married. She feels responsible.'

He began to laugh.

'No,' I said, 'don't.'

We went that evening for the first time to an hotel in Richmond, built upon a spur of the river. We were to go there regularly during the following year. Sitting in the cocktail bar, dimly lit for lovers, we looked out across the starless water, arrowed by ghostly swans.

Ned held my hand tightly, almost hurting me. 'You mean so much, Chris. I never thought I could feel like this. You don't know how happy I am.'

In the ballroom they were playing a popular tune of the day, gentle, sexual, invading.

I am always a little sorry for the man or woman sensitive to music, whose lover is deaf to it. A tune which, for me, contained and still contains the essence of ourselves together, because I had heard it in his company at some moment of heightened sadness or felicity, would mean nothing to Ned, for he could not tell it from another. To have it haunting my own past and to know it could have no place in his was, for me, a barrier between us. These mnemonic tunes need have no appropriateness to the moment in which they are first heard or apprehended; there is a trivial, facetious song, with a commonplace melody, which moves me violently even on the heights of the present, since it resurrects for me a moment twenty years in its grave; it makes me look down, and I am afraid of falling.

'What are they playing?' I asked Ned.

'Don't ask me. The only tune I know is God Save the King, because everybody stands up.'

Later, we walked on Richmond Green. The air smelled of grass and dew and of the river. ' "Unforgettable, unforgotten," ' Ned murmured, tightening his arm around my shoulders. 'You see, I can be literary, too, if I want to be. I'm not altogether a Philistine.' The lamplight shone upon the Georgian houses beautiful in their plainness and integrity, softening red brick to the rose of Emilie's cheeks. 'That's where I'd like to live one day. But we'll have to go slow at first.'

I had not contemplated going slow: I had seen my marriage in terms of stateliness and space and ease. But I was troubled only for a minute, for youth is ready to adapt itself to any new idea, and within a second I had established us both in a small but elegant little flat, three rooms and bath. It was a delightful idea, more delightful than the original one. Here I would work for Ned, showing him my love by my care for his well-being, the skilfulness of my domestic economy.

'I shall like it anywhere with you,' I said.

He swung me round. Few people were about; for him there might have been no one at all but ourselves. He said, again in the voice unlike his own, that disturbed and excited me, 'Will you? Do you feel like that? You've got to love me, Chris, as much as I love you, because otherwise I shan't be able to bear it.' He put his hand upon my breast. 'You'll find out.'

I said at last, excited by an emotion I had never known before, an emotion which seemed to demand a gift for the lover, and a great one, 'You're older than I am. If you don't want to wait . . . it would only be for you. I couldn't say it, except to you.'

He let me go. Before he spoke, I felt the frost that came from him. 'You're not a trollop. Don't be so silly. And don't ever say a thing like that again.'

None of this would have happened had I not been too young for him, and other things were to happen for the same reason; but as yet I did not understand it. I humbled myself; I assured him of my innocence. He said he did not doubt it, but that I must learn not to say things which might arouse doubtfulness in people who did not know me. I told him I would do whatever he said, that I would learn from him, that

I would trust my life to him. When he thought I was sufficiently conscious of my error he took me and kissed me until I was breathless with joy and on the edge of hysterical tears; but inside of me a small, cold critic sat aloof.

7

Next Sunday he took me to meet his family. He lived with his parents. He had a widowed sister ten years older than he, whom he seemed not to like very much. I was shy enough of this visit to ask for advance information. What were they all like? What did they look like? Would they be pleased with me? How did they wish to be treated? I could not be sufficiently prepared. When Ned told me his sister despised make-up but his mother didn't mind it, I begged him earnestly to tell me which of them I should try to satisfy, urged him at least to anticipate his father's casting-vote. 'It wouldn't matter a two-penny damn to me what any of them thought,' he said. 'And, anyhow, I like you as you are. You don't want to dress yourself up. Or down.'

Nevertheless, I spent over an hour upon myself that day, growing more and more nervous as I tried first one dress and then another, made-up my face, scrubbed it clean again, and attempted to do it differently. My hair would not go right. It sprang out at angles foreign to it, it was lustreless, it hung lankly out of curl. I felt I had not only a young look but a humble one. I was almost in despair, and so frightened by this time that birds seemed to be fluttering around in my stomach. Emilie did not help me by sitting mute on the bed, staring with mournful eyes at a patch of wall about a foot beyond my head. She was now in a state of melancholic resignation. It made her follow me from room to room, watching me as though she expected me to vanish suddenly into air, and making no comment except occasionally to remark, 'I don't suppose he meant it about letting me live with you. It was just for something to say.'

It was ridiculous but noble-hearted of Sinbad the Sailor to stop and worry because the Old Man of the Sea might be getting pins and needles. Emilie should have maddened me, but she did not. Somehow I felt her misery as if it had been my own, was endowed with such a degree of empathy that I could sometimes wish she had the power to persuade me not to marry after all, but to support her dismal loneliness for as long as she lived. Even when she was not with me, she hung around my mind like an importuning ghost; but I dared not console her openly for fear of making her worse. I doubt nowadays whether she was really suffering so much as I supposed; her misery was probably more of a passive than an active state, something necessary to her, something she would have been lost and naked without. I think perhaps we often suffer unnecessary torments of spirit by imputing to others griefs as intense as our own. If we did not, we should, of course, be happier – but then, we should be less than we are. For we cannot dispossess other people from our conscience simply because they are self-regarding, or even wicked. They may suffer in the same way as the most selfless, the most generous of heart; so long as we are unable to assess the degree of their pain, we must assume it as heavy as we ourselves can imagine, and treat it accordingly.

'I expect you'll be late, dear,' said Emilie, 'but don't be later than you can help.' She added, presenting me with a picture of woe, 'Have a good time.'

I was so anxious to appear gay and at ease when I arrived at Maddox Street that I succeeded in fixing upon my mouth a tight and aching simper. I knew it did not become me; I did not know how to get rid of it. My lips had a stretched feeling, as though they were chapped.

'Relax, relax,' Ned said to me, as he stopped the car.

'I am relaxed,' I answered in a strange, high voice, but the simper fell away, leaving behind it a small, uncontrollable twitching.

We climbed up a steep, uncarpeted stairway past several floors of offices. A little light filtered through the landing windows, an olivine and dusty light, unhelpful, discouraging. 'Let me get my breath.'

'What bad shape you must be in!' Ned exclaimed. 'You're snorting like a grampus. Why, I played rugger up to last year. I was about the best fly-half the club ever had.'

We came to the top floor. Before he opened it, he kissed me. 'I'm as proud as Punch.'

After the commercial dreariness of the approach, the flat seemed to approximate itself to my dreams of smartness. I was aware of light paint, gilded looking-glasses, damask hangings; the very tall, very lean woman who came to meet me was, to my eyes, a creature from the *Sketch* or *Tatler*. I thought she must be his sister, since she looked so young.

But her voice was not young, and a vision of Leslie's mother flicked up into my mind before I could formulate any reason why it should.

'Well, Christine, thank God my son's, found someone to take him off our hands.' She touched my cheek formally with her lips. 'I'm very pleased. Come along in.'

In the harsh north light of the drawing-room I saw that, despite her slenderness, her stiff bearing, she was an old woman. She must have been sixty – which was old to me then, but is not so old now. She had Ned's lofty, avian look and heavy eyes; her hair, which she wore in the eton crop of the 1920s, was still ivory-fair. She turned me about, studying me thoughtfully. 'She's a pretty girl, Ned. Has she the slightest idea what she's in for?' She added to me, 'My dear, he's always been a rolling-stone. This is his last chance to settle down, so mind he takes it, because he'll get no further help either from me or his father.'

Ned shrugged, and grinned at her with all the privileged influence of a favourite child; I wondered if he could, in fact, be her favourite. Yet she seemed no fonder of her daughter, a stout, sardonic-looking woman carelessly dressed, to whom she now introduced me. 'This is Elinor. She'll be more like an aunt than a sister, won't she? Nelly, do take that horrible dog from under my feet! He'll be the death of me one of these days.'

Elinor said how-do-you-do to me briefly, gave me a snap-shot glance and picked up from the carpet an old, clotted-looking Skye terrier. 'I'll put him in the hall, poor little devil. Nobody wants you, do they?' she demanded of it. 'Only your rotten old mistress.'

Mrs. Skelton asked me to sit down. Taking the chair opposite, she knotted upon her knees her rather large, arthritic hands, barnacled with rings, and gazed at me steadily. 'He's twice your age.'

'Come, come,' said Ned, 'four years short of that. Don't scare the child.'

She gave him the cold, experienced look I had so often seen Leslie's mother give her son; Mrs. Allbright give Iris. Ignoring him, she said to me, 'It's on your head. I hope you'll be happy. But you see he sticks to his work.'

We were joined then by her husband, who seemed to have been making his delayed entry for the sake of the effect and, I thought, justified it. He was short, grey, pug-nosed; he had an air of extraordinary cleanliness, as though he had just come from a Turkish bath. He was pink as a rose and walked springily.

'So this is Ned's surprise!' he exclaimed, clasping his hands within an inch of my face, bending his knees so that his eyes were level with mine. I did not know what to do. I knew

I should always rise in respect for women much older than I. But for men? I hesitated, then made an upward movement, awkward, tentative. Mr. Skelton put me back again. 'No, no, don't disturb yourself. So this is the little girl! I suppose you came in your perambulator,' he added, with a wink.

'Don't clown, Harold,' his wife said to him; 'people don't like it.'

Sighing, he rose up like a jack-in-a-box; his knees creaked. 'Well, well, well.'

Elinor came in. 'I'm getting tea. Is that all right, or is it too early?'

'Any time.' Mrs. Skelton lit a cigarette. 'When are you and Ned going to get married, Christine?'

I told her it had not yet been decided.

'I should do it as soon as possible if I were you. No point in hanging about. Besides, it's quite time Ned put his house in order.'

'We'll have to get a house first,' he said.

'My rude son has a maddening habit of picking up my words,' she observed to me. 'Perhaps you can break him of it. I must say it will be a relief to me to think someone else has charge of him.'

She was so far from my idea of the conventional mother-in-law whose instinct would be to hate and hamper me that I could not resist an impulse of warmth and gratitude; I told myself that her constant belittling of Ned must be a family joke.

Elinor brought in the tea and served it. To my surprise I found that Mrs. Skelton preferred to mix herself gin and French vermouth. The meal was rather a silent one, for Elinor addressed herself in murmurs only to the dog, who had followed her back again. Ned and his father discussed the state of the stock market, and Mrs. Skelton gazed absorbedly, with no appearance of feeling that she should say anything at all, into her glass. I had time to look about me more carefully and to perceive that my first idea of sumptuousness had been a deluded one. The furniture, the carpets, the curtains, these had been expensive enough originally; but over them all lay that shabbiness which comes not so much from shortness of money as from the housekeeper's utter lack of interest. A gas-fire spluttered and popped. The day grew darker. No one turned on a light.

At last Ned said he was taking me away again; he wanted to run out to Richmond.

'What fun, in the pouring wet,' Elinor observed.

'We'll be seeing a great deal of you, Christine,' said Mrs. Skelton, pouring a few drops of extra gin into her cocktail. 'You're "family" now. You and I must have a serious talk together one of these days. And you'd better try to think what you're going to call me.'

'Well, I call you Harriet,' said Ned, who looked oddly reduced in his own home, 'so I suppose Chris had better.'

Mrs. Skelton shrugged. 'As you please. It's up to you. *I* don't care what anyone calls me.'

Her husband had gone away. I was to learn that all his social appearances were hearty but extremely brief. He had not enough heartiness to last him long, and when he had exhausted it he relapsed into a smiling, far-away silence. He was rather like someone who has about a dozen phrases of excellent French and no more; who uses them at once to Frenchmen, amazing them, firing their admiration, and then takes his leave quickly before they can be disillusioned.

It was Elinor who went with me to the door. Ned had already gone down to the car to try to discover the cause of some fault or other he had detected in the engine. I had learned this afternoon that it was not his car but his father's, who let him have the use of it.

'Dullish lot, aren't we?' said Elinor, but she looked at me with kindness. 'I'm the oddest man out, because I can't stick London and live in Tudor squalor in Herts. Neddy's all right really; he's lucky to get you. But keep your claws on him, if you've grown them yet.'

She was very ugly, I thought, and she knew it. In her view any attempt at self-improvement would be useless; so she made no such attempt. Her thick glasses had old-fashioned frames, quite round, very heavy. She wore grips in her hair, and did not conceal them. Yet she had a sweet mouth, and I supposed it was for this that her husband had married her.

'I'll do my best, Mrs. . . .' I hesitated.

'Ormerod, if it matters. But you'd better call me Nelly, as the others do. They do it out of malice. Go on, your beau's waiting for you. See he keeps his temper, by the way. When he was a baby he used to lie and chew his fists with rage. He's better now, of course.'

It had been a discouraging afternoon in one way, since it had effectively laid my romantic fancies; in another way it was consoling. I had been approved. I had been liked. In fact, I had been liked a little too much for my taste; it seemed to me unnatural that Ned's family should instantly range itself on my side, as if against him. The critic within me had something to say; but I would not listen. Not at that time.

8

A formal engagement brings its obligations. Ned must meet my friends. I arranged an evening, inviting only the few nearest to me: Dicky, Caroline, Take Plato. I did not invite Iris – I was taking no chances.

I was apprehensive from the first. It was not that I worried as to what my friends would think of Ned – they could hardly, I felt, fail to be impressed. But what would he think of them? They seemed to me suddenly so young, the fun we had together so childish, that I loved them as never before while, in my mind, I hotly defended them against his imagined criticism.

'We had better have some sherry as well as tea,' suggested Emilie, who seemed as edgy as I. 'Ned will be used to it.'

'But one can't,' I said, with superiority, 'drink sherry after dinner.'

'Dinner?' she repeated vaguely. For her (as for me, hitherto) this was a meal taken at midday. 'Oh, I see. Should we buy some beer?' Teetotal herself, her militancy had faded somewhat since her doctor had made her break the pledge in favour of a small whisky at bedtime. Besides, she was in awe of Ned and of what she imagined to be his world. I think she sometimes regretted Leslie and his singular predictability.

The evening was as difficult as I feared. My friends sat stiffly about the room, laughing in a brief, isolated fashion whenever Ned made a joke. Dicky, having brought his ukelele, took one look at my fiancé and slipped away to hide it under the hallstand. Caroline, in whom my hopes had rested, since she at least was a married woman and presumably, therefore, of adult status, was a disappointment. Her usual easy, ribald ironies ceased to flow. She smoked cigarette after cigarette; she hardly spoke at all. I found myself resenting her because she appeared to have assumed the onlooker's rôle that I had reserved for myself.

Only Take Plato preserved much of his usual fluency, and I could have wished that he had not. (For it was by him that Ned appeared the most amused.)

'Nietzsche, for instance,' he announced, pushing back his black and tufty hair, 'influenced me for a while. But one comes to see through him. At least, I feel one does. One can't take too much of the world upon oneself.'

'I never could,' Ned agreed equably. 'Who did you find to take his place?'

'Schopenhauer wallowed along for about a week, didn't he, Reg?' Dicky enquired. 'But he didn't last. No. What we heard about then was Freud. *Ad nauseam.*'

'That, at any rate, was fruity,' Caroline murmured. 'It made a change.'

Take Plato cleared his throat. 'It is hardly possible to deny that Freud has been the catalyst of our day. Don't you think so?' he enquired of Ned, man to man.

'And what has the effect been?'

'Well . . . to know ourselves. Now we know ourselves as we never did before. And what is more,' my friend added with a kind of nonchalant shudder, 'the revelation is somewhat of a catharsis.'

Dicky hummed a song, squinted at the toe of his shoe.

'You're all too clever for me,' said Caroline. 'What is a catharsis, or whatever it is, anyway? It sounds like an opening medicine.'

'It is,' Take Plato told her eagerly. 'It's a kind of spiritual aperient. It is a clearance of the soul.'

It had occurred to me before that he was rather silly, though I had been too fond of him to care. Now he seemed to me ridiculous to a degree, and I found myself caring a great deal.

I tried to display him in a better light. 'Well, it was you who discovered Thomas Wolfe,' I said to him, for Ned's benefit.

'The divine Carolinian!' he exclaimed. He smiled, delighted by the opportunity I had afforded him for bringing out his newest phrase.

'You ought to read Wolfe,' I said diffidently to Ned. 'He's pretty wonderful.'

He stretched his legs. He had rejected the sherry, as I guessed he would, and (the only comforting thing that had happened so far) appeared to be enjoying the tea and also the bread pudding, which I should have countermanded, had I known Emilie meant to provide it.

He said to Take Plato, with the air of one disposed to be instructed, 'What do you do for a bit of light reading? In the train, for instance?'

'Actually I read verse.'

'God help us,' said Dicky. 'Now, a nice limerick—'

'The Latin poets,' Take Plato continued eagerly, his eyes translucent. 'What a discovery when one comes upon them at first! Can you wonder Shakespeare worshipped Ovid?' He quoted mellifluously, in the modern Latin we all learned at school, his accent impeccable, his quantities faultless:

> '*Terra tribus scopulis vastum procurrit in aequor, Trinacris a positu nomen adepta loci.*'

'I did that in my last year,' Ned said, somehow surprising us and casting us into consternation, 'only I never said "Wastoom". One didn't, in my time. It means something like – "The earth sticks out in three promontories into the water. The name of the place is Trinacris, which is not inappropriate." '

'You haven't got that quite right,' Take Plato began, blushing bright red, but Ned went on, as if he had not spoken, 'It doesn't seem particularly thrilling to me. What do you see in it? I told Chris I hadn't a poet's soul.'

There was a long silence. 'It's the *feeling*,' Take Plato said at last. 'If you can't sense it you can't.'

I could tell that everyone but Ned was relieved when it was time to go home. I was most unhappy. I had wanted him to like them; he seemed to have formed no opinions one way or the other. I had wanted them to like him; obviously they were not going to. The gap of fourteen years or so yawned more unbridgeably between him and them than between him and myself. I knew the shiver of desolation which is like the coming out of mild drunkenness into sobriety. I knew that, whatever happened in the future, I had that night bade farewell to my friends.

9

Yet the succeeding months were happy ones, for I was caught by the buoyancy of sheer newness. I had to learn Ned like a language; and the early stages of most languages seem simple and progress fast. I saw him nearly every day, either at my home or his – but more frequently at mine, firstly because his mother, though kind to me, seemed permanently sunken in derisive gloom, and secondly because I felt blackmailed by Emilie's unexpressed desire for my company. I never told Ned the real reason why I so often refused to go out of an evening; I knew instinctively the comment he would have made. Instead, I found all manner of excuses for staying at home – the office had tired me out, I had a headache, I had some work to finish that would keep me too late for a run out to Richmond. He accepted them all. He was content enough to sit with me, to make love to me, to draw from me small and ludicrous incidents of my childhood to which he would listen with his half-smile, now and then running a finger down my cheek. On these evenings Emilie sat with us very little: she was content simply to know that I was in the house.

Ned had now set up in business on his own. He had bought the goodwill of a house agency near South Kensington station. The gross profits, he said, should be about three thousand a year; he hoped to nett about half. To me, the thought of this half was a fabulous one; if I married Ned I should greatly exceed the ambitions of my mother, who had so often said, 'I should like Christine to marry a thousand-a-year man.' It was a phrase of mysterious overtones, an incantation to peal like a jammed bell through my dreams of the future.

'If everything goes as I hope,' said Ned, 'we'll get married in August. I hope to God it does. It may be tricky just at first.'

I do not know when I first sensed his lack of self-confidence, realised that it was as much a part of him as the marrow of his bones. I knew, then, that it was indeed a part of him; but, being young, I believed I could change it, that I could change him. I have never forgotten the way I tried to do so, nor the result. I remember it as one of the shames of youth which project their misery into age, of which it is impossible to speak and difficult even to write.

But before that something else happened.

One night, when the weather had turned hot and starry after early rain, Ned happened to leave his mackintosh behind at my house. I was not to see him on the following day, and as usual I was fretting – I hated days without him. I came home from the office, had my supper and was going upstairs to read, when Emilie stopped me.

She had a secretive, excited look, her mouth pursed so tightly that she seemed to be making a physical effort to keep her lips shut. I had seen her looking like this before, on the very rare occasions when she had had to nerve herself to be firm with my father. She came with quick little Japanese steps along the hall, shot out her arm and presented to me a dingy-looking piece of paper.

'I think you ought to see this.' She drew in her breath, held it.

'What is it?' I did not want to look.

'I found it on the floor under his mackintosh. It must have fallen out. It was lying face upwards, so I couldn't help seeing.' She had the grace to flush a little. 'I think you ought to know.'

She went rapidly away. I heard a door bang.

My heart lurched. It is never easy, when one is in love, to face mysterious pieces of paper; when one is also young, it is abominable. In later life we sometimes have the sense to glance at our findings with half-shut eye and half-shut mind, and destroy them before we have formulated a theory. We have learned, in fact, the superiority of uncertainty to certainty. But this day, holding in my hand the note Emilie had discovered in her idle pryings, I felt as if I were waiting for a bomb to explode. I was sick with fear of the future, as if one part of my life had come abruptly to an end long before I had begun to prepare myself. The note looked as though it had been folded and refolded many times. I saw one word – 'Beloved'. Then another – 'unbearable'. Stiffening my shoulders, drawing a deep breath, I read the rest. It was a short letter, undated, a letter of passionate reproach, to my young standards rather indecent. It was signed 'W'. It was obvious enough that the writer had been Ned's mistress.

Even if he had not mentioned Wanda to me, I should not have been silly enough to imagine that I was the first girl with whom he had been in love; and I think I had been aware enough, in the sensible but unexaminable depths of my thought, that not all his love-affairs were likely to have been as innocent as mine. But his behaviour towards me had been decorous as Leslie's, and so I had allowed the ridiculous idea to germinate that perhaps (this was a favourite phrase of my mother's) he had 'kept himself' for the girl he meant to marry.

Now that I knew he had done no such thing I felt betrayed: and I knew a rage of jealousy so swamping that for a second it was like the onset of some physical illness. For I envied Wanda the loss of innocence that made it possible for her to write with such violence. She made me look small to myself, young, silly, laughed at behind my back. She had taken advantage of me: by being 'bad', she had made herself far more attractive than I, who was 'good'. How unfair! How sneaking! I wished I, too, were wild, beautiful, disreputable – for I knew she must be all these things. My innocence seemed to mark me out like a dunce's cap, and I hated it.

I sat down on the stairs, folding the horrible letter smaller and smaller, till it was dirtier and more seamed than ever. Why had he been carrying it about with him? When had it been written? I jumped to the conclusion that he must still be seeing her, this dark Helen (Thomas Wolfe supplied the phrase, and by doing so became my enemy) who was trying to lure him back.

Hearing a door open, I jumped up and raced upstairs to my bedroom. I put the thing on the dressing-table and covered it with the lid of the powder-bowl, so that I should not be able to see it. As I lay face downwards on the bed I thought I heard it uncurl and rustle about in its prison.

Emilie tapped and coughed. 'Christine.'

'I'm working,' I said, on a high, airy, strangled note.

'Dear, I *had* to let you know. After all, I am responsible for you.'

'It's not important,' I shouted.

Emilie came in; I had just time to sit up. 'He's so much older than you—'

'It's not important, I tell you. It's all old history.' I did not believe this.

'Do think what you're doing, dear! I'm sure you're too young to marry yet awhile.' She looked excited and hopeful.

'Oh, don't be silly!'

'That's, rude, dear,' said Emilie, with the same mild inflection she would have used had I reached across her at the table. She went on. 'You needn't say anything *to* him. But you ought to know.'

I did not mean to say anything to him. I had steeled myself not to. When he came the next evening my manner was light and gay. I accepted his first kiss and avoided a second. I kept the conversation on the general plane, imparting to it a disarming sprightliness. Considering I had wept most of the preceding night and at intervals during the day (thank heavens it was a Sunday, as I could not have indulged myself so healingly at the office), I felt I was doing well. But I could not have been.

'Will you stop whatever game you're playing?' he said to me. 'You won't deceive a pussy-cat. What's wrong?'

I drew out the note and thrust it into his hands, assuring him incoherently that I had only glanced at it (because it had happened to be lying face upwards), that I didn't know what it was all about, that I didn't in the least care, that I couldn't think why men didn't prefer *decent* girls, that if he preferred this kind I wouldn't dream of standing in his way, that I was sure Wanda had been the right person for him really, that she was undoubtedly charming though not quite the type I was used to knowing myself, and that the whole affair was entirely trivial and none of my business.

'Ah, don't be silly,' he said. As I tried to move away he gripped my arm, holding me at his side. With his free hand, he uncrumpled the note and stared at it. 'Oh, *that*. Where did you get it?'

'It fell.'

'Fell? Where from?'

'Out of your mackintosh.'

'No, it didn't. Don't be an ass. *You* wouldn't go poking about, so I suppose dear Emilie did. I didn't know I'd got the thing: I thought I'd lost it.'

'So you're still seeing her. But, darling, I honestly don't mind. I'm like that. After all, one's civilised—'

'Extraordinary,' said Ned, still regarding the note.

'—though *I* don't think being civilised necessarily means behaving like a prostitute—'

'Stop it, Chris, stop it. Stop it, darling. Stop it, silly.'

'And if you want to see her—'

Tearing the note across, he threw it into the hearth.

'Look here, Chris. I told you I had to get rid of Wanda before I even began taking you out. I had this, and a couple of dozen like it, from her in February and March. Then she stopped. This was the last. I stuck it in the pocket of my mack and forgot about it. And as I sent said mack to the cleaners at the end of March, and then forgot it, and then they lost it, and I finally got it back at the beginning of last week, it should be perfectly clear even to you that I have not been seeing Wanda and don't want to.'

I do not know why I instantly accepted the story of the missing mackintosh – perhaps it was because I so much wanted to accept it. (It was lucky that I did, for surprisingly enough a chance remark of his mother's, six months later, proved it to be true.)

The flood of my relief swept away the old unease at the way Ned would speak of other women – 'get rid of her', 'not been seeing her and don't want to' – and I flung my arms around his neck.

'Idiot,' he said, 'idiot' – kissing me. But he was not content until he had made me apologise for my suspicions, had reduced me again to tears, had asked me wasn't I ridiculous, wasn't I childish, didn't I lack faith in him, didn't I deserve to be sent to Coventry, to be left alone till I had more sense, to be shaken till my teeth rattled – and had made me answer yes to all these things. The reconciliation was exquisite, but I tried not to think about it too closely, for in it was an element of something slightly shabby. I knew I had behaved stupidly: but I knew also that I had behaved as most girls of my age would have done, and that his eagerness to put me still more deeply in the wrong was somehow a disquieting augury for the future.

'But she was your mistress,' I managed to say, for a moment dragging myself away from him.

'If you want to put it like that.'

'How can one put it?'

'Darling, you must be more sensible. I'm thirty-two. You can't imagine I've lived like a monk.'

'I suppose not.'

'And there's no one but you now, and never will be. You know that? Don't you? Come on, don't you?'

'Yes.'

'Tell me you know it.'

I told him.

'Now tell me again.'

I wanted to ask him what she looked like, ask him to describe her beauty for me; but the scene had turned into one of those which, however engulfing in their delights, may suddenly fill the participants with an instinct to bring them to an end. So I did not ask.

That night, as I undressed for bed, I caught sight of *Look Homeward Angel*, lying with some other books on the dressing-table. I took it up, ran downstairs with it, and locked it in one of the sideboard drawers. I could not bear the sight of it.

This had been our first significant quarrel. The second, however, was far more grave and infinitely more my own fault. This is the one I do not find it so easy to write about.

The idea was put into my mind by Mrs. Skelton. It was near the end of June, and for several weeks Ned had been noticeably silent about the progress of his business. Once or twice, when I rang up his office, I failed even to find him there. It appeared that he was spending a good deal of time playing tennis and squash, both of which, he told me when I cautiously mentioned the subject, were a help in his kind of enterprise. You got to know the right kind of people.

One evening, when I arrived at Maddox Street for dinner with the Skeltons, I found only Mrs. Skelton at home. Her husband was away, inspecting a country property, and Ned was unusually late.

I asked his mother how she thought things were going. She gave her huge, Gallic shrug, poured herself another drink. 'Don't imagine my son talks to *me*. He may talk to his father, but I doubt it. If he did, I'd be the last to hear.'

I persisted: was Ned doing well? I had been worried.

'Has he ever done well at anything?' she demanded rhetorically. 'No staying-power. Nor has his father. We'd be in the gutter if it weren't for Finnigan.' This was a new name to me, and I did not question it. I learned later that it was the name of Horace Skelton's head clerk.

'No staying-power,' she repeated, 'no self-confidence. Selfish. Bone-selfish.' She leaned back as if in satisfaction; the lids, violet-ribbed, shell-shaped, shut slowly down upon her large, full eyes. 'You'll have to take him in hand.' She shrugged again. 'Not that it's likely to be any good. Tell him to do one thing and he does the opposite.'

Now it struck me that the most clever thing I could do to help Ned was to take advantage of this counter-suggestibility. I wanted him to succeed; I wanted us to be married as quickly as possible, for at the back of my mind I was frightened to risk a long engagement. Also – this on a pettier level – I wanted an engagement-ring. There had been some comment from Mr. Baynard that I was not yet wearing one: but when I timidly mentioned this to Ned he replied with unexpected and dismaying surliness, 'I didn't know I had to spring a ring right away.' The phrase stuck in my mind. I hated him for using it; it had a touch of brutishness and vulgarity which reawakened all my doubts. But I loved him – and I did want the ring.

10

The most-dangerous of all our plans are the ones we formulate right at the backs of our minds and leave to grow there, like water-cultures. They are the plans we never examine until we put them into practice. The moment they are exposed we realise our hideous recklessness. We realise the damage we have done.

It was a hot summer night, sticky and airless. Ned had taken me to a cinema near Victoria Station, saying he had had a hard day, his feet were sore, it would be cooler inside than out.

The film was not a very good one, but it passed the time. We sat in the back row of the almost-empty circle. Ned had his arm around me. Now and then he drew me hard against his shoulder. Sometimes I guessed that he was watching my face in the light from the screen.

I do not know why, at that particular moment, the mischief should have begun to work in me irresistibly. My cheeks felt hot, and my heart was beating. It was the moment for that bold stroke which had presented itself to me little by little, without my volition; the stroke I had not dared to contemplate in full consciousness, the stroke by which I believed I must gamble, if I were to help him, if I were, like the wife of Abraham Lincoln, to be the making of him.

In the row in front of us a couple rose and went out. Then a woman by herself, a dozen seats away. We were alone in the circle.

The culture in the dark jar, like a piece of human brain, like the white of a cauliflower, was gorged – full grown.

'You know,' I said, 'I've been thinking—'

'What?' His hand closed upon mine, caressed it. 'Darling. My darling.'

For an infinitesimal space of time I felt myself fall: too late now to grasp, to clutch, to be saved. I said airily (and I can hear my own voice now, the precise pitch of it, the precise inflection), 'You know, I haven't the slightest faith in you. I don't believe you'll make your business work. I haven't any faith at all.'

I meant: Darling, I have faith in you; I'd trust you always; I beg you to justify it, my darling, please; but that was what I actually said.

And when I had said it, I went, for a second, stone-deaf. I did not hear thunder. I felt it. His hand was still on mine, but the pressure of the fingers had relaxed.

I waited for him to say angrily, 'Haven't any faith? I'll show you, then. I'll make you take that back.'

He said nothing.

Two faces filled the screen – a man's, a girl's. They were talking passionately, but I did not know what they said.

My hand was free, hot from his pressure, suddenly cold in the air. 'Pins and needles,' I said.

He said, 'Come on', pulled me up. His voice was flat and harsh, thick with contempt. 'Come on.'

I followed him out of the circle, into the hot plush passage, down some stone stairs with EXIT in red letters at the bottom and a draught that rushed up to meet us, out into the street. He had not spoken.

I said, 'Darling, you mustn't think I mean—'

'If you haven't any faith in me, that's that. Come along, will you?'

He walked so fast that I had to run a little to keep up with him. I was sick with misery and fright. I wanted to tell him what my ruse had been, but was ashamed to because it would sound so ridiculous. 'I didn't mean it seriously,' I said.

'I don't give a damn what you meant.'

'You must know how I'm longing for you to get on—'

'It sounds like it.'

We were at the bus-stop.

'Here's yours coming,' he said. 'I won't see you back, if you don't mind.'

'Ned, I must talk to you!'

'There's nothing to talk about.'

I began imploring him to forgive me: he stood with his face averted. The bus came up.

'I won't catch this one—'

'Yes, you will. Go on.' He pushed me on to the step. 'Good night.'

'Ned!' I shouted it to him, for he was already walking away.

'Move along, miss, will you?' the conductor said. 'You're holding everyone up.'

I sat out my nightmare in the bright and sickly light, seeing and not seeing the joggling row of tired faces, white as fishes. A child cried miserably because it was so long past his bed-time.

This could not be true – that I had lost Ned. Not for one silly phrase. Not for one silly, romantic, childish idea. I had been a fool, but I had not been wicked! I was so much younger than he was: he must take that into account. Perhaps he was following on another bus. He could not let me go like this, could not. For such a little thing. He would follow me, catch up with me, scold me, laugh at me, forgive me, and it would be all right again.

I was in an agony of remorse, for I knew I had, after all, done a wicked thing, not merely a silly one. I had watched the idea germinate in its wickedness, swell up, come to fruition. I had bitterly hurt him. My fear was hallucinatory. Somehow I left the bus, walked down St. John's Road, past the bright and empty shops, up Battersea Rise to the sprinkled lights of the Common. I listened for his hurrying footsteps and I heard them, but when I turned he was not there. Far off, a train whistle drew a razor-slit across the night.

In bed I cried hysterically, cried because I had no father and mother to help me, because I could not talk to Emilie, because I was suffering this pain alone. I cried because I was an orphan, choosing this sentimental reason because I was too weak and scared to cry for the real one. It seemed to me, when I awoke fitfully again and again during that horrible night, that all the world should pity me because I had no father and mother. I was angry with them because they had died. What right had they to die?

II

Have you and Ned had a quarrel?' Emilie asked me at breakfast. 'You look so puffy. You look as if you've been crying.'

I was early at the office. I sat by the switchboard, waiting for him to ring. He did not. Well, I thought desperately, let him sulk. He's just being beastly.

It was a busy day; I do not know how I got through it. I remember that Mr. Baynard was happy because his sister had given birth to a girl. 'Such a funny little thing, Miss Jackson. You should see her; her face is no bigger than my watch! Uncle, she'll call me – Uncle Percy.'

I had no lunch. I went into the rest-room of a big shop and wrote Ned a letter – a calm, sensible letter of dignified apology, with a touch of lightness at the end. It was very long, perhaps too long. But I had no time to rewrite it. I posted it and felt better.

He did not reply.

On the third day I made a miserable confession of the whole affair to Emilie, because there was no one else. She understood nothing.

'Fancy him making all that fuss about a silly little thing! You let him sulk, if he wants to. He ought to be ashamed of himself. He'll come round in time, and if he doesn't you'll be better off without him. If he's going to make you miserable over trifles, your marriage will be quite impossible. You can think yourself lucky you've found, him out in time.'

Her face gleamed. She hoped she would now have me to herself, have company, until she died. Not for months had she shown less sign of melancholia. Indeed, she bought herself a new summer hat – mauve, for half-mourning.

Iris was the last person I should have told of my wretchedness, if I had not happened to meet her one afternoon in Piccadilly, when she was coming from rehearsal.

'Christie! We can go home on the same bus. Why have you been avoiding me, you pig? I won't steal your Neddy. He wouldn't want me. No one would want a hag like me.' Her prettiness, as usual, was making people crane backwards for another look at her. 'They're working us to death, darling, simply to death. My feet are so tired I'm sure my toes are going to drop off.'

We went up to the top deck. 'Oh, Christie!' Iris mourned loudly. 'I did want to sit in a front seat, but they're all taken.'

A man rose instantly. 'You sit here, miss; I'm getting out soon.'

'But how sweet of you! Are you sure? Are you quite sure?'

He told her it was a pleasure.

'There,' Iris said to me, 'that just shows you, Christie. You can usually get a nice seat if you really want it.'

She settled happily down and tucked her arm through mine. 'Tell me all about yourself. You let me do all the talking, as a rule, and tell me absolutely nothing. Tell me about your Neddy. And I honestly *won't* take him away, because I've got the most wonderful new charmer on the *tapis* – he's in the show – oh, and Victor's got a new girl, too awful, a sort of Simple Life girl, with bangles, and *Grecian* sandals and *hammer* toes. I don't know how he can. One can't keep one's toes clean in sandals, honestly one can't, not in London, but she doesn't seem to *see* that, and it's worse if you've got corns.'

The sunlight, refracted from the windows of buildings and buses, flashed on her sparkling face and magnified the golden graining of her skin. I felt desolate.

'All right,' she said, with scarcely a change of note. 'Tell. Tell Iris.'

When I had done so, as barely as I could, she turned to me with her usual little bounce of interest, her self-conscious concentration upon the love-affairs of others. 'My dear, just let him come round!'

I told her he would not come round, because it was all my fault.

'Well, you've said so once, haven't you? If he won't listen to you, that's that. I think he's being quite *revolting*. Do you adore him? I suppose you do.'

I said nothing.

'My dear,' Iris continued with a strange, quaint, motherly look, 'suppose for the moment he's not coming back.'

The words wrenched my heart.

'Don't make faces. Suppose he isn't. Don't you even feel, right down deep, that it's rather nice to be free again? That no one's going to kick up horrible fusses and make your life miserable?'

The conductor asked us for our fares.

'Oh, you will be cross with me!' she told him confidingly. 'I've only got a pound note. Now you'll be *furious*!'

He grinned and said he would manage somehow, but that she would have to wait for her change.

'I could have lent you fourpence,' I said.

'Nonsense. It's good for them to have to oblige the public.'

She turned again to my affairs. 'Listen. Isn't it nice to be free? Free as a bird? Dicky says *you* said Ned didn't like you writing poems. But you adore writing poems! Isn't there any fun in knowing you can write reams and reams if you want to, and simply spit in his *eye*?'

Strangely enough, all this was to have its effect upon me, not then, but after Iris and I had parted on the edge of the Common. It was true that I could make myself feel a touch of relief, a touch of joy in freedom. Down the hill, behind the spires, the sky was a delicate, duck-egg green, very even and pure; and just above the cross of Saint Mark's a single cloud floated, little and rosy, serene, unparented, unfriended, beautifully free. The light was brilliant on the roadway, a Venetian light turning to copper the faces of the grammar-school boys toiling upwards on their bicycles, late after games, after detention.

That night I slept well. Emilie had put new sheets on my bed; they were stiff as paper and smelled of lemons. I knew the peace that is a savourable pleasure in every limb, a refreshing of bone and muscle and flesh. Over the ceiling the headlamps of passing cars fanned their lime-coloured beams; I watched them until I fell asleep, experiencing that fall, slow and delightful as the fall of Alice down the rabbit-hole; I had time to put out my hand and touch the shelf of each potential dream as I floated past it.

In the morning I awoke as serenely, to find I had scarcely stirred in the night. The sheets lay stiff and smooth over my breast. It was some time before the anaesthetic began to disperse, before the first shaft of coming pain heralded itself by an uncomprehended movement of my memory. Remember what? I knew, but I would not remember yet.

All that day and the next something of the serenity persisted, although by now I was consciously repressing any thought of the future, fighting it as an enthralled dreamer fights against awakening. Dicky called, and we walked on the Common.

The weather was still hot. Though it was nine o'clock, the little bare boys still darted among the gilded island leaves and flashed in and out of the water.

'Aunt Emilie's looking pleased with herself,' Dicky said. 'The cat who's eaten the canary.'

'We're having the telephone put in at last,' I told him. 'They're coming to do it tomorrow.'

'Is that why she's so pleased? Is she going to phone people all day?'

I told him she was pleased because Ned and I had quarrelled.

'I see.' He looked grave. His attitude both to me and to Iris had always been gentle and brotherly. It had been a shock, two years ago, when she had showed me in great secrecy a note written by him, beginning, 'I am not exactly a sheikh in flowing robes, but I still think you're wonderful.' He, at least, I had believed, did not care for her particularly; but although he had only cared, apparently, for about a fortnight, he had been like the rest of them. 'Is it really all off?'

'I don't know.'

'I never much took to the fellow,' said Dicky, putting the whole matter into the past. He picked a tiny caterpillar from his wiry fair hair, knelt down, and deposited it safely on a blade of grass. 'He's all right, I suppose. But not for you. Have you got your phone number?'

I shouldn't know it till tomorrow, I replied; and felt suddenly miserable because we should have a telephone and I should not hear Ned's voice over the wires.

A naked child skipped yelping out of the water, a second child in pursuit. The two of them played tig around Dicky's legs, depositing damp and mud on his new fawn trousers. He picked the bigger boy up and held him out at arms' length over the pond. 'Look what you've done to me, you little devil!' The child screamed with hysterical joy, struggled and fought. Dicky dropped him in, and stood by laughing while the smaller boy went to the rescue. They abused us happily and tried to splash us as we walked on.

Dicky took my arm. 'You'll get over it.'

'I don't want to.'

'We'll all have good times together as we used to do.'

'There's nothing to stop that, whether I marry Ned or not.'

'I suppose not.'

'My friends are my friends,' I said with firmness and dignity.

'He's not exactly yearning for them to be his.'

I told him angrily that he was simply prejudiced; that none of us were children any more and could not go on playing as if we were. 'If you wanted to get married I should love it. I shouldn't say I couldn't get on with her.'

'I'm not getting married.'

'You will, some day.'

'I tell you what,' he said thoughtfully. 'If we both happen *not* to be married by the time we're forty we'll marry each other. We'd get on all right in middle age.'

'Why in middle age?'

'Not so much *love* and all that stuff. I say, Chris.' He stopped on the edge of the Parade, shielding his eyes against the sun to see if the road were clear.

'What is it?'

'If you're miserable you can always come and tell me. At any time.'

We crossed the Parade into a field of grass and clover. The white flowers were tipped with brown, as if the sun had scorched them, and they smelled sweet. I felt at peace with Dicky, as I always had done. We walked on in silence and tenderness.

12

I wrote a Byronic poem about the end of love and was pleased with it, but editors were not. I felt they must be shallow men.

A week went by. Caroline asked me to tea in her rather overdressed service flat. She never asked her friends when her husband was in, because, she said, he would not say a word to them but simply sit in a dark corner swinging his foot and squinting down at it till their resistance was broken and they went home. 'We get on pretty well when we're by ourselves, in a stodgy sort of way,' she explained rather anxiously, as if not wishing me to pity her overmuch, 'only I don't like being by ourselves all the time. I can't help being sociable, any more than he can help not being.'

The disappointments of this marriage had not, strangely enough, impaired Caroline's looks. She had never been pretty; but the compensating quality of high-floating elegance and unconcern (she had often reminded me of a flag fluttering from the mast of a ship on a clear, cool day) was becoming more and more distinctive. Also, she had more money for her clothes, more than I had ever hoped to have, even with my thousand-a-year man.

It occurred to me to try to write a poem about Caroline, from a male point of view; most of my love-poems at that period, with the exception of the Byronic one, were from men to women. I was writing a great deal and reading a great deal. Freedom from Ned, I told myself, would give me freedom to cultivate my mind and my talents. What worried me was the suspicion that there was something false in this sudden fertility, that the work itself was not good. Still, I was not unhappy; the anaesthesia had not entirely worn off.

'If you're only writing,' said Emilie, 'perhaps you could lay the table.' Both writing and reading were, to her, activities specially designed for interruption.

I put the poem aside with apparent bad grace but inward relief; it is good to be called from work that is not going well.

'And you might get out the other cloth, the one your mother embroidered. I don't see why we shouldn't have nice things, even when we're by ourselves. It's in one of the sideboard drawers.'

While I was looking for it, I came across *Look Homeward Angel* and for a second wondered what it could be doing there among the napkins and knife-boxes. Then I remembered, and at the same time was invaded by a rush of memory so intense that I had to cling to the sideboard until the occupation was complete. I could see nothing but the wild dark face of my disreputable enemy, the woman he had loved before me, to whom he would surely, if I did not intervene, return.

Hardly knowing what I did, I went to the telephone and dialled his number.

'What are you doing, dear?' Emilie called from the kitchen. 'You haven't time to begin a chat now, whoever it is. The eggs are done.'

The bell rang and rang down the dark and gaseous tunnel of space and time.

At last the operator told me there was no reply.

I was sick with relief. I pushed the receiver back and returned to the dining-room, where I found my mother's cloth and threw it on to the table. What a fool I had almost made of myself! I said a prayer, thanking God for saving me from the consequences of my own weakness.

During the meal the telephone began to make an extraordinary noise, something between a growl and a crunching of gravel. I answered it; I was trembling.

'You have not replaced the receiver properly. Will you please replace the receiver properly.'

Which I did. But by now I was awakened from the ether-dream, awake to panic and pain and longing. I should have to write to him. It would be a dignified letter, like the last, but with my pain written between every line in the heart's invisible ink. The only trouble was just how invisible I should make it. I wrote and rewrote that letter. I even took one version out to the pillar-box. But I could not post it. Afterwards I was glad I had not, for I had just reached the office next day when he telephoned me.

His voice was slurred and cool. 'Hullo, you. If you've quite stopped being silly we could run out to Richmond tonight. But only if you're certain you have.'

I was much too young to realise the extent of my triumph, to know that I had it in my power to do with Ned as I pleased. Indeed, I did not even recognize this telephone-call as a surrender. I was simply shaken to tears and incoherence by love and relief. 'Darling,' I said. 'Oh, darling.' I repeated, 'Darling.'

I presented myself to Ned that night with a smoothed and smarmed meekness, a prettification of humility that I was ashamed of; but it is a mistake to suppose that a stronger emotion cannot reduce shame to acceptable proportions, that it cannot simply be taken on board and endured as a passenger.

He said little to me at first, kissed me briskly, told me to hurry up,, as we were late already; but in a quiet and leafy road he stopped the car and made love to me in a fashion that delighted me, for I felt he was at last treating me in a way more appropriate to Wanda than to a child. It was disturbing, worrying and glorious. It made it easy for me to abase myself more thoroughly than I had intended over the matter of our separation, and he listened to me until I was done, with the satisfied smile of an emperor receiving agreeable economic and military reports from his various dominions.

He made, however, one concession. As he started the car again he said, 'We made a nice little profit on a sale this week, old girl. Things are looking up.'

'I knew they would!' I cried, trying to tell him with my eyes that my faith was infinite and my love entire and at his disposal. For one shaking minute it occurred to me that I might be looking like Dog Gelert – but comedy, I knew, could only be fatal that night of all nights.

Later, as we sat in the bar over the river, he grew mysterious, saying little, returning short answers to any remarks of mine and looking at me with a concentrated interest rather reminiscent of an expert shopper contemplating a purchase. My sense of power and of unease grew together, like separate creepers that suddenly knot and become as one. In the dark of the gilded glass upon the wall were sunk stratum upon stratum of little lights, the citron candles on the walls, the glowing tips of cigarettes. I saw myself, made rosy by the velvet on which I rested and by his steady gaze upon my face.

He said suddenly, awkward in the fashion that worried and most moved me, 'I've got something for you. I knew you wanted it. I hope you like it.'

First the table before us held nothing but ashtrays and glasses: and then there was the little red box, the focus of all light, all moments, of all my years. I could not touch it.

Ned put his finger to it and it sprang open; and there was the ring, and before I could think about it there was the ring on my finger, the ring with rivets to his side, frightening; but worse, disappointing.

The Dutch boy put his finger to the breach in the dam and he stemmed the sea, but the sea held him prisoner. I was caught, I was done for, I was frightened – what other word? Not terrified. Not panicked. Simply, as a child, frightened. It is frightful to be caught by your future in a corridor of youth, to feel its hands of iron across your eyes. Caught you! Did you think you could go further? There are corridors and corridors, rooms and rooms, gateways that open on to gardens orientally bright with peonies and singing-birds, but they aren't for you. You've been caught right at the beginning of the game. This is your end, this is the end for you.

'It was Nell's. I had it reset. It was better than anything I could buy for you.' His voice shot up in alarm. 'Dear! What is it? You're not crying?'

We must not be sorry for ourselves in the present: that is a luxury we cannot afford, and to learn this is the first of the stoical lessons. But we may fairly be sorry for ourselves in youth, for that is the same as being sorry for another person – since we are built up of a succession of selves, so that we may never know what we truly are until our life's end; and if there is any sort of revelation then, it will come too late to be useful. None of us is one person, but many: the one may wonder at the other, and, if there is enough time between, may pity.

Youth in love tends to seem snobbish, since the material things connote a sort of security not yet within the comprehension of the spirit. In youth we are afraid to lay our lives within the hands of another person. Into this far-off country to which he will take us it is a comfort to bear the things we know, the silken carpet, the golden bowl, the coin inscribed with the familiar face. Money we know; 'position' we know, or think we know. We may yearn for these things not because we are greedy but because we need comfort. It is only when we are mature that we ask nothing of love, when love is itself the far country that is also home.

Because I was afraid to marry Ned, because I was afraid to hold him or let him go, I had clung to the things that, for me, were symbols of maturity (and, as I believed, safety – not knowing then that there is no safety in' maturity nor anywhere in life, until the sexual spirit dies): the dignity of a woman marked by a ring, the dignity of a woman married, having a home of her own, and the word 'mine' for material possession. I supposed that these things would compensate me for the bitterest disappointment, if disappointment came. For they would give me a public face to wear about the world; and only when we are young are we so positive about the value of appearances.

'Green is your colour, isn't it?' He was anxious. 'You wear green a lot. It's a real emerald.'

It was a little stone between little pearls, a fleck and two dots. I was not, as he had thought, crying, but I wanted to cry, and as he spoke I did so.

I supposed I was crying because of disappointment with my ring, but now I know I cried for more than that. I cried because the future had caught me too early in the game, because, though the game would go on, I was 'out' – and it was unfair, a cheat, an injustice; I cried because of my first revelation that life is frequently unjust and it is no good for us to demand that it shall be otherwise.

'It's lovely,' I said, 'but I didn't expect it, not tonight, and it's been so horrible these last weeks.'

'I was angry with you. But it's over now.'

'It was horrible,' I repeated, and could not look at him.

He begged me not to cry. It was over, it would never happen again. He asked if I were happy, and when I said I was, laughed at me because I looked so woebegone. 'Let's go and dance.'

I shook my head. I wanted to talk the weeks of misery away. He was gentle and kind; seeing my need to talk, he coaxed me on. Had it been so very bad? I must have known in my heart, he said, that it was all right really. I told him how I had gone for a walk with Dicky and how he had comforted me.

'But you won't need any more walks with Dicky now,' Ned murmured, smiling. 'I'll do all the comforting. Dicky's nose will be out of joint.'

I had to smile back at him. 'Poor Dicky!' I remarked.

'Yes: Dicky's nose, and Peter's, and Hugh's. All of their noses.'

Peter and Hugh were adolescent boys long lost, long forgotten, that I had told him about when he had made me amuse him with the tale of my childish love-affairs.

'And Take Plato's. I nearly left him out. Now come and dance. It will make you feel better.'

13

We left the bar and went into a high bright room where a few people were dining and a few couples dancing. The noise of the small band was hollow in so much space. As we danced, I felt myself rising out of the morass of fears and disappointments. I began to feel excited. I loved Ned. The ring did not seem so little after all; in fact, I liked it because it was not showy. It was in good taste, even though Miss Rosoman might not recognise taste when she saw it, and Mr. Baynard's ideas on jewellery would be so hapless that I need pay no attention to whatever *he* might say. But though the ring might be little, it seemed to weigh heavily upon my finger. I was almost painfully aware of it. And it seemed to me strange and alarming, the thought that I must wear it until I died.

When the music stopped, Ned walked over to the band and asked for the same tune again – 'as this is a special occasion,' he added in his clear, rather harsh voice. He put his arm around me. The leader, glad of any incident to break the monotony of playing for hours to so small an audience, broke into a great white smile. He bowed, congratulated us both. We danced again.

'We'll have a drink,' Ned said, 'and then we might make them play it a third time.'

I told him I did not think I ought to drink much more.

'Champagne hurts nobody,' he informed me, 'and that's what we shall have.'

I felt all eyes upon us. I was both pleased and upset. The whole evening was now curiously out of focus; everything was strange.

'Where did Wanda live?' I asked him suddenly, as if she were dead. I could ask him anything I liked. I was full of power.

'Wanda? Oh, round about here, somewhere.'

'Did you bring her here?'

'Once, I believe. Why?'

'I only wanted to know.'

We drank the champagne, and danced in what was to me a darkness filled with splintering lights, to a music that came from all sides, from above, from the ground. I was glad to sit down, because I was tired.

'You wouldn't have a photograph of Wanda, I suppose ?'

It was delightful to hear myself asking this so lightly. I began to feel that I had at last arrived upon that plateau of sophistication from which such questions may be lightly asked.

Ned stared at me. 'I don't carry one about with me.'

'But have you got one?'

'I may have, at home. I don't know. I've got a lot of stuff.'

He passed the question off.

A week or so later, not forgetting what I had said (he forgot nothing), he did show me a snapshot of two girls in cotton dresses, blinking their eyes against the sun. I looked at the beautiful young woman, lean and dark, hair springing geometrically from her high and lovely brow. 'So that's Wanda,' I said.

Ned said, 'Give it here.' He glanced at it, caught the direction of my gaze. 'You're looking at the wrong one; Wanda's the fair one.' She was the one in glasses, short, inclined to stoutness, the very last of women (in my imagination) to be described as a mistress. 'Oh, I see,' I said. My heart sprang with joy.

But that, as I say, happened a week later. At this moment I forgot the photograph I so much wished to see, could think of nothing but the experience of a strange happiness and a strange tiredness, intermingled. Yet I could have danced till morning.

I was suddenly sorry for Ned because his face was flushed and he seemed upset. 'Ask for our tune again,' I said. This time I did not mind the thought that all eyes were upon me – it was delightful. I was only sorry that somehow the room was so dark.

He took my arm, called the waiter. He said to me in a voice that seemed unnaturally clear and slow, 'I think we ought to be going, or we shall scare Emilie stiff.'

My own voice was clear, too. I thought it sounded very pleasant and silvery. I told him I did not care how scared Emilie was, that I was tired of being treated as a child, tired of her waiting up for me and coming inevitably to sit in rooms where I was. It was easy to talk a great deal, and I was sure Ned was amused by what I was saying.

But somehow we did not go and dance, for we were in the car again, and I was a little worried because I could not for the moment remember by what stages we had got there. Ned, I noticed, was rather silent, and replied without much appearance of interest when I tried to make him see how romantic were the squares of lighted windows high in the night; how charming the road-menders' lamps clustered together like red currants on the trestle barriers; how pretty the illuminated 'Left Only' signs at the roundabout, where the pavements swung around the car as if we were at the hub of them. It was easy to talk; and then it was easier to be silent. When had I last spoken? I could not remember. I was sure I should bore him if I could find nothing to say, but nothing seemed possible. Then at last I did say something, without premeditation. I said, 'Please stop. I feel dreadful.'

We had to stop again and again. I was foundering in a darkness so black and swinging that I wanted to die. Ned was somewhere. He said comforting words, but he sounded almost angry.

My own voice said in a kind of liturgy,' I am so ashamed, I am so ashamed.'

'Don't be an ass, Chris! It happens to all of us. It doesn't matter.'

I said, 'We'll never get home; we'll never, never get home.' The cold critic within me was perfectly stable, observing me with customary detachment.

'We'll never get home,' I repeated. Ned was pushing his handkerchief at me. I took it and wiped my face; I was streaming with sweat.

And then we were home; he had taken my key and was opening the lower door. 'For God's sake brace up!'

I saw Emilie, very small in a pink dressing-gown, coming to me down a great funnelled corridor. She was saying that it was late, she had some cocoa for me.

Ned was saying very brightly, 'I'm afraid Christine's eaten something that's upset her. It may be a touch of food poisoning.'

Emilie was asking me anxiously what I thought it could have been – lobster was often upsetting, or crab. Had I eaten any lobster or crab?

I said bravely, 'It may be crab', and pushed past her to the stairs, the stairs so far away, so infinitely desirable, leading up and up into oblivion. I climbed them; I gained the upper hall.

I heard Ned's voice: 'I'd better not wait, perhaps. She'll be all right, I'm sure. I'll ring up in the morning.' The door closed.

It was a desolate sound, a destroying sound, the last sound in the world. I could go no further. I sat down upon the cold tessellations leaning my head against the wall. Emilie was calling me. She would come and ask me about the things I had eaten. All I had to do was to keep calm (for even this rocking horror must cease some time) and insist upon crab. The light sprang up. She was crouching over me; her apple-face was an enormous size.

'I am drunk,' I said. 'Aunt Emilie, it is awful! I am drunk!'

14

She never forgave him. To the end of her life she did not. As she looked down the precipice of the past, which did not make her giddy at all, for it seemed to her only a little hill, she would still say, 'You were a young girl. He should have taken better care of you. He had no right to let you do it.'

I think this was unfair. It was only half a bottle of champagne that I shared with Ned, but after two cocktails it was too much for me. I was a very poor drinker, but I do not see how he could have known this except by observation. Where I think she might have blamed him (she did not) was for losing his head and deserting me. He should have taken the blame, I think, even if he had not deserved it.

The incident, however, had a curious consequence; for Emilie, in her anger at Ned, seemed to decide that he owed her some very practical atonement. From that day forward she began to talk openly of living with us after we were married. She did so with a prim, defiant air, staring us between the eyes as she spoke, as if defying dogs to bite. Hitherto she had not taken Ned's offer to share a home with her at all seriously. Now the idea never seemed absent from her mind. She no longer tried to impede my marriage; she simply included herself in it.

It was now accepted by everyone that we should marry at the end of the year. Mrs. Skelton was for ever trying to urge us into making the date earlier; but Ned was against it, for no reason he seemed prepared to give, and I had an impulse to cling to my freedom for the period at first appointed. Also, I rather resented his mother's urgings; I had believed all proper mothers hated to lose their sons, and this unnatural behaviour on her part (or so I considered it) filled me with misgivings. I did not know how the business was going, and Ned did not tell me. He seemed cheerful enough. A month ago there had been the selling of some sizeable warehouse premises in Sutton; I presumed other things had been sold, since, after all, it was for such transactions that property agents existed. As for the amount of time he spent in sport or in driving around the country, I could only imagine that the duller matters were dealt with by subordinates.

In the meantime I had all the excitement of looking for a flat, deciding what I should wear for my wedding and whom I should ask to it. We were to be married in church, but I was not to wear white. 'It's so damn silly in this day and age,' Ned said, 'and I should feel a prize ass with a lot of bridesmaids prancing after me. It's much better style not to fuss.'

I believed I was in cordial agreement with this. When Emilie complained, 'But a young bride in white is so beautiful; and you're only married once', I grew disproportionately angry. 'I'm not a pagan,' I said, 'I don't want all sorts of primitive rites' – which she did not understand and which saddened her.

I hated Emilie to be sad, though I knew she displayed sadness only as a kind of moral blackmail. One night, indeed, she left her bedroom door wide open, so that on my way to the bathroom I could not help seeing her at her prayers or hear her say, in a piercing mutter, 'and make Christine a good Christian following the laws of Church.' It was maddening. Yet her little, stubborn, pleading face never failed to touch me, and I vowed that if I were to be burdened with Emilie all my life I would do my best not only to endure that burden but to enjoy it. I think I might have persuaded Ned into letting me wear white for her sake if she had not prayed at me. It was a pity she sometimes went too far, and a pity I was too young to understand that 'going too far' may often be the most pitiable plea of all.

On the whole I was very happy. I had set all else, all other interests, aside for Ned. I was learning him better now, learning to know where his nature was most tough and most sensitive. I had caught the style and rhythm of his rather rough humour and could laugh at the same things as he. I realised his tendency to bully and rather enjoyed it, for I was sure I should be able to check him if ever my enjoyment grew less. I realised that a certain kind of woman was markedly attracted by him; I had seen this in the cocktail bars, at the sports meetings and dances to which he took me. This woman was usually about five years older than he, she was married, she liked a good time, she liked to talk and drink with men, she played games well, danced well and had the assurance of success. I did not realise that for Ned she had no attraction at all, that she was not in his style; and so my love for him was constantly nudged on by jealousy. I knew he loved me. I did not believe he could possibly love me as I loved him, with that kind of obsessive love that will cherish an old bus ticket if the lover has held it, or revere like a shrine the particular platform at Victoria Station from which he catches his usual train. I did not realise, in fact, that any love except my own could be in its whole nature a little idiotic. There were things I longed to say to him that I dared not say, lest he should think me absurd. And my diffidence, my unsureness, bred his own jealousy in a fashion that suddenly became alarming.

We were sitting downstairs in the dining-room one night, both of us excited to a kind of bantering passion by the thundery heat of the weather, when the telephone rang.

Now it was typical of Emilie that she had obstinately insisted on having it installed at the bottom of the lower stairs, in the darkest and draughtiest place in the house, because she was sure it was the one place where everybody would hear it. One could, of course, hear it in the kitchen and the dining-room; on the upper floors it was almost inaudible, and if it did ring when I was in bed late at night, and I did happen to hear it, I had to run down two flights of stairs in the dark before I could reach the switch in the top hall; and even so, usually had to answer the caller in the half-dark, as the switch nearest to the telephone was several yards further along the passage.

On this occasion the caller was Dicky, just back from a walking holiday in France and eager to tell me all about it. I was as eager to hear it, for I had never been out of England, and Ned had made a half-promise to take me to Paris for a week after we were married. The conversation went on for a long time, and would have continued longer had Ned not walked out of the dining-room, his hands in his pockets, and by violent shakes of the head indicated that I was to bring it to an end.

I told Dicky I could not stop longer but that I would see him soon, and I hung up the receiver.

'Who was that?'

I told him.

'You might tell your friends I'm here another time, and then they may not take up your entire evening.'

I said Dicky had just returned from France, and it had all been very exciting.

'So I gathered. And I don't want that youngster on the telephone morning, noon and night. Things are different for you now, and he'd better realise it.'

I had to laugh at this. 'But it's only Dicky!'

'I don't care if it's Mussolini,' Ned retorted; 'you'll please make, things perfectly clear.'

I said nothing; I thought this was a spurt of irrational temper, prompted perhaps by the electricity in the air. This nonsense would blow over, and Ned would come to his senses. But it did not. Within an hour Dicky rang again, to ask me if I could lend him some book or other, and Ned began to quarrel. It was so disagreeable that I took the first occasion to ask Dicky never to telephone me on Mondays, Wednesdays, or Fridays, for it was then that Ned was usually at my house. It made trouble for me, I said.

'Look here,' Dicky protested, 'I don't think much of a fellow who carries on like that! You tell him not to be an ass.'

'I daren't,' I replied, feeling a certain emotional luxury in not daring.

Dicky gave a disgusted shrug. 'I don't see how any girl could stand it.'

'It's natural to be jealous.'

'But not of me!'

'That's what I told him.'

'I don't know how anybody could be jealous of *me*,' Dicky pondered simply. I thought how unfair it had been for him ever to be suspected of 'fastness'. He was the least mature sexually of all my friends, I loved him the best, and could never have thought of him for myself.

'No,' I agreed, 'nor do I. I can't imagine it.'

'Oh, come,' he said, with a spurt of injured dignity, 'perhaps that's going too far. I'm not Quasimodo, or anything.'

'Of course you're not. But don't telephone, will you? Not on those nights?'

He did not. But two days later, when I was with Ned, the bell rang again and when I answered it my blood ran cold.

'Oh,' I said, 'you. It's funny to hear your voice again.'

Ned had come to stand by the door, his lips folded and furious.

I tried to make the conversation anonymous as possible, and all the while my thoughts were running round in search of an escape.

I said, 'I'm sorry, but I'm rather busy now. Perhaps some other time.'

By the most wretched chance my caller was the young boy Hugh, of whom I had told Ned in fun. When Hugh and I had walked on the Common, giggling, pushing at each other, clumsily pursuing our rudimentary flirtation, he had been fifteen and I a year younger. I had not seen him since. Now, having returned to London from Ireland, he had been impelled by some malign fate to look me up.

I came back to the dining-room. Ned followed me. 'Who was that?'

'No one of any interest. A girl I used to know.' I was really frightened.

'What's her name?'

'Betty,' I improvised. 'Betty Hughes.' I began to chatter. This girl, I said, was a friend of Caroline's. I had never liked her much, she was rather a bore. She lived in Dublin. She had come back to London for a job. She was a dressmaker. Rather a good dressmaker; even at school she had made her own clothes.

'Shut up.'

I looked at him. His eyes had a propped and staring look. His face had a high, irregular flush. I made some feeble protest.

'You're a liar,' said Ned. 'Who was it?'

'I told you. Some girl—'

'Liar. Liar.'

He took my shoulders gently, and as if he were turning me for blind-man's buff directed me towards a chair. He sat down in it, pushed me on to my knees before him.

'Who was it? Do you think I couldn't hear it was a man's voice? Was it that Dicky lout?'

I told him he was upsetting me, that I could not answer him while he looked like that.

'Damn what I look like. Was it Dicky?'

'No.'

'Who was it?'

I told him the truth. 'But I haven't seen him for years! I haven't even heard from him!'

'Why did you lie?'

'Because you get so angry.' I tried to put my head down on his knees, hoping he would pity me. I burst into tears.

'I'm always angry with liars. I hate lying.'

'Oh stop it,' I said; 'I'm sorry.'

'What's the good of being sorry? Look at me. Go on, look at me.' He jerked my head up. 'No use crying. The, harm's done.'

I was swept by desolation. I should lose Ned. We should never marry. I should have to tell everyone about it. Nobody would ever want me again. Frantically I assured him I was sorry, begged him to forgive me, promised never to do such a thing again.

'At the moment,' said Ned, 'I could hit you.'

I held his arms so that he might not; I almost believed that he meant what he said.

'You should trust me!' he shouted out, I thought unreasonably. The inward critic, though having no power to help me, informed me that he was unreasonable.

'I do,' I wept, as ludicrously. I tried to stare straight at him, to show him how profound my trust was; and I caught the glimmer of a smile. It was no more than the suggestion of light, flashed off again as soon as perceived, so that reason doubts it; but it gave me hope. I flung myself on him, laughing and crying, telling him archly that I would be good now, that I would never fib again.

'Never lie again,' said Ned; 'let's use the right word. You're a liar, and that's that.' His face was like stone.

At this moment Aunt Emilie came in with a tray of tea.

'Well, children,' she said with her air of sad merriment, 'the cup that cheers.' She put the tray down. Then she looked at us appalled. 'Oh, Ned, what's the matter? Have you been upsetting Christine ?'

'It's a pity Chris wasn't brought up to tell the truth. I suggest you start training her, even if it's late.'

I burst into ungovernably absorbing sobs. They were a luxury; they were so interesting in their reflex violence that they made a refuge for me.

'Ned,' said Emilie, blushing and trembling, 'I don't know what this is all about, but you should be ashamed!'

'Ask her to tell you. I'm going.'

He got up so abruptly that I stumbled backwards and almost fell. He took my arm and pulled me up. 'Can't you stand on your own damned feet ?'

'I must know the meaning of this,' Emilie cried feebly. 'She's upset; she's only a child.'

He had left us. I heard him snatch his raincoat from the peg, open the door, run up the steps to the road. I called after him.

'Oh, what is it ?' Emilie demanded. 'You must tell me!'

I went out. Ned was not there, not in the car. I looked left and right, saw him walking slowly across the road to the Common. Far away behind the trees the faint silent lightning flickered. The eye of the sky flashed open and closed again.

I raced after him; I caught him by the waist; I said his name.

He turned and pulled me into his arms.

'It's you,' he said; 'you don't know how I feel. You never did. I get scared.'

'I didn't mean to lie. I was scared of you.'

'I'm too old for you, Chris.'

'No, you're not.'

'I hate you to feel you have to lie.'

'I won't again.'

A hot wind shuffled the tree above us like a pack of cards. I felt weak, as after a long illness. He was asking me to forgive him now, but I could not care. I wanted to go to bed and sleep. I was so tired. But I should not be able to go to bed until I had made up some sort of story to satisfy Emilie.

'I am so tired,' I said.

He kissed me in a manner peculiarly gentle and benedictory. It was like a laying on of hands, and it filled me with peacefulness. 'Then go straight up to your room. I'll talk to your aunt,'

It seemed to me wonderful beyond words that he should be so understanding.

'Chris, I promise I will try and be a good husband to you. I'll make up for all this, you'll see.' He turned the little green ring on my finger so that only the gold band showed. 'There! Then we'll be safe.'

'Safe,' I repeated. It was comfortable in the hushed and stormy dark. I could have slept then, upright, my head on his shoulder.

15

I ran into your friend Caroline last night as I was leaving the office,' Ned said, 'and bought her a drink. She's a lively one, isn't she?'

He often used these odd terms, which had for me an old-fashioned ring.

'Blackguarding her old man right and left. How long will that last?'

I said I had no idea. Caroline had always had a singular capacity for endurance – or, rather, for regarding trouble as if it were something over the other side of the road, interesting, but not really any concern of hers. Touched by jealousy, though not strongly, I asked if he found her attractive.

'Not my type,' said Ned. 'Too much of the good-time girl.'

I thought how pleased she would have been to have heard him. It was how she would most wish to be regarded, though she did not have a very good time and her hope of one in the future was slender.

'Good fun,' he added, 'but no depths to her. She thinks you're the wonder of the world. By the by, she wants to know if you'd like an electric-kettle for a wedding-present.'

It was the beginning of September; it really seemed as though we should marry at the end of the month. We should have followed our earlier intention if Ned had not insisted that he must wait till business looked more stable. I had found a flat for us in Avenue Mansions, upon the north side of the Common. It was a comfort to me to know that I should not be going far away from the world of my youth. Emilie had put our house up for sale, and was crying every morning at breakfast with the sorrow of having done so. 'Everything going! Nothing left!'

She was not to live with us. This was a worry to me and a nagging guilt. Ned, who had suggested that she should, who had apparently made all our plans as if to include her, had suddenly turned round and told her quite clearly that it was better for couples to begin their married lives alone. He had found her a room with kitchen and bath in the same block of flats. 'You'll be able to see Chris every day, Aunt Emilie, so there won't be any nonsense about loneliness.' He often put matters in this harsh-sounding way; it was less through callousness than through an inability to shape a sentence softly. Whatever he was, Ned was no hypocrite.

He told her this at supper at our house, on a night when Mrs. Skelton and Nelly Ormerod were there. Emilie, taken aback, flushed up to her eyes. She seized her little string of metal links interspersed with turquoises and garnets and twisted it so tightly that it left a red mark on her neck. She said nothing.

Mrs. Skelton added more lime juice to the small quantity of gin in her glass. It was one of Emilie's unconquerable obstinacies never to provide more than a quartern bottle for the entertainment of Ned's relations. Smoking between courses, Mrs. Skelton thoughtfully placed an empty matchbox at her elbow to serve as an ashtray. 'You've got to let them fight it out alone, Mrs. Jackson. There's nothing else for it.'

'Christine is so young,' Emilie mumbled. The tears gathered on the rims of her eyes and rolled along the lashes, not falling. I was hot with pity for her.

'You've got to lose her some time.' Mrs. Skelton gave her an opaque glance, half sardonic, half sympathetic. 'It comes to all of us. We're not getting any younger.'

'No one in their senses would want to live with Ned,' said Nelly with a false, comradely bark. 'We're all glad to see the back of him.'

'You know you love me, Nell,' he said. They exchanged a look unusually intimate, almost affectionate.

Emilie rose, with some inaudible excuse, and left the table.

'It is hard for her!' I said. 'She has nothing.'

'Nor have any of us,' Mrs. Skelton replied. 'Not now. We've had it all, such as it was. She's had her youth. She must let you have yours.'

I did not feel I wanted my youth. At that moment I would have given it all to Emilie, had it been any use to her. I felt myself against Ned, against them all.

'Look here, Chris,' Nelly said sensibly, 'I know you think we're a lot of brutes. But look at it like this. There is a difference of age between you and Ned. You'll have to get used to each other, and the first year's never easy. My first year with Edgar was frightful, but we fought it out and in the end we were happy.' Her eyes, behind the thick glasses, were swollen by the memory of joy. I wondered if she had seemed good-looking while her husband was alive, whether she had simply let herself become ugly after his death since she had no more to offer any man. 'You know that poor old Emilie, fond as we are of her, is pretty well melancholic. She'll hang around you at all the wrong moments. She'll want parts of your life that you owe Ned. If you don't give them to her there'll be ructions from Auntie.' Her turn of phrase, like her brother's, was often crude in its humour. 'And if you do, there will be ructions from Ned.'

Unexpectedly she rose, came round the table and put her arm round me.

'You know I like you, don't you, Chris? You know that what I'm saying's really for the best?'

'Things that are for the best always mean the worst for somebody,' I said, and was astonished by my own epigram.

'You should write plays like Lonsdale,' said Ned.

Emilie came back. She put in front of Mrs. Skelton a cloisonné ashtray fetched from the drawing-room and shiny with new cleaning. She had cleaned it so thoroughly, I noticed, that she had even managed to remove a brown stain which had been on the rim ever since I remembered it. I thought of Emilie scrubbing and scrubbing away in the kitchen, trying to quieten her sorrowful heart by this manual effort.

'Oh, thank you, Emilie,' Mrs. Skelton said in her surprised, gracious tone. 'How kind! You shouldn't have bothered.'

Emilie took her place again at the head of the table. She stretched out her hands before her on the cloth, looked at them, locked them. For a moment she seemed to have a chairman's authority; everyone waited for her to speak.

She said, 'I am sure you are right about me. I daresay I shall like having a little place of my own to potter about in.'

'That's the spirit!' Ned exclaimed, with a touch of that real affection which is born of relief.

Emilie looked at me. 'And Christine will come and see me.'

'Every day,' I said, feeling stifled with pity.

'Not every day. You will be too busy with your new home. But quite often.'

So there it was. My life was ordered. We sold our house for a fair enough price, and Emilie decided what she would want to take (little enough), what I should take (there would be no need for Ned to buy much furniture, which was fortunate, as money seemed rather short again), and what we should put in store. She would sell nothing, not a single white elephant. My father had known them all – had touched them all.

The wedding was fixed for the last day of the month. Ned's friend Harris, whom I did not care about, was to be his best man. Apart from Aunt Emilie and the Skeltons there were to be no guests but Dicky, Caroline and Miss Rosoman. I agreed, with a doubtful heart, that it was idiotic to 'splash'

(Ned's word) on a reception money we would need to make our home nice. It was all very sensible.

A fortnight before the wedding was to take place I went to Kensington to buy my dress, and I took Caroline with me. Her presence made me cheerful and full of hope. She could not have appeared more excited if the marriage were to be her own, to someone with whom she was in love. 'Damn superstition, Christie! You're not going to prance around in nasty powder blue. It's so minnie-ann. You buy green – it suits you.' I hesitated over the fantastic luxury of green shoes; they would be no use to me afterwards. 'Darling,' said Caroline, exuding her sweet breath and her familiar odour of *Paris Soir*, 'you're not going to get a bloody old kettle from me. I'd be *sick* if I gave you a kettle. I'm going to give you the shoes.' She added, 'You'll get the kettle, of course. Peter' (her husband) 'will give it you. He's got to show willing.'

Tall, fair, flippant, courageous, full of humour and impenetrable within, having come to terms with her own defeat, she rushed me up and down the great shop, making this an adventure for us both. I loved her. She was no older than I, but so far removed from me in experience that she gave me a feeling of permanence and safety.

We sat down, exhausted, to a tea of rich cream cakes.

'You haven't introduced him to dear Iris again?'

'No,' I replied firmly.

'I don't think he'd like her. But I shouldn't take risks, if I were you. Do you know,' Caroline added, hitching her fur as she had seen smarter, more carefree women do, blowing the smoke out thoughtfully from her broad and rose-coloured lips, 'that *if* Iris were defunct, she would be the one Dead of whom I could speak ill without a shred – a shred, darling – of compunction?'

She added, 'If she only took what she wanted I could bear it. But she will persist in taking what she doesn't, and mauling it round in her little hot paws till it's all messy, and then handing it back to you with a lovely generous smile. Not, mark you, that little So-and-so was worth my tears.' She never mentioned the name of the young man Iris had spoiled for her.

'I don't think he was,' I said.

'I know he wasn't. But it's the principle of the thing.'

The band, behind a fence of golden basket-work, played a Strauss waltz. Most of the women around us were middle-aged or elderly. They wore hats with much trimming. They had flowery, powdery faces which, among the gilt, the glitter, the asparagus fern, the clustering of rosy lights, looked like blots of blossom in a herbaceous border. The atmosphere of tea-time intimacy gave me courage to ask Caroline the question I could have asked nobody else.

'Oh, that.' She took a moment before replying, anxious to do her best. 'Well, darling, it varies between person and person, I believe. I'm entirely Pro myself. But don't expect to have a good time right away – perhaps not for a couple of months, even more. If people would only realise that it would save so much fuss and flap.' She looked at me, considering, weighing up what she knew of my physiognomy and temperament. 'I expect you'll be Pro, darling. In fact, I'm sure you will.'

I was comforted. I had never known Caroline so eloquent in order to be kind; for her, this had been a long speech. I asked her anxiously how she had found Ned when he took her for a drink.

'Oh, I think he's a dear old thing,' she said, not meaning to refer to his age at all but rather to assure me that she could speak of him in the same terms in which she spoke of Dicky and Take Plato. 'Simply sweet.' It was the idlest of comments, but well meant. 'He's madly in love with you. Only one topic, dear, on and *on*; it would have been boring if you hadn't been my co-mate.' (This was our private word for friendship, ever since, as children, we had been taken to *As You Like It.*)

The last jealousy was allayed. I smiled at her as she made up her mouth.

'We won't lose each other, will we,' I asked her, 'after I'm married ?' I told her she was the only close friend I had ever wished to have.

'We don't get in each other's way,' she replied, 'that's what it is.'

It was true. We did not. We had no need to. We did not even have to see each other often; our intimacy would always begin again at the moment where we had left it off, smoothly, without any introductory fencing. I was glad Ned liked her, and that she seemed mildly to like him. This, at least, was left me.

At the office there was much whispering behind my back. They were planning my wedding-present.

'It's a roody great basket of a clock,' Hatton confided in me at lunch-time; 'ordinary, that's what I told them. I wanted to give you a picture. I saw a beauty going cheap, down my way, sunset on the snow, whoo! You could imagine you was there.'

Miss Rosoman seemed more excited than I was. 'I don't know how you can keep so calm! I wouldn't be able to type a line.'

Mr. Baynard, inexplicably cross as usual, made a point of speculating, with every appearance of delight, upon my successor. 'I expect we'll get a real Junior, junior-trained. A nice little girl, fresh from Pitman's or Gregg's, that's the idea, only *he* will go to these agencies and get ones too big for their boots. I expect the new one will really enjoy our filing-system. You don't see many like ours.'

I could not forbear to point out that I had instituted it.

'Well, if it pleases you . . .' he said with a false, indulgent smile. 'We all have our little vanities.'

In order to subdue mine, he sent me to an hotel in Kensington on an errand that could as easily have been run by Hatton. 'I don't like the messenger carrying jewellery,' he said; adding illogically, 'Money's different.'

16

I had to take to one of our clients some earrings Mr. Fawcett had had valued for her. It was half-past four when I left the hotel, and I had been told that I need not report myself back to Mr. Baynard that day. It occurred to me to pay a surprise call upon Ned.

I had been to Ned's office once or twice. Now, as I went in, I was greeted by Hignett, his clerk, a thin, smart young man, with a counter-jumper's air and a neck slightly awry.

'Out,' he said.

It was the one word. I looked at him in astonishment. Hignett had not, on previous occasions, been wanting in the courtesy I felt it natural to show to the future wife of an employer.

'Mr. Skelton's out? Will he be back soon?'

'Not today, if I know him.'

I looked about me. The office was neat as usual, but had a curiously deserted air. There were few papers about. The typist was painting her nails. She gave me an eager smile. 'Gorgeous weather, Miss Jackson! Makes you want to be on the river.'

I asked Hignett where Ned was. To my further astonishment I saw him indulge in a slow, histrionic grin exaggerated in its smugness.

'I'm not in the secret, don't think it. Perhaps *he's* on the river.'

'He can't be!' I was indignant.

'Or playing games. Bats and balls, that's what it is. What a nice life! It would suit me. Suit us all, wouldn't it, Jessie?' This was to the typist.

I felt indignant and ashamed. I did not know what to do. I was too young to rebuke him and too scared. Besides, rebukes were Ned's business. But I promised myself I would tell Ned about it later. 'Please tell him I've called,' I said, 'if he does come in.'

'If ifs and ands were pots and pans,' said Hignett. 'Oh well! Do my best for you. Ta-ta,' he added, as he opened the door for me.

When I told Ned that night how I had hoped to surprise him at work and how insolent the clerk had been, his face tightened. 'Master Hignett,' he said distinctly, 'is under notice to go. He's been sacked. This was his last day – hence the milk in the coconut.'

I asked why.

'Because he's lazy as mud and wants too much money.' He paused. 'And look here, Chris, I don't want you dropping in and out.'

I was bitterly hurt. Why on earth shouldn't I call on him? I demanded. For one fantastic second I imagined that the typist Jessie might be his mistress and that he was afraid of me finding it out.

'Because woman's place is in the home, my girl, and mine is on the job. Also, because I say no. And that should be enough for you.'

We began to quarrel; I could have cried with mortification. Then, adroitly, Ned turned the whole thing into a joke. I found myself laughing at him, at Hignett, at myself. He held me tightly, talking into my hair. 'You come when you like, silly, only there's nothing to see. And half the time I'm out taking people over houses. But of course you can come. I was only joking.'

He knew well enough that I should never again call there uninvited – and I knew it, too. I had been snubbed. He had had his way. But my nerves were too tender for me to pretend to myself that I had had other than a triumph.

17

A night or so later Ned and I were walking across Richmond Green. It was ten o'clock. We had been quarrelling since seven about nothing in particular, and Ned had made me cry. We had had a reconciliation almost as violent as the quarrel itself. He walked with his arm around my shoulders and his face was young and appeased. The aftermath of quarrels always had this calming effect upon him; it was as though every worry and weight in the world had fallen from his shoulders, making his step so light that he hardly bent the grass as he trod. For me, however, these aftermaths were an appalling confusion of spirit. They made every nerve in my body twitch and sting. They raised the beat of my heart. I was always afraid, after these scenes, to eat or drink.

It was a mild night. A harvest moon, rust-red, hung in an indigo sky powdered over by the river mist. The lights shone in the windows round about, between or behind the curtains. One window was rose-coloured. I fancied that behind it there existed some mysterious achievement of peaceful love, secret and content, and I longed so much to be in that high room that my eyes filled again. Once, later in my life, at a time when I was very unhappy, I found myself in the National Gallery before an Italian landscape of prussian-blue distances that stretched far away behind a little Abraham and Isaac playing out their minuscule drama in the foreground; and I felt the same aching desire to step through the picture frame, to walk and walk away into that undiscovered country till I was lost from everyone's sight, that I felt that night on Richmond Green to step through the rose-coloured window and be lost for ever in the peace awaiting me there.

Ned did not speak. He was too deeply wrapped in his own kind of contentment. A street lamp shone on his imperious, bird-like face, carving it out upon the dark. His hand moved down my breast, my nerves leaped, and I heard myself say in a voice full, confident, that did not seem to be my own, 'I can't marry you.'

His hand continued to move upon me, rhythmic, affectionate. 'You'd have to give back all those kettles and table-mats.'

'I mean it,' I said. 'Dear Ned' – for I was pierced with compassion for him, though not at all afraid – 'I can't marry you.'

His hand rested. I knew he had heard me.

'Don't be silly,' he said. He drew me on.

I began to tell him, quite coherently, that I was very, very sorry, but that I knew we should be unhappy. There was time to draw back, and we must do it.

Still we walked on. 'I was a pig tonight, I know,' he said. 'I upset you more than I meant to. But it's been a strain for me, all these months, and I can't help taking it out of people. When we're married it will be all right.'

'I'm not going to marry you,' I said.

At last he stopped. He faced me. He had a mild, bewildered air, as if awakened suddenly, by some sound of innocent portent, from a peaceful dream.

'Don't be silly, Chris. I've told you I'm sorry. But you know as well as I do that we love each other. You do love me?'

I took the common refuge of childishness. Yes, I did love him, I said, but not in *that way*; not as he loved me. I loved him, he was dear to me, but I had realised that I was not 'in love' with him.

'That's a bloody thing to say,' he said slowly, still with the same bewildered look.

I felt within me an absolute authority, and it was very strange. It was not in the least disturbed by the pity that rose in me granular and hot, like sickness. I said nothing.

Ned said restlessly, 'Let's go back and have another drink. It will seem different indoors. We shall stop talking nonsense.'

But I would not go in. We walked down to the towpath. The orange moon was doubled in the river; the reflection hung from it like a fob from a watch. Above it a golden cloud burned golden and still, the charred edges smouldering upon the thick dark blue of the sky.

'It's beautiful,' Ned said, holding me tightly to his side, his thigh against mine. 'Isn't it?'

I nodded.

He told me that he loved me, more than he had ever hoped to love. He needed me; I was good for him, I would help him, I should be able to make him as I wished him to be.

We sat down on a wooden bench.

'Don't, Chris, don't,' he said. 'Please stop now.'

The air had turned chilly. I was glad of his nearness and his warmth. My need of it weakened me a little. 'We won't see each other for a week. I want to think. We can put the wedding off for a little while to see how we feel.'

'Idiotic!' he cried angrily. For the first time real doubt entered into him. He pressed me to assure him of my love, to tell him I had simply been trying to punish him for his bad treatment of me, for his quarrelsomeness. 'I know I deserve it, Chris, but, damn it, I'm doing my best to make it up to you.'

It all seemed so easy. No, I insisted, it wasn't that at all. I had simply seen quite clearly that we could not be married – 'so soon,' I added, out of the weakening. I told him we must stay away from each other for a while.

And then he shocked me, for he put his head on my shoulder and began to cry. I had never seen a man cry before. I had believed that never to cry was a discipline of male life as obligatory as not striking a woman. My pity was flooded with alarm and contempt. What sort of a man was he? I did not know then that in love men and women are much the same; they are jealous in the same fashion, they live the same kind of fantasy life, they are moored to love in the same way by its fetiches: the tree in the lover's street, the light in the lover's window, the odour of the flesh, the special secret smile, the fleck upon the finger-nail. Nor had I realised that only in the most profound, the most matured love, is it possible for a woman to honour a man for his tears.

When we are young it is impossible for us to believe that we may be passionately loved. There is no magic for us in our own image; only our own desire is real. It seems strange to me now to realise how blind I was to the reason for Ned's crying, which was a perfectly simple one. I believed he was playing out a distasteful charade in the hope of winning me back. I could not, or perhaps did not want to, believe that he was sincere. For even if life with Ned had shaken my faith in my belief that I should only be happy with a master (mastery and bullying were dangerously equated in my mind by now), I still could not endure the thought that I was destined to be the strength of any man, lonely and angry above his head while he brought his sorrows to my lap.

I stood up. Ned sat quiet, dejected, hands hanging at his sides. He took out his handkerchief and passed it over his face. He said, 'Where are you going?'

He ran to catch me up.

'Where are you going?'

'Don't come with me.'

'Don't be an idiot.'

I told him, with all the force of this curious authority, that he must not follow me. I did not wish it.

Why he did not I still cannot be sure; but I think there is a kind of authority unpremeditated, unselfconscious, that few people in any state of stress are able to resist. I ran along the path, and the moon ran with me.

'Where are you running to, darling?' a man's voice called, idle and amorous.

I ran on. After a while I stopped, breathless, and looked back. There was no sign of Ned. I pictured him sitting there still, on the wooden bench by the river. I walked easily, calmly, on towards the station. Ned had kept our tickets. I had to buy another one for myself.

I sat in the train. My head felt light and empty; emptiness was pleasant. It would be rather like this in heaven, I thought – that quiet place where nobody felt intensely about anything at all.

'Stuffy night,' said the only other traveller in the compartment, an elderly man, small, Jewish, in a fawn trilby hat.

Ordinarily I was afraid of advances by strangers. That night I was worried by nothing. Even if I had been, it would have been unnecessary; he simply wanted to talk. He was a natural talker. He told me he was in office supplies. I told him I worked in an office.

Did I like it?

Not very much.

What did I want to be?

The train rattled over the points. Smoke blew backwards in a gust of fresh, wet silver. The moon raced alongside.

I wanted to write, I answered him.

'You'll need paper for that,' said my new friend practically. He had an earnest, good face. 'I can let you have it at cost.' He gave me his card. 'Carbons, too.'

The train stopped at Clapham Junction and I got out. He was going to Victoria.

For twenty years I have bought paper from his firm; he is dead now, and his son has taken over. It is an odd reminder of that night with Ned at Richmond, the night when I gained my false freedom, when I was sure enough of myself to walk away and make him stay where he sat, powerless to follow me.

18

For a week I avoided him. I would not speak to him on the telephone. I read his letters, the most obsessive he had ever written me, not touched at all now with his affectionate, rather condescending irony, and I was unmoved.

Meanwhile Emilie, to whom I had said nothing, but who guessed that there was trouble between us, did not rejoice. A month or so ago she would have been delighted to see my marriage checked; but now, with the house sold, the flat rented, her own room in the mansions half furnished, she was terrified of any breakdown in our practical arrangements. She would not know which way to turn. I think she saw herself evicted in the street, a pathetic figure crouched on a heap of packing-cases, no roof over her head. Her anxious, timid, forget-me-not gaze followed me, seeking, imploring reassurance.

The week was up. I answered Ned's call.

'Well?' he said roughly. He was afraid. I heard fear in his voice.

'I don't know.'

'You ought to know. We're getting married today week, and that's that. I've given you your head; now show a bit of sense. I'll be round tonight.'

I told him I was not ready.

He was silent for a minute. Then he said, 'Look here, then: we've got to break this damned silly ice, I suppose. Let's meet at some place of public entertainment' – he gave this phrase a portentous sarcasm – 'where we can't row, and then see how we feel afterwards.'

'All right,' I agreed.

He said he would take me to dinner at a restaurant in Leicester Square; it was a place far smarter than any to which we normally went. 'Eight sharp.'

'Yes,' I said.

'And, Chris' – his voice was coaxing – 'wear the yellow frock, the one I like.'

I dressed myself very slowly and carefully. I did not yet know what I was going to say to him, except that I must find a way of telling him once and for all that we could not be married. There would be a terrible scene; and I felt I could endure this more calmly if I looked my best. I bought myself a little spray of slipper orchids (it would mean only a bun and a cup of coffee for lunch on two days of the following week) and had my hair waved. I could not help feeling a little excited now about going to so smart a place to dine. Even Caroline was never taken here.

He was waiting outside for me, very stiff in his dinner-jacket, a red flower in his lapel, his fair hair glossy under the row of coloured lamps. Coming forward, he kissed me on the cheek. 'You look nice.'

I thanked him.

'I've missed you, Chris. I think you've done enough to me.'

His eyes momentarily clouded over, as if he were thinking of some point in the future. I believed that if I were to take him back (which I had no intention of doing) he would revenge himself upon me in some way for having exerted power over him; the thought of this, for a second, was not displeasing. Even at a cost to myself, I should have liked to see him back on his pedestal.

We went downstairs into the big, hot, glittering room. He had booked a table by the dance-floor. 'If there's a damned cabaret one may as well be able to see it.'

He ordered the most expensive food for me; I could not touch it. All the time I was pretending to eat he watched me. I could not bear to meet his eyes, for they were lonely and frightened. We were frightened of each other. Meanwhile, he drank a good deal.

I have never known Ned drunk: that was not the word for it. His speech, his gait, were never affected. But having had too much to drink gave him an air of what, in a woman or even in a man of regular features, I should have called beauty. It blanched all colour from his skin, making his eyes and his lips darker; it smoothed away all lines; it made his flesh appear transparent, delicate as glass. It made him sit very still. Always economic of gesture, he now seemed hardly to move at all, and this very immobility made him impressive.

We had finished our perfunctory meal. We had been talking little, and always idly, talking about the flat, the wedding, as if they were realities. It did not seem strange to me that we should be doing this. We had to talk about something, and anything would do.

He said at last, 'Well?'

'Dear Ned, dear Ned,' I replied, 'it's no use.'

'I don't understand you. I don't understand you at all.'

I said he must have realised that for a long time things had not gone well with us.

'We have rows,' said Ned. 'The best people do.'

'It's worse than that. I'm not happy. I never can be, with you.'

He spread his small hands on the table. The veins shone blue as flax through the fine skin.

I took off my ring and pushed it across to him. He fitted it on his little finger, stared at it, polished up the emerald with his sleeve. Then he grasped my hand, and forced the ring back on to it. He said, with quiet violence, '*I won't look a bloody fool for your sake!*'

He stared at me, the lashes sticking out around his eyes. He was trembling.

'We don't care what other people say.' I believed this. 'That doesn't matter.'

'Of course it matters! Chris, for God's sake, you've got to stop it. You've got sense. You know as well as I do that girls do get upset before their weddings – it's common enough. You love me. You've said so. And I'll turn myself inside out to make you happy. I'll do anything. But don't—' His voice faded; he cleared his throat. 'Don't go on with this. You must marry me.' He looked down at the cloth. 'There's nothing for me without you.'

I said, 'Ned, I can't.'

The cabaret had begun. Three American negroes in sailor suits were dancing with a grotesque, compulsive slackness from hip to ankle that made me think of men at the end of ropes dancing on air. Ned ordered some whisky. We could not talk. We were too near the band. The trumpeter was splitting the air in two.

I was glad I had drunk almost nothing. Sobriety gave me confidence. I felt taller, statelier, older. I knew I looked well. Even in these horrible moments – and for all my detachment I knew that, looking back upon them later, I should find them horrible – I was excited because Ned's sad, angry eyes admired me.

The negroes danced off. The band broke into a muted tune, catchy and neat. Three girls came on and one of them was Iris. They wore tight black gowns, blacks caps with paradise plumes, white furs. They minced into the middle of the floor, struck attitudes of elegant indecency, and began to sing something about 'Three little ladies from Leicester Square'.

Iris caught sight of me. I saw it in the slight twitching of her mechanical smile.

'Suffering somewhat from wear and tear,' she sang, having a line to herself. Her little, true voice was thinner than I had remembered it.

'If those are meant to be whores,' said Ned, 'give me the parson's daughter. God, what muck!'

'The middle one's Iris,' I said.

'Yes, I know. Your famous friend. I don't forget faces.' He paused. 'What do I care, anyway? Damn her eyes.'

He was ugly in his misery now, wanting to hurt me by coarseness, or, for that matter, by any means in the least likely to succeed; but he could not find a means. He was still speaking quietly, and he sat without stirring; yet I felt people were covertly watching us.

Iris paused for a second before our table, winked very slightly at me and sang her final line straight at Ned.

He looked back at her. Any means would do; any chance must be taken. He smiled.

The girls went off, and the star of the evening, a French *diseuse*, appeared. Ned and I watched her in silence. I had spilled a drop of wine on my dress; I dabbed and rubbed at it with a corner of my handkerchief which I had dipped in the water-jug. I was glad to have something to do.

The first part of the show came to an end. People started to dance.

Ned rose, took my hands in his and made me dance, too. The band was playing the tune he had requested again and again at Richmond, on the night I had disgraced myself, and I resented it because it weakened me. Yet for the moment I was happy simply to dance with him to this sad music, to feel his body supporting my own, to be one with him at this hour of parting. I found myself saying, 'I do love you, but not in that way. I told you that. You must *see* it.'

It is only when we are young that we hope to give comfort by this sort of distinction to a lover we no longer desire; yet many years later the same kind of thing was to be said to me, in terms more subtle, by someone far older than I; and I was to know the shame of accepting it and the never-ending regret that I had done so.

Ned said nothing at all.

When we sat down we found Iris at our table. She still wore her stage make-up, but had put on a blue evening dress. She looked self-consciously mischievous; she had the reticent glitter of a handful of diamond chips.

'Caught you!' she said to me. 'Christie, you're caught out. Now you'll have to introduce me to your mysterious Ned, won't you? Though actually we've been introduced before.'

'Yes, I remember.' His voice was flat.

'I didn't know you were playing here,' I said.

'My dear, nor did I till last week! Someone fell out and I fell in. Isn't the show awful? Such an awful song. And that costume makes me looked like a horse.' There was something so perennial about Iris that it was rather a comfort, like one's certainty about the cycle of the months. 'Didn't you think I looked like a horse?' she demanded of Ned. 'All dressed up for the circus, with feathers on. All I want is a dear little nosebag.'

She turned on me again. 'Christie! You pig! You shouldn't have hidden him away like that. It's greedy. I adore Christie,' she went on, giving Ned her simple look; 'she's my *very* best friend.'

I asked her if she came on again later.

'But thank God, no! *Mille fois non*, darling. I'm through for the night. I just rushed into my things to join you for a few minutes.'

Ned asked her if she would have a drink.

'A wonderful orange-squash,' said Iris, who never touched alcohol, 'just to drink to you both. Is it true you're getting married next week? You unspeakable *beast*, Christie, not to invite me.'

I said, rather feebly, that we had meant it to be very quiet.

'But I can come! Say I can! Neddy – I'm going to call you Neddy – you invite me, and then I can go and sit with the *bridegroom's* friends on the *right* of the aisle, and no one will be able to turn me out.'

He smiled and said nothing.

'It may have to be put off for a little,' I said. I explained that there were complications about our new home. Ned went on smiling. I had to remind him to order the orange-squash.

'Oh, poor you! But remember, Iris is to come. She has said it.'

To my surprise Ned asked her to dance. I saw her flush, as she always did when greeting the success she felt was her natural right. 'But we can't leave poor Christie all alone!'

I said I didn't mind.

'Well, a tiny dance, then.' Iris rose and gave herself into Ned's arms with the benevolent air of the chairman of a factory presenting an aged foreman with a marble clock upon the occasion of his retirement. I sat and watched them, feeling nothing but amazement. As they danced she talked, her face brilliant with animation. Ned looked out over her head and appeared to reply only brusquely. She rested her left hand on his upper arm, as her habit was: as if she were too small to reach a man's shoulder. Once she threw back her head in a fit of laughter, bringing him to a halt. She disengaged her hand from his and waved to me.

When they came back to the table Ned seemed to me whiter than ever, but very cheerful. He was no longer monosyllabic; he teased Iris as if he had known her as long as I had.

I thought how lucky it was that I no longer needed to be jealous. Ned would not care much for her, of course, though she might amuse him. Certainly I doubted whether he had ever seen anyone prettier. Still, it startled me to find him so suddenly at ease.

'Christie,' she said to me, 'that yellow is your colour, definitely. It makes you look so frail.'

'If you mean,' I said with what I felt was a degree of stateliness, 'that it makes me look sallow, you may as well say so straight out.' For I was free of Iris, no longer under her spell, no longer to be loved, cajoled, threatened or deprived by her.

'Mee-ow! Oh, puss, puss, puss! Neddy, isn't Christie *too* unkind?'

'Chris is all right,' he said. They were staring at each other.

She said, 'Now *what* a beautiful flower! Neddy, you have a most gorgeous flower in your buttonhole. Iris would like it. She presses flowers in a little blotting-book.'

He hesitated.

It was as though the whole focus of that night, that week, of my whole life, had shifted. I was in love. I was in danger. I felt cold and sick.

'Christie wouldn't deny her friend a flower,' Iris said. She touched my hand. 'Would you?'

'It's Ned's.'

I could hardly speak. It had always been like this. Nothing had changed. There was still the same fret. You let her take everything from you, poor Keith had said.

'*Why on earth do you let her take everything?*'

Iris had her finger-tips to the carnation. She looked merry and secretive. As she glanced quickly at me there was real affection in her face, the affection that often spurts up between rivals. 'Shall I?, Or shan't I?'

'You may have it if you want it,' said Ned, 'but it's a bit on the faded side.' He took her hand and held it down, removed the flower himself and put it behind her ear.

'You perfect sweet!' she cried. 'Christie, he *is* nice. You're a lucky, lucky girl. You must bring him round to see me – promise!'

I found myself promising. I was near to tears. I was not, as I had thought, grown-up and strong, and I hated her for weakening me. All I wanted was for Ned to take me away.

'I'm dead tired,' I said.

He called for the bill. 'All right.' He turned to Iris. 'Can we run you home? I've got the car.'

'Oh, how lovely! But I can't. I've got to go on to a silly stupid old party, and if I don't run along now I won't have time to change my face.' She gave her high peal of laughter. 'And it does *need* changing! I'd like to change it altogether, I swear I would.'

She leaned over to kiss me. Her lips smelt of the violet cachous that she ate, strangely enough, simply because she liked them. 'And I think he's a great dear,' she said, as if we were alone together, 'and I wish you both oceans of luck, and you're not to forget your poor old spinster friend who adores you.' She looked speculatively at Ned. 'No, I mustn't kiss *you*. We're not sufficiently acquainted.' She touched his cheek with the carnation he had given her, and scampered away, making diners look after her in admiration and amusement.

'Come on,' Ned said, his cheerfulness gone.

He said, as we drove home, 'That's a ridiculous young woman.'

I believed he said it to deceive me. Like the rest of them, he had been instantly charmed by her, charmed away from me. She would even take Ned, whom I had not wanted.

'*I* think she is,' I replied stiffly, 'but I can hardly expect a man to.'

'Ridiculous.'

'She's extremely pretty.'

'Chocolate-box type. No character.'

'You were willing enough to give her that wretched flower.'

'Elementary politeness.'

'Oh, nonsense,' I said, my heart bursting. I was sure now, for no reason, that they meant to meet again. They had arranged it while they were dancing.

He stopped the car. We were halfway down Grosvenor Place, the leaves from the palace trees rattling above us in a sudden stiff wind. He held out his arms to me, and I put mine around his neck.

'Next week,' he said, 'as arranged.'

'Next week.'

It was the first time I had known physical desire so strong. I was invaded by it, and frightened.

'It will be all right,' he told me; 'we'll be happy together.'

'Of course.'

'It's not been easy for me,' he said, and, putting me away from him, drove on.

I went to bed in a rapture, a turmoil of thought, that made me think I should not sleep. Yet I slept at once, slept without dreams until six o'clock, when I awoke in the grey room that was hurrying to shrink back into the normal contours of day before I could catch it exposed in the secret transformation of the night. I sat up in bed, sober, fearful, longing for someone to come and talk to me, to reassure me – anyone, even Ned whom I did not want (how could I ever have wanted him?) – because I knew now what Iris had done.

She was the goddess in the machine, the descending mischief – idle, malicious, affectionate, who had taken the matter of my life out of my hands.

She had committed me.

PART THREE

I

Hatton had warned me that I should not like my presentation gift, but he was wrong. It was a handsome sunray clock, chosen by Mr. Baynard who had remembered me admiring the one in the office more than a year ago. In my already emotional state this evidence of thoughtfulness from an unexpected quarter so touched me that I was hard put to it not to cry. I had never liked the office. Now the time had come for me to leave it I felt I was being torn away from safety and from friends, from the known to the unknown. I stood in Mr. Fawcett's room, the others grouped around me with their glasses of sherry, and tried to find words that were not lame.

The mood of the ceremony was transformed, however, by the discovery that the clock was far too heavy for me to carry home on the bus. Hatton said he would go with me and lend a hand; Mr. Baynard told him sharply that he couldn't, because he had to pick up some money from a Mrs. Phipps at Claridge's and could not be spared. Mr. Fawcett, after suggesting that Miss Cleek should assist me (her eyes filled at this, for she had arranged to meet her very first young man at Ken Wood that afternoon) experimentally raised the clock himself and decided that it was too much even for two girls to carry. So he decided that Hatton must fetch a taxi and put me and the clock into it. 'I'll pay for it, of course,' he added. He looked at his watch. 'I'll have to be off now. Goodbye, Miss Jackson, and the best of luck in your future life.'

'Time and tide wait for no man,' said Mr. Baynard; 'and if I dont buck up, too, my wife will have something to say. We're always punctual in my family.' He had a parting shot. 'And the new Junior had better be, too, or I'll know the reason why.'

He was gone. Mr. Fawcett was gone. Miss Cleek, to whom I was already part of the past, had slipped away to joy.

So there were only Miss Rosoman and Hatton to wave to me as I set off in the taxi, my gift at my side. Somehow it seemed to me unkind that the others should not have waited. This was so important a break in my own life, and there are some importances which are only endurable if veiled with ceremony; but it was important to no one but myself, and I felt lonely and belittled because it was not. I told myself that I should be happy to leave this trudging, unpromising life for the excitements and hopes of marriage; yet as I looked out of the window at Regent Street falling away behind me, at the trees of St. James's Park swaying in the hot and dusty wind of autumn, at the horsewoman of Constitution Hill looming larger as she rode up the sky, I was inexplicably sad. I took hold of one of the sunrays which was poking through the green baize and held it, as if it were a finger, for comfort.

The last days of my freedom seemed to me now too fast, now too slow. Sometimes I was taken, especially if I woke at the first light, by a panic so energising that I wanted to grasp the intangible hours, and, by checking them minute by minute, force them to go slowly; sometimes I felt the days would never pass. And then, suddenly, the day had come and was speeding by me, inapprehensible, immemorable.

I had come to this marriage, half in doubt, half in the deceitful exhilaration of hope; yet it seems to me now that it is mistaken to describe any wedding at all as 'memorable' – at least, for the two persons concerned. They are too busy trying to feel the whole of this climactic experience to feel anything whatsoever; they are beyond observation, except of a kaleidoscopic nature. The most recognisable emotion they are likely to know is that of surprised, astonished disappointment that they are unable to 'make the most of it'; there is so much to make the most of, and yet somehow the whole essence of the occasion has eluded them, has half-concealed itself between one of the Chinese screens of consciousness and will not be drawn forth. At my own wedding in St. Barnabas' Church, on a mild yellow day in autumn, I found my attention concentrated upon a single detail; the shoes that had been a present from Caroline, satin shoes that would be no use to me afterwards, a luxury bestowed out of friendship and understanding. They made me love Caroline. I clung for steadiness to the thought of her.

I do not believe I can have looked well. It is another mistake to suppose that a girl looks her best upon her wedding-day. As a rule she does not. She has been too anxious about herself; she looks strained and bewildered. At her dressing-table she has been filled with the gnomic belief that some inspiration will occur to her whereby she can make herself more beautiful than she has ever been before. It does not occur. She labours with her appearance; when she looks in wild hope into the glass it shows her her everyday face, no better, no worse. Cheated, she rises with something of a swagger; people will have to take her as she is, without the miracle. Added to the lines of strain is the small line of discouraged vanity.

At the reception held in Aunt Emilie's flat (which seemed to me as crowded as a ballroom) I could feel at first only a hostessly fret about whether everyone had enough to eat and drink. 'Happy?' Ned whispered to me. I was not unhappy, certainly. I was simply strange to myself. And yet, as the time went on, I knew, beneath this confusion, the stirring of an excited pride. I was, I told myself, a married woman, not yet twenty years of age. Unworthily, it pleased me that I should have been married before Iris. I wanted to find an opportunity for signing my new name. And once, as Ned looked straight at me in momentary forgetfulness of the others, his face open with love, I was in love also.

It was an afternoon of curious lacunae; I found myself losing little patches of time as one may lose them on a summer afternoon in long grass, between sleeping and waking. Now and then I was puzzled and a little mortified to observe how quickly the conversation passed from Ned and me to general topics: as years later, at the first night of a friend's play, I was puzzled to find the audience discussing anything but that play during the intervals and even after the fall of the final curtain as they poured out into St. Martin's Lane.

I heard Ned whisper to me, 'I think that in just about ten minutes we might make a move.'

I had cut the cake. Mr. Skelton had read aloud a batch of telegrams. Most of them were from Ned's friends; I had an affectionate, umbrageous one from Iris, reading, 'All wonderful luck darling from your old absent friend'; and another from Take Plato that the telegraphist had transcribed imperfectly but which should have read, 'Cras amet qui nunquam amavit.' This Mr. Skelton did not read, but, with a remark about 'Double Dutch', passed it to Ned, who passed it to me. 'I don't think Take Plato will be my favourite guest of the future,' he observed. I was saddened. It seemed unlikely that many of my friends would be likely to rank as such.

Somebody murmured in my ear that the car had come; and, with the mysterious prescience of wedding-guests, they all came around us, sensing, though they had not been told, that we were about to leave them. They were around us, ready with their farewells; and then, as if a moment of time had been blotted right out, these farewells had been said, and everyone was gone, and Ned and I were alone.

I said, 'Poor Emilie! She was crying.'

'People always cry at weddings. It's part of the fun.'

'She looked so lonely.'

'Nonsense. We're not going to Timbuctoo.'

The car passed along familiar streets, through the familiar, unregarding crowds.

'Don't look so worried,' he said. 'I love you very much.'

In the train we had a compartment to ourselves. He put his arm around my shoulders. We looked out of the windows. The reflected smoke of the train over the fields seemed to me like a file of azure angels soaring upwards with linked arms. I wished I could feel excited, but I was not excited at all; I was becalmed.

'You are a frightful responsibility,' said Ned.

I asked him if he had enjoyed the wedding.

'It all went so quickly one couldn't really think about it.'

I told him that I had felt this, too: we were unified by the mutual experience of experiencing nothing at all.

'*Not* to look worried,' he insisted.

I assured him that I was not.

We were to spend a week at Bournemouth. Paris was out of the question for the moment, Ned had told me, since things were not as bright as he had hoped; but if they looked up again, as they should do shortly, we might go abroad in the spring.

The spring, I thought; I shan't be there – and had been shaken and distressed for a moment at this invasion by an irrational denial so unpremeditated, apparently *so obvious*, that it had nearly reached the tip of my tongue.

'We can go for longer in the spring, too,' he had added. 'I can't leave the business for more than a week just now.'

When Ned signed the hotel register and I saw my new name I knew a stirring of unease, and was glad; I did not want to be calm. It was wrong to be calm. But the unease refused to persist. Alone with him in the bedroom looking out on only half the sea (riot the orange-scented vastness I had imagined), I kissed him and began to unpack. Ned sat on the edge of the bed and watched me. I felt his gaze lying along the nape of my neck and down my spine. My movements, I believed, were very neat, unflurried. He would be able to guess, from them, what an able housewife I should be.

The curtains were still open, and beyond them was the black, patient, unharmful night. 'It's extraordinary,' I said, 'but I don't feel in the least tired.'

He came to me with a swiftness that suggested a spring. My nerves leaped. Ned laughed. 'Darling, you've been reading books about monsters, and you are looking like a martyr. Come and have dinner, and don't be silly.'

I began to cry.

'You are an ass,' said Ned. 'You are, you really are.'

2

Those autumn days by the sea are clear in my memory, sweet, like new linen. They were Ned's days and mine. In this brief certainty we loved each other.

For the first time I understood that the waiting-time had been hard for him. His nature was direct and sensual; it was not possible for him to live happily, like some men, on the romantic promise of joy. Yet he treated me with a gentleness, a good humour, a selfless consideration that filled me with a gratitude I could not express; and despite Caroline's warnings, which I had borne talismanically in my mind, he brought me quickly to the understanding of pleasure. I felt for a while as if the earth had steadied itself under my feet, as if I had grown taller, as if I should make no more mistakes.

The weather was fine for us. The sun sparkled out all day from a white sky, and there were no shadows on the sea. We lay on the beach, went walking through the close and odorous pine trees, danced at night in the Pavilion. We were in high spirits and tranquil, hoping for nothing, because hope is only necessary when one is afraid.

On the day before our return I told him I had some shopping to do.

He got up. 'I'll go with you.'

'No, don't,' I said. 'You stay and finish your book.' I explained that my purchases would be dull ones, and that I did not expect to be away for more than half an hour.

What I wanted to buy I did not know, except that it had to be something heavy. I went into the ironmongery department of a large shop and considered the saucepans. I rejected aluminium and bought a big cast-iron one, suited to a family of ten.

'Do you want it sent?'

Certainly I wanted it sent, I told the salesgirl. (That was the whole object of my shopping.)

'Where to?'

I gave her my address.

She said there would be an extra charge for postage.

She asked me my name.

And I could at last satisfy the small, persistent desire that had been nudging me since my wedding day.

'Skelton,' I said, 'Mrs. Edmund Skelton. S-k-e-l-t-o-n.'

Satisfaction ran through me like a warm drink on a chilly night. I saw my life simple, solid and plain; it seemed the right sort of life for me, and I was content.

The early days of a youthful marriage are rather like a charade; a girl plays housekeeping. I went self-importantly about the new flat, doing the work so briskly and with such good will that by half-past eleven in the morning I usually found myself with the rest of the day on my hands. Unaccustomed to so much leisure, I hardly knew what to do with it. I did not feel like writing; I had, I told myself, dwindled into a wife, and proper wives should have no need to express themselves in verse. I read until my eyes ached, read the books of which Ned was fond and which he kept on the bedroom shelf: Scott, Conrad, Wodehouse, Kipling and, rather oddly, Joyce's *Dubliners.* I wanted to become as much like Ned as possible, to share his tastes.

Emilie intruded upon me little. It was as if the honeymoon, which, for the first time, had deprived her of me entirely, had set her free to find a new interest of her own. She had returned to the nonconformity of her youth and was centring her life around the Congregational Church, where there was a minister of exceptional personality and vigour. She had transferred to him something of the loving reverence she had felt for my father. He was, she told me, not only good but exceedingly clever; it pleased her that he should sometimes preach sermons 'above her head'. He was a man of cultivated tastes, and was in the process of transforming the literary and musical into a centre of the arts remarkable by any standard. Emilie took me to a recital given there by William Primrose, and she sat through it in a state of entrancement, beating the wrong time to the music with her gloved hand for the best part of two hours. 'Quite a musical feast,' she told me afterwards, giving me her new, timid, uplifted smile.

Ned was cheerful and, so far as I could judge, busy. He only played games on one day in the week. I heard nothing more of the temporary embarrassment that had prevented our honeymoon in Paris.

One day, after we had been married for three months or so, Mrs. Skelton came to tea with me. I had not expected her, so had nothing but tea for her to drink. She drank it in a suspicious, lowered fashion as if it had been some exotic brew that no Englishwoman could really trust. She had been talking with her customary distaste of her husband ('He has simply no conversation and never had') and of Nelly ('Why must she be so hopelessly unsmart?'), and now conversation was at a standstill. Her long body relaxed in an armchair, she sat with closed eyes. Then the eyes shot open; the pupils contracted. 'Are you and Ned going to give me any grandchildren? It would be something to amuse me.'

I told her he thought it would be better for us to wait for a while.

'Why? What for? Much better to have them while you're young.'

I explained that he wanted us to enjoy ourselves for a year or so before we were tied down; and also that he felt we ought to be on our feet properly first.

'And aren't you on your feet? Why not? How's that business going?'

I said I did not really know; I supposed it was all right.

'Doesn't he tell you?'

'I don't ask,' I replied with dignity. 'I feel that's his life, and the house is mine.'

'Parrot-talk,' said Mrs. Skelton disconcertingly. 'I suppose he told you that. If I were you I'd make it my job to find out.'

This did not, however, disturb me. Ned was still in high spirits; we were having a good time. It was true that money seemed rather short, and that during the past few weeks we had gone less to the theatre and cinema; but I felt it was wise of him to be cautious, and that perhaps he had turned over a new leaf in being so. Caution had not seemed a conspicuous feature of his life till now.

I was more concerned by Mrs. Skelton's raising of the question of children, for I should have liked to have them. As I say, time was inclined to hang lavishly upon my hands. I spoke about this to Caroline, with whom I was having dinner one evening at the beginning of the New Year. Both our husbands were away – hers on some business abroad, Ned on a tour of Suffolk houses with a client who wanted to settle there.

'My dear,' said Caroline, 'you have them if you can. Apparently I can't. Anyway, I've had no luck.'

She looked, for a moment, quite distraught; it was disturbing to see: such a change in her.

'But you haven't been married so long,' I said.

'Long enough to be anxious in. Not that I'd be so anxious, but he is. He appears to see himself smothered with happy little ones, all smearing jam in his hair. And his kindly view is that I am barren.'

She spoke to me more frankly than she had ever done, her need to talk, to be consoled by a responsive indignation, overcoming her natural evasiveness. Her husband, I gathered, could think of nothing but their childlessness, talk of nothing else. 'I must admit I've wondered if it could be his fault, but honestly, darling, without being crude, no one could possibly think so.'

Neither of us knew much about the problems of sterility.

'It's a mania with him. I tell him, give me a chance, I'm not twenty-one yet; but he says that if I were normal that would make no difference. I am beginning to feel,' said Caroline, with something of her old, stoical airiness, 'like a circus freak.' She turned the subject abruptly and asked me how Ned was getting on.

I told her he was getting on well. (I had that day, in fact, a special reason for thinking so.)

'Does he let you have the boys and girls round?'

'He would,' I replied loyally, 'only somehow I seem to have grown out of all that.' I told her how much I missed him while he was away.

'I wish I could say the same of mine. But when I know he'll stalk in and instantly start peering at me, counting up the days, I can't say my heart will beat with joy.'

For all her desire not to speak of him further, she could not abandon the topic. She told me more about him than I had ever known; that his open and generous manner with his own friends was quite different from his manner towards hers; that his temper was unpredictable, and his bouts of sensuality even more so; and that he had the habit of compulsive and unnecessary secrecy. 'When he gets his letters in the morning he snatches them up and runs off to read them in a corner with his back to me. It's just like a squirrel with nuts. As if I care who the devil's writing to him – even if I didn't know they were mostly about his stamp collection! Does Ned let you read his letters?'

I replied proudly that certainly he did; that when he went away he liked me to open them and to forward only those that seemed to me important.

'What trust!' Caroline remarked. 'How lucky you are!' She added broodingly, 'A damned squirrel with damned nuts.'

One of the letters I had that morning opened for Ned had given me great comfort and reassurance.

Now I had never had a banking account of my own and, as Emilie had kept all our financial affairs in her own hands, was unfamiliar with the appearance of a bank statement. I had glanced without interest at Ned's and had been about to put it aside for him, when my eye was caught by the figure that appeared to sum up his position; three wealthy-looking digits written in red ink. Well, I thought, my anxiety appeased, his mother is quite wrong. Everything is going splendidly.

When he returned, relief had made me as light as air. I even felt inclined to be playful. The mood never, I felt, really suited me, but there were times when it charmed and amused Ned.

'I want you to give me something,' I said. I was sitting on the arm of his chair. 'Promise me.'

'No blind promises,' he said cautiously. 'What is it?'

'I wondered if I could have a fur coat. I do feel the cold so much. It would only be a cheap one,' I added hastily.

He looked at me. 'I would if we could afford it, Chris, but we can't. You wait till we get out of the wood.'

'But we're not *in* the wood!' I said triumphantly. 'Darling, I've found you out. And I think we're doing very nicely.'

The expression on Ned's face was curious. He asked me what I thought I had found out. Still playfully (when I think of myself now I shrink a little, for it is easier to endure the memory of having looked ridiculous yesterday than of having looked ridiculous in the delicate days of our youth) I went to the desk, took out the bank statement, put it on a cushion and presented it to him with the flourish of the herald who offers the glass shoe to Cinderella. 'There!' I said. 'We have eight hundred and forty-two pounds seven shillings and five pence. Do you mean to say I can't have a coat out of that?'

He picked it up. For a moment he had lost all expression; he might have been sleeping with open eyes. Then his face reddened and seemed to swell. His mouth tightened.

I was still holding the cushion. Ned knocked it out of my hands. 'You imbecile!' he said. 'Is this your idea of a joke?'

I was scared and at a loss. 'I was only playing.' I thought he had meant the business with the cushion. 'I thought you'd be pleased.'

'Why the hell should I be pleased?'

'Because we'd got some money. It must be all right if we've got all that.'

'Do you seriously imagine—' he began. He stopped. 'Yes, I believe you do. You are an imbecile. I've never seen anything like it.'

I begged him to tell me what was wrong. It was our first disagreeable scene since we had been married.

'This isn't money we've got. This is money we owe the bank.'

I could not understand. Ned, in a quiet, patient, furious voice, explained to me the meaning of the red ink. 'So you see,' he concluded, 'it would have been damned odd if I had been pleased.'

I saw it now. But while he had been talking I had felt, growing within me, the courage to counter-attack. I had had time to resent the way in which he had received my foolishness, the roughness with which he had spoken to me. I was no longer a girl whom he could flatter with the love of his maturity: I was his wife, and I would not be browbeaten.

'Then it's a pity,' I said, 'that you've let us get into this state.' I walked to the far side of the room. I felt safer there.

'Mind your own business!' he said in a kind of astonished shout. He got up. 'You stick to the house! When I want your advice on my affairs I'll ask for it.'

I told him not to talk to me in this fashion; I would not bear it.

I thought he would follow me, but he did not. He said, in a softer tone, 'It's only that you can't understand it, Chris. I've had bad luck. No one can help that.'

'You could have helped it; you were hardly ever at the office. You left everything to wretched people like Hignett.'

'One has to go out after work.'

'You weren't going after it. You were playing silly games.'

He sat down again. His hands hung between his knees. I wondered what he would say next.

He said at last, in a strange, young voice, 'I never wanted to go into the damned thing. I wanted to be a soldier.'

Perhaps there would be a war for him one day, I said, and in a second was sorry, because, for the first time, I had sounded shrewish. 'I didn't mean that.'

He took no notice. 'They always drove me the way they wanted – the lot of them.' He paused. 'I'm so tired. I feel dog-tired, Chris.'

'What are we going to do?'

'Struggle on. The bank won't bother me for the time being.'

'I'm sorry, Ned,' I said. 'I'd help you if I could. I could always go back to work.'

'I don't want the family to know.' He ignored my last suggestion; he had always refused to hear of it.

I asked him if they would not be forced to help us in the long run, if our difficulties became too great.

He shook his head. This was, he told me, his last chance. He held out his hand to me. We stood in silence. He looked really exhausted, the lines of his face grey and deep. I knew I had won a victory, but it brought me no pleasure. I had not wished to win victories, not over a lover. I needed to look up, to admire, to be tutored, to be led and comforted. Now I saw the shape of my marriage clearly, and wished to think of other things, so that my mind would be clear and fresh for the readjustment I should have to make.

3

It makes us scared of life, aware of its disequilibrium, when we first realise that the moment of a cold truth is most likely to fasten upon us during an hour of contentment.

After the quarrel over the bank statement Ned and I had somehow slipped into one of those pockets of mutual confidence which, in any ill-adjusted marriage, are apt to make their inexplicable appearances. He was sorry he had upset me and was more than usually eager to please me; I had been delighted to have him in so compliant and loving a mood, had been tricked by it into a new hope. We both knew the happiness of the body, were matched in our fevers and in the easy acceptance of sleep. Nothing was wrong there. Ned's attitude towards sexual desire seemed to me compounded of cheerful matter-of-factness and a kind of reverent astonishment; his own pleasure appeared to afford him an unfailing source of delighted surprise. For my own part, I believed I had discovered the nature of love – that it was one part of physical pleasure to two parts of friendly conversation. It was a disappointing discovery, and I felt that literature had somewhat cheated me; but it was also a relief. This, then, was love: the problem solved. Anyone with a little sense could deal with love once he or she realised the essential simplicity of its composition.

It was in one of these states of calm (which, in youth, follow the imagined solving of one of the great philosophical questions with something of that fulfilled, yet fretful, loose-ended pleasure most writers know when they have finished a book) that I went to walk on the Common one afternoon towards the end of the winter. Everything had gone well that day. We had risen contented after love, discussed the news in the paper without a trace of conflict, Ned had gone cheerfully to work, and I had had a successful morning's shopping, by Machiavellian skill saving at least tenpence on the week's expenditure. An accomplished housewife, all my affairs in order, my mind quiet and self-congratulatory, I walked over the hawthorn field towards the pond, hearing the crackle of the frosted grass under my feet, admiring the salty and glittering trimming of the naked twigs. The pond lay under a grey film of ice that took from the bright grey sky the bloom of steel. The trees on the sugar-loaf island were shapely in their bareness, the skeleton of summer laid plain. The thinner branches were merely salted over, like the hawthorns; but along the thicker ones lay knife-edges of snow. All was clear, hard, unmysterious. A few birds, black on the general lightness, drank from the jagged rays of water along the rim of the jetty, where the ice had thinned and crumbled.

I was fully conscious of peacefulness, which is a dangerous thing to be. Peace was lying along the still air, like the smoke from my cigarette. No one was in sight. I was able to consider eternity without being troubled, for it could only be like this, the perpetuation of nothing happening at all. Well, I thought, here I am – as if I had arrived after a long journey at a dreaded destination, only to find there was no news of any kind, good or ill, awaiting me, only a place to rest, a meal to eat, a bed to lie in and a sleep without dreams.

And I thought, Well, is this anything to be feared? Isn't this enough?

A bird alighted on a branch, casting a little light plume of snow into my lap.

Though there seemed to be no wind at all, it must have

been blowing from the north-east, for the chimes of the parish clock fell clear into the afternoon. I had half an hour in which to sit there, on my seat under the tree, by the frozen pond, and then I must go back and make ready for Ned.

Tomorrow would be the same as today, as calm, as friendly, as little to be feared. And so on, always, till youth had passed unnoticed, and middle-age (the unimaginable) also, and at last old age (which the young think they can easily imagine) had become a harmless reality, with dying at the end of it all as the only fear and the only real excitement. Enough for anybody.

I felt the tears stacking in my throat before I understood them. What was there to cry about, when there was nothing to be afraid of?

The Common awakened suddenly with the swish of a car through the icy sludge of the Parade, the drone of an aeroplane across the sky, a drive of wind that sent the snow flying off the island trees to scamper over the ice. And it was dreadful to be alone with nobody near, to understand that for me such peace was not and would never be enough, that the body in itself would never be enough, and that I had done wrong. I had done wrong in marrying Ned, not only to myself but to him. I felt myself shaking, not with cold, but with the surrender to a fear naked as the trees were naked, now that the wind had blown. I was afraid of the effort of enduring, of the effort to make myself into what I was not (it was not for what I was that Ned loved me), of the effort to believe, now I knew that my marriage had failed, that it had not failed at all.

I had so far knapped my thoughts over the head, like Shakespeare's eels, and kept them down. Now they were all upon me, swarming in triumph, and I was helpless. Mysteriously, without warning, by some agency I could not conceive, I had been suddenly pushed out of the shelter of childishness and had been forced to grow up. Yet, the hidden critic remarked, you have this comfort: children cannot endure, for they cannot make resolutions and abide by them. Adults can. You can, of course. And must. And, of course, will.

4

I began to find changes not only in myself but in others. It seemed to me that the lightness of my youth had left me as a flush of light disappears from a wall when the sun goes in, leaving all things more plain, more real, more grey. If I were growing up (I thought of this process not as a forward step but as a coldness and a loss), so perhaps were my friends also, for when next I saw Dicky, meeting him by chance in St. John's Road on a shopping day, he seemed to me to wear his old, shy, sheepish air, but with a difference. It was as though he himself had recognised it as engaging, had studied it as he might have done in the personality of a stranger, and was now using it consciously for the purpose of pleasing. 'Which way are you going? I'll slope along with you.' He used his familiar schoolboy idiom, but behind it there was a smile of appreciation of its absurdity. 'Here, give me the basket. I have to carry the wretched thing for mother, so I may as well for you.'

We walked along, dividing as the crowds parted us, coming together again. 'How are things?' he asked me.

They were all right, I said. I had no special news. Had he?

'As a matter of fact, yes. I've changed my job.' He told me he was now employed by a music publisher and was very content. He was doing simple clerking for the most part, but once or twice they had let him try his hand at the arrangement of popular songs. 'You know, sometimes we get a tune, but what's underneath it is hell. I can usually tidy it up a bit.

I may even have a future.' He looked up into the sky. 'Fancy me with a future!'

I asked him about one or two of our acquaintances. Nothing much had happened to them. Take Plato was in his second year at Cambridge; it seemed that he was doing brilliantly. 'That poor chap is so generous in throwing his brains around,' Dicky said, 'that one never imagines he can have any left. I never really know why we laughed at him; for sheer intellect he knocked spots off the rest of us.'

Privately believing myself superior, at any rate potentially, to Take Plato, I reserved my opinion.

We walked up the Rise together. It was a sparkling, cold Saturday in March. The cries of the stall-holders floated across to us from Northcote Road. In the front gardens new buds, sharp as emeralds, were prodding their way through the grime of the winter privets.

I asked about Leslie, but there was no news of him at all; no one had seen him.

'But I expect he's doing something terrific,' said Dicky, referring not to reality but to Leslie's heated imagination; 'rum-running, or starring in *Rigoletto* at Covent Garden.'

He paused. 'This will surprise you. I've got a new girlfriend.' It was the phrase of our time, our milieu. No one in those days spoke of 'a new young woman'. 'Lady' was an outmoded, class-conscious word, 'woman' a little discourteous; a 'girl' was any woman under fifty.

I asked him to tell me about her. Life is so odd that it is hard for us to sustain the mood of our conclusions; here and there the kingfisher hope flashes up, brilliant, leading nowhere. In these days any romance, however vicarious, gave me a sense of warmth and excitement, perhaps even a moment of irrational forward-looking. Every night in bed I told myself how lucky I really was (could I only see things straightly) to have my life settled for me while I was still so young. There were to be no more uncertainties. My physical love for Ned existed still in its continual recrudescence; the understanding of our bodies was complete. Also, I had my duty to him, and I believed I was proud of that duty. Later, when he had hauled the business back on to its feet, we should have children: and I should come quietly, without noticing the transition, into contented domestic middle-age. I knew I should be grateful, but at twenty it is easier to recognise the need for gratitude than to feel the gratitude itself. I despised my inner restlessness, and promised myself that this, too, would pass away.

Dicky, however, having been uncommonly communicative, now found himself unable to say much more on the subject of his girl. He had met her in the office. She was twenty-two. Her name was Baba, which, he admitted, was a little ridiculous.

I asked him if this was serious.

He gave his stage-yokel's look, scuffed his shoe on the pavement, smiled sideways at me. 'You know me. I'm not much on love. But I'd like to know what you think of her.'

We stood outside the mansion flats where I lived. I said, on an impulse of freedom, for once determined to do as I pleased in harmless matters such as this, 'Bring her to see us one night. What about Wednesday?' I did not care what Ned thought; all that was over. I was going to have my friends after all.

'How will He take that?' Dicky never referred to Ned by name.

'How will who take it?'

'Come, come.' He grinned. 'Don't be stuffy with me.'

'I ask whoever I like,' I said. 'Ned likes me to have people in.'

When Ned returned that evening I told him, with the greatest authority I could muster, that I had invited guests for coffee the following week. He hardly listened. 'Do as you please.'

We had a silent meal. I thought that, despite his air of unconcern, my assertion of will had made him angry; and I did not care if it had, though I was still a little afraid of him. But it was not that. When I came back from washing the dishes he rose from his chair, kissed my cheek and said, 'Get your coat on. We'll go for a walk.'

The night was sharp and clear. Thousands of stars prickled the sky above the big field. Ned walked with his arm around my waist, as he had not done for a long while.

'Old girl,' he said at last, 'I'm afraid we're sunk.'

I was frightened. 'Oh, what has happened?' (Though I knew. But I had believed that a decline could go on indefinitely without reaching the nadir, as acceptable, as easy to bear – once it had become familiar – as a steady progress on the horizontal planes.)

'I've been hoping against hope,' said Ned. 'I didn't want to worry you before. Especially,' he added, with a bitterness that seemed somehow irrelevant and did not touch me, 'in view of your well-known faith in my capacities.' His face was sharp in the starlight. I saw his throat move. 'We can't go on.'

I asked him what would happen.

'I saw my father today. I hoped he'd give me a last chance and haul me out of the mess for the time being. God knows he's got the money. But not a bit of it. I heard his terms – with Harriet putting in any of the bits he might have left out – and I've had to accept them.'

We stood still in the middle of the rough field, the field where I had sat with my friends on those soft violet evenings so long ago (my father tipping his cap with a smile as he passed the forbidden circle of deck-chairs), and Ned put both his arms around me and held me to him so that I could not see his face.

He told me his father would take him back into the family business, not as a partner, but as an assistant to Finnigan. He would pay Ned a salary on which we could manage without changing our way of life, but there would be little over for luxuries. 'Pretty, isn't it? It's a punishment. It's not nice to be punished when you're in your thirties.' He added, in hatred, 'Damn them!'

When we are bound to a person there must be moments when we feel, however sparse love may be between us, the clutch of unity. We are one with them; we feel their injuries in our own flesh. Sheer rage on his behalf, which was rage for myself also, made me speak before I had had time to consider my words. 'Mr. Carker the Junior!'

Then I wished I had not spoken, quickly taming a leap of panic by reflecting that Ned would not know what I was talking about.

But he had read his Dickens. 'Thanks, it only wanted that.' Letting me go, he walked away from me. 'A help-meet,' he said, as I caught up with him. 'My God, you are the perfect help-meet!'

I held his arm in both my hands. He was so unhappy that I could not bear for him to suffer further through me. I begged him to believe that I had not been jeering, and as I did so felt a visceral stirring such as I once had known in the quarrels of love, when, in all hostility, there had been the hint of joy refreshed. There was no joy in this. Nevertheless, the body, inevitably out of date, persisted in remembering.

I begged him to believe that I had not been jeering. I had thought only of the cruelty of the firm of Dombey, forgiving the defalcations of the young clerk and taking him back again, but on the condition that he should never rise from his place; that he should sit upon the same humble stool until he was grey and old, the Junior, the butt of men above him who were young enough to be his grandsons.

'I didn't mean it unkindly,' I said. 'You must know I didn't. I'm so angry for you I could cry!'

But I knew I had done wrong again and that it was precisely these sillinesses of my youth that he found it so hard to forgive. I was moved by the memory of the night in the cinema, when I had stupidly tried to stir him to action by announcing my lack of faith; and at this moment I needed him to forgive me as I had needed him to forgive me then, but now because of his suffering, and not of mine.

I looked up into his face. He looked down at me, still bitter in his humiliation. I did not know what was about to happen to either of us. But then the bitterness faded. Weariness pacified him. 'All right,' he said, 'we'll get on. We'll manage somehow. Anyhow, we've got each other.'

5

Next day, while he was at his office winding up its last tattered affairs, I telephoned Mrs. Skelton asking her if I might come to see her. I did not wish her to tell Ned about it.

'I never tell him anything,' she said shortly, as if I should have known this long before.

'Will you be alone?'

'Nelly's up for the day. You sound mysterious.'

I told her I was not feeling at all mysterious, only miserable.

'It would probably be better to go to the pictures than come here, then. I'm never much good at cheering people up. And Nelly's had to have the dog put to sleep.'

I said I would be with them at three o'clock.

When I got there I found my mother-in-law stately and lazy as usual, a magazine in her lap, a glass by her side, and Nelly still blotched from weeping.

I told Nelly how sorry I was.

'Sorrow's no use. He's gone, and that's that. You can't keep them when they're suffering, I suppose.'

I replied formally that obviously one could not.

'But the damnable thing,' Nelly said, 'is that I'd have been happier if I'd still had him with me, even if he was in pain, even if he wanted to die. That shows you what people are.' She added, 'Or what I am.'

'You'll have another,' Mrs. Skelton consoled her.

'Oh yes. After a bit. I'll have another, and get as fond of it, and go through the same kind of hell. On and on.'

'Christine says she's miserable, too.' Mrs. Skelton smoothed her ghostly fair hair, turned her heavy gaze upon me. 'What a family we are!'

'I suppose Chris is feeling upset about Ned,' said Nelly. 'I thought she would be.'

This understatement gave me courage. Ignoring her, I turned to her mother: and I pleaded for Ned as I have pleaded for no one else in my life. It did not matter to me that she and I had never been on terms that were more than formal. I told her I knew she had enough money to help Ned once more, to let him try once again to make a success of his own life. He had been disappointed in his one romantic desire, the passion of the restless man for soldiering, which meant not only moving in the breadth of the world but the hope of controlling himself through the discipline of controlling other men. He was trying to settle down in the one thing left to him: he wanted to be (he did not, but I was too carried away by distress to be finicky about the truth) the son she had hoped to find in him. He was a good husband (as I spoke I did not doubt it), and in future I would help him, we would work together, together we would succeed. I finished, 'Don't make him a clerk. You can't!'

She looked at me unblinking for a few seconds. She was troubled. Her loose body tightened in a way that made her more formidable and more human.

'Oh, Chris,' she said. She passed me her cigarettes. 'Oh, my dear, I thought you wouldn't understand.'

'How would you feel, Nelly?' I cried.

'Bad. As bad as you do. But I think I'd see sense.' As she talked to me, she was, without knowing it, tapping the side of her leg as she had done so often when wanting the little dog to come to her, trot to her side, jump into her lap. She explained, against the background of her mother's silence, that I didn't know Ned as they did. He had done this sort of thing not once but, in various and more minor forms, many times. It would be idiotic to throw good money after bad. His business was beyond saving; his father was not doing too well and did not really want an addition to his own firm at all. Ned's position would not be defined; he would simply take some of the work from Finnegan's shoulders and make himself useful.

'If things do look up, which they ought to do if we get rid of Snowden,' Mrs. Skelton intervened, 'and Ned still hates working for the family, he could try and get himself a job with one of the big people. He's got the experience, and we shouldn't tie him down.'

I did not know what to say. It all sounded sensible enough when they put it like this. I still felt it was cruel.

Nelly said kindlily, 'We both think you've done him a power of good. When he's with you he's positively civilised. We like you, Chris, you know that. But we're not going to make fools of ourselves over our wandering boy.'

They refused to continue or to reopen this subject. I choked down my tea, said goodbye to Mrs. Skelton. 'We're not dragons, poor child,' she said; 'we're business people. We have to be.'

Nelly went to the street door with me. We walked in file down the narrow, dusty, rickety stairs. 'I'm sorry about your dog,' I said again.

'I should have had children. Then I wouldn't be making myself silly about animals. There's something repulsive about animal-women, I always think: they get a doggy smell. Probably I've got it. I suppose no one would care to tell me so.'

She patted my shoulders. 'Things will work out all right for you. You'll make them. You just prop him up and make him stay up.'

The twilight was sifting along the street, filling it with the promise of metropolitan night. A light drizzle had fallen, and the windows of the shops were reflected in their mandarin colours upon the roadway. There was a sweet smell in the air above the acrid smell of smoke and petrol fumes, a smell of limes or flowers or of the sea that sometimes seems to pervade a London evening. It took me back to my dreams of W.1; of the smart women in the little bars; the small, secretive restaurants glowing in the side streets; the music of a song of those days to which all the crowds had drifted in time, as they went upon their mysterious pleasure-seeking.

I said, out of a twist of anguish too great to bear in silence, 'I'll never forgive you, any of you!'

'Oh, you will one day, Chris,' Nelly said sadly, 'when it's all over.'

6

In the following days I had a sense of the calm that comes from pure exhaustion; the taking of my decision to plead with Mrs. Skelton and the acting upon it had worn me out.

Ned, also, was outwardly peaceable; in a way, we were living more easily together than we had done for weeks past. The friendliness that comes of sharing a common trouble still sustained us. Though we spoke little of it directly, we fell into the habit of applying to it some of our old, half-forgotten jokes, as if our best hope of minimising misfortune was to make it all seem a little ridiculous. Yet underneath the calm the stress persisted, like a muted ground bass. It was with us, however mildly we endured it, by day and night.

I had forgotten my invitation to Dicky and his new friend until the day they were expected, and by then it was too late to put them off. I reminded Ned of the visit, and apologised.

'Oh, let them come. I don't mind. It might take us out of ourselves.' He walked in his familiar perching way about the room, now and then stopping to peer at a book, a vase, a chair, as if he were one of those men (he was not) who like to criticise a wife's housekeeping and catch her out in some petty sluttishness. 'We'll go to bed,' he said; 'we've got a full hour.'

It was one of Ned's ominous habits to decide suddenly, at some inconvenient time, to make love; it usually meant a new worry. Worry may destroy for many people the idea of physical love. It was not so with Ned, for whom the latter was an unfailing anodyne.

Afterwards he seemed lively again, and it was not until our visitors were due to arrive that he said suddenly, on a bark of furious laughter, 'You can't get upsides with them, you know. You really can't. They defeat the imagination.'

'Who do?'

'My family. I saw the old man today. The latest is to tell me I can't use the car any more. Mother has decided she wants it herself at the week-ends.'

The bell rang.

'Here they are,' said Ned. 'Let 'em flow in in their hundreds.'

Dicky's girl was just the kind I imagined he would choose. She was at the same time slender and sturdy, her back rather long, her breasts small and high. She was quiet, pale-faced, dark-haired, and she wore glasses. Her best feature was a large, beautifully-shaped, somewhat derisive mouth. When she laughed, which she did often and silently, she showed teeth as white and fine as Dicky's own. She appeared to be shy – which was not unnatural, I felt, since, having once introduced her, Dicky behaved as if she were no responsibility of his; as if, perhaps, she had followed him through the door by accident. Luckily, her shyness gave Ned a desire to please. He was more amiable than I had seen him towards any acquaintance of my own, and the evening I had dreaded showed signs of becoming a pleasant one. Dicky's usual assumption of ease became a reality. After I had served coffee, Ned produced a bottle of gin.

'Only a little,' said the girl Baba, speaking for the first time of her own accord and not in response to the usual sociable questioning. 'I readily become disgusting.'

She said this with a quaint, vicarage air that made Ned laugh aloud.

I was pleased to see him so taken out of himself. Tonight he was as easy as he had been in carefree days, in the company of his own friends; and it comforted me to see him enjoying the company of mine. The veiled, amused look that had once attracted me had come to him again; he looked at the girl as if he were surveying her from a vantage point, through opera glasses, and I thought it would be fun to discuss her when the evening was over.

'Oh, but I do. Dicky will tell you.' Folding her hands in her grey silk lap, so that they were like virtuous hands in some Flemish painting, she flashed a tender, ironic smile in my direction.

Dicky smiled, shifted his feet, said nothing. It was as though, having brought her to us, he had retired completely, had made her over into our charge.

She watched abstractedly as Ned gave her the volume of drink he would have poured for himself. 'Oh dear, that's far too much!'

'I can always gauge a girl's requirements,' he said. His eyes met hers. She laughed. 'Well,' she murmured, 'on your head be it.'

I followed him out into the kitchen on a pretence of fetching more lime-juice. 'You'll make that poor girl drunk! What on earth are you doing?'

'My foot,' he said, 'don't tell me. I know that type.'

As I went by him, he caught my waist and kissed me.

But Baba would not permit her glass to be refilled. While Ned drank a good deal (growing rosier, his smile steadier) and Dicky far more than he was used to, she entertained us with quiet and funny little stories of life at the office. She had a demure wit and the gift of presenting a very clear picture of herself while speaking, ostensibly, only of others. Dicky gazed at her in lazy pleasure. He did not mean to talk much, for, though he would make a clown of himself within the limits of his own choosing, he did not really like to look a fool; and whenever he had been drinking, which was rare, took care that drink should not betray him. He had gone to sit in a chair by the window, a little apart from us. He seemed proud of his girl, proud that we – especially Ned – were entertained by her.

She thanked us at last for a delightful evening. She was no longer playing comedy; she was shy again, mouse-like, deferential.

'Will you get home all right?' Ned asked her. 'Do you live far?'

'I'll be seeing her home,' Dicky said with a fond smile. He rose rather cautiously, as if he had pins and needles or was testing the floor to see if it would bear him. 'The trouble is, whether I'll get a tram back afterwards.'

'Oh, they run awfully late,' the girl assured him. She was obviously unaccustomed to dissuading young men from their full duties as escorts.

She took my hand and held it. 'I do wish you'd both come over and see me one evening. Will you? I've got a little flat of my own – quite poky, but not all repulsive.'

'I suppose there's no one to sit up for you with cocoa as there was for me,' I said. 'I envy you.'

'Do you know,' she said, her eyes wide-open behind her glasses, 'I simply worship cocoa. Not many people do.'

Dicky began to hustle her into her coat. Despite his pride in her, he did not want to walk home by himself from the outer suburbs of London.

When they had gone Ned's spirits fell again. 'Oh Lord, I'm tired.' I asked him, with the triumph of a successful hostess, whether he did not think the evening had gone well.

His face lit with a reminiscent flicker. 'Not bad. But Baba may prove a bit much for poor old Dicky.'

These adjectives, belittling though they were, at least held a friendliness I had never yet heard him display in speaking of anyone whom I knew; somehow they made our future together seem a little brighter. I had struck this small blow for liberty; he had reconciled himself, even in this trifling way, to accepting my own likings. I believed we might come to terms with each other; be generous with each other, perhaps, through tolerance and tenderness; cease to take life so hardly.

It would be better if we took it as easily as possible, for I knew that in itself it would, for an unguessable period, be hard as stone.

7

We had spent so much anger and distress before-hand over Ned's return to the commercial roof of his father that when the time actually came for it it had not seemed so bad. He did not talk much about these new days at the office and I did not question him. One of the danger signals in any intimate relationship is a sudden inexplicable inability or disinclination to ask questions: happy lovers do not watch their words. Whether Ned realised the distance that had grown between us I do not know, for certainly it was masked by amity and a kind of outward ease; but I realised it myself and recognised every symptom of it. Yet life seemed to hang in suspension, like a cloud that will not discharge its weight of rain; and this suspension itself was a comfort to be clung to. I think I had no conscious frets at that time but the fret that money was so tight. It seemed impossible even to replace a cracked cup without debating the cost.

I heard nothing more of Dicky till he telephoned me one day early in May to tell me (among other things that seemed to him more interesting) that his affair with Baba was now a thing of the past. When I asked what had happened he replied, 'Oh, we just drifted. You know what I am.'

With this I had to be content. Anyway, it was hardly likely to stay long in my mind, for I had a fresh worry of my own and a grave one. I had been too anxious about Ned to notice the passing of the days, and did not realise what had happened till I was unwittingly awakened to it by Caroline.

She had called to see me one morning on her way to her mother's. I thought I had never seen her so jaunty, so smart, or looking more strained. 'I could do with coffee,' she said, answering my question, 'hot and strong and black.' She threw herself down on the sofa, head on a cushion, her legs dangling over the arm. 'Darling, doom has descended. I really must tell somebody, and you've had a line on the affair up to date.' Lighting a cigarette, she blew some steady, handsome rings. 'My dear husband,' she said, 'has received a grave blow to his self-esteem. I couldn't stand the "barren woman" charges morning, noon and night, so I took an outside chance and said I'd see a doctor if he would. "What rot," he says loftily. "*You* go. I'm damned if I will." Whereupon I say I'll only go if he does. Row, row, row, row. You can't imagine what it was like. In the end we both went – great strength of mind on my part, darling, you simply can't imagine.'

She heaved herself up from the sofa and put herself in a hard chair. 'Better for my posture, dear. And, anyway, I can't sit still for five minutes. Coffee first, and I'll tell you the wonderful result.'

She made me wait. In those days it was never easy for her to talk; but at last I learned what had happened. Caroline was perfectly able to conceive and to bear children; her husband was sterile.

At first he had refused to believe it. He had shouted at the doctor, had tried to impress him with accounts of his potency ('which nobody could deny,' Caroline put in wearily), had jeered in shock and bewilderment on hearing that this was often entirely irrelevant. He was going to get another opinion; he wasn't going to believe what the first medico tried to tell him. 'He was so rude, darling, and I was so ashamed. Because you know how I hate scenes of any sort.'

He had sought another opinion, and another one, both for Caroline and himself. The findings were the same.

'And now,' she said, 'there comes the maddest complication of all. He can't beget little ones, so he refuses to try. He absolutely refuses. Honestly, I think I'll go mad. We live just like brother and sister.' She turned her head away. 'Which is hard for me. As I told you, in my crude way, I was distinctly Pro.' She added, 'A sickening sort of joke, isn't it? Of course, it will stop him ticking off the lunar months, which is one good thing.'

It was at this moment that my own fear struck me, struck me with such force that for a minute or so I was unable to speak. I could not care for Caroline, who had exposed herself to me as she could have done to no one else; could not pity her for this new irony of life or for the stoicism that had set the jauntiness of middle-age upon a face still so childishly formed, a brow still bare and round as a baby's.

I managed at last to tell her how sorry I was. My words sounded stilted. Yet stiltedness of response was pleasing to Caroline, who could never endure compassion to be emotionally expressed.

'Oh, well,' she said. She stood up. 'So now you know. And now I have to go and see Mummy, and be bright and breezy and never breathe a word. Because to Mummy all this would be quite incomprehensible. She's so simple, poor lamb. She'd never understand.'

I went downstairs with her to the door. She looked across the common, green with the spring. Some children were playing on the railings, hanging upside-down, exposing ragged knickers and wishbone thighs. The ice-cream man, with his harlequin cart, was shouting his wares. A little solitary maybush on the edge of the big field had broken out all over in freckled and honey-scented flower.

'We did have good times, didn't we?' Caroline said wistfully. 'Do you remember our first high heels? We were so proud of them. Oh dear, here's my bus.'

When she had gone I stayed by the gate, looking at nothing at all, conscious only of the irrelevance of the steady sun upon my face. My calculations could be wrong – I had made even an adding machine go wrong, so I might easily be mistaken with mental arithmetic. But I knew I was not.

I waited for Ned to notice. He noticed nothing; he was insulated from interest in all about him by the feverish determination to work hard, to make his parents sorry they had misjudged him. So at last I had to tell him myself.

I timed it badly. I had been trying to amuse him by an account of Dicky's break with Baba, and how characteristically he had taken it. He had listened abstractedly, smiling politely now and then as if switching a light on and off. Without my volition the words came, rapid and fearful. He stared at me, the mosaics of his eyes drained of expression. Then he flushed, the colour plunging down in spearheads from his cheekbones to his throat.

He said, 'You've damned well done that, when you know how rotten things are!'

He believed I had deliberately cheated him: I could not convince him that I had not, that something had simply gone wrong. He threw up at me the times when I asked him to let us have children. Even in my despair I was astonished to learn how accurately he seemed to remember everything I had ever said to him.

'Don't lie to me,' said Ned. 'You used to lie like the devil, but I thought I'd broken you of it.'

'Do you think I'm happy about this?' I demanded.

'Of course you are. And you don't care who suffers.'

'We'll manage somehow.'

'Parrot-talk.' (It was his mother's phrase.) 'How?'

'People do.'

'How you could do this to me, I don't know! You're bone-selfish. You never give a damn for anyone but yourself.'

I wanted to speak to him, and I wanted him to listen. I knew a sickness of anger and disappointment and pride. When I spoke I wanted my voice to sound strange to him, so that it would enforce his attention. I waited. Ned was loping up and down the room with a stride which, I thought, began to falter a little as the silence went on.

'Well?' he said at last.

I said, 'You're making it seem like a bad dream. I'm expecting a child, and it's yours.'

'Who else's would it be?' He could not resist the automatic gibe.

I told him to be quiet, and I heard the strange voice, the voice that was not mine, the voice that silenced him.

'I'm expecting a child, which is a dreadful shock to me, knowing how you feel, and you're behaving like a brute.' He should be ashamed of himself, I said. How dared he say I had cheated him?

'Well, it seems damned queer.'

I asked him again how he had dared to call me a cheat, a liar, to accuse me of thinking of no one but myself. I asked him – and it did not sound like weakness – to remember how much younger I was than he; and to treat me with decent kindness.

He got up and went out of the room.

I picked up a magazine. I was not going to cry. I was going to read quietly till he came back again.

He did come back. He told me he was sorry for what he had said – he had not known what he was saying. We should, of course, manage somehow, as I had said; people did. Harriet would like a grandchild – it might soften her a bit. I was to go to the doctor, just to make quite sure, and take care of myself and put my feet up. He fell into a kind of stricken tenderness, smoothing me, patting me. Then he had an inspiration: he told me he had only spoken cruelly out of concern for me. If anything happened to me he could not bear it. That was the truth of the matter, if only I would see it: he was afraid I would die in childbirth. 'Because I love you, Chris; you've got to understand that.'

I was too tired to refuse his plea that we should stop quarrelling, to refuse to forgive him. I pretended to accept his story of a care that was only for me. After a while he grew lively, almost hilarious: we must drink to the baby. We should have to find a name for him. We nearly quarrelled again over the names suggested; the whole evening took upon itself a kind of anaesthetic unreality. We began to behave towards each other with a kind of sly amorousness, as if we had only recently met. The hours were very long, the hands of the clock lagged round the dial. I thought it would never be time for sleeping, to weep in the dark.

Next day, while Ned was at work, I went to see the doctor, who confirmed my pregnancy and arranged for me to pay him monthly visits.

I walked back across the Common from West Side in the hot morning sun. I realised that until now I had not, despite myself, really believed it could be true, and the sense of final captivity sprang upon me. Now I was trapped; from this there could be no way out. Ned and I would have to learn to live as happily as other people and content ourselves with watching our child grow up. I sat down for a while under the trees to wait till the moment of panic had passed, as I knew it must pass. The air was still. The white dust that overlay the hawthorn leaves was turned to dry and sparkling gold by the sun. The grass was dry as hay.

A woman went by, pushing her baby in a little wooden chair. It lolled over the strap, reared up again, gazed blankly and bluely up into the roof of the sky. And this was enough. Fatalistic, beyond tears, I walked on; I had known already the edge of that joy Ned had not let me feel when I had told him my news. I had wanted a child; I still passionately wanted one, and I thought how long the months were going to seem.

I called in upon Emilie and told the news to her. She seemed dumbfounded; it was as though she had imagined up to now that Ned and I had lived (in Caroline's phrase) 'as brother and sister'.

'But you're so young!' It was her old protest. 'Well, dear, I'm sure I don't know what to say. I can't really take it in.' She took my hand and patted it steadily. 'It's such a shock, really. There wasn't a hint of it, was there?'

Her first coherent idea was that she should do some knitting for the baby. She would go out and buy wool that very day – in fact, immediately. Indeed, she was so eager to escape to the shops for this purpose that she almost pushed me out of her flat. To Emilie adjustments came slowly, and she needed solitude in which to make them.

When I got home again it seemed unnaturally quiet and rather dark, though the sun was still blazing down. I did not know what to do with myself, was confused between a resurgence of the panic and a stronger resurgence of excitement. I tried to read, but could make sense of nothing. This, of course, would be the worst day. Tomorrow I should be steadier, more used to the idea of this enormous change that had come to me so suddenly.

I was having a sandwich lunch on the edge of the kitchen table – I could never be bothered to cook for myself in the middle of the day – when the bell rang.

On the step was a door-to-door salesman, with an attaché-case full of brushes, combs, hairpins, rolls of elastic.

'Good morning, madam! Can I be of any use to you today? I have a very fine line of . . .'

His voice trailed off.

We stared at each other.

He gave a backward stagger, and said, from his deepest chest-notes, 'My God! You!'

It was Leslie. He wore the same little bowler hat, or perhaps it was another bowler of the same pattern. His face looked longer, more foxy than ever before; his great, vacant eyes protruded. 'My God!'

It was not an easy moment.

'Well, how extraordinary,' I said. 'Won't you come in?'

The whole atmosphere of life had changed for me; this intrusion of the farcical made me light-headed.

He had recovered himself. He gave a harsh laugh. 'Come in? Into the hall, perhaps. No further. That's my place.'

He strode over the threshold, dumped the case on the hall table, and stood by it, bitter and brave.

'You see, I have come to this!'

'Oh, it's a job like any other,' I said. 'How are you?'

He ignored me. He had a wild look; he did not seem to be any less 'touched' with the passing of time. 'A job, yes. All a grateful country can find for a man who has done it, perhaps, no mean service. Oh, have you a cat?' His voice changed surprisingly into its natural tones, as he dived down under a chair. He had always been fond of animals.

'It's not ours. It comes from next door.'

'I see.' The cat eluded him and ran off through the open door. 'Puss, puss, puss!'

'What service did you do for your country?' I asked, giving way to curiosity – not for the truth, but for what his imagination could contrive.

I had to wait for an answer, for he had dropped his hat and had to retrieve and brush it down.

Then he looked at me, put a finger to his lips. 'Confidential matters. I'm not allowed to talk. Secret service, as a matter of fact,' he added light-heartedly.

I told him this sounded very exciting.

'It was, rather,' said Leslie, with an air of reminiscent satisfaction. 'Yes, not – er – unexciting. And, as a matter of fact, this lowly job I am doing now is not quite all it seems – but I can't tell you more about that.'

I asked him if he would not come further in and have some tea.

'No, little Christine,' he replied, putting unnecessary weight into his refusal. 'No. Your husband might object.'

'He's out,' I said, and at once felt I had been fast.

But such slips never impressed themselves upon Leslie. 'I heard you were married. I happened to run into Reginald during the Long Vacation last year.'

It took me a few seconds to realise that it was Take Plato to whom he had referred in this stately manner.

'But I did not know,' he continued, 'where you were living. I thought it best not to enquire.'

I asked him why he had thought it best.

'Let the past bury its dead,' said Leslie. He paused. 'Let the past bury its dead.'

I enquired about his mother.

His face clouded. 'Oh, Mater's her old self, you know. Still the *grande dame*. But as I can't tell her the truth about myself there's a certain misunderstanding between us. My father died last year.'

I said I was sorry. 'A superb musician,' Leslie said. 'We shall not see his like again.'

Awkwardly, I told him it was lucky he had called, because I did, in fact, need a clothes-brush.

'Do you think,' he replied, curling his lip with something of an effort, 'that I could behave as a huckster to *you*?'

I persuaded him that business was business.

'Oh, well,' said Leslie, forgetting his audience, 'here's a nice little line. Real hog's bristles. You'll see nothing like it anywhere for the money.'

I asked him how much it was. I saw his calculating glance flash over the hall, over what he could see of the dining-room, over my dress. 'To you, eight-and-six.'

'Far too much,' I said.

He assured me that I would nowhere find an article as fine as this going so cheaply. He was offering me cost-price because he knew I appreciated good things when I saw them. I offered him five shillings. He said I might have it for seven-and-six. Eventually I paid him six-and-six, which was sixpence more, as I knew, than a similar brush in the window of a shop on the Rise. This transaction concluded, Leslie reverted to his chest-notes.

'Tell me,' he said, as he shut the attache-case, 'are you happy?'

I said I was.

'Truly happy?'

'Certainly,' I replied in a loud and, I hoped, conclusive voice.

'You could never deceive me. I know you too well.' His hand was at the door. He seemed to ponder, his head hanging low, the bowler in place. 'So you are happy. Yes.' This seemed rather a foreign construction. I wondered if Leslie had by now persuaded himself that he was really a German count; he had always been fond of the U.F.A. films. 'You are happy. But life is queer, little Christine. I want you to know that if ever you need a shoulder to cry on – mine is here, waiting for you.' I thanked him. I was in haste for him to go lest he should see that I was not, in fact, far from tears. For a moment the past had weighed too heavily. He added, with little logic,' Goodbye, my dear. We may never meet again.'

I watched him as he ran down the stairs, the suitcase jolting in his hand. Poor Leslie, the first to love me, to give me confidence in myself; Leslie living in his dream-world, free to travel where he would on his Ruritanian passport; poor Leslie, fortunate Leslie, who would know poverty, worklessness and despair, but never know himself except as he most desired himself to be.

I closed the door and did not think of him afterwards.

8

In those days the neighbourhood bordering between Clapham and Battersea was like a village, with all the village intimacy and cross-cuttings of class. The small professional middle-classes living along North and West Sides shopped along the Rise and St. John's Road; sometimes, for the sake of cheapness and perhaps liveliness as well, they shopped along the stalls of Northcote Road, where bargains were to be found under the naphtha flares on Saturday nights. They drank coffee at Arding & Hobbs; the young ones who were in love walked around the specimen 'furnished rooms' of that shop, pretending to be in a home of their own. The young ones not yet in love, perhaps, and studious, worked in the cedar-smelling quiet of the Reference Library on Lavender Hill; the General Schools Certificate was always just around the corner. And whenever one went out, one met a friend.

On the Rise one day Mrs. Allbright came on me out of nowhere and said (not forbearing to glance at my waist), 'You never come to see us nowadays.'

It was a thundery day in August. I was tired. I did not want to be kept standing. I said I was sorry, but that I had been busy: a remark that sent a flicker of lubricious light – hardly a smile – across her face. 'Iris says it's hard to be deserted by all her best friends. You never come, any of you.'

Her sensitive nose moved at the tip. Despite the warmth of the day she had a pinched look, a blueness about the narrow nostrils.

I decided to be honest with her. I reminded her that only recently she herself had greeted Caroline, who had called on Iris unexpectedly one afternoon, with the announcement that her daughter would not be 'receiving' till four o'clock. 'Caroline was rather hurt,' I said.

'And why?' Mrs. Allbright bridled. 'She works later hours than the rest of you. Naturally she has to get her rest during the day.' She paused. 'Of course, she'd be at home to *you*. Her oldest friend.'

I said I would try to look in.

'I expect *she* feels,' said Mrs. Allbright, 'rather hurt that her oldest friend withholds her confidence. She only heard in the most roundabout fashion that you were expecting.'

'I never kept it secret. But I haven't been going about much.'

'Due about Christmas,' Mrs. Allbright persisted. She knew everything. She added, in a burst of bitterness, 'To think she's still left on the shelf, with the rest of you married and settled down!'

I wanted to go. My legs were aching and the coming thunder was like a weight on my head. But I said,' I thought you didn't want her to marry early in case it spoiled her career.'

'Not any Tom, Dick and Harry. But there's a stage-door Johnny after her now, and I tell her she's a fool to play fast and loose with him.' She gave me an account of him, half reverent, half ironic. He was rich, not too young, a diamond merchant of Portuguese extraction, who waited for Iris to leave the theatre night after night, who smothered her in flowers and delightful, not too expensive little gifts that it would have seemed priggish to return.

'Suppose,' said Mrs. Allbright, facing the worst, 'that her career does not turn out as we hoped?' Her voice sharpened: it was an effort for her to express her long fear in words. 'In that case she would have something behind her. Thousands,' she added, in case I should not realise what this something was. 'But of course, she's Miss Hoity-Toity, Miss Pick-and-Choose. I say to her, "Christine didn't pick and choose. She took what she was offered, like a sensible girl." '

'I did choose Ned,' I told her, young enough to be 'drawn'.

She gave a wide peculiar smile, but made no comment.

A common acquaintance, stepping almost upon us out of a shop, saw her and quickly crossed the street. Dicky had once said it was always possible to know when Mrs. Allbright was coming, from the preliminary going to earth of the neighbours.

'Iris,' she went on, 'is rapidly coming to the crossroads. She has made her first film. If she succeeds – well, who knows? There may be no need for Jaime.'

She pronounced this name so accurately and with such *empressement* that I had to ask her to spell it.

'Only a small part,' said Mrs. Allbright, 'but a little "plum". It will be released next month. She has to sing an old English ballad.'

Now she had given me her news she was willing to let me go. But I had not moved five yards away from her when she caught up with me, her eyelids flickering, her nose pointed. 'You come and see the girl and put some sense into her head! She's always relied on your opinion. She worships you. You tell her a bird in the hand may be worth two in the bush.'

But I did not call upon Iris: all that seemed dead and gone, as faded as her pierrot doll and as grimy.

When Ned and I saw her film we realised what a short distance, in fact, her career was likely to take her. The extreme small delicacy of her features seemed insipid, with no colouring to emphasise it. Her recorded voice had a trace of the genteel that I had never noticed when talking to her; and yet, perhaps, it is only the blind who truly hear a friend's voice, since they are unable to associate it with the smile, the charming mouselike flicker of a facial muscle, the darkening or lightening of the eyes. Her small part had obviously been made smaller in the cutting-room; her song had been cut out altogether.

Yet it seemed to me, that night, wonderful that she should appear on the screen at all, wonderful that there should be millions of people to see her and perhaps ask her name. I found myself looking at Ned with a touch of jealousy renewed. We had been more or less content together of late, for there is a moment, not infrequent, even in the most unhappy of marriages, when everything seems well enough, when even the sharing of ordinary domestic exchanges brings something like a touch of sweetness. Sometimes a common sense of failure is enough to give the illusion of a unity of success. And in my own marriage, ill-adjusted, wrong from the beginning, these things were true also. Sometimes Ned and I were near to each other in the thought of the child.

For all that, he seemed not so much in love with me. His endearments were more brisk, more formal. He touched me less. He expressed an interest in the baby, what its sex would be, which of us it would take after; but he looked at me without ardour.

I was not yet very big and I thought pregnancy had not made me plain. Nevertheless, I found myself envying girls who could be pretty, that hot summer, in their ordinary dresses; and found myself wishing that even Ned would reassure me, would tell me I was still as pretty as they, as pretty as I had ever been.

As we left the cinema we walked towards Piccadilly Circus. Coloured letters ran along the sky. A golden bottle lavishly decanted stars into a golden cup. Over the rooftops the sky burned with the permanent rust-red sunset of London. I felt very heavy and tired, but I tried to walk lightly; I was determined not to adopt the occupational waddle of many women in my state. In fact, I cared for my looks as I had never cared for them before; even in the days of gramophones and dancing and the hopeless struggle to compete with Iris on the romantic Sunday afternoons of adolescence. I wanted Ned still to admire me, not to feel I was uninteresting and a drag; for though I was no longer in love I felt a selfish need for him. Only he was left to me, and I could not bear to feel alone. Without him, I should have nobody at all.

9

Ned stopped me suddenly. 'We'll give ourselves a little treat,' he said. 'Why not? I think we deserve it.'

He took me without warning into one of the cocktail bars that had once so delighted me, had made me feel that I, too, was a part of W.1. But tonight, though I tried not to show it, I went there reluctantly. In my anxiety for the child I would not touch alcohol at all, and among the slender women I felt shapeless, somehow disgraced. Never had my life (that handful of days, so easily expended) seemed to me less profitable. However, we sat there in the rosy gloom, our faces flatteringly reflected in the pink-tinted glass along the walls, and I drank lime-juice.

'Oh, go on,' said Ned, 'you need something stronger to cheer you up.'

'I am exceedingly cheerful,' I said, on the edge of tears.

I heard him mutter to himself. Then he gave a sudden, strange, bright smile. 'I expect all girls feel like that; they all have their moods when they're in your condition.'

'I expect they do.'

'When it's over you'll be quite all right again.'

'I'm sure I shall.'

He listened to the music coming from the restaurant upstairs. 'There! You say I'm tone-deaf, but I bet that's the thing we used to hear at Richmond, day in, day out.'

'No, it's not,' I said.

'It sounds like it to me.'

'Well, it's not.'

A silence fell; we might have been quarrelling.

Then he patted my knee in a kindly fashion, put his hand on mine. 'I'm proud of you, you know. It's just that I can't realise it.'

'Are you proud?' I could not help asking. I wanted him to desire me, and was frightened that he should see this in my face, for it made me ashamed.

'Of course I am,' he said pacifically, patting my knee, 'I've just said so. I'll spell it if you like.'

'Yes,' I began, 'but—'

'But what?' he prompted me. He looked pleased.

But this I could not tell him. For some reason, perhaps because he was afraid of harming the child whom he now appeared to want, he would not touch me. For weeks he had not come near me. And I was strained with desire. It was not the desire of love; it was a harsh bodily need, that made me contemptuous of myself and also, curiously, of him – an anticipatory contempt, as if I had asked him for satisfaction as some hot and needy woman might ask a stranger, and he had, as to a stranger, derisively given it. I might have been driven to hint at something of this need had I believed I could still attract him; but I felt the resentment of the woman who, carrying a lover's child and for his sake losing her looks, realises that this is the last sacrifice he can possibly be expected to thank her for.

'I don't know what I was going to say.' I smiled at him because, at this moment, he was happy and I could not hurt him.

'Funny girl,' he said, not at all curious.

'Do you remember us coming here once before?'

I remembered it well enough: on that evening we had fallen from pleasure in each other's company into an anger which now seemed to me inexplicable. We had made up the quarrel, but it was marked out for me as being the first quarrel to leave a sad, stale aftertaste in the mouth.

'You had a hat I didn't like. A red one. Garish,' he added, with one of his lofty looks, as if he were the arbiter of all taste. Then he took my hand. 'But you looked pretty, even if a trifle ridiculous.'

'You told me so,' I said, suddenly recalling the trivial cause of a misery that had been quite new, quite bewildering 'It was tactless of you.'

'My dear girl,' said Ned with something of his old, imperious jauntiness, 'when you get to know me better, which may still take some years, you will realise that I am only tactless *on purpose*. I have no patience with people who don't work out their tactlessness beforehand.'

This, he thought, contained a truth of some weight, and perhaps it did; but the only words to hold my attention were '*some years*'. Years and years, I thought, and I am so tired. Yet I said, to quieten the last of a jealousy that had now no relevance, 'Did you think Iris looked pretty?'

'So-so. Nothing special.'

I suggested he had thought her special that night when she had made him give her the carnation.

'No, I didn't. I never liked her much. But then, that evening, I wasn't much liking you.'

Our next news of Iris came at the beginning of December. There was an announcement in *The Times* that she had been married in Paris to Jaime Silvera de Castro, of Brazil.

I telephoned Caroline to ask if she had seen it, but she had not. She had no news.

'Oh well,' I said, 'we shall have to wait.' For I did not think Mrs. Allbright would remain umbrageously uncommunicative for very long, and so it turned out. One morning she called upon me. She was wearing new furs and a great deal of make-up; her manner, too, was different. She swayed towards the sofa as if she were unaccustomed to walking at all, being brought from point to point, perhaps in a sedan chair; and when she sat down it was with something of the deliquescent grace of a candle in hot weather.

'My dear Christine, you must forgive us both for our secrecy. You must be generous. But it was all so sudden and we were in such a whirl. . . . 'She gave me a quick look to see whether I believed it.

'Iris,' she said, 'has sacrificed her career.'

'I'm sorry to hear that,' I replied, to help her on.

'Sacrificed it, just as it was coming to fruition. Just as C. B. Cochran was showing an interest in her.'

Mrs. Allbright closed her eyes and let her mouth tighten for a moment in pain and regret. She opened them again. Leaning forward, she put her hand earnestly upon my arm. 'But never mind. Jaime is such a dear, even if he is rather old-fashioned – he can't bear the thought of his wife performing in public – that Iris makes the sacrifice *willingly*.' She added, in quite a different tone, 'Now she can go and ruin her figure with babies, for all I care. She was always dog-lazy.'

Drawing out a little gilt case, she opened it to display pastel-coloured cigarettes, blue, pink and green, tipped with gold.

'She is going out with Jaime next month. They will settle in Buenos Aires, where his work is. I only hope,' said Mrs. Allbright, weary again, 'that riches won't spoil my little girl. All I ever asked her to be was *natural*.' She paused. 'May I tell her you wish her every good fortune?'

'Of course,' I said, and knew a pang of envy. Ned and I were not rich. I should never be able to go even to Paris now, let alone to the Americas. I thought: She will go and see nothing at all, it will be wasted on her. What I could have done with it! What I could have seen! 'I'll write to her,' I added. 'Will you give me her address in Paris?'

Mrs. Allbright wrote it down for me. 'I shall join them eventually, when Iris has her own home. I shall be a poor relation, shan't I? Though Jaime has been very generous. He has helped me already.' She glanced at her furs. 'I have to *force* him not to give me things.'

When she rose to go she held me apart for a second and studied me. 'You must be near your time.'

I confirmed this.

'How exciting it will be for you! Well, Christine, you may turn out to have had all the luck after all.'

I asked her how this could possibly be.

She said, in a curious, thick voice, 'It's not as if you'd had a career to give up. *She* could have got on. She knew I wanted it. I could have seen her name in lights.' Her eyes were magnified by tears, the great, rainy tears that Iris wept so easily; but these were tears of anger and disappointment. She burst out, 'But she was up against me, always. Whatever I wanted she did the opposite. After all my dreams for her, she marries a greasy man old enough to be her father, or nearly – you married one a good deal older than you were, but then, you hadn't anything to lose.'

She looked old and sick. She shut her eyes tight while the tears squeezed themselves like seed pearls between the lids.

'It's just that you're upset, losing her so suddenly,' I suggested.

'Yes, that's it. That's all it is. I'll get over it.' She pulled out a heavily scented handkerchief and dried her face. 'Mothers are so selfish!' she cried, as if repeating in scorn words that had been flung at her – and she went away.

December was a month for news. Within a few days of this visit Caroline rang me up to tell me her husband had left her. 'He's got another woman,' she said, in her edged way, 'who doesn't know his dread secret. So he can be easy with her as he can't be with me: do you see he point? He's left me the flat and all that dwells therein.'

I said I supposed she would divorce him.

'Such complications, dear, you simply don't know. I could, I suppose. But he wouldn't like it. You see, he's a Catholic.'

I was amazed by this. She had never even hinted at such a thing.

'Oh, we kept it quiet, because my people hated it and his were furious, and we had one of these awkward mixed marriages where I had to promise to bring the children up R.C. – very funny, that, when you come to think of it.' She hesitated. Then she said, 'That's why we never asked anyone. I expect everyone was huffy. I bet you were, really. But then, my marriage was shrouded in gloom, in any case, so I suppose no one really noticed.'

'Why did you never tell me?' I asked.

'You know how hard I used to find it, telling things. I've been somewhat cured of that by events. Now I positively babble.'

I asked her if I should come and see her.

'You're my co-mate,' said Caroline, 'and if I wanted anyone it would be you. But at present I just feel like sitting very quiet with the blinds down. Wait till I'm better company, and I'll ring you.'

10

It was the middle of the night, warm in bed, cold without, frost ticklish as snuff in the room. My watch had phosphorescent hands. I had timed the intervals: twenty minutes – then fifteen – now ten. Not indigestion.

'Ned.'

A heave in the trough of sheets.

'What is it?'

'I hate to wake you – I wouldn't if I could help it.'

'Well, then, don't.'

'I think it's beginning.'

'What is?' Another heave: then the light flashing up, showing us to each other. 'Oh, my God!' He was out of bed in a bound. 'I'll fetch Emilie.'

'Don't be silly. Just ring the doctor!'

'But Emilie ought to be here.'

'I tell you I don't want Emilie.'

'Oh God! The doctor – what's his number?'

Ned blundering across the room and out to the telephone, one pyjama-leg rucked above his knee.

He came back. 'He says you'd better get to hospital. I'll ring them up.'

He did so: returned again. 'How do you feel?'

'I am quite all right,' I said, feeling set apart, calm, enthroned upon the edge of this adventure. 'I should like a cup of tea while I dress.'

Everything was packed: the list of necessities had reached me months ago.

I tried to smoke, but that made me sick. Ned was white and solemn. We sat side by side on the bed, our arms around each other's shoulders. We did not talk much.

'There it goes again.'

'There what goes?' Ned said, jumping.

'The pain.'

'Oh God!'

'It's nothing. It's hardly anything yet.' I relished the thought of the pain to come. It would be exciting. There had been so little excitement lately, not for me. For Iris, and for Caroline, if you called it excitement. Not for me.

'I'll put on the fire,' Ned said. 'It's as cold as the grave in here.'

'It's funny,' I said, 'but if you look at that box on the cupboard from this angle it's exactly like a head in a top hat.'

'Very funny.'

'You do see it?'

'Yes, yes, I see it all right. Have some more tea.'

'We've done nothing about Christmas,' I said.

'We don't have to hang paper-chains.'

'You'll be all right at Maddox Street.' We had arranged that if the child came before Christmas Ned should go to his family.

We waited. The time seemed very long. Then the door bell rang and for a little while there was activity. Ned came with me to the hospital and was almost at once dismissed and told to telephone. I was examined by the doctor; a little fat nurse came to carry out the humiliating preparations for childbirth. Then I was given more tea and told to ring if I wanted anything. I had a small room to myself, the walls painted a smooth and shining grey. There was a chair, a locker, and against the far wall a white cupboard with a touch of

Heppelwhite grace about it that bore the words 'Eclamptic Equipment'. In the ceiling a white light burned brightly and sometimes swung in a high draught, throwing over the walls a reflection like a tolling bell. It had been cold in the ambulance, or perhaps I had been afraid without knowing it. Here I did not feel lonely: I still felt enthroned, apart, dedicated. All the same, I badly needed something to read, so I rang the bell.

This time another nurse came in, an Irishwoman with coppery face and hair, and a look of constantly expecting some wonderful surprise.

'You gave me a fright you did!' she said, when I told her what I wanted. 'I tore along like mad, thinking you'd hurried yourself up.' I understood that she was scolding me; but nevertheless she went and fetched me an old magazine, with a girl in a bathing-dress upon the cover.

Beyond the frosted window the darkness had thinned away. There was an upper pane of clear glass, and soon I could see beyond it a single fraying cloud, streaked like a daisy with pink. I began to wonder if Ned would come soon to see how I was getting on, for I felt it would be a comfort to talk to somebody. I tried to think about him, about our life together; and as I lay in the growing dawn, in that quiet waiting-room of birth, it seemed to me that ours was a very ordinary life, perhaps no more unhappy, no more happy, than the lives of most married people. It struck me now as remarkable that few women seemed to speak with any excitement about their husbands. Marriage was perhaps unexciting in its essence; probably everyone but myself had known that already. I tried to take comfort from this thought, but a shadow of depression lay about it, and I turned over on my side to read the only part of the magazine I had not already read, which was the advertisement page.

The Irish nurse came in to ask me how I was getting on, and if I wanted anything.

I told her I was all right. I should have liked her to stay and talk to me, but she seemed very busy. When she had gone, I thought how odd it was that nobody should seem much interested in me or my baby; yet why should they have been? Birth, of course, was as common here as butter in a grocer's shop. All the same, I felt a sudden wish to cry a little because time was so long.

I think I must have slept for a little while. At last I grew aware (having consulted my watch) that I could reasonably ring the bell again. 'It's every *four* minutes,' I said.

It was better now. I had something to occupy me, something in which I could participate. They let me walk about the room. Between the pains I was perfectly calm; indeed, for three and a half minutes out of the four pain was unthinkable. I did not know how anyone could possibly have felt it. But in a while I knew the first touch of panic; for the pain I was now experiencing was not easy to bear, and I felt, indeed, that if it got any worse I should be hard put to endure it.

The nurse who had brought me the magazine studied my face thoughtfully. 'I think we'd better get you along to the labour ward.'

They put me on a trolley, and I set out on a strange, dizzying, half-hilarious progress (Macheath to the gallows, I thought), down corridors of light and dark green, into a room all white and silver. 'That's the girl!' one of the nurses called to me. She had the jolly, rather uneasy smile of somebody playing a practical joke. 'One, two, and oops we go! Doctor will be here in a minute.'

When he came the Irish nurse told him that I was having good pains. I thought it a strange adjective.

After that there was hustle and attentiveness; they touched me when I dreaded to be touched, rallied me, applauded me, told me I was doing well. I thought: Tomorrow must come. Before I know where I am it will all be over, and I shall say to myself, 'Why, it happened the day before yesterday.' Time has to pass.

I found myself panting, a harsh and ugly noise. 'Degrading,' I managed to say.

I heard the doctor laugh. He told me to go on panting: that it was good for me.

'Like a steam-engine,' I said, proud that my voice sounded so normal. Then I was engulfed by an agony so extreme to my experience that it felt like some preposterous insult.

'That's right, that's right,' said the doctor. 'You're doing fine.'

In front of my eyes was the lightning-edged scarlet of pain, which is like the colour that lodges under the lids when one tries to sleep in the sun. I did not think of the child, only of pain, only of myself, only of being brave or not brave. I had a fear of being torn in two. 'But don't worry,' said the cold critic, still present within me and unassailable, 'nobody ever is torn in two.'

'I think,' said the doctor, 'that we shall now put you to sleep.'

Another man was standing at my bed. I could see the edge of his white coat.

'Thank you,' I said, as if I had been offered theatre tickets; 'that will be nice.' I added, in a gabble, 'Just wait till this pain passes—'

'We'll make it pass. You've been very good. Now you shall go to sleep.'

The beautiful anaesthetic was like the fall of velvet over the photographer's camera. I was the camera under the velvet, observing with the dark behind me. I saw a green mountain and a river with a water-snake of blue glass, swimming with kingly grace towards me. Then, almost at once, 'Well, there you are, you can wake up; you've got a nice little boy.'

'Have I?' I said. 'Oh, good.'

I saw him held up above the basin, a struggling puppet of vermilion satin, all mouth; his roars split the room. He was wrapped in a blanket and given to me, his small face tight and sulky as if he had been turned out of heaven during a party.

Well, I thought, well.

I kissed him; he did not seem to belong to me. I touched his little hand and loved him, whoever he belonged to. Then I felt I could kiss the doctor, the anaesthetist, the midwife nurse; I was full of triumph.

'Thank you,' I said. 'Thank you very much, doctor, nurse.' I was glad I was in a fit state to be courteous. I was proud of such courtesy.

But the doctor was not there, nor was the anaesthetist. 'Gone to get their breakfast,' said the nurse. I felt it a little callous of them to hurry off so thoughtlessly to their meal. I had a sense of anti-climax.

The baby had disappeared; I could not remember it being taken from me.

I was back in my room. The sun shone brightly through the clear glass and filled the frosted panes with stars of fawn and gold. They brought me some tea and I drank a little.

I thought of Ned, and was suddenly tormented by the idea that all this time, all these hours, he must have been worrying himself sick, that he still did not know it was over and that we had a son.

I called out, as loudly as I could, since there seemed to be no one about, 'Will somebody tell my husband?'

A face popped up from the floor. A wardmaid looked at me, a humble little girl in a pink dress. 'I'll go and ask nurse, if you like.'

Nurse appeared from nowhere. 'Your husband knows all about it, Mrs. Skelton. I've been on the phone to him. He's like a dog with two tails, and as soon as you've had a sleep he shall come and see you.'

Then it was night again, or perhaps evening. I had had something to eat. I had powdered my face, combed my hair. My body felt strangely soft and flat and light. From the kitchen along the corridor came the rattle of china and cutlery, the pervasive and repulsive smell of cauliflower cheese.

Ned came in suddenly, on tiptoe, looking scared. He was not at all like a dog with two tails, and I was surprised at the nurse's invention.

'Thank God.' He kissed me quickly, as if he were shy. 'Was it awful?'

I told him it had not been too bad and that I should not dread doing it again.

He shuddered. 'Not on your life.'

I said that if he would ring the bell for me I would ask them to fetch the baby.

'Not for a moment.' He held my hands tightly. 'Oh, Chris, it was so awful. If you knew what I'd been feeling.'

I made a commonplace, tinny little joke about men suffering at childbirth.

'I was afraid you'd die. I did get Emilie up. I couldn't be alone.'

'Of course I wasn't going to die!' I quoted the maternal mortality rate. He damned it.

'It's very low,' I said.

He sat stroking my hair.

He found nothing to say except that he was pleased the baby was a boy.

When they brought it, still sullen in sleep, a spire of fair hair sticking up from the blanket, minuscule hands knotted beneath its chin, he barely seemed to look at it.

'Very fine. Very nice. He looks like you.'

Ned could hardly wait until the nurse had taken the child away and we were alone again.

Then he told me he loved me and that I must always love him. We had had a bad start, but now we must manage our affairs better, have better times, go for a holiday.

Out of my first disappointment, that he seemed unable to share my love for this little, mysterious boy sleeping out his first day away from me, came an obscure pleasure that the child was my own, entirely mine. As Ned looked at me with something of Dicky's sheepishness, half-wanting to go and half to stay, I felt a fondness for him that appeared to me deeper than the love I had lost. There was no noise now from the kitchen; only the refrigerator gave out, at intervals, its lurch and grind. In the still light, the ethereal quietness, I took comfort from him and was very glad to hold his hand.

II

The first sleep of a child after birth, like the sleep of a traveller at the end of a long journey, is solemn, unlined and deep. During it the child lies between his unguessable past and his equally unguessable future; the blanketing of both is about him. But when, refreshed, he floats free of that dark, warm memory, until nothing is left of it except the position in which he now lies, tortoise-wrinkled hands clasped beneath his chin, his knees drawn up to those hands, his eyes regard only the future. Then, every day, he shows new evidence of his budding; perhaps only in the flash of a new colour across the eye, in a little grumble almost too faint to hear, in the sudden stretching out of fingers that must learn to *touch* but do not yet know where touchable things are to be located.

I found so great a fascination in watching the manifold changes of Mark, as we called our baby, that I could watch him untiringly without thought of time. I tried to make Ned see how infinite, in fact, was the variety of each new day – but he could not. 'I'll like him when he's old enough to talk and stagger around a bit. At the moment he's just a blob.'

It was meant to be funny; and it chilled me. I wanted him to share this new experience, this curious research; wanted him to check my findings, assure me that they were not imaginary, that not only every day but every hour this progress towards sentience continued. But he could not. After his self-imposed abstinence he longed for me again. He was impatient until the baby was bathed, fed, and put back into his basket. He wanted to be alone with me, to feel alone with me, as if we had never had a child at all. And he was eager for me to be well enough to receive him again.

The nurse, who was staying with me for the first month after my return, infuriated him. She was a great, moustached, cleanly chatter-box, excellent at her job, and given to open condemnation of all men and their ways.

'I shall be damned glad when she's gone,' he said to me, as we watched her from the window wheeling the baby out into the front garden. 'My God, how pleased I'll be to see the back of her!'

'I won't,' I replied. I still felt weak and dreaded the moment when I must take full responsibility for the child.

He looked at me oddly. 'Shall I tell you why you won't?'

I said it must be quite obvious.

'Oh no,' said Ned. His face was flushed. 'It wouldn't be obvious to most people. It is to me.'

What he said then astonished and bewildered me. However well we may think we know another person, we can never tell what bizarre resentments they may hide within them, how curious may be the whiplash of the inner tongue that speaks to them as our own inner tongue speaks to us. We do not know what may be driving them to destruction, until the inner tongue sounds suddenly through their lips, betraying them beyond forgiveness, and altering the entire shape of our belief in them. Ned told me he knew perfectly well why I would not let him make love to me again. It was, he said, because the nurse hated the thought of sex, despised it, revolted from it. In my usual hypersensitive way – hypersensitive to everyone's feelings but his own – I would not let him come near me while she was still in the house. He knew all this, because he had seen the look in my eyes.

'It's not five weeks,' I said. I did not know how else to defend myself against this farrago, so preposterous that it made him seem a stranger, someone to be feared.

'That's not all of it,' said Ned, 'and you're perfectly well aware of it.'

The baby began to cry.

'Leave him alone. He's only yelling to attract attention. You listen to me.'

I walked past him into the little nursery and shut the door.

'All right,' he called out to me. I heard him go to the telephone and dial a number. He spoke briefly to somebody, but I did not hear what he said. I only heard him laugh.

He did not refer again to what had happened between us until after our evening meal, when the nurse had gone off to do some washing for the baby. 'If you've no use for me I'm not going to be tied to the house. I'm going out, and I may be late. Don't wait up for me.'

I did not question him; I supposed he was going drinking with Harris or another of his friends. But he did not return at all that night. I kept waking hourly to turn on the light, look at the clock. When the nurse brought the baby to me at six o'clock she said sharply, 'All on your lonesome?'

I told her my husband was away for the night on business.

'Oh, is he? Well, we're always better off without *them*. What with their ins and outs, and their bad tempers. I envy you that dear little baby, Mrs. Skelton, but not when I think what you had to go through for it.'

'I had an easy time, really,' I said, thinking she was referring to my confinement.

'I didn't mean that,' the nurse said, with a kind of lubricious grimness, 'I meant something else.'

She watched me feeding the baby.

'I don't give up easy, Mrs. Skelton, but you'd better ask doctor what he thinks about the bottle. Our little Packet's not gaining as he ought, and in my view that's because you're a worrier. Not that you haven't enough to worry you.'

The baby fell away from the breast and began to cry; the nurse and I between us had one of those curiously undignified and slightly brutal struggles to make him take it again. She seized the top of his nut-like head and appeared to screw it on to the nipple, as if she were screwing the top on to a bottle. 'And the state you're in tonight! What good do you think that's doing him? You've got to be quiet to feed them, quiet as a cabbage. Which you're not.'

We all struggled on for the best part of an hour. At the end of it I was utterly exhausted and my head was aching.

The nurse bore the baby off for a test-weighing, bore the bad news triumphantly back. 'Two ounces, that's all he's had! I'm going to give him a supplementary feed, poor mite; I won't have my Packet starve.'

I thought, as I fell asleep, how strange it was not to care about anybody; not for Mark, not for Ned.

But I woke to an immediate sense of wrongness. I remembered the lonely night, Ned's disappearance, the nerve-racked struggle with the baby. My headache was still acute.

'You look a wreck this morning,' the nurse said, bringing me tea. 'How fit will you be when I leave you at the end of next week? You want a regular nanny, that's what you want.'

I told her I could not afford this. 'Maybe you can't, but it's what you want.' She added abruptly, 'You stop in bed this morning.'

For she was kind; she had guessed that I did not know where Ned was, that I was worried about him. She tried to comfort me by such cossetting as she could achieve.

I lay in the quiet bedroom, watching the orange sun of winter measuring out the corners. A saffron fog hung about the sky, no more than a gauze. It was a hushed, enclosing day, a day of suspended time. I tried to write a poem; it was the first time I had written anything for over a year. There were six verses, irregular in metre. They seemed good to me when I had first completed them. Half an hour later I read them and found them lame, stale, obscurely shameful. Yet I could not bear to destroy them; I put the sheet of paper away in the empty cigarette-box that stood on the bedside table, the box I had always meant, in the first days of my marriage, to keep filled for its proper purpose, but which was now a receptacle for an odd collar-stud, a hair-grip, a laundry receipt.

The nurse was out, doing some shopping for me.

I telephoned Ned at the office.

'Where have you been?' I burst out.

There was a pause. 'Nowhere interesting.'

'You must tell me! I've been so worried.'

'No need. I can look after myself. I told you I'd be late. I simply couldn't get back.'

'Where did you spend the night?'

'Nowhere of interest.' His voice was stubborn and level, the kind of voice that seems to be steadied by a ruler.

I told him angrily that he had no right to leave me like that; I had been upset and frightened. How would he feel if I behaved like this to him?

'That's different.'

'Why is it different?'

'I can't talk now. We're busy. See you at the usual time.'

When he came in we could not talk, for the nurse was everywhere.

At the meal he was quiet and courteous, even putting himself out to please a little.

I could not eat.

'If you don't do better than that, Mrs. Skelton,' the nurse said, 'you won't be able to do our Packet much good. The trouble with your wife' – she turned purposefully to Ned – 'she's a worrier. And people who want to be kind to her ought to see she's got nothing to worry *about*. That's what they ought to do.'

In the bedroom afterwards I rounded on him.

'You must see I've a right to know!'

The nurse was lustily singing *Jerusalem* in the kitchen.

'I'm not going to tell you,' Ned said. 'You'll have to trust me.'

And he refused to say another word.

In the obstinate silences, the cold politenesses, the parody of normal domestic behaviour that filled the next few days, I was torn between two emotions. Oddly enough I was stirred by some recrudescence of my early romantic feeling for Ned into faintly admiring him for his refusal to speak. Perhaps, after all, he was proving as 'strong' as I had hoped he would be. But a more realistic sense told me that his obstinacy was stupid and cruel: that whatever the truth of his disappearance and however unpalatable he thought I might find it, a kindly man would have taken trouble to find a comforting lie for me.

As the weeks went on I brooded over it all less and less; sometimes I only thought of it once or twice in a day, for the baby was now in my sole care and all my love was turned towards him. Sometimes I would be taken by a rush of irrelevant jealousy – irrelevant, because it was the kind of jealousy we usually know only when we are in love, and I was out of love, living deliberately from day to day, allowing myself no hope in anything but the capacity of life to change itself utterly at any time through one of its incalculable miracles.

12

I think I might have filed Ned's disappearance away into the small drawer of my mind reserved for insoluble mysteries if I had not had an odd encounter with Nelly Ormerod.

Emilie was looking after the baby for the day so that I might go shopping in the West End. Though I had little enough to shop with, the idea of the change was stimulating, and the idea of putting on my best dress.

It was April; a sticky spring day, unnaturally warm for the time of year, a day of brief showers and hot sun. Oxford Street was full of the reek and steam of mackintoshes. I was looking at the jewellery counter of a big shop when I caught sight of Nelly. She was examining watch-straps with a troubled air, fitting one after another upon her thick wrist, shooting back the cuffs of her tweed suit each time she did so. She stood with her legs widely planted, a pale-blue, unsuitable town hat well to the back of her head. I ran and caught her by the arm.

'Oh, hullo!' She stared at me. 'Fancy seeing you.' She coloured. 'How is everybody?'

I asked her if she was in London for the day, whether she would come and have tea with me. 'Well, I don't know—' she began.

Just then a small, eton-cropped woman, little more than a girl, thin and raven-like in a tight black costume, pounced on Nelly from the opposite side. 'Dearest, I *will* buy you a brooch! I insist!' Her voice was harsh and passionate. 'It's so damned silly to be proud—'

She saw me, and waited for an introduction.

'This is Miss Fisher,' said Nelly. 'Joy, this is my sister-in-law.'

'Oh,' said the girl, flashing out a long thin hand darkened by the sun, 'I've heard about you.' I had not heard about Miss Fisher. 'Were you two going to tea? Do, if you want, and I'll meet you later. I've got to have my feet done.'

'No, Joy,' said Nelly, whose colour had not subsided, 'there's no need for you to go dashing off like that.'

'But you can't sit there while they cut my corns, can you? Where will you be?'

Nelly mentioned a tea-shop nearby.

'I'll be back in about an hour. So long.' Miss Fisher disappeared in the crowds, walking with a stiff back as if she had somehow been affronted.

'She lives near me,' said Nelly. 'I've known her since she was a schoolgirl.'

As we went towards our tea she asked me the ordinary questions: How was I? How was Emilie? How was the baby? She was all right. She'd got a new dog, but it was rather a sickly creature – she could not feel for it in the same way.

Her troubled look did not leave her for a long while. She said unexpectedly, 'Well, you look pretty, but I can't say you look smart. Money tight? You're not to mind me asking.'

Indeed, I did not. I had no one now to whom I could speak in intimacy, for Caroline never wrote or telephoned, and I heard little of Dicky. I had always found Nelly's physical bigness a comfort. I had often wondered whether I might not make a real friend of her.

'Of course money's tight,' I said; 'it couldn't be otherwise.'

'Tighter now the baby's here? I think Harriet ought to help with him.'

'We can manage.'

She gave a little sigh. Her face was clear now, clear and smiling. There was a teasing look in her eyes, warming, but somehow rather disconcerting. 'Oh dear, you proud young people! Well, we shall have to see. How is Himself? Sticking to the grindstone?'

'In my opinion, he's doing his very best,' I told her, wondering if he really was.

Nelly did not take this view. Ned, she told me, was doing just enough work to make it possible for his father to employ him without all the office eyebrows shooting up. 'There's no log-cabin-to-White-House about your husband, my dear. If only he'd put his back into it Father might be generous. But he won't. Still, I think you've improved him a bit.' She opened her mouth as if about to say something, closed it again.

I watched her; I knew an incomprehensible touch of unease. Her eyes were still bright, still teasing; but it was as though, below the surface expression of the retina, another expression had been slotted in, like a slide into a magic lantern.

She said, 'Anyhow, you seem to have kept him off the women.'

This was so startling that for a second I did not feel the implication of betrayal. 'Women?' I said.

'Now, Chris, you must know him by now. And he'll have told you all about his past, if I know him.'

The hurt was beginning; I felt my heart sink. I tried to speak lightly. 'I know about Wanda, of course.'

'Oh, her! She lasted longest. I suppose he doesn't still see her? He never could get off with the old before he got on with the new. That's what led to some of the complications.'

I could not believe this was happening: that I was sitting with forthright, ugly Nelly Ormerod in a teashop in Oxford Street and that she (not a tactless woman – like Ned, she was only 'tactless on purpose') was trying to torment me. I realised that the expression in her eyes was one that I had seen before in the eyes of people frustrated, luckless, who, normally kind, will suddenly seek relief from their own dissatisfactions through outbursts of motiveless malice. This impulse to upset me was obscurely connected, I believed, with Miss Fisher and the brooch Nelly would not let her buy: I had simply appeared at the wrong time, though I did not know why it should be wrong, nor what silent pool I had muddied by my stumble.

I said, 'I do know Ned. That's why I can't think of him as a Grand Turk.'

'That may be putting it strong. But, my dear girl, the debts he ran up on account of them!' She paused. 'You didn't think it was gambling, did you?'

I said nothing.

'Oh Lord,' Nelly murmured, her face softening into the disguise of innocence, 'don't tell me I've bothered you! What I was saying was, you've got him over all that, and more power to your elbow. You'll be the making of him yet.' She looked sated now, as if she had eaten richly and desired only to doze away the afternoon.

We talked of other things; she kept looking at the clock. I told her I could not wait for Miss Fisher to return, but that I must go home to relieve Emilie.

'Good luck,' said Nelly, 'and we'll see if we can't help about the baby.'

All the way back in the bus I repeated to myself the hints she had given me, repeated them till it was a hideous luxury to do so, till I was trembling with something between anger and love reawakened.

I waited for Ned to come in. I could not sit still. I walked about the flat, the muscles of my legs quivering beneath me. He was rather early. He came cheerfully into the room, bringing with him a Penguin detective story and a bowl containing two goldfish.

'Here you are, silly. They may draw the line at pets here, but I thought these two would lie doggo enough. A chap was selling them on the Rise.'

'I know where you went that night,' I said. My mouth felt dry and evil-tasting, as if I had been sick.

Ned put the bowl down. He looked at me, gaining time. 'What night?'

'The night you didn't come back. I know where you were.'

'Tell me,' said Ned, 'fire away.'

He sat down.

I said, 'You were with Wanda.'

I could not mistake his expression; it was one of pure, open surprise.

'The hell I was!'

I told him not to lie: though I knew he was not lying.

'Of course I wasn't with Wanda! I haven't seen her for nearly three years.'

It seemed to me now that if I refused to believe him he would be obliged to tell me the truth. 'That's a lie,' I said.

He caught my knees, pulled me towards him. Gripping me tightly, he put his head to my waist and closed his eyes. 'I was not with Wanda.'

'Who were you with, then?'

He said, in a kind of rage that was not for me, 'It makes me look a fool. And if you don't believe it, it makes me look worse.'

'Who was it?' I said.

I was not prepared for the answer. 'I went out with that girl of Dicky's.'

I cried out.

'I rang her up. I'd thought about it once or twice before. I knew the kind she was when she came here; I spotted it at once.'

I asked him, as if hoping to prove his own story was untrue, how he had known her number.

'She told us she had a flat of her own. I looked her up in the book, and there she was.'

'Go on,' I said.

Still gripping me at the knees, so that I stood over him, he told me he had arranged to take her for a drink. He had met her in Hatchett's, had gone home with her afterwards, had failed to ask her what he had half intended and what she had thoroughly expected. 'I couldn't do it to you. And, what's more, it all seemed silly. I bade her a tepid good night and went off. I got back on the last tube to Piccadilly but couldn't get home from there without walking. So I stayed the night at Maddox Street. You can check that, if you want to.' He paused. 'And all that is footling and dismal and true. Of course, I should have telephoned you, but I was angry.'

I heard myself asking why he had done this.

He raised his head. The light fell on his eyes, making them beautiful in colour and very clear. His hands moved over me. 'Because you don't care. I thought I'd like an hour with somebody who did.'

I believed his story. It was unquestionably true; it had the ring of truth, which is often a dull one. In his face I saw a strange hope that with this confession our troubles might melt like sugar in a teacup; that by some miracle we should be together as we had been for that short period after our marriage.

I thought: After this we shan't be able to go on together. Whether sooner or later, it will all be the same. *I cannot bear it.*

For I had realised that the last jealousy had left me. I should have been angry and jealous; it was degrading to be neither, and it destroyed the last shred of hope. So long as I could feel with any glimmer of intensity about Ned, whether with desire or bitterness, hope had remained alive.

I wanted even now to be kind, to be gentle, not to dishonour him; but I heard myself saying very clearly, 'No, I don't care. I can't help it, dear. I don't. I wish I could.'

He let me go. Rising to his feet, he shook his head violently. He seemed quite lost, not knowing what to do next. He looked at the bowl. One fish, carrot-red, was lying half way up, mouth opened and white upon the glass. The other, pale yellow, was motionless at the bottom. Ned stirred the water with his finger and they both swam around. He felt in his pockets, brought out a paper bag and put it down beside the bowl. 'You feed them with this. The man told me how to clean them out.'

He tipped a little of the food into the water; it puffed into a dust, resettled and sank. 'Hungry as hunters,' he said.

He put his arm round me, drawing me to stand by him, so that we could look at the fish together.

'You don't mean that,' he said. 'Of course you don't mean it. *I* know.'

PART FOUR

I

Mark was a beautiful child, a firm, square baby, sweet as a beanfield to smell. He had Ned's blue eyes, but they were happy ones. The soft hair over the fontanelle, the colour of a new penny, changed colour like wheat with a wind in it; it was strange and rather frightening to me to behold this beating life in the crown of a head. He was a 'good' baby – which means, one that gives little trouble; he ate well, slept well, and in his waking hours lay contentedly under a tree in the front garden, watching the branches move, the birds fly, or playing with a silver bell that Emilie had given him for a christening present and which had once belonged to my mother.

He was, as I say, 'good'; yet for the first eight months or so of any baby's life the mother's sleep is broken. Although I would put him back in his cot at half-past ten, after his feed, and he usually slept through the night to six or half-past, I seldom slept soundly. I was afraid of not hearing him; or, if I had lain awake long, became obsessed by the idea that it was scarcely worth going to sleep at all since he would rouse me again so soon. And the routine of caring for a baby, day in and day out, is very tiring. Emilie came sometimes to help me, but she did all things these days in so faraway a fashion, her eyes as vague, hopeful and innocent as if she perpetually beheld a formal grouping of angels harping by a glassy sea, that I never cared to trust Mark long in her care.

Ned had decided to ignore my confession of lovelessness as if it had never been. Not at all a histrionic man by nature, he now seemed to be acting the part of a cheerful, ordinary, humdrum husband in an ordinary, cheerful, humdrum marriage. He went about the flat whistling to himself with a bright, uplifted look; the strain lay far back in his eyes. Each morning and night he came to look at the baby, put out a finger to him, paraded all the clichés of fatherhood. A baby, he said, was 'woman's work'; he could not understand chaps who consented to push the perambulator. It was only under protest that he would hold Mark for a moment while I went to fetch rusks or orange juice – 'I shall only drop him.' It was as if he saw himself standing apart from us both, admiring, mildly amused, but insisting that his part in the affair had been over long ago.

I was tired these days, locked in discouragement. When the baby smiled at me or held my fingers I felt he was the agent of some supernatural comforter; I began to feel supported by, dependent upon, this child still too young to sit or speak. When I was with him I was happy, for his radiance and beauty absorbed me. I could have worshipped him, as if he were God. But in long evenings, when Ned was either out or sitting about the flat re-reading his books – he seemed to have come to an end of all literary adventuring – I found myself falling sharply into self-pity.

I never know why self-pity is considered especially disgraceful. It seems to me neither a virtue nor a vice, but simply an inevitable emotion. The sympathy of others is an uncertain thing at best. A friend may be genuinely sorry for us for an hour, but forget his sorrow the moment affairs of his own divert him – which is perfectly natural and right, but no consolation to us, in whom unhappiness may endure day in and day out. We have to be sorry for ourselves: nobody else can sympathise with us as steadily, as loyally as we, and it is from such sympathy that we draw strength to put a decent public face upon our misfortunes. 'There's a brave girl,' says the mother to the child in the dentist's chair who has just let out a roar of terror at the mere sight of mirror and pick; whereupon the child, proud of the accolade bestowed, will probably exhibit some genuine if minor bravery during the next ten minutes.

I was sorry for myself because I was getting shabby, because I had no one to talk to, because I could never go dancing or to the theatre. I was still, of course, not twenty-one. My self-pity was at that time valuable, for it kept hope alive. Had I sturdily said to myself, 'You have made your bed and you must lie on it, serve you right', I should have accepted this as the last word on the subject and have sunk into despair. As it was, I could feel, now and then, the tingle, of some irradiating hope, of some sudden joy in the dazzle of a spring morning, the all-immersing light of a full moon, the trembling glimmer of a cyclist's lamp rimming the edge of the common. In one of these hopeful moods I sent the poem I had written on my night of worry to an editor whom I had not been ambitious enough to approach before. Once again I began to wonder whether I might not, after all, have some sort of a 'career'.

Ned was gentle with me, and once a week took me to the cinema. As Mr. Carker the Junior he had received no increase of salary this year (though Finnegan and the typists had); he did not seem bitter about it. He had fallen, so far as I could see, into a state of general acceptance that might last for ever. The newness had faded and shredded away from our home. There was no money for flowers. Mark seemed to me an astonishingly expensive baby.

One Sunday in May, when Emilie was in the flat for tea and Ned was lying on the sofa re-reading *Nostromo*, Mrs. Skelton rang up. 'As it's such a nice day, may we pay you a state visit? We don't want anything to eat. Just tea, or a drink.'

'Who was that?' said Ned.

I told him.

'What the devil do they want? There isn't any drink, so Harriet can go without.'

'Perhaps I'd better leave you,' Emilie suggested.

'No you don't,' Ned said quickly. 'You stay here.' He hoped we could induce her to miss church and sit with Mark while we went to the pictures – very occasionally, upon a Sunday, she would give us this liberty. 'Now what *are* they up to?' he repeated.

They arrived in the car we were no longer permitted to use, and I watched them coming up the path; Mr. Skelton with his bantam strut, his social beam which, like a torch with a fading battery, he could not long maintain; his wife with her graceful, weary, lagging step, the lids half down over her full eyes.

Mr. Skelton hailed me loudly. 'Well? And how's the baby's baby? I must say *you* look blooming.'

'We saw the baby,' Mrs. Skelton said, in her slow, edged way; 'you know we saw him, Harold. We looked at him in the garden. He looks very fit. So he should with all Chris's care.' She spoke to Aunt Emilie with poorly acted enthusiasm and stretched herself in an armchair.

'No gin,' said Ned. 'We're out of liquor and it's Sunday.' He glared at his mother, who looked scornfully back at him.

'Such a charming greeting,' she said to me. 'Can't you civilise Ned a little?'

'The baby's baby,' said Mr. Skelton, 'that's the idea. Ought to be in rompers yourself, Christine. Isn't that so?' he demanded of Emilie. 'Aren't I right?' – of Ned. The battery failed. The torch went out. He sat down on the sofa and picked up Ned's book.

I could not help feeling myself on Ned's side. The unity of marriage, even an unhappy one, is rooted in a kind of pride, and I could not bear that his parents should humble him, since in doing so they humbled me also. So I told myself that I was not going to be cordial at all. They had made him despondent, me shabby; they knew how I felt. I should not pretend to feel otherwise.

'My dear Chris,' Mrs. Skelton said, 'haven't you any felting under this carpet? It's beginning to wear shockingly. You ought to have it repaired at once before you're entirely threadbare in that patch.'

'Repairing carpets costs a lot of money.'

She looked at me. 'Letting things go costs more in the long run. But I'm not interfering. This is your home.' She peered at the bad patch again. 'I'm afraid they sold you a pup with this.'

Emilie, who had had the kettle on the boil, brought in the tea. I thanked her.

'You must be a great help to Christine,' Mrs. Skelton murmured. 'I'm sure she wouldn't know what to do without you.'

'We must all do what we can, however little it is,' Emilie replied breathlessly, as she watched the musical angels. 'Sugar?'

'No milk, no sugar.' Mrs. Skelton raised her voice to a languid, commanding tone. 'Ned.' No answer. 'Ned, I am speaking to you!'

'Sorry.'

'Would you have a *lemon*?'

'I'll get one,' I said. 'There's one in the kitchen.'

'My son will get the lemon,' Mrs. Skelton announced. 'Sit down, Mrs. Jackson!' – for Emilie had wavered in the direction of the door.

Ned said to me furiously, 'Where's it kept! I don't know where you keep the things.'

I went to fetch it myself before there could be more discussion.

Mrs. Skelton squeezed the juice into her cup. 'Thank you, Christine. But you mustn't wait on Ned. It's all wrong. It's bad training.'

I was furious with her; I felt she was belittling my husband in the same fashion (though less bizarrely) as Leslie's mother had belittled her son. 'Ned waits on *me*,' I said, 'but he knows I like the kitchen to myself. He always helps me.'

'I'm glad to hear it,' she replied.

'So am I,' echoed Mr. Skelton, far off.

When Mrs. Skelton had finished her tea and had lit her first cigarette she broke into the rather turgid flow of general conversation. It was pleasant to chat, she said, but they had come for a purpose. I might have thought that she was interfering about the carpet, but it was not so at all. It had simply reminded her of what she had come to say: that she and her husband realised money must be short with us, and that though they had done their utmost for Ned and could do no more . . .

'I'd touch my cap if I had one,' Ned interrupted, with a curious lively smile at her, almost a friendly one.

. . . there was one thing they were prepared to do. They were prepared to pay the entire expenses of my confinement, to pay for the perambulator, for the cot, for the cost of the first month's nursing. Furthermore, they would make us an allowance of one pound a week to cover the baby's food and clothes. 'This,' said Mrs. Skelton, 'is our grandchild, and we have a right to help.'

I was surprised by my own immediate reaction; it was one of relief. The gracelessness of being hard-up had, in itself, depressed me; a little extra money would make a great difference to us. If the Skeltons reimbursed us for what we had already spent there might be a new dress for me, a new suit for Ned, a new coat of paint in the living-room, and sometimes, perhaps, a few flowers in the vases. My second reaction, coming rapidly upon the first, was one of anger that their largesse should be thrown at us in this manner. I realised many years afterwards that the Skeltons could never have been as well-off as I had supposed and that indeed during the slump they must have been hard put to it to keep their business going at all. (Even the unnecessary job they had made for Ned must have been a drain on the falling profits.) But at the time their offer seemed to me not only insulting but parsimonious. I said nothing at all. I looked at my mother-in-law, who had folded her hands and closed her eyes. The smoke rose straight up from her cigarette to swivel grey and violet on the still air. Mr. Skelton was staring at his feet.

'No, thanks,' said Ned. 'Very nice of you both, but, as you say, you've done your utmost for me. Chris and I can manage on the utmost very nicely.'

His mother shrugged. 'What does your wife have to say?'

'I agree with Ned. We do thank you, of course.'

'All right.' Her eyes snapped open. Taking out powder puff and lipstick, she busily set to work with them. 'All right. But the offer's there. Whether you take it or not is up to you. What do you think, Mrs. Jackson?'

Aunt Emilie jumped. She had tried to remove herself spiritually from this family conclave, to shrink smaller and smaller inside her bones, to make herself so little that nobody could see her at all. She was aroused so suddenly from this dream of smallness that she had no time to think. 'Oh, I think they're being silly.'

'What!' Mrs. Skelton smiled widely. 'You do?'

Emilie flushed into her brown-rose patches. Her answer had been a true one. She meant to stand by it. 'They do have a hard time. I know they didn't like Ned going back into the job you gave him. I mean, when you offered him what they didn't like they were very upset. I don't see why they should be upset when you offer them something they ought to like.'

Mrs. Skelton clapped her hands softly. The ravaged handsomeness of her face was striking in the late sunlight. 'Bravo! Thank God somebody's got some sense.'

'It's amends, in a way,' Emilie said hopefully to Ned.

Mr. Skelton was roused to protest. 'Oh, now, now! I don't admit that. We've nothing to make amends for. This is just because we want the baby to have a decent chance.'

The suggestion that this plump, lovely, hungry, happy child was not getting a decent chance enraged me.

'Thank you,' I said, 'but we can't possibly accept.'

I looked at Ned. He was silent, his hands in his pockets. He balanced upon the balls of his feet.

'It *is* kind,' I repeated.

His mother smiled faintly. 'All right, dear, I've said it's all right. In my opinion only Mrs. Jackson is showing the slightest nous, but there you are. Harold, we must be going.' She reminded him that friends were expected at six.

As they both rose Ned said thickly, 'Mark's perfectly all right – Chris does marvels for him. And I don't think we can stand any more favours.'

I wished he had not sounded so graceless. I was torn. 'No, let's not put it like that,' I said. 'Please, let's not.'

'My dear,' said Mrs. Skelton, kissing me, 'we know your heart's in the right place. We even know it's made of flesh and not of indiarubber. I'm sorry you won't support your aunt, but there it is.'

Walking up to Ned she gave him a sudden, affectionate buffet on his arm. 'Silly fool, aren't you? Well, it's the way you're made. I never knew such a boy.'

He said nothing.

The Skeltons had shaken hands with Emilie and me and were just going out, when he spoke. 'Chris and I will see you down.'

We took them across the grass to the shady tree. Mark, eyes full of secret gaiety, of jokes only he could understand, was laughing to himself. He had kicked off both socks and, like a netted bird, had got his feet caught in the broad mesh of the perambulator net.

'He's most like Ned, I think,' Mrs. Skelton said judiciously.

'There's the boy, what a boy!' her husband crowed, taking out his tie and waggling the end of it at the baby. 'Say dad, then: can't you talk yet? Say dad-dad.'

'I think there's a touch of Nelly about the mouth.' Mrs. Skelton lowered herself further over the pram, frowned, nodded to herself.

I freed the baby's feet, pulled the net away and kissed him. His cheek was firm and resilient. It smelled of powder and flowers.

'All right,' said Ned loudly, 'you know we'll take it. You know we haven't any option. We both thank you very much.' His face was convulsed with anger; the rising blood had stopped at a line halfway up his forehead. He might have been out all day in the sun, watching cricket. His eyes were enlarged, as if by the lens of tears. He said tightly, 'We are very grateful.'

2

After that Ned paid even less attention to the baby than before. He was my child and Mrs. Skelton's. I cared for him. She paid for him. I think Ned felt that Mark no longer had anything to do with his father.

So far as I was concerned I did not much mind. There was a little more money coming into the house. I bought two new cotton dresses that gave me more pleasure than any clothes I had ever had in my life before. Looking sentimentally at the reflection in the looking-glass of myself holding Mark in my arms, I hoped people would think, A pretty mother and a pretty baby. I began to fall back upon the fantasy life of my childhood; it was pleasant to move in those sparkling marine depths, among the delicate corals of imagination, to move slowly, flowingly, against the pressure of the waters. And though I could still see Ned clearly, I saw him through a clear glassy barrier, as a goldfish sees human beings through the bowl.

Perhaps he, also, was removed from me by dreams of his own. Often, as he sat over the newspaper while I cleared the breakfast dishes, he would remark that he didn't like the state of the world; he wouldn't mind betting that there would be trouble again some day. He sounded gloomy, but his eyes brightened. He was thinking of war; his own desires made him far-sighted. 'One never knows which way the world's going to jump. I tell you, I'd never be surprised' – he beheld distances, marching men, a life he could understand – 'to find myself back in uniform again.'

But, unlike my own, his fantasies were sporadic and short-lived. I always knew when he had emerged from one of them because of the shortness of his temper; his angry, hopeless spurts of endeavour to find a new path for himself. Once or twice, unknown to his father, he tried to find work with other firms; but business was still bad, the stock markets were still low, nobody was buying much property, and nobody wanted Ned.

I realised that he had indeed been unfortunate. If he had had his wish – to soldier, to see the world, to command and to obey, to live life by numbers – he would have been a different man. His physical courage, I had learned from his mother, had always been of a high order. He was easy and good-humoured in the company of men like himself. He could have been successful. He could have been serene.

My dissociation from him, however, had grown so extreme that I was beginning to forget what his ordinary reactions were like. A year ago, had I received this letter from the editor, telling me he liked my poem but wanted to see me about it before going further, I should have concealed it from Ned and not thrust it upon him in unthinking delight.

'Are you up to that stuff again?' he said.

I told him that it was only a poem.

'I can see it is. I thought you'd grown out of all that.'

I tried to impress him with the distinction of the periodical.

'Nobody reads it.'

'It has,' I said professionally, 'quite a large circulation.'

'You don't want to get into those circles,' said Ned.

I asked him what was wrong with them.

He replied rather surprisingly, 'Messy morals. A lot of half-men who don't wash.'

I told him indignantly that the private life of this editor was beyond question, and that his magazine was run by higher-grade literary persons almost like civil servants in their personal cleanliness.

It struck me as sad, even as I spoke, that the lighter moments of our life together should arise only out of friction. When Ned was angry he lost his sense of the ridiculous; I regained my own.

'Well, you're not going.'

Even from him this was preposterous. I asked him not to behave like a Victorian father.

'The Victorians washed,' said Ned, apparently obsessed by salubricity. 'And I don't want you getting into queer sets I don't know about. They'll take your mind off your home and your children,' – he used the plural for sturdier effect – 'and you'll find yourself involved in all sorts of muck.' He paused. 'Is this chap married?'

I realised that he was driven by jealousy, that jealousy was taking a fantastic shape. A year or so ago this would have excited and pleased me: now it appeared no more than idiotic.

I said, as calmly as I could, that to the best of my knowledge the editor had been married for fifteen years and had three sons.

'All the same,' Said Ned, 'you write and tell him you can't get away and that he can say what he has to say on paper.'

He rose abruptly, fetched his hat, jammed it not quite straight on his head and went away.

Now if many of us know the pressures of the inner critic, many of us also recognise – though not until his task has been carried out – the activities of the secret planner. We are unhappy in the prison of our lives – we want to break out. And so, without realising what we do since it is the secret planner who thinks for us, we slowly lay our schemes for escape.

When I went to ask Emilie if she would look after Mark that afternoon (I was, of course, going to see the editor) I had to wait for ten minutes till she could talk to me, as she was having a bath. Emilie had no books – she had never seen the need for them – so I had to divert myself by reading her church magazine. And it occurred to me that she might be far happier with the church on her doorstep, instead of a bus ride away.

When she had agreed to take Mark after his midday feed I asked her whether she would not rather have a flat in Clapham Old Town. 'Wouldn't it be far more convenient to you?'

The idea appealed to her at once; but she could not see that it would be practical. 'I shouldn't be nearly so much help to you, dear.'

She was not often a help to me in any case, but I did not, of course, say so. I told her I could always bring Mark to her if I wanted some free time, and that it would be less troublesome for me to do this than for her to cross the Common twice on Sundays and once or twice in the week.

'But I'd never find another place,' said Emilie, 'and I don't know that I could face moving.'

'I'll look out for something,' I told her, 'and help you all I can.'

She looked in timid bewilderment about her flat, as if she were being forced to leave it within the hour.

The editor was hardly worth my gesture of defiance.

He was a young-old, aunt-like, eagle-featured man, who treated me rather as though he had forgotten sending for me and could not remember why he had done such a thing. He was courteous and prim; even Ned could scarcely have been jealous of him. It seemed that he did not like my poem well enough to print it (I swallowed disappointment like a draught of aloes) but that he thought I might be worth encouraging. He wondered – this appeared the final insult – whether I had thought of writing prose? If I should have anything else to send him (they were somewhat overstocked with poetry just at the moment) he would be interested to read it. He rose and bowed me out, curving his height over me as if he were a lean-to shed.

I should have confessed my disobedience to Ned had the result of it not been humiliating. I should have gloried in defiance had I been able to add that the editor was printing my poem next month and that he had not seen gifts comparable with mine since he first discovered Ezra Pound. But to tell Ned I had defied him and had then received a gracious dismissal was too much. I said nothing at all. Ned assumed that I obeyed his orders, and for several days afterwards he went about with a strange, fattened look of satisfaction, treating me with uncommon tenderness.

At the end of May Dicky telephoned me. It was months since I had heard from him. He had been for a walking tour in Germany, he said, and was longing to tell me about it. What a country! There was going to be trouble. Already he had seen a sign in a park: 'Dogs and Jews not admitted.' It had made him think of poor old Take Plato – one had never thought of him as being a Jew, had one? How revolting people could be. But he thought Hindenburg would come down pretty smartly on the Brownshirt mob when the time came.

I asked him to come round to the flat. Ned was at his club, playing squash; he rarely went there nowadays, as he could not afford to buy people drinks. 'I'll be alone,' I said, 'so we can have a good talk.'

It was one of those evenings of mysterious promise, hot and still, a faint blue mist overlying the green mist of the common. The lamps along the Parade, the watered gold of orange juice, were just visible through the trees. I opened the windows wide, and the scent of may and petrol fumes were borne into the room.

Dicky came in with his old, sly slouch and gave me a kiss. He had never done this before. It did not mean that he had fallen in love with me; it meant that he was growing-up, that he was adopting the easier social customs of a generation a little older than our own.

'This is cosy,' he said, settling himself in one of the chairs I had set before the window. 'That takes me back to old times.' He waved his hand towards the big field, from which came faintly the sound of music. A cluster of glowing cigarette-ends were like fireflies in the dusk. Some boys and girls, like the boys and girls we had been, had brought out a portable gramophone.

'The Rachmaninoff,' Dicky observed, 'his own recording.'

He turned to me and began to talk about his holidays. He was excited, but genuinely perturbed. I noticed, as his voice ran on, that in speaking of what he had seen he did not use his old schoolboy slang.

'I don't like it, Chris. I really don't. There's something there as ugly as the devil.'

I stretched out my hand to switch on the table-lamp, but he stopped me. 'Don't. It's nice as it is.'

The boys and girls were singing, their voices scooping as wistfully in space as the voices of others who had sung the songs of the last war.

'That's a new number,' Dicky said attentively, slipping into the jargon of his trade. 'It must have come out while I was away. What is it?'

I said I did not know. I did not listen to the wireless. Ned did not care for it.

'You shouldn't have married that fellow,' Dicky said abruptly.

'If I hadn't I shouldn't have had Mark.'

I could just see his face pallid in the beam of a street lamp.

'You'd have had a baby you'd have liked as much. You wouldn't have known any better.'

'I can never believe that,' I told him.

'Are you getting on more or less all right?'

Even to Dicky I said, 'Quite all right.'

'Shouldn't have married him. Sh!' He held up a hand to check my reply. 'I can just hear a word or two – something about apples and trees . . . quite a good number. I'll have to mug up all my backwork when I get back to the office. Mind you,' he went on without a pause, 'I don't suppose we'd have got on any better. We've known each other too long. We should have liked the same things, though.'

He took my hand for a moment and held it. 'You'll be all right. Good luck.'

We were more intimate than we had ever been; I knew he had to conquer his shyness in order to speak to me like this, to touch me, and I was moved by the kindness that was so deep in his nature. We sat together in a quiet that was like the quiet of love. The common was black now, but over the rim of the farthest trees the sky was a pure and lovely green. The evening star trembled and spurted its silver as though somebody had twitched a wire. Still, from the dark field the voices rose in mournful and delectable song.

The outer door slammed. I switched on the light. 'There's Ned,' I said; 'earlier than I thought he'd be. I suppose I'll have to make fresh coffee.'

He came in, stared at Dicky. 'You, is it?' He said to me, 'What on earth were you sitting in the dark for? The light wasn't on when I came by.'

'The sunset was so nice,' I replied, 'we wanted to watch it.'

'Hullo, Ned. Nice to see you.' Dicky had risen and was standing slightly on one foot. He was not feeling guilty – there was nothing to feel guilty about – but in Ned's presence he always tended to parody his own boyishness.

'Dicky's just back from Germany,' I said. 'He's got an awful lot that will interest you.' I began trying to interest Ned.

Dicky said fatally, 'Oh, and we've been yarning about old times.'

Ned looked at him silently. I wondered for a moment if he had been drinking too much – but he had not.

'I suppose I'd better slope along,' said Dicky. He whistled softly under his breath, moved his foot in a limited tap dance.

'Yes, I think you had.' Ned's voice was very clear. 'It's late.'

I could not bear to be so humiliated. Nonsense, I said; it was not half-past ten. I would make more coffee, and Dicky would talk about Germany.

'No, look,' Dicky murmured, 'I really shall have to wallow along. Got to be up early to work.'

'If you come again you might make a point of coming while I'm here,' Ned said.

I told him sharply not to be silly.

'I won't have you coming when I'm not here,' Ned repeated. 'I damned well don't like it.'

'Look here, Ned,' said Dicky, 'you've really got the wrong end of the stick. I'm not like that. I'm not a Don Juan.' (He might have been seventeen; I was reminded, with a touch of the irrational jealousy we may feel for people we do not love ourselves, when they show love for others, of that schoolboy's letter to Iris: 'I'm not a sheikh in flowing robes.') Between Ned, and Dicky and myself, the years rose like bars of iron. 'You ask Chris. She'll tell you.'

'I don't need to ask my wife. I am telling you to come when I'm in and not when I'm out.'

'I asked him here,' I said.

Dicky was quiet. We both watched him. I saw a change in him, that made me feel I had never known him before. For a moment I was as scared of him as I was of Ned. We do, not know people. We cannot know people. We are always wrong.

He said to Ned, in a light, unfamiliar voice, 'You're behaving like a lout.'

Ned flushed. He had expected attack, but not of this order; its very touch of schoolboyishness put him at a loss. And his reply was oddly like a schoolboy's.

'It's you who's the lout. You get out of here and don't come back.'

Dicky turned to me. He seemed easier now, in control of himself. 'I'm sorry about this, Chris. It's beastly for you. It's a pity I'm the cause of it.'

I said meaninglessly, 'Oh, it doesn't matter.'

'You get out of here,' Ned said. He put a hand on Dicky's arm.

Dicky stepped back. 'If you like to come out with me,' he said, 'I'll damned well fight you. You can't hit a chap in his own house, or so I'm told, and you can't hit him in yours, so there's nothing but the Common.' He sounded rather as if he were a little drunk; his words were slurred.

Ned smiled. He touched my shoulder, as if to make us associates. 'Aren't we a bit old for that sort of tomfoolery?'

'I'm not,' said Dicky.

They looked at each other in a sparring silence that was curiously like one of the silences of friendship.

'I'll come with you,' said Ned.

I said, 'No, you won't. If you knew how stupid you both looked!' And indeed I was angry enough to include Dicky in my disgust.

'Now, Chris,' said Ned, 'you mind your own business.'

I told Dicky to go. He looked at Ned, then back at me. Ned stood silently. A big brown moth, flown in from the Common, dashed itself against the light.

Dicky shrugged his shoulders, gave me his old, sidelong smile; it was the bumpkin smile, disguising, derisory. 'If you say so. We'll see each other some time, I hope.' Switching out his hand he caught the moth, listened to it for a second as it whirred within his palm, and put it out of the window. 'Poor fellow! Well, I'll slope along.'

When he had gone we both listened until the sound of his feet had died away along the road.

'Lout,' said Ned uneasily. He looked in the coffee-pot, swishing it around.

I said, 'You won't let me write; you won't let me meet new people; you've driven all my friends away.'

'Oh, he'll be back, worse luck.'

No, I said, he would not. No one would come back.

Then I told him I was unhappy. We had failed, I said, a long time ago; he must know that.

'I don't admit it.'

Even at that moment domestic responsibility seemed important. Taking the pot from his hand, I said I was quite prepared to make some more coffee. All he had got there was a lot of grounds.

'Damn the coffee,' said Ned.

He looked thoughtful, but no more so than if he had been puzzling out the best way to get from A to B on a map. It was hard to talk to him.

I told him I wanted to be free, that I had come to the end of life with him. He must divorce me (I knew a touch of grown-up pride as I said the word) and we would both try to part without pretending a misery neither of us could really feel.

'Oh, don't be more silly than you can help,' he said, still in the same restrained and moody tone.

'I wouldn't,' I said, 'want to take Mark right away from you. We could share him.'

It was curious how unreal all this seemed, even to me; and yet I knew that it was in fact a reality, that I had come to the end of pretence, of the dreary fantasy that I could live a life of sober and hopeless endurance.

'What should I divorce you for?' Ned asked me in a light, almost cheerful voice. 'Adultery? Who shall I cite? Not Dicky. I'm prepared to admit that.'

I told him we must talk about this seriously. He must realise that I was in earnest.

'You can't, of course, divorce me,' Ned went on. 'I've done nothing and I don't propose to. And you couldn't expect me to perjure myself. I'm an honest man.' He paused. 'So you see, I'm afraid all that's washed out.'

I said, 'I mean this. I can't live with you any longer. You'd be happier without me, too.'

He caught my arm. 'That's where you're wrong. I shouldn't.' He looked at me. His eyes were thick with anger and distress. He blinked them rapidly, as if he were finding it hard to see. 'Stop this,' he said, 'and don't let's have any more acting.'

3

The secret planner began to work hard for me, quite in the dark at first – I did not realise fully, until later, what had made me find Emilie another home a mile away and help her immediately to move into it – and then a little more openly. I told myself that my reason for making tentative enquiries about a return to office work was that I needed something to break the monotonous tension of my life with Ned. After all, Mark could be cared for during the day; if I were earning a salary again I could afford to pay for help. Ned would be angry with me, I knew, but I did not think he would try seriously to stop me. He was prepared to please me in any way but the one I longed for. He was making love to me with a kind of feverish deliberation, almost as if he were going to the wars and we had only a little time left. He was taking me out and about. Once or twice he had bought me some flowers.

My first enquiries were tentative indeed – no more than a casual glance at the clerical employments column in the paper; a letter sent in answer to an advertisement for a girl more qualified than I – a letter to which I did not expect or really wish to receive an answer. It was too early for conclusions.

I fancied Ned had hinted to Maddox Street that there was some kind of trouble between us, because I saw none of my relations-in-law. The days dragged on into July; and as I look back at them now I am surprised to remember my own temperate, almost cheerful, spirits. It was, of course, the cheerfulness of determination. I had made up my mind. Nothing might appear to be happening, but under the quietness was a steady undertow.

I telephoned Caroline. Did she feel like seeing people again? How was she? I had missed her.

'Darling, I *will* come around soon,' she replied, 'really I will. I'll make the effort. At the moment I never seem to get anywhere. How's Ned?'

I told her briefly that we had failed. She did not seem surprised.

'And what's going to happen?'

'I don't know,' I said, 'but something will.'

'Aren't you in love with the poor old thing, not at all?' she enquired, in something like a parody of her old, flippant manner.

'No,' I said, and felt sorry for Ned and for me. 'I hate being out of love,' I added.

'Oh, I don't mind that,' said Caroline. 'I told you I was Pro – you know what I mean; but I was never romantic. Not like you. It's simply that I'm at such a loose end.'

She meant that she was lonely: but it was a loneliness against which she seemed unable to act. She asked me if I had looked at the morning paper: Iris had had her first child, born in Buenos Aires. 'I bet it's in a frightfully unhealthy basket,' Caroline added, 'all air excluded by muslin and blue bows. She will probably have photographs taken of it sticking out of a boot, like one of those soppy kittens.'

She promised she would come and see me soon, she did not know when. As I hung up the receiver I felt that she, like all my friends, had gone forever.

One morning when I had gone to the West End to shop – this was my weekly entertainment, my comfort, my illusion of release – I found myself walking without premeditation down Waterloo Place. Something told me not to think at all, to let my feet carry me where they wished, to deal with a situation when I actually came face to face with it.

I got into the lift, conscious that my face was hot and flushed, that my heart was beating. Outside the door I paused, and read the gilded letters as though I had never seen them before.

It was half-past twelve. Mr. Baynard should be at lunch, Mr. Fawcett indoors with Miss Rosoman.

The familiar smell caught me, the smell of sandalwood, Jeyes fluid and carbon paper. It penetrated the joining of the doors, sifted through the keyhole. I went in.

Nobody was there. The sunlight sparkled in its familiar way upon the bevel of the looking-glass, threw its golden squares over the parquet and across the three clean blotting-pads upon the counter, pink and white and green. There was a cover upon Miss Rosoman's machine, a sheet of paper in the typewriter that had been mine. I was reminded of Ambrose Bierce's story of the deserted city and was about to make my escape, when Mr. Baynard came out of the inner office.

He stopped short. 'Well, well! What a surprise! Well, Miss Jackson – Mrs. Skelton, I should say – we'd given up all hope of a visit from you. Come through, come through.'

He swung the gate for me and I stepped through into my old pasture behind the counter. Drawing up a chair for me beside his desk, he explained that he was holding the fort, that he was head cook and bottle washer. Mr. Fawcett was away on a business trip to America and had taken Miss Rosoman with him – 'and very nice for her, too! I told her she was a lucky young woman.' Fortunately it had been a very slack summer, otherwise he, Mr. Baynard, would have been overwhelmed. Hatton had left. They had a new man, from the Corps of Commissionaires. Miss Cleek had left, too – her father was sick, she had to nurse him. There was a new Junior,

Miss Fenwick, a very bright little soul. (He sounded as if he liked her better than he had liked me.) At the moment she was out to lunch.

How was I? This was like old times. He believed I had a youngster – his tardy congratulations. Well, well, much water had flowed under the bridges.

He had always looked older than his years; now – he could not have been more than thirty-seven – he seemed dry and shrivelled as a nut. His fair hair had thinned away from the crown of his head, which protruded from the rest of his skull like the top of a cottage loaf. I saw that he had been reading *The Thirty Nine Steps*. I remembered him reading the same book three years ago, and found myself wondering whether this was a second reading or whether it had indeed taken him all that time to reach the two hundredth page.

'I had hoped to see Mr. Fawcett,' I said.

'He'll be sorry to have missed you; you must call on us again. Is there any little service I can render? You must make use of us as if you were a real client these days, you know.'

I saw that marriage had immeasurably improved my status in the eyes of Mr. Baynard. He chattered on about his wife, his children; told me how he had understudied Wilkins in the local society's production of *Merrie England*. 'I nearly sang it one night, too. The fellow got a heavy cold and said he wouldn't be able to sing – but, bless you, of course he did. They'd rather make a mess of things than give another fellow a chance. Jealousy, jealousy – you find it everywhere.'

He brooded on his disappointment. ' "The lobster and the stickleback . . ." ' he hummed under his breath. He looked at the clock. 'I'm sorry you won't meet Miss Fenwick. She's got to go straight from her lunch to the Passport Office. Yes, she's a good girl, but, like all good girls, she's getting married. The moment you've broken them in, off they go. That's the way of it.'

The secret planner forced me into the open. I heard myself say, 'I am thinking of going back to work myself. Would there be any chance for me here?'

The moment I had said it I was overcome with shame that I should have made such an appeal to my old enemy. I tried to sit gracefully, nonchalantly on my chair, to look out of the window as though my remark had been quite an idle one, the response of no consequence.

To my surprise Mr. Baynard said in the shocked voice of one familiar with hierarchical matters, 'But, Mrs. Skelton, you couldn't come back as a Junior! Not now you're a married woman!'

I said I supposed so, though I hardly saw why not.

'Surely you could find something better! After all, I imagine you only want something to pass the time. I don't really approve of women going out to work, but sometimes my wife says to me, "You don't know how dull it is, Percy, to be stuck in Streatham all day! I often wish I had a job." '

I guessed by the shadowing of his face that this was no uncommon complaint of Mrs. Baynard's, supposed that theirs was the kind of marriage which had endured desirelessly but without question, that there was little pain in it and little joy, but only a great deal of tedium that seemed to them both like contentment. And it was to this that I refused to come.

I felt the courageous adrenalin forcing itself through me before I had realised what use I was to make of it. I was hotter than ever, the room more still.

'I don't want something to pass the time,' I said. 'I want something I can live on. I haven't been lucky with my marriage.'

He stared at me and flushed. I must have seemed to him a visitor from that half-world where marriages were spinelessly accepted as failures, where people ran off with each other's husbands and wives, and where the wages of their sin was usually – and unjustly – a very good time.

'Oh dear!' he said in a hushed cathedral voice. 'Oh dear! I'm sorry to hear that. That's sad news. I'm very sorry indeed.'

A noisy, iridescent blue bottle was blundering up and down the window-pane, trying to get out. Mr. Baynard rose. He took his empty tea-cup from the desk, poured the dregs into the saucer and clapped the cup over the fly. 'Give me an envelope, will you, Mrs. Skelton?' he asked me. I gave it him. He slipped the envelope under the cup, removed the insect gently in its prison, clambered on his chair and released it through one of the upper frames. He climbed down. 'Poor things! I hate it when they get trapped, but I can't bear to touch them.'

Reseating himself, he stared at me again. 'Well, well, this *is* sad. I won't ask questions. But are you quite serious about wanting work?'

I told him I was in deadly earnest, and that I should be grateful if they would consider me for my old job.

'But look here,' Mr. Baynard said, a picture of embarrassment and worry, 'if you came back here as the Junior it would be hard for me to treat you differently, which indeed as a married woman . . . Why don't you go and work somewhere quite new?' he asked me hopefully.

I told him, better the devil I knew than the devil I didn't. This pleased him. A smile more natural, more relaxed than I had ever seen on the face of Mr. Baynard, brightened his eyes and mouth. He liked to be called a devil.

'It might be awkward.'

'I don't see why.'

'This is so sudden,' he murmured, turning his head this way and that as if I had proposed marriage. He got up. If I were likely to come under his command again, then it became his right to terminate interviews. He was getting into practice. 'I'm afraid I must get back to my work. If you're still serious – and mind you, I hope this only an impulse on your part – I suggest you write to Mr. Fawcett. He'll be back at the beginning of August. It's far better for him to deal with these things.' He did not open the door of the counter for me. I passed through it, once more stood on the other side, temporarily restored to my married status. For a moment he looked desolate, as if something other than my affairs had troubled him; and this look made me say, 'I expect you think badly of me. But I promise you, it can't be helped. I have got to be free.'

'If some of us had said that earlier—' His voice was strained; he hesitated. 'Well, I suppose the whole foundation of family life would be undermined. One doesn't expect life to be a bed of roses, Mrs. Skelton. One has to put up with things.' He added, sadly and grandly, 'I often think happiness is an illusion.'

I said, 'No, it's not. We must have known happiness at some time or other, or we wouldn't spend so much time struggling for more. You can't fight for what you don't know. So it must be real.'

'You young people want everything your own way,' he said.

I was standing by the back wall, just by the door. The girl who came in, a small, plump, raffish-looking girl, saw Mr. Baynard but did not at first see me.

'I'll have to go back later, Percy. There's a queue a mile long at the Passport Office. Had a good lunch?'

It was not only the use of the Christian name which made me understand, startling enough though it was from a Junior to Mr. Baynard; it was the easiness, the ironic domestic intimacy of the voice.

He coloured. He said loudly, 'Miss Fenwick, I want you to meet your predecessor.'

She saw me; she betrayed no embarrassment. She held out her hand with a comradely flourish, jokingly suggested that she must be a poor substitute for such a paragon as myself, from all she had heard. And all the while he looked at her in hunger and in hopelessness.

As I went away, I knew that for whomever I might work it must never again be for Mr. Baynard. I knew too much about him now, had discovered this small, sorrowful romance that had come to him too late, that he would never attempt to pursue. Ugly, fussy, unattractive, he had somehow managed to engage the passing affection of this spirited-looking girl. It was one of the ludicrous miracles of love that are repeated again and again in life, every time causing the same smile, the same incredulity. We shall never know what people 'see in each other'; it is stupid to enquire. At a time when he had come to think romance impossible, a thing only for hot-headed boys and girls, this attraction had come to him; and, ruinously, had brought him hope. For without hope he could have lived comfortably enough in his nice little house, with his capable wife, his two growing girls, his amateur-dramatic societies. Now that the crutch of hopelessness had been taken from him he was fearful and lost. He would never be the same again.

A year ago Mr. Baynard's private grief would have diverted me from my own affairs: now, however, I pursued them remorselessly. I went up Regent street and called upon a rival of Mr. Fawcett's with whom we had occasionally done a little business. I saw the manager, who had always been inclined to treat me with flirtatious indulgence; and without beating around the bush I asked him if he were likely to need another typist. He was a sardonic man, permitting himself to be surprised by nothing. He said that I might have called at the right time; his girl (an elderly woman, well-known to me) was retiring at the end of

August. He might give me a trial – a month's probation: what about that?

I said I could not be too sure of my plans, that my enquiry was for the moment tentative, but that I would let him know.

'Well,' he said, 'that's up to you. But don't leave it too late.'

4

I could not leave it too late: yet there were days when it seemed fantastic to consider deserting Ned at all, when the realities of the present seemed to stand all around me like a fence far higher than my head, blotting out the prospect of any other kind of life but the one I lived. Sometimes it would seem to me, as I bathed and fed the baby, or played with him on my knee (his beaming, anticipatory face, eyes sparkling, lips open ready to laugh when he knew I was coming to one of our favourite jokes), that I was sufficiently happy in possessing him; that he was all I could possibly need. He was seven months old, a sweet-tempered, jolly child, increasingly responsive to me and to his small, comfortable world with every passing day. I felt for him a love that was at the same time protective, sensuous, visceral and comradely; it seemed to me, mysteriously, that we understood each other. Physically, he delighted me; the sweet springiness of his flesh, flushed through with rosiness like sunlight in coloured glass, was lovely to the touch; his hair was soft as the feathers on the breast of a bird. His hands, which he used with the unconscious and inimitable grace of infancy, were like mine; it was strange to see how, in him, my own third and fourth finger, leaning closely together, my own short, backbending thumb, were reproduced on so small a scale. And when he turned his head suddenly the shape of it, so like Ned's, disturbed and weakened me.

If Ned had seemed really to love Mark, I could, I think, have gone on; but he did not. Lately he had displayed a renewal of pride in him; he wanted to know how much he weighed, how soon he would talk, how soon he would stand alone, and sometimes, to please me, he would hold him for a little while. The moment Mark began to cry, however, Ned thrust him back upon me, pursing his lips as if the noise were something I could hardly expect him to endure.

One night he turned suddenly upon me in a new jealousy that I had not suspected.

For some time past he had been making love to me rarely and always suddenly, in silence, as if solely for his own easing. Afterwards, at once, without a word, he had slept. I had accepted this mechanical love with half my mind elsewhere; he had appeared to find it enough. I might have been any woman. But in the past week or so I had noticed that he was looking at me with a curious, smiling steadiness, as if he were recognising me again at the end of a long journey. In the dark he spoke to me with a hot tenderness, asking me the questions of love: but hastening on before I could reply. He was needing me more and more; he was using his own need, his own driving impulse, in an effort to awaken love again. And as I felt the weight of his head on my shoulder, his arm thrown across me (as if, like Mark, he were seeking comfort and reassurance), I wept.

But he was tiring me bitterly with these forcing renewals; they made me both pity and dread him. For I had not for months been sleeping well, and Mark still woke me between five and six of a morning when I had had perhaps only four or five hours of rest. One very warm night in the middle of July, knowing Ned was out with one of his friends and was likely to be late, I had gone to bed early, determined to read for half an hour, take some aspirin and, if I felt I could manage it, get to sleep before he came back. I had just put out the light when I heard him enter the house. In a few minutes he came into the room.

'Are you awake?'

'Only just,' I said.

He switched the light on again, sat upon the edge of my bed. He had the triumphant look of a confident lover. 'Sleepy?'

'A little.' But I had never yet denied him, and would not.

He undressed himself, humming a tune as he did so. His face was open and cheerful; I did not believe in this openness. 'You look nice, Chris. Something smells nice. It is that cream you use?' He bent to kiss me. 'Make room.' He said, in an odd, questing voice, 'My darling?'

Mark burst out crying. His cries, gasping and harsh, cut through the wall between us.

Ned took no notice.

'I must go to him,' I said.

'There's nothing the matter with him.'

'It's his tooth. I was expecting it; he had a red patch on his cheek today.'

'Let him get on with it, then.'

I tried to pull away, to reach for my dressing-gown.

'He'll cry it out,' said Ned.

I said,' He can't. If I give him a little water it sometimes helps.'

'Leave him alone. You can go later.'

Mark cried with the pain of misery and desertion. I pushed Ned from me, jumped out of bed. 'I can't leave him. He works himself up into such a state. He feels so lost,' I added.

Ned said, 'All right. Go.' He lay down and closed his eyes.

It was nearly an hour before I could quieten the baby. I walked up and down his room in the faint glow of the night light, holding him first over my shoulder, then against my cheek, whispering to him, singing his favourite songs, giving him sips of water, stealthily slipping him back into his cot, and then being forced to take him up again as he roared in misery renewed and gnawed at his fists.

At last, exhausted, I returned to Ned. He was back in his own bed, and he did not speak until I had lain down. I had hoped he was sleeping, but his voice came sharply out of the dark. '*I* won't be made a slave to that child, if you are.'

I told him it was a necessary slavery. The baby was in pain. It was a commonplace pain, and probably it would, to us, be trivial: to him it was an outrageous pain and a great one.

'We're going to get a nurse. You can get a working nurse fairly reasonably. I'm just about fed up with seeing you worn out and fit for nothing.'

'I haven't let you suffer,' I said, knowing what he meant.

'You throw a dog a bone.'

I was so tired that this petty unfairness made me burst into tears. 'You can't say that.'

'What are you crying for? I'm the one who should cry. I wanted you. You should have stayed with me, not jumped at any excuse to go running off. You're going to think more of your husband in future and less of that kid.'

'Stop it!' I said. 'Stop, stop, stop!' I could not check the uncontrollable wrenching of my own tears.

'Certainly. But tomorrow you'll get a nurse.'

My nose and throat thick with sobs, the tears salt on my lips, I burst out that I had tried to please him; that not once during this past fortnight had I refused him. I told him what it was like to be aching with tiredness, to sleep only a few hours, and then drag up again, hardly knowing what I did, to look after the baby. I reminded him that, despite this, I had tried to please him. That I had taken pleasure from him, and he must have known it. But I could not let him make love to me while the child wailed in pain and in fright because I did not come to him.

'All children teethe. They've got to get over it. We all did, and none of us died of it.'

'Ned,' I said, 'I must go to sleep. I have got to go to sleep.' And, indeed, the thought of sleep seemed like some unimaginable happiness, more desirable than any other human experience. I craved for it.

'Tomorrow you'll get a nurse.'

Desperately I told him that even now, if he still wanted me, I was ready; but that afterwards he must let me rest.

'I must sleep,' I repeated; 'I've got to.'

'Thank you,' he said. 'It's very nice of you, but I think not. I don't enjoy being tolerated.'

His voice sounded very near. I put out my hand and the light sprang up. He was leaning across from his own bed, his face close to mine. It was quite white, and the sweat on his forehead shone white also.

I said, 'You know there's nothing left for us! Why don't you let me go?'

'I'm going to get you over these hysterics, my girl. We're going to settle down and live decently, make up your mind to that. Less of the baby, and more of me.' Then, surprisingly, he weakened. He put his hand to my cheek. 'It will be all right, Chris, I promise you. We'll make a go of it.'

I got out of bed again.

'Is that Mark?' he said. 'I don't hear him.'

'No. But I'm going to sleep in his room.' There was a divan there. I had used it several times before, when the baby had been smaller and had needed me more often.

'No, no. Don't. Please stay where you are. I'm sorry I upset you.'

'I'd rather go.'

'Please, Chris. I swear I'm sorry. I was disappointed, and I lost my head.'

I told him I was no longer angry with him, no longer particularly distressed, only tired; and that if he wanted to be kind to me, he would let me go, just for that night.

He said nothing more. I crept into Mark's room, lay down and slept at once. At six I awoke and fed him, slept again. At eight I found Ned sitting beside me, his face mournful, his eyes red as if he had been weeping. 'Come back with me now.'

Outside the rain was pouring down, the noise of it like an interminable rush of breath.

He half carried me back to my own bed and lay down beside me – but he did not touch me. He buried his face in the pillow, near my own, and was silent.

5

This scene with Ned was not in itself a crisis, though it meant a new fear for me – the fear that he would somehow separate me from Mark. Most of the real crises of life take place in the imagination; around the main thread of worry the accretions of fear, of anticipation, of resolve, cluster secretly, thicker and thicker, till the thread snarls and knots beyond untangling, and we realise that the time has come to cut it clean away. During the last two weeks of July Ned left me much to myself, going out early in the morning, returning late after the office and often going out again immediately after dinner. He was quiet, amiable, rather remote. He did not try to make love to me. I said to him once, in a flash of hope, 'Let me go, Ned – you must see how it is with us', but he gave me the same reply as before.

Mrs. Skelton called one afternoon. I had not in the least expected her; it was a long time since we had met. I had had a bad night with Mark, who was teething again, and had just lain down in the hope of an hour's sleep, though it was always difficult for me to get to sleep in the day. When I went to answer her ring I was dazed, untidy, upset at being disturbed. She told me she was just passing and had taken it into her head to drop in for a little while – an odd fiction from Mrs. Skelton, who was usually logical in all things. I knew she was acquainted with no one else in the neighbourhood and must have made the journey on purpose. She must, I thought, be worried enough not to bother about acceptable pretences.

For a few moments she talked of nothing in particular. She walked about the room, glanced at a new frock I had bought for Mark, picked up my library book, observed that my hair was not cut as well as it might be, and that she knew a good man, surprisingly reasonable, in Conduit Street.

'I should never find time for it,' I said, feeling all the exasperation that is aroused by someone incapable of understanding the exigencies of one's daily life, together with a spurt of irritation that she had made me seem dowdy and ill-cared-for.

'Your aunt could take the baby,' Mrs. Skelton told me. 'I don't think you ought to let yourself go.'

I said nothing.

'What's wrong between you and Ned?' She spoke casually, as if most of her interest were concentrated upon the book she still held in her lap. Then she raised her eyes and looked straight at me. She was thin, old and handsome. For years her life had been without joy. I realised that she would be impatient with anyone less stoical than she.

I told her that our marriage had failed, that we had nothing in common, that we were bitterly unhappy, but that Ned refused to make an end of it.

'I warned you before you got married that he was difficult.'

I accepted this I-told-you-so meekly. 'It's my fault as well,' I said. 'I'm not right for him. He might be happy with someone else.'

She smiled. Her face was kind and contemptuous. 'You young people think you can break marriages as easily as breaking teacups. You really haven't any stamina, any of you. I wanted to leave Harold years ago, but I didn't. There were the children to consider.'

I was young enough to be diverted by this; I was curious. I asked her why she had wanted to leave him. She grinned. It gave her pleasure to answer me, to amaze me. 'Because he's a hopeless womaniser. He always has been. One damned woman after the other. I thought I'd break my heart at first; and then I got used to it. It was better after I stopped him talking about them, though he hated that. Part of the pleasure was coming home to me and weeping on my shoulder when the affair was going badly.' She told me she had been afraid Ned would turn out to be like his father, but that I had made all the difference to him. He had been entirely faithful to me; she knew this by instinct. She would have known at once had it been otherwise. He would always be faithful to me, and she thanked God for it.

Without hope, I asked her to persuade him that he must let me go.

'Oh, don't be silly,' said Mrs. Skelton, looking and sounding so much like him that his spirit might suddenly have taken possession of her. She put her hand on my bare arm. I felt the flesh withdraw from her touch. 'You buck yourself up and think of the baby. Your duty's to Ned. You've steadied him up. You've given him some sort of a decent life, and I intend to see one of my children reasonably happy.' She paused, tossed the book down on the sofa, as if it had served its purpose and added, 'I thought Nelly was going to be. Then her husband had to die; and now her life's a complete stupid mess. Dogs, and silly hysterical friendships. Oh, *I* know. I know everything. You wouldn't think a woman could be such a fool.'

When she left she kissed me; it was a rare gesture, and she offered me its rareness in the hope of taking the edge from the finality of what she had said. Despite her expressed contempt for Ned, despite the way in which she would let him down in public, she passionately wanted him to live an ordinary, contented life. She wanted to salvage something from the wreck of her hopes for him. When he was a child she must have loved him with a hard, secretive force: her baby, her son, better looking than her lumpish girl, a boy of promise on whom to fasten her ambitions. Now she believed he might still become the child of whom she could be proud, and that if this happened it would be through my agency. There was no help to be had from her. She would fight on his side.

When she had gone I was taken by so strong a sensation of being trapped that I walked about the room beating my fists upon the walls as if they were really made of stone. In a month I should be twenty-one. Before me lay fifty more years, perhaps, of life like this. I looked at the knuckle of my right hand. I had broken the skin, and it was bleeding a little. For a moment I knew a faint sense of comfort that my distress had driven me to so violent a physical expression; for I needed distress to be strong, to be the driving force in which lay my only hope of release. I was standing before the window, seeing nothing, when a change in the summer weather suddenly arrested my attention and filled the whole of my eyes.

It had been a lowering grey day, heavy and warm, drawing all the colour from the fields and bushes, dulling the surface of the roadway. But now, far off, the sun broke through an unsuspected crevice in the clouds and spread long fingers of light downwards to touch the furthest trees. Outside the window a few drops of rain fell. The fingers broadened, widened, stretching the crevice, tearing through the grey silk of the sky, and all at once the weather was transformed. The sun blazed out in lemon-coloured rays, each melting one into the other; all of a sudden the sunlight itself began to roll forward, field upon field, closer and closer, bringing up the sparkle of colour as a kerosene rag brings up for a moment the miraculous colours of a painting that has faded. It was like a golden army advancing and singing as it came. And it stopped halfway across the big field, slicing it in two. On the line of an intersection was a solitary hawthorn bush, half of it now in blackness and the other half of it shivering, jewelled and glittering as a bush in heaven.

I *saw* – as for three years, I had not seen; experiencing the fullness of sight as if it were the fullness of love. It seemed to me that I should not be defeated after all, for it was essential for me to see like this again, to see innumerable wonders all my life and, as the child grew up, to make him see through my eyes till he acquired a greater vision of his own.

That night, as I sat reading, as Ned lay on the sofa with his own book, now and then making some friendly, indifferent comment as though both of us were peacefully settled for ever, I decided to write the letter that must be posted by the beginning of August if it were not to be too late. In any case, I said to myself, he wants me to get a nurse for Mark; and if I do, then there is nothing to stop me working. If this must go on for us both, at least I shall have a wider world to live in.

I wrote it, and concealed the answer. I had arranged to take up my business life again in September. Still it seemed unreal. I might have arranged it; I still could not believe it.

On the following Friday Ned brought Jack Harris, who had been our best man, home for a meal and told me they were going to Frinton for the week-end to get some golf. Harris had not been to see us lately; he was a big, amiable, facetious man whom Ned seemed to find amusing.

'It's women like you drive husbands away,' Harris said to me, following this by a timid ha-ha, less like mirth than some kind of nervous affection. 'Ned says you ought to shut up shop and come with us.'

'What's the good of asking her? She'll only say she can't leave the boy. I've asked her again and again to get a reliable woman in.'

'Boy doesn't need you as he does,' said Harris, ducking his head sideways in Ned's direction. 'Come on, Chris; we'll all go together and have a high old time.'

Ned looked at me. I knew he had only brought Harris here in the hope that an outsider's persuasions might prove more effective than his own, though why he should have hoped for any such thing I did not know. 'Take the baby over to Emilie, why don't you?'

'I can't, not suddenly, like that.'

'Damn her, chasing over the other side of the Common. God knows what she wanted to do it for. She was comfortable enough here. Now one can't even get her on the phone.'

As I changed the dishes I saw the two men through the open door of the dining-room, silent together, nothing to say to each other. They looked forlorn.

But Ned had made his effect through the medium of Jack Harris, though it was not one he could have anticipated. For some reason I cannot explain, he looked to me far lonelier, far more pitiable in the company of a friend than he ever looked to me when he was by himself. The shine had gone from his hair, from the flesh of his cheeks. He seemed older than he was.

I made up my mind that when he came back from Essex I would steel myself once again to accept this marriage and to make it endure. I would honestly try. I had, as his mother had said, a duty to him. I thought of the countless people who had forced out of a duty a tolerable way of living, who had even been reasonably happy. It was a starry night, the stars swarming like silver bees over the black hive of the sky. I thought painstakingly of other worlds. With so many people, uncountable as the minutes in eternity, living out so many unguessable tragedies and comedies, it did not seem to me that my life was of the slightest importance to anyone but myself; and what, in these immensities of so many suns and moons, could I possibly matter? I decided that I did not matter at all; and though the thought gave me courage, it also made me cry a little.

I shall never forget that week-end. It is one thing to screw one's courage to the sticking-place, quite another to see that it stays there. It is the metaphor of the lutanist; the strings are stretched till the wooden peg holds them at the proper tension, ready to sing. But lute-strings may wither or snap. It was an intolerable strain and soreness, trying to keep my resolution in tune. I tried not to think any more of Ned, to think only of the baby and of my delight in him. This, I said to myself, should be enough for anyone to live by: a beloved child.

Yet there are many natures for whom one kind of love, no matter how strong, is not sufficient. Feed to repletion one mouth of the spirit, another mouth starves. I did not know, until I was much older, that it was so with myself; and before I recognised it and accepted it I suffered from a rotting sense of guilt, often hating myself because I believed I should never have borne children at all, since I could not give myself to them utterly.

That week-end I tried to force my own nature into a shape I was afraid it would never take; but then, I meant to do impossibilities. I was determined. On the Sunday night I hardly slept. I did not sleep till the early sun was flickering its water-shadows on the window-pane. When I woke again I felt calm and refreshed, ready to tell Ned that all was well with us, that we would begin again, patient of each other, and be as happy as other couples were.

I did not know what time to expect him. He had not told me. Since he did not come in the morning, I supposed he had gone straight to the office and would be home about half-past six, as usual. I put on one of my new dresses, made myself as pleasing as I could, although – as on my wedding-day – the glass would not perform a miracle and left me, as before, with lines of strain under my eyes. It was disappointing. I had wanted him to admire and love me as never before, so that the force of his love should be sufficient for the two of us.

He was late; the meal I had prepared spoiled in the oven. I took it out, and found some cold meat that we might have instead. Nine o'clock, and ten. I knew well enough that he would not return at all that night, but until past midnight refused to let myself believe it.

He did not come next morning, nor the next night. Early on Wednesday I put Mark in charge of the daily woman and went across the Common to see Emilie.

At once she saw that something was wrong. 'What's the matter? You look ill.'

I told her I was not ill, but that I was bringing the baby to her that day and that she must take us both in. I told her of the failure of my marriage, of my sudden decision to retrieve it, of Ned's non-appearance, and my final decision, at all costs, to break free, whether he would divorce me or not.

'You were married in church,' said Emilie, bursting into tears, 'in church.'

I told her the plans I had made, how I had included her in them. I had made her leave the flat where we lived because I wanted a place of refuge if the need should arise. And it had arisen. I was going straight home to get a taxi. I would bring the cot and the perambulator, the minimum of clothing for Mark and myself. I would send for the rest later.

'How can I do it?' Emilie moaned. 'I wish your father was here.'

I said that I did, too, though I did not think he would have been of much help.

'He would have been fifty-four today if he had lived,' she cried out, putting her handkerchief to her mouth. But even she, in this moment of crisis, could not linger too long upon his anniversary. 'Oh, Chris, you know you can't come here!'

I said, 'There's no one else to help me. And I'm coming.' I kissed her; she looked at me, her lips trembling, her eyes distraught. Then she seemed to grow quite calm, mistress of herself. 'I'll try to help you,' she said. 'I'll try. I shall always do my best.'

On the way home I had no thought for anything but practical details. Could I get the baby's clothes, his napkins, his bottles, his various tins, jars, powders and brushes, into one case? Would the driver let me put the perambulator on the roof of the cab? Should I need more for myself than one extra dress, a change of underwear and a nightgown?

I found myself pushing open the gate. The daily woman, in her hat and coat, was standing under the tree. 'Mr. Skelton said it would be all right for me to go now. He's just come in.'

I ran up the stairs and into the flat. He was standing with his back to the empty grate, his hands in his pockets, his bird-like head thrown back as if, for twopence, he would break into a whistle. But he was as pale as the wall behind him, and when he saw me did not budge from his position.

He said, 'All right. You can have it your own way.'

At first I did not understand. I even asked him what he meant.

'I'll let you go.' His eyes evaded mine. 'I'll do whatever you want, send you hotel bills – God, I don't know. . . . What is it one does? You must find out what they want me to do.'

Then he did look at me, and I saw in his face a contempt that was not for me but for himself; he was utterly unnerved by it.

'But what has happened?' I cried out to him. For a moment I felt a violent desire to hold him, to tell him he need not give way to me, that we would, after all, make a new beginning.

He said, 'What the devil can that matter to you? You've got your own way. Take it.'

He told me he was going now, that I should find him at Maddox Street if I wanted anything. He broke away suddenly and went into the bedroom. I heard him moving about the room. It could not have been five minutes before he came out again, carrying the suitcase he had taken to Frinton and had not yet unpacked, and a smaller one borrowed from me. 'You'll get this back some time.'

I said, 'Ned, surely we shall have to talk!'

'We've talked quite enough. I'll arrange about money.'

I told him I had planned to go back to work.

He coloured. It was as though he suddenly realised that I had accepted what was happening; yet I knew he had meant me to accept it. 'That's your affair,' he said after a moment. He looked as if he were about to say something else. He took a step towards me. I believed he would touch or kiss me.

Then he said violently, 'Yes, all right. Go on! Look! Stare away!'

His eyes were faceted with tears. Unblinking, he let them spread across the pupils before he smeared them away.

'I wasn't staring,' I said. I looked down. I saw the pattern of the carpet, the zigzag of dark blue upon fawn, in the discreet and nervous taste of our day.

He had stepped past me out of the room. I heard the door close. I went to the window. He walked steadily down the path. I thought he would go and look at the baby, but he did not. He did not even glance in the direction of the tree under which Mark slept in the dark-green lacing of shadow. Unable to watch him any more, I held my hands to my eyes and felt the trembling in my wrists. When I looked again the road was bare of him. A bus swept by, stirring up the white dust, whipping a newspaper along with it and then letting it go, to flutter backwards and flatten itself upon a lamp-post.

I am free, I said to myself, but could not believe it. I longed for Mark to cry, so that I could bring him in and care for him. I wanted his company. I wanted to hold him. I wanted something to do. For at the moment the horror of sheer emptiness, the horror of finality, was upon me, and it was too great for me to meet.

Down the abyss of time this moment sticks out, a hook upon air. I look at it and cling to the cliff face, till the giddiness passes. For around it is nothing, no cloud, no rim of distant sea. It is a hook upon whiteness without shadow, a cruel shape, infinitely lonely, infinitely sad.

6

(The Door Opens)

Silent, smiling, Iris stretched out her arms and, as if we were children, hugged me. She stepped back. Clasping her hands under her chin, she stared at me. 'Christie! After all this time!' She dropped her arms. 'Well, well,' she said, 'come in. We can't stand in the hall for ever.'

It had seemed to me, in that first moment, that she had not changed at all; that she had admitted me not into the present but into yet another cell of the past. She was still slender. She had still the same air of bunched and tidy prettiness, of cultivated, self-conscious mischief. For a second I felt something like my old dread of her, felt she had still the power to shadow and to deprive me. But then, as we came into the high, clear room, I saw that she had changed beyond my imagination, for she had lost her light. There was nothing now to shine through the shell of her beauty. She was lustreless. Her dress was the kind of dress she had worn in her girlhood, dainty, pale, a little over-elaborate. Out of some kind of vanity, perhaps, she wore no make-up at all; it would have helped her, but she had rejected it. I remembered my own strange vanity of more than twenty years ago, when I had stripped myself of ornament in the hope of looking stately and distinguished at the sports club dance.

'Christie, you make me quite *sick*! You haven't altered one little bit!'

'Nor have you,' I said.

'Darling, I look a horse! You know I do!' She embraced me again. Her flesh had still the same flowery and delightful odour, reminding one with an association of sight rather than smell, of the crystallised violet and rose petals that had always adorned our birthday cakes. 'How do you like my flat? A come-down, dear, after foreign glories, but it suits me.'

She had told me already in her letters the outline of her life. She had borne four children, of which two had not survived; the two living, a boy of twenty, a girl two years younger, were married, and had settled in America. Her husband had died in 1950. Iris, who had looked forward to a very comfortable widowhood, discovered that they had been living on capital for years and that the money remaining to her after payment of death duties and some astonishing debts was just sufficient to provide her with an income of ten pounds a week.

I looked about the room. It was so much the old Iris, even more like the girl of the past than the woman now displaying it to me, that I wanted to cry. This was the same elegant, pastel clutter, almost, but not quite, spotless; everything was frilled that could be frilled; and on the divan, so much a survival of the nineteen-twenties that I could not imagine where she had found it, was a brand-new doll, a toy with long soft legs protruding like tentacles from the crinoline rucked about its waist, and with hard, dead azure-lidded eyes painted on pink canvas, so that the whites were pink also.

Seeing me look at it, she snatched it up and held it to her cheek. 'You're my new baby, aren't you, pet? Say hullo to Aunt Christie and ask her to write in your autograph book.'

I had taken this for whimsicality, and was surprised when Iris produced from a drawer a silk-covered book filled with cachou-coloured leaves, on the front of which was written the doll's name. 'All my friends have to write in it. You too, Christie. Do it now, because I might forget, once we start talking. She's the only baby I've got left,' she added, and clenched her teeth in a smile, as if to hold back a sorrow she had long since rejected but of which she needed me to be aware. 'Aren't you, my love?' she said softly to the doll, touching its cheek to her own. She gave me the book. 'Write her a pretty message.'

When this ceremony was disposed of, Iris brought in tea. 'Now,' she said, 'we'll really get down to old times. How you've got on, haven't you? Right over the other side of the world I've been thinking, "That's *my* friend, doing all that. That's my own Christie." ' She gave a great sigh. 'Do you know, the very week poor Mummie died she sent me a cutting about you from a newspaper?'

Iris bounced up from her chair and came to sit beside me on the divan. She looked at me thoughtfully, with a trace of her old, flirtatious air. 'And very smart, Christie, too. Would I look nice in that hat, or like a hag?'

'Iris,' I said, remembering another incident, 'we aren't even going to experiment.'

Probably she also remembered, for she laughed, and pushed at my shoulder. She asked me about my husband. Was I happy? I looked as if I was.

As I replied it seemed to me that the sun had flashed up all around the house, and that the present was with it, there in those ragged fields, lying along the intersecting paths and over the leaves like light itself; and I longed to escape to it, away from this room stifling with memory, close with the shames, the shifts, the hopes, the guilt, of my youth.

'I'm glad,' Iris said, 'I'm glad you are. You always deserved things, Christie. Do you ever see anything of the old people? The people we used to know?'

I told her Dicky was dead, that he had been killed in North Africa; that I had not seen Caroline since her husband left her, but that I knew she had married again and left London.

'Oh, I've seen Caroline,' said Iris. 'I ran into her the other week. We had a terrific heart-to-heart. What about the others?'

I had never heard what had happened to Take Plato. I had never, as he had prophesied, set eyes on Leslie again.

'Poor Leslie!' Iris cried on an upward rip of mirth, 'He was such a mutt! Honestly, darling, I never knew how you could.'

I reminded her that in those days my area of choice had been restricted.

'Oh, nonsense! You could have had *anyone*, just *anyone*!'

She asked me about my son. I told her proudly, as pleased to speak his name as, in my youth, I had been pleased to speak Ned's, that he had just left Cambridge, triumphantly, with a First.

'A what?' Iris stared. She burst out laughing. 'Oh, darling, I thought you said a *thirst*. I am ridiculous! What is a First? You can't expect me to know these things. Is he very handsome?'

No, I replied, but his colouring was bright and his face lively.

'Is he like Ned?'

'Sometimes. Not so much now as he used to be.'

Iris withdrew from me along the divan and tucked her legs under her. Her eyes glittered. I felt uneasy without knowing why; then recalled that as a girl she had sat like this, looked like this, when anticipating the joy of imparting disagreeable news. Yet, I thought, she could have no news for me, not now, with a score of years lying between us. She could only ask questions. 'Tell me, does he ever *see* Neddy?'

No, I told her, not these days. Ned had taken the boy out occasionally while he was still at school, but always as if he were in a hurry, with a train to catch, more important matters waiting for him. Since he had married again (at last, barely two years ago) he had not expressed a wish to see Mark at all. 'Does G— adore Mark?' Iris enquired, characteristically referring to my husband, whom, of course, she did not know, by a diminutive nobody had ever used. 'I'm sure he does. Oh, you are lucky, Christie! You always were.'

I said nothing.

'Well' – she amended her statement – 'perhaps you weren't, right at the beginning. But Neddy did let you go in the end, didn't he?'

'Yes,' I said, 'and I never knew why.'

I had never known, had never guessed what had made him change his mind that week-end in July. And I had been too grateful to wonder. But now, betrayed by my own thoughts into offering Iris half a confidence, I was suddenly on guard. For her lips were tight upon a secret smile; she could hardly contain herself.

'Anyway,' I said, 'it doesn't matter. It was all so long ago.'

'Of course, I only met him that once,' she said suddenly, as if excusing herself for something.

I stared at her.

'What's the matter?' said Iris, opening her eyes wide in a simple look.

I reminded her of the evening at the restaurant. 'When you were in the cabaret. You came and talked to us.'

She looked thoughtfully down. 'Cabaret.' Then she looked up again, smiling. 'Oh yes, of course. I'd clean forgotten.'

She was telling the truth. Of the incident that had for so long directed my life, driven my inclination awry, thrust me into a misery I need never have known, she did, in fact, remember nothing at all. I should have liked to remind her of it still further; yet even now I was ashamed that she should recall a petty triumph over me.

'It was that silly song about the tarts!' she exclaimed radiantly. 'I had that awful frock – my dear, *never* shall I forget it!

It made me look spavined.' Reminiscently she hummed a tune; yet even as she did so her face changed, grew shuttered and secret. She stretched out her arms over her head, clasped her hands and smiled at me steadily.

I wanted to get up and go away, out into the sunshine and into my own now fortunate life. She was forcing me to look behind, to look down the vertiginous fall of the years.

'I could tell you, if you really wanted to know,' she said.

I asked her what she could tell me.

'Oh, why. The whys and wherefores.' She kept the same posture, taut, anticipatory.

Iris? It could not be. He had not even liked her. Yet the thought that it might, after all, have been Iris to whom he had turned made me feel sick and young and betrayed. But she had said, 'I only met him that once', which would have been a stupid lie if she were going to confess to such a betrayal. And then I remembered that at the time she had not even been in England. She had married by then; she had been far away over the other side of the world. In any case, what did it matter?

Her hands parted. She gave a rushing sigh. Slowly she brought her arms down to shoulder level, then let them fall and clasped her hands in her lap. With the light of her beauty faded, she still had beauty's audacious and meaningless graces.

As I did not speak she said, 'I *always* admired your Neddy – and you, too, of course. Even though you did hide him away, I tell you, he made a *deep* impression on me.' She grew solemn. She raised her face so that I could search it, lifted her hand with a faltering gesture, as if she were acting the part of a blind girl, and touched my cheek. 'I don't know if I ought to tell you. As you say, it *is* so long ago.'

'Come on,' I said, 'out with it. You always told me things in the end.'

'I don't suppose you'd *mind*,' said Iris, 'not now.'

I could not speak. Outside this house, outside this room, I should be free as a sleeper awakening; but I could not endure the way she had trapped me in this withered dream.

'Only I do happen to *know* why Neddy let you go in the end. I was told. Recently. I won't tell you if *you* don't want to know.'

'Of course I want to know!' I cried.

A faint smile moved along her mouth, lingered at one corner.

'It was Caroline.'

If Iris had hoped to be rewarded by my entire amazement she must have been satisfied. I could do nothing but repeat the name.

Having told her secret and been placated by the result of it, Iris suddenly relaxed. The girlishness left her. She looked a tired, bored woman, who had had nearly but not quite what she desired; whom life had treated fairly enough, but with a touch of stinginess.

'Oh, nobody else could get anything out of her, but I could. She always told me things in the end. That's why she started avoiding me – because she couldn't help pouring things out. Besides, she's still got a guilty conscience about it. "Oh, don't be so silly," I said; "it's all dead as Queen Anne. And, anyway, you did Christie a good turn." '

'Come on,' I said, 'come on. Tell me all about it.'

And she told me the confidence Caroline, only a week ago, out of some ancient compulsion, had disclosed to her. It seemed that Ned, on his way back to me from Essex, had met Caroline by chance and on an impulse had gone to her flat. (He had always liked her; she was the only one of my friends whom he had ever admired.) Miserable, desperate, he had told her that I was tired of him, no longer in love with him, that I wanted him to divorce me. Caroline, equally wretched and lonely, finding physical deprivation more and more intolerable, had tried to comfort him. They had sat drinking till late; till it seemed far too late for Ned to go. That night, not out of love but out of the ache of solitude, they had slept together, and the next night also.

'So there it is,' said Iris in rather a loud voice. She looked a little scared. 'Caroline said she couldn't have done it if she hadn't known *you* didn't want him. She said she never cared for him and she never saw him again after that. But afterwards she couldn't look you in the face. Because she loved you,' Iris added in something like a tone of anger. 'She *did*, you know; she loved you far better than she loved me.'

'It doesn't matter,' I said.

A bird had alighted on the window-sill. I could just see the quilled and silken head bobbing over the rim of the glass. Over the common the clouds floated like fingerings of cotton wool across a strong blue sky.

'Still,' Iris said, 'I still don't see why he need have changed his mind. He could just have kept quiet.'

She did not understand him; but I did. I knew that he could not have kept quiet. His fidelity to me had given him, in his own mind, a moral advantage. He housed me, clothed me, fed me, was faithful to me – he was not going to parade a concocted guilt for my benefit. But the moment he had, on a violent impulse, lost this advantage, he could not hold me. He had judged himself harshly, contemptuously, and found himself guilty.

'I suppose he could,' I said.

Iris murmured that she hoped I was not upset.

'No,' I said. 'Don't worry, I'm not upset at all.' And it was true, for in a moment strength had returned to me. Even in that room I felt the present like a wall at my back and all about me. Even as I looked at Iris, she began to turn into a stranger; as I, as a girl, was now a stranger to myself. She had been talking to that girl who had escaped her, who was no longer there.

We talked for a while of other things.

'It has been lovely to see you,' Iris said, rather fretfully, as I rose to go. Her eyes filled. 'Don't let's lose sight of each other. Old friends shouldn't, should they? I know you're busy, Christie, and have thousands of people to see, but promise me you'll come back.' She picked up her doll and talked to it. 'She'll have to come back to see you, won't she, my pet? You never let people get away, do you? Not when they've signed their names in your little book.' She kissed me, holding her lips open against my cheek, leaving it a little moist. 'Now the children are gone, everything's so empty. You mustn't desert me. Not my best friend.'

I did not wait for a bus outside the mansions, for I thought she would watch me from the window, as I had watched the boy and girl saying goodbye. I told myself I would indeed visit her again, since she had so little and I so much – but I knew I should not. It was not that I was any longer afraid of her, or that I was selfish enough to care nothing for her at all. What I did fear was the yesterday she bore with her as inseparably as her own shadow. All the past is our enriching. But we must live in the present if we are to remain real; not to ourselves, but to other people about us. It profits nobody whom we have injured simply to be sorry for them, to acknowledge our guilt and suffer for it, to regret words spoken in cruelty or actions done meanly under the disguise of courage or honesty. All it does is to put us on better terms with ourselves; we preen ourselves because we are repentant. If we can make practical amends, well and good; if we cannot, we should forego the luxury of the secret abasement, let the past bury its dead (as Leslie had put it) and refuse to let that past cast its smear from ourselves into the lives of those who have nothing whatsoever to do with it.

I walked along North Side, past the place where Ned and I had lived, past the church where we had been married. The Rise streamed in silver and brass down from one common to St. John's Road and up towards another. The masonic minarets flashed and twinkled in the brilliant light. I found myself looking forward in love to a homecoming, a greeting, to the day's news, to the evening's exchanges. How had things gone? Was he tired? Had any letters come? Anything interesting?

A boy on a bicycle came toiling up the hill, swaying on the saddle, schoolcap on the back of a round fair head, face burnished with sun and sweat, lips rounded in a gasping whistle. It was so like Dicky as he used to be that for a moment I was almost recaptured by time; but then he dismounted to speak to a girl, and his voice was a stranger's. He was nobody I knew, no part of anything I had known. The whole neighbourhood was suddenly unfamiliar; I had no business in this place; it had no business with me. I saw a new name on a shop front.

A stranger there myself, I was free.

Pamela Hansford Johnson

Pamela Hansford Johnson was born in Clapham in 1912 to an actress and a colonial civil servant, who died when she was 11, leaving the family in debt. Pamela excelled in school, particularly in English and Drama, and became Dylan Thomas' first love after writing to him when they had poems in the same magazine. She went on to write her daring first novel, *This Bed Thy Centre*, aged 23, marking the beginning of a prolific literary career which would span her lifetime.

In 1936 she married journalist Neil Stewart, who left her for another woman; in 1950, she married novelist C.P. Snow, and for thirty years they formed an ambitious and infamous couple

Johnson remained a productive and acclaimed writer her whole life, and was the recipient of several honorary degrees as well as a CBE in 1975. She was also made a Fellow of the Royal Society of Literature. By her death in 1981, she was one of Britain's best-known and best-selling authors, having written twenty-seven novels, alongside several plays, critical studies of writers such as Thomas Wolfe and Marcel Proust, poetry, translation and a memoir.

Praise for Pamela Hansford Johnson

'Very funny' *Independent*

'Witty, satirical and deftly malicious' Anthony Burgess

'Sharply observed, artfully constructed and always enlivened by the freshness of an imagery that derives from [Johnson's] poetic beginnings' *TLS*

'Miss Johnson is one of the most accomplished of the English women writers' *Kirkus*